GEARS

AND

GLORY

Fabiana Pennimpede

AOS Publishing, 2024

Copyright © 2024

Fabiana Pennimpede

ISBN: 978-1-998662-15-9

Cover Design: Meredith Lindsay

Visit AOS Publishing's website:
This is a work of fiction. All characters and places are fabricated and any
resemblance to any real persons is unintentional.
www.aospublishing.com

*This is for the sixteen-year-old girl who wanted
her dreams to come true. We did it.*

TABLE OF CONTENTS

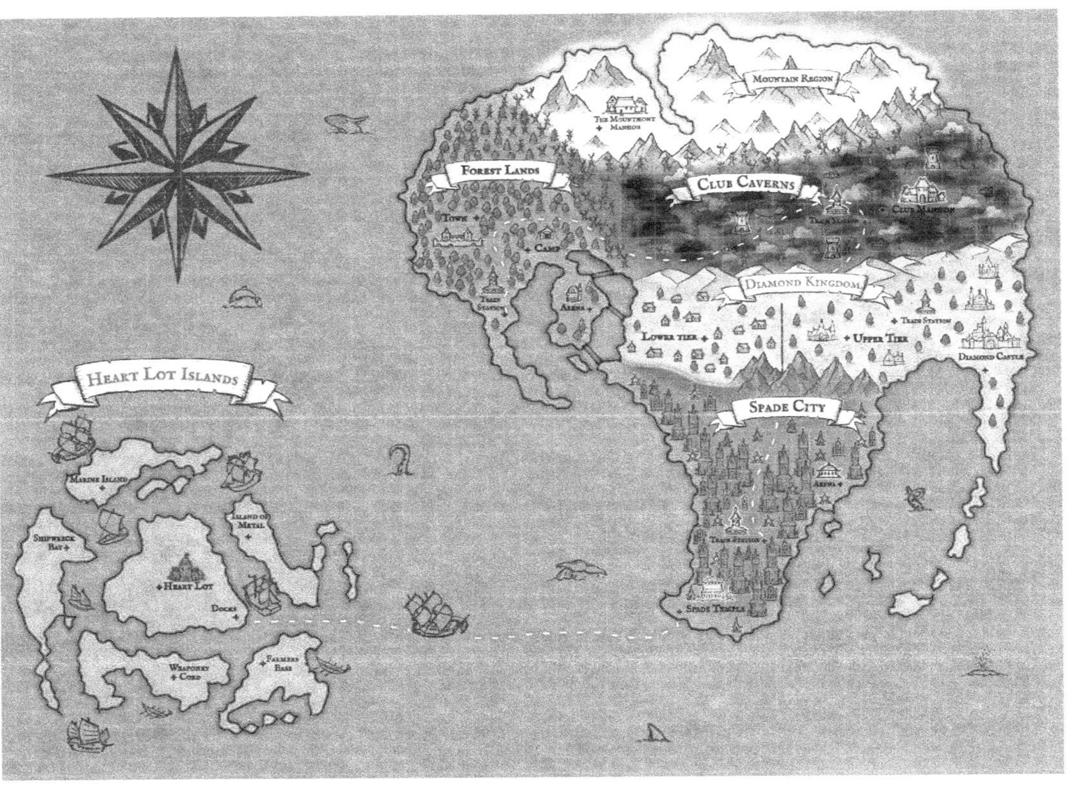

Mountain Region
The Mountfront Mansion
Forest Lands
Club Caverns
Club Mansion
Town
Camp
Train Station
Arena
Diamond Kingdom
Lower Tier
Upper Tier
Train Station
Diamond Castle
Spade City
Arena
Train Station
Spade Temple
Heart Lot Islands
Marine Island
Shipwreck Bay
Island of Metal
Heart Lot
Docks
Weaponry Cold
Farmers Base

CHAPTER I

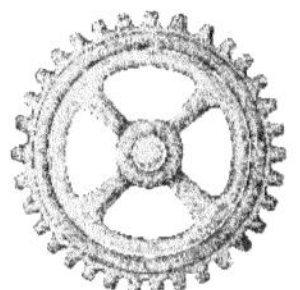

Sometimes dreams are better than reality.

Dreams can be filled with excitement and reassurance, while reality is filled with the unexpected.

That particular morning Cassandra refused to acknowledge the sun, wanting to dive deeper into her dream, away from reality.

In this dream, she found herself in a beautiful meadow near her family's estate, her head resting on her mother's lap as she sang sweetly. Cassandra could recall the captivating colour of her mother's crisp blue eyes, her delicate complexion, and the gentle freckles adorning her nose and cheeks. She had always believed that her mother was the most beautiful woman in the world—that no one could ever compare. Red hair tumbled down her mother's shoulders as she continued to sing. This precious time was when Cassandra felt the closest to her, believing it was her mother's spirit that temporarily dwelled in her thoughts, keeping her company for a fleeting moment before vanishing into the reality of the day.

The curtains were drawn back. The image of her mother vanishing from her mind as Cassandra's drowsy eyes squinted against the blinding glare of the sun that flooded her room. The once-quiet morning now buzzed with the sound of her maids scurrying about. Still groggy, she was yanked from her warm bed and forced into the cold bathtub. A gasp escaped her lips, muscles and gears awake at the feel of the water.

Forced once again to move, Cassandra was wrapped in a fluffy robe and was placed in more appropriate attire. She silently wished her mother farewell until the following night.

Cassandra's maids hummed and twirled around her, preparing the Princess for the day ahead. She tried to forget, nearly forcing herself to. The creeping realisation of the days ahead settled on her shoulders. Tomorrow would mark the departure for the Forest Lands, where the Triumph Games were being held: a gruelling two-week competition that Cassandra now wished to avoid. If she had a choice, she would much rather retreat to her mother's library, escaping reality once more within the comforting worlds of her novels.

One of Cassandra's maids fumbled with the old radio in the adjacent room. Its rusting knobs emitted a screechy crackle before settling into a faint melody. Then, like an otherworldly presence, the voice of the channel's radio host pierced the room with his amplified words. His daily ritual unfolded before her ears, his promotion of the impending Triumph Games, resounding through the airwaves. He urged the listeners to tune in or, for the daring few, to embark on a two-day long journey to the Forest Lands. For the inhabitants of the land, it meant restless anticipation before setting out for the grand event; however, Cassandra viewed it in a different light. Bound by her brother's involvement as a participant, she found herself entangled in a dreadful four-day trip to various cities and kingdoms, forcing her to confront her nation's rivals.

Savannah, the Princess's head maid and friend, directed the bustling maids. Her light brown hair was pulled into a tight bun, accentuating her fair tanned skin. With an elegantly raised finger she pointed at each servant, expertly guiding their movement. Three of them tended to Cassandra's day gown, a stunning maroon with an elegant sweetheart neckline. Their nimble hands expertly smoothed out every crease. Meanwhile, the two hair maidens curled and sprayed Cassandra's dark red locks, ensuring that every strand remained perfectly in place. Seated in a velvet armchair beside a towering wooden bookshelf, Savannah's piercing green eyes observed everything, making sure things were done right, her way, and never wrong. From her vantage point, she offered corrections like a conductor orchestrating the grand performance of preparing Cassandra for her day.

Savannah glared at the radio. "That man seems disturbingly cheerful for such an ungodly hour," she murmured. "I cannot imagine two full weeks with him."

"Let us not forget my father and brother." Cassandra glanced at her maid through the vanity mirror, a sigh escaping her lips. "They will be just as loud. Now you understand why I wish to remain within the Lot walls."

The radio host began to recount the events of the last Triumph Games that occurred fifty-two years ago. His words bounced off the walls of her bedchambers, detailing the challenges each competitor faced and reminding the audience of the three Princes and the lone representative from Spade City. The host did not forget to speak of her father's legendary match, a victory in the hand-to-hand combat sector. Cassandra took a deep breath, feeling the constriction of her corset tightening around her waist. The radio soon became a distant voice.

The Triumph Games were originally created for amusement, intended to showcase which nation held the strongest leaders. However, after the War fifty-six years ago, the games had transformed into something much more profound. They became a fierce competition, a test of resilience and power among nations with rankings that would last for generations.

Cassandra found herself being transported back to her childhood—the days filled with her mother's captivating stories, the memory bittersweet like a melody that played in the depth of her heart, both soothing and haunting. Growing up, Cassandra would listen to her mother retell the story of her father's legendary showdown with King Albert, a tale that was often told before bedtime. Cassandra begged her mother to retell it for weeks until fate took her away, leaving a void that could never be filled. She could almost hear the gentle hums of her mother's voice, feel the warmth of her delicate fingers brushing her hair, and see the flickering firelight reflecting in her own eyes, the same shade of blue that had been passed down to Cassandra.

While being a guest in the Sky Box, a privileged vantage point reserved for the royals, her mother made sure to watch Cassandra's father, the figure of strength and bravery. Every moment was etched in her mother's memory and she recounted each thrilling event to her wide-eyed daughter. *"The crowd roared his name,"* she had once said. *"Their cheers shook the very foundation of the Arena. Your father would raise his arms, waving to the crowd. In his right hand, he carried a formidable metal spear, a weapon that was unmatched. In his left, a staff adorned with the Harth Family Crest—a masterpiece forged by the island's most skilled blacksmiths."*

Cassandra was consumed by her mother's words, and even now she stood picturing her father's victory. Her mother's sweet smile was the last thing Cassandra held dear, mainly due to the fact that her father had told her countless times that she has her mother's smile.

"Across the ring stood his opponent, Prince Albert Dimond, from the Diamond Kingdom. Oh, he was a worthy opponent. Stood just as tall and strong as your father did, but he was different all the same. He remained

composed and calm. In his left hand, he wielded a golden hammer, rumoured to be crafted from pure gold. However, Prince Albert had an advantage, for, you see, he had a new spinal extension that he personally designed to also be a mechanical arm—one that served as an additional limb."

Cassandra always pictured the now-King Albert as a spider with a long robotic arm on his back, one that would pop out as if the King himself could control it. She would have never known for sure but she did wish to find out, once the games began, if the King's son Benjamin held the same back extension.

"The winner for third place had been announced," she remembered her mother saying, her eyes glimmered with delight as if she was transported back to the thrilling games. *"This would prepare the audience for the main event. Dimond versus Harth. Diamond Kingdom versus Heart Lot Islands. Battling it out to see who will be the winner of the Triumph Games."*

It was Savannah's gentle voice that brought Cassandra back to her senses, remembering that she was in her bedroom being dressed and hearing the radio host's voice louder than ever. Savannah questioned Cassandra's tired appearance and blamed it on the lack of sleep; however, she brushed it off, claiming ignorance, but Cassandra knew the truth about why she was so tired lately. It had been due to the extra reading she was doing every night, sneaking into her mother's library and grabbing every history book imaginable; specifically, the ones that spoke of the Triumph Games and their history. It all fascinated her deeply and she craved to learn every detail.

The game was held every fifty-two years, spanning a lifetime for one person to witness them twice, marking the entrance of a new heir. Each nation's King would send their eldest son or a chosen representative to compete in the event. Specifically, the regulations explained that the *oldest son* rather than *oldest child* was permitted to participate.

This rule frustrated Cassandra, as she knew there was a loophole that was being overlooked. She was the eldest child of King Jaronas but her gender led to her dismissal. Both the title and fame went to her younger brother, Grayson. This realization always enraged her, it tormented and bothered her. If only she was born a boy, she would have the crown and the opportunity to participate in the Triumph Games.

Cassandra always found a way to reject the societal norms imposed upon her, and so did her father in some ways. He allowed her to train with her brother, but there was always a limit. It remained the traditional route of protection—this also led for her educational courses to being limited to history, literature, arts, and armoury, rather than the education that came with the title of future heir.

Some part of her believed she was a better fit to rule, but part of her also knew it was wrong to take that away from her brother. Yet, she did not care. She was the firstborn.

After all, it was only a few days ago that she and Grayson had their weekly shooting range challenge. It was routine: they would meet at the crack of dawn, strategically place small targets around the fields, and conceal them in the most obscure spots. The objective of the game would be to hit the bullseye consistently, and the person who hit the greatest number of targets won ultimate bragging rights. Cassandra had maintained her lead for the past three weeks and this streak continued as she flawlessly struck each target without a single miss, extending her winnings into a fourth week. Grayson struggled with the final target that Cassandra strategically positioned, nestled beneath a branch of trees with its leaves slightly covering it, visibility being the true element that would cause Grayson to lose.

It was a dirty play, a wrongful move, but it did not matter to her. It was the one thing she was able to win over him, the one thing that was hers and that made her better than him.

Clapping hands pulled Cassandra from her thoughts, bringing her back to reality. She watched as Savannah's fair skin shone in the morning sun and her eyes narrowed at the maids she directed. Barking more orders, Cassandra was dressed in a day gown, her red hair cascading in gentle waves and her cheeks flushed in a rosy hue. Savannah looked down at her wristwatch, eyes widening as she quickly escorted Cassandra to the Dining Hall and exclaimed she was to be last for breakfast with the King. Cassandra clutched her history book, eyes roaming the pages as she absorbed every bit of information that was written for her. Savannah guided them down the halls; their footsteps echoed on the marble floor as she shouted for the workers to move out of their way.

When they came to an abrupt stop, Cassandra bumped into Savannah, who snatched the history book from her hands. "Save it for after breakfast," her friend advised, flashing a sweet smile. Cassandra rolled her eyes in response as Savannah signalled the guards to open the large steel doors of the Dining Hall.

As they entered, Savannah gave a deep curtsy to King Jaronas, whereas Cassandra gave a half-curtsy before quickly getting up and making her way to her seat. His keen brown eyes scanned the newspaper before him while a servant stood nearby tending to his large beard. "You are late," her father said from his seat at the head of the grand wooden table that was filled with various foods. His eyes followed his daughter as she took a seat to his left. "A lady must never be late."

Cassandra rolled her eyes. "You know much of that I take?"

"I am sorry for being late, my King," Savannah apologised, which caused Jaronas to chuckle deeply.

"My dear, it is not you who I am scolding." Jaronas gave a look to Cassandra. who shrugged. "Seems that my daughter is responsible for the lateness. Having to drag her out of bed every morning."

"Here we go," Cassandra muttered as Jaronas retracted his mechanical arm, allowing his speared arm to shine through and stab the fried fish in his plate. Cassandra gave her father an odd look, not understanding why he chose fish for breakfast.

"You must understand that a—"

"That a lady is never late," Cassandra finished his sentence as she pulled fruit into her plate. She was frustrated at her father. It was a daily conversation, him criticizing her about how late she was, yet her brother's seat remained empty in front of her, her father saying nothing about his precious son.

Her father gave her a look. "A lady should always be on time. It is not hard. Your mother was always on time."

"Well Mother isn't here anymore."

There was a long silence in the hall. The servants stopped moving, Savannah held her breath, and Cassandra sat there nibbling at her fruit. Her father stared at her and Cassandra could not decide if he was shocked or angry by her choice of words.

"You went to her library," her father finally said. Realization crossed his face, causing Cassandra to know where this was going. It would end one of two ways—an argument or a conversation about what she had read.

Her father placed his newspaper on the table, huffing as he rubbed his eyes with his other hand. "Alright. What did you search for this time?"

"Whatever do you mean?"

"You seem more irritable than your typical morning demeanour, Cassandra. This suggests that you have been up all night reading something. What captured your attention this time?"

"Nothing extraordinary."

Her father gave her another look.

Cassandra straightened. "I have been delving into the usual subjects, exploring reasons behind the societal expectations that confined women to more delicate roles, particularly why royal women are excluded from participating in the Triumph Games."

"Cassandra," her father said sternly, causing his daughter to chuckle. She knew this was going to happen. With a radiant smile on her face, a glimmer of excitement, Cassandra was eager to annoy her father. She wanted more than anything to tell him of her recent findings. She wanted to express the interests of the historical books she found and how she found that being in her mother's library made her feel closer to her. She savoured every second of it, almost imagining that her mother was in the very room with her, helping her turn the page and read the words as she once did when Cassandra was young.

She opened her mouth, prepared to speak, but her father only shook his head. "You must stop with this silliness. There are rules placed for a reason. They are meant to prevent you from getting hurt."

"Father. There has never been a female competitor. *Ever*. That is not fair. Queen Suzume is a living example of that, needing her father to call in a representative from their nation to replace her in the games."

Jaronas grew angry, frustrated, and annoyed by his daughter. Not understanding why, she always pushed for this, but Cassandra knew that history was written for men, making them seem superior. She wanted nothing more than to speak of the history of the world's four nations, and how the Triumph Games were initially meant for amusement and peace.

"Rules are rules" was all he said.

Cassandra retracted her mechanical arm, allowing her sniper to shine through. Anger consumed her, emotions guiding her state as she raised her arm and prepared to fire a shot to tapestries on the wall before her.

Jaronas returned to his newspaper, shaking his head, muttering, "My point exactly."

She put her arm down, sniper still on display for the room to see. She tried to control her breaths and found Savannah across the room widening her eyes. Her friend demonstrated how to catch her breath and calm down. It was something Cassandra struggled to do, controlling her anger and rage.

Instead, Cassandra calmed herself by thinking back to her most recent reading. It always helped her. She thought of the Triumph Games and how they were created. It spoke of an age requirement for the heirs to the throne, emphasising that they must be between their late teens to their late twenties. She nearly scoffed at how ironic it was for her brother to have only turned of age to compete not too long ago. Her brother beat her by being two years younger; if he had just remained in his early teens, maybe she would have had a chance, but it would always be just that—maybe.

She thought back to when her father once spoke to her about his experience in the Triumph Games. She remembered clinging to his words. Her father's stories brought history to life before her. She remembered how her father's tone shifted when he spoke of the War that had taken place nearly fifty-six years ago. How it had begun with the Prince of the Diamond Kingdom declaring war on Spade City, due to the recent assassination of his wife. That was when the Diamond Kingdom and the Heart Lot Islands formed a new alliance, while Spade City turned to Club Caverns for aid.

"*The games were postponed during those dark times,*" her father once said. "*The war changed the world and to this day we cannot decide if it was for the better or for the worst.*"

That was when her father had gone into detail about the missing parts of history. How the truth was not truly it.

"*It was never recorded,*" her father once said. "*Never dated and never spoke about how it was or who it was. There was a deranged scientist, nearly mad, who aligned with the Clubs. A genius who created weaponry by using steam-power, gears, and the human body, permitting them to forge together."* She remembered her father touching her mechanical arm, tapping on the metallic piece, the double-barrel sniper hiding beneath.

"This scientist sold his inventions not only to his allies but to all his enemies, reaping vast wealth in the process. The War transformed into a chaotic scramble for survival once these deadly inventions arrived on the battlefield. It marked the beginning of a new era, one that showed each nation how to defend themselves independently and no longer rely on alliances for their protection." Her father's gaze turned distant as if his mind replayed the events of the past. *"My father, your grandfather, was the first to be spared from the conflict. The Diamond King was enraged, for he found himself at a disadvantage against the new weaponry. Eventually, the Club King discovered the scientist's hiding place and condemned him to death. Yet, on the night of his execution, he vanished without a trace as if swallowed by the very shadows he dwelt in.*

"And the most astonishing part," her father had continued, *"was the existence of two treaties. The first, a public peace treaty that spoke of the war's end and its reasons. Then the true contract, hidden from the public, which aimed to conceal the real motives and events. The Kings were forced to sign both, bound to secrecy. Unfortunately, your grandfather had a loose tongue and revealed the truth to me as soon as he returned from Club Caverns."* She remembered the concerned look on his face as he told her this. *"Remember, Cassandra, this is our secret, you must not tell anyone. No one else knows of this."*

Cassandra had agreed to not say anything, and to this day she found it off that her father entrusted her with this piece of information instead of his precious son.

The doors to the Dining Hall swung open, causing Cassandra to look up from her plate. She watched as Grayson strolled into the room, his dark red hair pulled back into a tight low bun with strands poking out in the most random of places. His clothes were dirty, as if he had been training for hours.

"Ah! Good morning!" Grayson greeted his family, his arms extended as he bowed playfully before them. He moved to Cassandra first, planting a gentle kiss on the top of her head. "Cassy." Then he circled around their father and gave his right shoulder a squeeze. "Oh, Father. You seem tense."

"Hmm." Their father playfully brushed off Grayson's concern, focusing on the newspaper once more. "How was training?"

Grayson flopped into his seat to the King's right. He possessed an impeccable physique, built like a true Heart Lot warrior. Among the Harth family, he stood out as someone who had remarkably few attachments with the sole exception being his bow. Cassandra often marvelled at how he, like many other residents of the islands, seemed to have minimal attachments.

With a soft mechanical click Grayson's left arm retracted the bulky mechanical bow, allowing for his mechanical arm to come forth, resting it behind his seat. "Father," he began, reaching for a strawberry in the bowl that was placed to his left. Jaronas lifted his eyes from the paper, acknowledging his son. "You must have a word with the trainer. He insists on altering the techniques for the fencing component, which is becoming overly complex and causing me to doubt my abilities." He flashed a mischievous grin at Cassandra then popped a strawberry into his mouth before reaching for another. "Sister, please disregard this conversation, as it is not something you need to be bothered with." He swung around his strawberry as he spoke. "After all, men must attend to the finer details in life, to enhance themselves."

As Grayson chuckled, Cassandra swiftly raised her arm and shot the strawberry out of his hand. She did not care for his words, as most of the time they did not make sense, however she did care for the way he spoke to her. It was rare he did such a thing, playfully speaking down to her. No matter how playful it may have been, Cassandra found no amusement in it. Grayson sat in shock, while his sister simply smirked and blew smoke off her sniper.

Jaronas shook his head at his children, ignoring their banter before reassuring his son that he would excel. Words of encouragement were exchanged, and he reminded them to not let such little things affect their behaviours. "We are Harths!" Jaronas began, setting his newspaper down. Dark eyes locked onto Grayson, who had stopped whining about his personal trainer. "Your grandfather won the Triumph Games, as did I. Now it is your turn, Grayson. It is your turn to claim the title!"

Despite her father's words, Cassandra sensed her brother's nervousness. She saw the hint of fear and worry in his eyes as he nodded his head. "Yes, Father. I will do my best."

He was no fit for this tournament. She knew it, her father knew it, and Grayson knew it, too. Her brother trained his entire life, but nonetheless, he was not mentally prepared for it. He never understood the true cost of losing, never cared for the duties that came with the title that was given to him.

Their father nodded, rising from his seat. "We leave at dawn." With that he left the room, leaving his children quiet. Cassandra silently ate, waiting for her brother to say something, but he sat silently staring at the food before him, clearly lost in his own thoughts. Whenever Grayson needed someone to speak with, Cassandra was always there. No matter how much she hated the system, she could never hate her brother.

She swallowed her food and calmly sipped from her cup of tea. "You will be alright."

"You have no idea what it is like," Grayson seethed, the weight of his emotions evident in his voice. His eyes narrowed, locking onto hers with a fierce intensity. "The expectations imposed on me since birth—the relentless training, day after day. Pushing myself to the limits and never being enough—it never seems to end. Everything I have worked for is about to be placed on a stage for everyone to watch and sometimes I stand there knowing that none of it will ever matter to me, it only matters to him, and I know I have to do it for him even when I know I will fail." Grayson shifted his gaze to the closed Dining Hall doors. "I will be nothing but a disappointment to him."

"You are not a disappointment to him," Cassandra scoffed. "Trust me. You're his precious Prince."

Grayson glared at his sister. "Yes, and that comes with unrealistic expectations."

Cassandra forced herself to not grow angry. To compose herself. How could he say such a thing? The only unrealistic thing would be her trying to compete, yet here he sits, with everything she has and wants, and he is ungrateful for it all.

She forced a tight smile. "You will do great. Besides, it is not that hard. You are simply being dramatic." She nonchalantly took another sip of her tea, satisfied with her answer.

Her brother scoffed, disbelief etched on his face. "Not that difficult? Are you even listening to yourself?"

"You are overreacting. It is simple—hit your target, run, shoot, fight. Well, I admit the fighting part might present some challenges…"

"You are of no use, no help at all." Grayson abruptly stood up. "Be thankful you were born a woman; you could never understand the position I find myself in right now."

"Oh, yes, because the books Father bestowed upon me were such a blessing!" Cassandra shot back, her voice tinged with bitterness. "Forced to observe from the Sky Box and mingle with those foolish rulers when I would much rather be participating in the games!"

"This is not about you, Cass!" Grayson began to stride toward the door. The Princess swiftly rose from her seat and fired a shot at the wooden door, her anger getting the best of her. Her brother's movements ceased; his mechanical bow activated with a resounding click. A fiery expression of anger consumed his face as he pivoted towards her, his arm raised and ready to retaliate. "You nearly shot me!"

"Just sit," Cassandra huffed, gesturing for him to return to his seat, but he remained rooted by the door "Alright. Understand that I am not trying to make this about my issues, but you are putting an immense amount of pressure on yourself. You will be extraordinary, unparalleled by anyone else." Cassandra smiled as she slowly stepped to her brother. "If it helps, once we arrive at the Arena, can we practise shooting together? Or, better yet, I could try to convince Father to allow your trainer to accompany us? We could arrange additional training sessions before each section?"

"You would truly do that for me?"

Cassandra approached her younger brother, placing a reassuring hand on his shoulder. "We share the same blood. I would do anything for you, including ensuring that you remain as relaxed and composed as possible."

Grayson shook his head. "I may not be as good as the other competitors, there is a chance of me failing and disappointing him. I cannot do such a thing. We have a legacy to uphold–"

Cassandra tightened her grip on Grayson's shoulder, pain creeping up in her chest. "You, Grayson, are no failure. You are perfect in every way, shape, and form." Her gaze filled with confidence. "Remember that."

With a short nod, he smiled lightly. "I am perfect, then?"

She laughed. "You are impossible."

CHAPTER 2

Cassandra surveyed the chaotic scene before her. Shoes scattered on the floor, books stacked on her bed, divided by genres and use, and dresses carelessly flung about. Some hung off the edge of the bed while her most elegant dresses remained in her armoire. Cassandra continued to divide her dresses by use. Debating if she should pack more or less. Marching to her dresser, she examined the trousers and shirts, still debating whether she should pack them. She was determined to pack on her own. She had dismissed her maids without considering the unfamiliar terrain of the Forest Lands–the temperature, the weather, or any practicalities for her packing.

A sudden knock on her door shattered her focus on the disarray before her. Cassandra silently hoped it was Savannah coming back to her aid, however it was Grayson who entered, wearing a smile that stretched from ear to ear. "Father granted permission for my trainer to accompany us," he announced. That morning at breakfast while Grayson trained, Cassandra had fulfilled her promise and successfully convinced their father to allow his trainer to join them on the expedition. However, she was obligated to bring Savannah, as it was deemed inappropriate for a Princess to travel without her maid.

"You had my word. Now you can relax and pack for the trip," Cassandra reassured Grayson.

"You do know we have maids to handle the packing, right? There is no need to do it all on your own." A hint of amusement was in his voice as he surveyed the chaos on her bed.

Cassandra let out a frustrated huff, tossing some books back onto the pile that had accumulated on her bed.

"Would you like me to get Savannah?"

Cassandra nodded her head. "Yes, please."

Once Savannah had returned, Cassandra decided on three books to bring along on her journey.:*History of Our Nations, Beginning of the Triumph Games*, and a self-help guide called *How to Become a Lady*. Each carefully picked and essential for her travels. She considered them easy light reads, however it was *How to Become a Lady* that filled her with unease, as she knew she would be expected to mingle with the elites at the games. She blamed her father for bestowing this book upon her, and instructing her to bring it.

She felt utterly unprepared. No matter how many times she attended her manners sessions, she never quite excelled. Initially, her mother had been the driving force behind those lessons, sitting with her and imparting wisdom, but after her mother's passing, the session seemed pointless and her governess was a horribly bitter woman.

Savannah swiftly packed the rest of Cassandra's things and guided her towards the copper carriages waiting at the front of the Lot. Unlike the grandiose castles of the past, Cassandra's home was a humble abode, constructed entirely of wood, with large glass windows and interwoven copper accents. As she took one last look at her home she realised this journey marked her first separation from it. Despite its simplicity, Cassandra cherished her home; it was always a place that welcomed her people with open arms.

The copper carriages represented a new era of technology for the Heart Lot Islands. These steam-powered carriages with large rectangular windows wrapped around their copper frames. They boasted ample space, comfortably accommodating a family of four. Positioned at the front of the carriage was a mechanical horse, its entire body adorned in copper hues to match the carriage. The horse's face, though, seemed more like an artificial construct, resembling something born in a laboratory rather than nature.

Climbing into the carriage alongside her brother and father, Cassandra kept her gaze on the Lot, watching as the carriage slowly carried the Harth family away.

Cassandra's eyes lingered to the grand cabin gradually receding into the distance and becoming shrouded by trees. She continued to observe her lands, witnessing the homes that scattered throughout the villages and the crowds bustling by. The homes consisted of wood or stone, while very few were built of iron and metal. Cassandra did not hesitate to gaze up to the bright sky being clouded with the occasional blimp transporting goods to other nations or simply supplying food for the people of the Heart Lot Islands. She realised how much she would miss her home during the short period of time that she will be away. Part of her would miss walking along the familiar roads of her village, however she was excited to see what was going to happen in the next upcoming weeks. Hoping to come back home with memories and stories to tell.

Grayson nudged her, offering a nervous smile.

Jaronas cleared his throat, adjusting the crown atop his dark red hair, and with an air of authority he commanded the attention of his children, preparing them for the journey ahead. He spoke of the destinations, the visits to the nations, and the importance of adhering to strict guidelines. His gaze lingered on his daughter as he emphasised the significance of the guidebook and the rules she must follow. Her father had high hopes for Cassandra, but he knew the complexities of their world. First impressions were very important, and he wished for her to make a lasting impact.

Cassandra straightened her posture as they arrived at the docks, the Royal Ship looming before them like a formidable beast ready to set sail to Spade City. She observed the final preparations being made by the workers of Shipwreck Bay. The imposing ship before her was covered in a rich, dark red that caught her eye. Massive gears adorned its sides, promising swift propulsion on the journey to Spade City. This vessel was a collaborative creation between Shipwreck Bay and Weaponry Cord. Its sleek exterior concealed an array of mechanical weaponry, ready to be deployed at a moment's notice. Three imposing white sails bore the Harth Family crest at their centre.

As the crew activated the ship and harnessed the wind's power, the flags billowed and the gears spun at a breathtaking speed. Cassandra's eyes scanned the marines that stood on the dock. Their disciplined movement was a testament to their unwavering dedication. In the sheltered enclave nearby, beneath a gazebo adorned with chairs and fans, sat five councilmen, trusted allies to her father. Each councilman hailed from a different island, their roles integral to the prosperity and defence of the Heart Lot Islands.

Florian, a native of Farmers Base, oversaw the cultivation of crops and the fishing trade, and the occasional salt trade, ensuring the islands' sustenance. Loris, hailing from Shipwreck Bay, commanded the construction and enhancement of the nation's warships, transforming ruined ships into formidable vessels. Ruben, a resident of the Island of Metal, held the best blacksmiths, forging iron rivets and crafting essential parts for the ships. Dirk, from Marine Island, commanded the military forces and served as the first line of defence, responsible for safeguarding the islands from external threats. Lastly, Mees, the resident of Weaponry Cord, specialised in crafting advanced weapons tailored to the ships and the royal family, as well as fine-tuning their gears with precision.

These councilmen, with their distinct expertise and local commitment, formed the pillar of the Heart Lot Islands' strength and unity. As Cassandra observed them, she could not help but feel a surge of gratitude and pride for the collective effort that ensured the security and prosperity of their nation.

Accompanying them were their sons and daughters, who were also close companions of Cassandra and Grayson. They were not sitting in the shade like their fathers but laughing and sitting on barrels. Cassandra nudged her brother, pointing to their friends. They were all there, all nine of them, to wish the royals farewell. The carriage rolled towards the gazebo, stopping mere feet away from the steps leading in.

Jaronas, wearing a wide smile, was the first to step out of the carriage once it came to a halt. He warmly greeted his friends as he stepped into the shaded area. He emphasised the importance of promptly notifying him of any issues during his absence. Trusting these men implicitly, Jaronas knew that the nation would be in capable hands in his absence.

When Grayson emerged from the carriage, a piercing scream shattered the air. Cassandra's eyes snapped towards the commotion, witnessing a swarm of women flocking towards her brother. They were his adoring admirers, just a few of the many he effortlessly enticed with his smooth words and captivating smile. Determined to protect her brother from the relentless attention, Cassandra swiftly descended from the carriage and dismissed the women with a wave, summoning the guards for assistance.

As the guards intervened and escorted the sobbing women away, their friends rushed to them. Mila, Florian's daughter, was the first to Cassandra's side. She embraced Cassandra tightly, radiating a regal presence that surpassed herself. Tall and graceful, with cascading golden locks and deep blue eyes, Mila possessed a captivating beauty that radiated from her.

"Do you really have to leave? I was prepared to plan a field party in our family barn!" Mila's voice rang out, akin to a soothing song. She released Cassandra from their embrace and turned to Grayson next, giving him a warm hug.

Grayson chuckled, his deep voice resonating. "I must admit, a field party sounds far more appealing than the tournament." Mila's gatherings were legendary, an annual event that drew an elite crowd. She had transformed her family barn into a sanctuary, a haven where they could escape the suffocating constraint of their daily lives. Nights and days were spent laughing and feeling free, with the taste of her father's secret rum lingering on their lips. Cassandra knew she would miss those carefree moments but she also knew that more adventure awaited her on this journey.

Yara, daughter of Mees, reached out to embrace Cassandra next. The two were inseparable, always by each other's side. Yara, with her short brown hair and matching brown eyes, stood in stark contrast to Mila. "Oh, Mila, please." Yara rolled her eyes at her friend's comment before hugging Grayson in turn. Mila let out a frustrated sigh; the two never truly got along but remained polite due to their fathers' close bond.

Next in line were the twins, Jan and Nora, children to Loris, bidding their farewells to the royal siblings. Nora had blue eyes while Jan's were a rich hazel. Jan, towering over his sister, possessed a similar height to Grayson and to the two oldest sons of Dirk, whereas Nora remained of similar height to Cassandra and Adriana.

"Shall we come and watch you?" Jan said as he pulled away from Grayson and approached Cassandra. "Our father mentioned the possibility of sending us on a ship."

"Would our fathers be joining us?" Yara asked over Jan's shoulder.

Jan turned from Cassandra and smirked. "No! Just us."

Grayson smiled as he embraced Nora tightly. "As long as your father constructed and repaired the ship, and not you, I do not see why not." Nora could not help but chuckle at his remark, while Jan shot a disapproving glare at Grayson, playfully irritated.

Lars, the son of Ruben, forcefully shoved Jan aside and extended his arms dramatically. "I shall cross the seas gladly to see Cassandra once more!" Cassandra squealed as Lars lifted her off the ground, twirling her around.

Mila panicked. "You are going to make her sick!" Lightly tapping Lars on the shoulder, Cassandra noticed Yara rolling her eyes again, sharing a similar distaste for Lars as she did for Mila.

Last were Dirk's children; the four of them stood tall and proud. They had been instilled with a strong sense of discipline. While the older two had already commenced their marine training, soon to be placed in a Camp, the younger siblings had yet to begin their training, as they waited to complete their educational training. Bran, the eldest, was never one for displays of affection, a trait shared by the two oldest sons. Bran stood tall, with buzzed light brown hair and dark brown eyes; he shook Cassandra's hand firmly and gave Grayson a friendly pat on the shoulder before joining Yara's side. The two were engaged and destined to marry after the tournament, an arranged marriage by their fathers, yet seemingly a perfect match. They stood side by side, adopting a military stance with their hands behind their backs. Hendrik, the second son, bore a striking resemblance to his older brother. He followed in Bran's footsteps, adhering to the same disciplined demeanour. Micha, the youngest brother, had lighter hair than his siblings, which fell messily around his light green eyes. He leaped towards Cassandra, planting a gentle kiss on the top of her head and wishing her a safe journey.

Adriana, the youngest and sole daughter, embraced Cassandra with a gentle yet somewhat reluctant hold. Her light brown hair was neatly braided, accentuating her light green eyes inherited from her mother. "How dare you leave me," she whispered softly into her friend's ear, her voice tinged with a mixture of sadness and playful reproach.

"Yes, yes, Cass is leaving, but I am the one competing in the tournament. Where is my goodbye hug?" Grayson extended his arms, expecting his hug.

Adriana, with a hint of mischief in her eyes, simply patted his chest. "There," she said, teasingly. She then returned to stand by Cassandra's side, intertwining their arms together.

"I've got you, brother!" Jan exclaimed as he enveloped Grayson in a tight bear hug. Micha soon followed suit, joining the embrace. Grayson tapped both of them, signalling to be released.

Mila joined Cassandra and Adriana, with Lars trailing behind her. Yara, known for her blunt remarks, referred to Lars as a love-struck puppy, clearly amused by his infatuation. Placing her hands gently on Cassandra's shoulders, Mila requested, "Please, do write to us." Yara promptly joined Adriana's side—someone she genuinely enjoyed being around unlike the light-hearted group before them. "Tell us about your experience, the people you meet—"

"And especially thePrinces from the other nations," Nora interjected, winking as she walked over and rested an elbow on Yara's shoulder.

Cassandra offered a sweet smile, attempting to disregard Yara and Nora's secretive whispers and the mischievous smirks on their faces. She knew what was in store and how they were prepared to tease Mila for their own entertainment. "I promise not to leave out a single detail." Cassandra smiled.

Yara began speaking, providing instructions on staying aboard the ship and maintaining composure during storms. Nora joined in, sharing knowledge about the location of emergency boats. Mila frowned at the sudden change in atmosphere, dampening their cheerful farewell, and soon the three of them found themselves bickering.

Adriana followed Cassandra's gaze to the group of boys. "I worry about him," she admitted. Her brother was laughing without a care in the world, his head thrown back. Micha, the youngest and shortest among them, stood in the centre of the circle, gazing up at his older siblings and friends. "I fear that something unfortunate may happen during these games and my father will blame himself for it."

"I understand your concern for your younger brother, but it is time to learn that sometimes letting go is all that is needed. He will be fine. He has trained hard and will excel in these games," Adriana sighed as she glanced towards her brother. "Micha has yet to grow, and Father worries he will remain short. However, Mother is not concerned, as she believes he will grow in due time. He will blossom when he becomes strong and excel when the time is right. Grayson has already grown; it is time for him to shine and put his hard work to use."

Cassandra gave Adriana an odd look, not knowing what she had said. Before she could say anything, her father summoned herself and Grayson, indicating it was time to depart.

With tearful goodbyes, the group of friends bid each other farewell as the royals stepped aboard the Royal Ship, accompanied by Grayson's trainer and Savannah, who were already on board. Savannah informed Cassandra that her belongings had been placed in the Princess Suite. Giving a nod of acknowledgement, Cassandra turned her attention to her brother.

As the ship slowly drifted away from the dock, the captain barked orders to his crew, and the sound of a horn on land marked the final farewell.

With a surge of excitement, Cassandra waved vigorously. They were bound for Spade City, arriving by the end of the day, and the anticipation of the journey ahead filled her with an overwhelming sense of joy.

CHAPTER 3

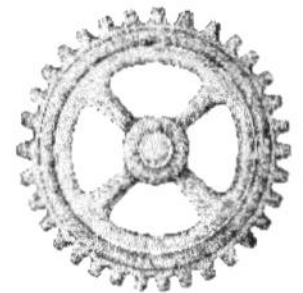

Cassandra settled on the captain's deck, her back turned to the vast expanse of the sea. The salty breeze caressed her face, a gentle reminder to find solace in the moment. Taking her seat, she surveyed the ship and its crew. Within seconds, her attention was absorbed by the pages of *History of Our Nations*, the book she held in her hands. The weight of anticipation made it impossible for her to delve into the other two books she had brought along, but history, with its timeless essence, remained a constant refuge she could always turn to.

As she delved into the words on the pages, her mind embarked on a deeper exploration of the histories that shaped her land. *"The Heart Lot Islands, composed of six individual islands, stood as guardians against foreign threats."* Her reading revealed their reliance on steam-powered blimps for the transportation of salt and sea life to the mainland. *"Known for their fishing, sailing, and marine activities, the Heart Lot Islands engaged in trade with all nations, acting as mediators and acquiring valuable resources in return. Gold, diamonds, protection, and advanced equipment flowed into their grasp."*

While immersed in her reading, the clanking of metal, the grunts of men, and her father's resounding voice pierced through her concentration. Jaronas was displeased by Grayson's fencing stance, irritated and displeased. The sounds of their practice echoed across the ship. Cassandra's gaze shifted downwards, landing on the deck where men lounged and conversed, others diligently attending to their duties and few observing Grayson and his trainer. The relentless training continued until dinner, her father's voice an incessant source of irritation. Cassandra reluctantly set her book aside, tearing her gaze from the pages to peer out at the vast sea surrounding her. The boundless water, an endless expanse of blue, seemed to muffle her father's shouts as the waves crashed against the ship.

"We are just days away from the tournament and you still cannot hold your foil properly?" Jaronas berated his son, who set down his sword in frustration. "Bend your knees, lunge properly, keep your back straight and your arm tight." Grayson sighed, enduring his father's complaints until he allowed him to continue.

Cassandra knew her brother's fencing skills were lacking, often having to instruct him in the proper stances herself. Yet, she could not resist intervening, smirking at her father as she retorted. "If it is so easy, why not give it a try, Father? As I do remember reading about your last fencing challenge." She clicked her tongue as she turned a page in her book, shaking her head. "Third place."

An awkward silence fell over the ship. Cassandra knew she had crossed a line and spoke out of turn, but it was said, and she still had some leftover anger from the day before that needed to be unleashed. Jaronas turned slowly, his gaze piercing. "Excuse me?" he questioned, his voice firm.

Cassandra held her head high, refusing to back down. "Well?" she replied, unyielding. Her boldness allowed Grayson to find some respite from his nerves, making fewer mistakes with their father's attention diverted.

Her father said nothing, storming off the deck and slamming the door to the Captain's Quarters. They heard loud crashes and glass shattering, and Cassandra saw the Captain gulp; however, she did not care, and shot a reassuring thumbs-up to her brother, who nodded gratefully.

"Peace for once," she muttered, drawing a chuckle from the Captain.

The rest of the evening passed on the deck with the crew and Grayson. Her father remained in seclusion, allowing her brother to practise more freely and improve his fencing stance.

Once again, Cassandra demonstrated the movements, tugging at the maroon fabric that covered her legs to reveal the proper foot placement to Grayson. They eventually settled against the boat's ledge, watching the sun slowly set, a blend of orange, pink, and blue hues filling the sky. Time slipped away and darkness descended, putting an end to Grayson's training.

The Captain's voice ran out into the dark sky, informing the crew that they would soon arrive at Spade City and to prepare accordingly. Confused, the two royals exchanged glances as they noticed bulky goggles with dark tints being handed out. Their father emerged from the Captain's Quarters, taking a pair of goggles from a crew member. Placing a hand gently on each of his children's shoulders, he began explaining that they were close to Spade City. Cassandra was prepared to give a snarky remark; something along the lines of "*Yes, the Captain just told us that,*" but Grayson gave her a look indicating to not push it. She rolled her eyes. They both knew that by their father's approach it was his way of apologizing for the earlier events.

Cassandra and Grayson continued to stare at one another, silently debating who should speak to their father first, but that was when she heard it—the pulsing music blasting from speakers, flashes of white and blue lights. Grayson gasped while Cassandra stood with her mouth wide open. The two were in shock about what was before them.

Their father chuckled at his children's astonished expressions, drawing them in closer with a smile. "Welcome to Spade City!"

Spade City held a reputation steeped in danger. It was a place where individuals were moulded into lethal killing machines, holding deadly skills and nurturing intellect like a dark art.

The city was known for making dangerous trades, such as dealing weaponry with her Island. The blacksmiths made no less than a thousand weapons for the city once a week, and in return, her home demanded for their advanced technology. The city did the same with the other nations. They extracted gold from the Diamond Kingdom to create coins in exchange for protection. In Cassandra's home land, they exchanged salt and fish for inventions that were being created with Club Caverns.

As the Royal Ship edged closer to Spade City, Cassandra's eyes widened in awe. The sight before her was overwhelming—a forest of towers, giant skyscrapers that seemed to defy the heavens themselves. The city's cacophony of loud shouts, the mesmerising play of lights and smoke rising from various corners, almost as if the city itself were breathing fire, stirred a mixture of fear and fascination within her. The sprawling buildings surrounding the towers formed a labyrinth, concealing secrets within their imposing structure.

Their father stepped away to speak with the Captain when Grayson slid over to his sister. "Tonight, I intend to attend the Mercenary Games," he said in a low tone.

Cassandra's gaze sharpened, her mouth forming a pronounced frown. "There is no such thing, it is nothing more than a myth."

"That is your belief," Grayson replied. "But I am determined to find a way to witness those games. This is your final opportunity to join me."

Cassandra's heart raced within her chest. She had researched those infamous games, hearing different people speak of its true existence or not, along with various books that briefly spoke of these deadly games. They were considered a darker version of the Triumph Games, an unholy competition held in the remote corners of Spade City. This event involved a deadly game where the thrill of killing became a sport.

Whispers of these games had first reached Cassandra through the siblings' shared friends, who spoke of it with an unsettling excitement. Competitors supposedly willingly surrendered their lives as if accepting their fates for these games. The thought of her brother participating in such a gruesome event weighed heavily on her mind. However, part of her remained intrigued by the possibility of these games being real. It was a once-in-a-lifetime opportunity.

As the ship drew nearer to the outskirts of Spade City, Cassandra found herself lost in contemplation. She mulled over the various ways things could end horribly. Several troubling scenarios crossed her mind. However, when she turned to her brother, she gave him a decisive nod, signifying her final choice. Grayson responded with a radiant smile and enveloped his sister in a tight embrace. Cassandra was aware that Spade City harboured dark secrets; although Grayson was determined to uncover one of them, she was resolute in her decision not to let him face it alone.

They stood on the ship's deck, their gazes fixed upon the towering structures that lay ahead. These colossal edifices made them feel minuscule, akin to ants navigating a city of giants.

"Look there," remarked one of the crew members beside them, his head turning to his comrades. He extended his arm towards the foreboding circular building in the distance. Its exterior was adorned with gleaming white tiles, and it was bathed in an eerie display of white lights flickering around it. "That is where the Duelists undergo their training."

Cassandra turned to Grayson once more, who was listening intently to the crew members.

Another man made a derisive sound at the sight. "I wonder what those assassins do inside there."

"Rumour has it that the Spade King permits them to spar against his son. It has been going on for years," offered the first man.

"How do you know this?" questioned a third crew member, narrowing his eyes. "You've never set foot in Spade City in your entire life."

The first man chuckled. "It is called gossip. The ladies are experts at it; most of the time, they are right."

"Most of the time," echoed the other man with a chuckle.

"Do not think about it," Cassandra mumbled to Grayson, who did nothing but flash her a bright smile. Before he could respond, the ship's docking process commenced.

Waiting below were two royal carriages welcoming the Royal Harth family to Spade City, and there stood the King, Queen, and future heir.

Standing in the middle was Kenji, the King of Spade City, his features etched with an air of authority. Both he and the Queen looked nearly as young as her father did. His oval face, defined cheekbones, and strong jawline exuded an aura of power. His straight, shoulder-length black hair framed piercing black eyes that seemed to analyse the arriving ship with an intensity that sent shivers down Cassandra's spine. A whip-blade replaced his right arm, a formidable weapon befitting his fearsome reputation. The handle of a black dagger, bearing the Spars family crest, rested at his side, his left hand brushing against it with an almost habitual touch.

Beside the King stood Queen Suzume, a woman of equally formidable presence despite her petite stature. Her pale skin and blank expression seemed to conceal a well of hidden emotions. Her black eyes betrayed no excitement as the crew secured the tethers to the dock. The wind caressed her long black hair, wrapping around her like a protective veil. Her dress, a mesmerising shade of dark blue silk, draped gracefully over her, but what truly captured Cassandra's attention was the sight of the samurai sword, ancient and formidable, securely fastened to the Queen's waist with her robotic fingers gently touching its leathers, as if ready to be drawn at a moment's notice.

A sense of awe washed over Cassandra as she caught sight of the extraordinary sword. She could not contain her excitement as she turned to her brother, urging him to share in her admiration. "Do you see that? On the Queen's right," she whispered. "That is the Spars family sword. Forged with the sharpest steel and holding true dragon leathers. Yara told me all about it! I must write to her at once about this marvel!"

"What is so special about it?" He asked, his dark brows furrowing in curiosity.

Cassandra glared at him, her voice carrying a hint of exasperation. "That sword is the embodiment of the entire Spars family's legacy. The Queen is a true royal by blood and it was bestowed upon her by her father, serving as protection from an assassin hired by the Dimond's to place a bounty on her head." Cassandra's gaze remained fixed on the sword as she casually mentioned, "They say that before King Kenji ascended to the throne, he was the most formidable assassin in all of Spade City, taking on contracts from anyone willing to pay the right price."

Grayson raised a spectacle brow. "How do you know such things?"

"It is called *reading*, brother. If you had not spent your days training and remained in Mother's library with me, you could have learned a thing or two about the other nations."

"But that is what you are here for. To inform me on such things," Grayson said with a smile, causing Cassandra to roll her eyes and playfully shove her brother. Their father's call echoed through the ship, causing the two to scurry to him. Together, with their father leading, they walked down the ramp, stepping onto the dock.

Her father smiled through his thick beard, his dark brown eyes gleaming with joy as he greeted his old rival, King Kenji. The two monarchs met halfway; they clasped their hands firmly in a handshake. "It has been too long, old friend," Jaronas said. The three royal children stepped closer, cautious of these new people.

"Why is he kind to our rival?" Grayson asked his sister, who shook her head wondering the same thing.

The Spade King nodded. "Much too long, Jaronas."

Jaronas exchanged smiles with Queen Suzume and nodded towards the Spade Prince, whose face remained as cold and impassive as his father's. Cassandra did not comprehend her father's warm greetings towards their rivals. In her eyes, every nation posed a potential threat, regardless of the trade agreements made. It was a treaty signed years ago when the nations were once allies, but times had changed.

"I do not believe you have met my children," Jaronas said, extending his hand. It was the cue for the siblings to share an uncertain glance, but they drew closer to their father nonetheless. Cassandra and Grayson performed their respectful bows as Suzume approached them with a delicate smile.

Cassandra could not take her eyes off the legendary samurai sword hanging at the Queen's waist. In a hushed voice, but loud enough to be heard, Suzume murmured, "Gifts." Her gesture prompted the two guards at the Queen's side to present gifts to the young royals.

In Spade City it was customary to present gifts upon welcomed guests, and it was considered improper not to do so. Cassandra remembered her father questioning her and Grayson a few weeks earlier, demanding to know what intrigued them most about Spade City. Cassandra had passionately discussed Queen Suzume's sword for hours before Grayson had intervened, expressing his admiration for the intricate crafted lethal leathers they had read about before rushing off to a training session.

In a small silver box, Cassandra received a metal bracelet—a miniature replica of Queen Suzume's samurai sword. It was an enchanting and thoughtful present. "Your father told me you are fascinated with my family's sword. I do hope you enjoy the gift," she remarked.

The bracelet fit perfectly and Cassandra expressed her gratitude with a warm smile. Grayson unwrapped his gift—a black leather band with a metal bow—and learned it was meant to tie his hair. Suzume smiled lightly as he thanked her. Soon enough, it was the Harths' turn to present a gift to the Spade Prince. Cassandra watched closely as her father signalled for a crew member to hand him the gift.

Taking the opportunity, Cassandra examined the man before her, whose reputation as a dangerous being preceded him. Grayson had informed her of the Prince's name. Sebastian Spars was born and raised to be an assassin, much like his father. He stood tall and broad, with black hair pulled back in a similar style to her brother. She noticed the metallic components on his face and the robotic arm on his right side. The concealed daggers around his body intrigued her, but what captivated her the most was the dagger he was nonchalantly playing with. Cassandra had listened to stories of this dagger, crafted with true steel and dragon leather, just as sharp and lethal as the samurai sword.

As she gazed at him, his dark brown eyes shifted, taking in the presence of the three new royals in his nation. Their eyes locked and she felt a sudden chill run down her spine, unable to break free from the gaze that held her.

Cassandra was momentarily lost in her thoughts until Grayson's hushed whisper pulled her back. Their father presented the gift to Cassandra, silently urging her to pass it on to Sebastian. With a nod, she took the small, neatly-wrapped maroon box.

As she moved closer to him, her heart quickened, intimidated by his deadly skills. Holding the box out at a cautious distance, she observed Sebastian as he reached for it, their fingers lightly brushing as he took hold of the gift. Stepping back, she watched him unwrap it, revealing a black metal ring intricately designed with twisted waves symbolising sea life—a creation by Mets.

Sebastian bowed in appreciation, expressing gratitude to the Harths.

Soon, they parted ways, each group boarding separate carriages, the adults in one carriage and the children in the other. Grayson pressed his face against the carriage window, utterly captivated by the new city. On the other hand, Cassandra sat quietly, her hands neatly folded in her lap—a posture the chapters of her guide on *How to Become a Lady* incessantly reminded her to adopt. It hurt her back to sit in such a way, especially with her corset poking into her side. However, all her focus remained on the assassin seated before her. She did not like the sudden change in carriages, did not like the idea of her father alone in another carriage. Anything was possible— much like anything was possible in that very moment being alone with Sebastian.

Sebastian's piercing gaze locked onto her once more, as if he heard her thoughts. It was not long before Grayson bombarded Sebastian with questions about the city's towering buildings and its people, drawing comparisons to the Heart Lot Islands.

Cassandra continued to ignore her brother, her attention held firmly by Sebastian. She could not help but notice the slight differences in his facial features compared to his parents'. While they possessed almond-shaped eyes, Sebastian's were wider and circular, often hooded. She wondered about the reasons behind these distinctions, but the thought of inquiring directly felt too impolite. Try as she might, every attempt to speak to Sebastian failed, her words held captive by a strange mix of nervousness and fascination.

Her heart raced each time his gaze met hers, rendering her speechless and disoriented. The turmoil in her stomach left her feeling both queasy and anxious.

Before she could gather her thoughts, Grayson directed a question at Sebastian, seemingly oblivious to the underlying tension. "Do you know where the Mercenary Games are being held tonight?"

Cassandra widened her eyes in disbelief, and promptly slapped her brother's arm, a subtle plea for him to cease his inquiries.

"There is no such thing" Sebastian replied smoothly, his gaze unwavering.

She could not help but smirk, her head slightly tilted as she engaged in this verbal dance. "Why the sudden defence? Seems to me that Spade City is hiding something."

Sebastian scoffed. "You do not know what you are talking about."

"Alright, then what is the Arena for?"

"For training the Duelists."

Cassandra narrowed her eyes at his quick response. "Are you sure? Are you positive there is nothing else happening within that Arena?"

"I think I know what happens in my city."

She did not like his response. In retaliation she clicked her tongue, watching as he cringed at the noise. Smirking, she leaned forward. "Let us say, at night, where no one is nearby, we were to enter the Arena."

"Regardless of what you may think, this is none of your concern. Last I checked, you were a Heart Princess, not a Spade Royal," he retorted with an air of finality, but his eyes locked in an unspoken challenge.

In that tense moment, with locked gazes, Cassandra revealed in the exhilaration of this little game he was trying to play. The secrets and mysteries that swirled around Spade City beckoned to her and she could not help but be drawn in further.

The carriage moved in silence. She looked out her window once more. The only sound was the murmurs of life on the bustling streets of the city, the city being so different to the fields she was used to.

Cassandra could not help but steal glances at Sebastian, his dark eyes wandering over her frame while he maintained an unwavering composure. She found herself questioning the person before her—how could someone as lethal and dangerous as him also possess such undeniable handsomeness? It bothered her, gnawing at her thoughts. Her brother's voice broke the silence, a mutter under his breath as he turned his face to the window, tapping his sister's arm to pull her away from Sebastian's intense gaze.

"What is it?" she inquired, puzzled by his sudden interest in the surroundings.

Grayson did not answer, merely pointing towards a majestic temple perched atop a slight hill, its gates firmly shut. "You live here?" her brother asked with evident excitement.

Sebastian nodded, somewhat puzzled as to why they were so fascinated by his home. Yet, he could not comprehend the thrill that seemed to electrify them both, the exhilaration of leaving their familiar island and exploring this new world.

As the carriage passed through the imposing iron gates and approached Spade Temple, Cassandra noticed the grandeur of its four large pillars at the front, the elegant windows, and the three steps leading to the entry of the house. Servants dressed in traditional Spade City attire—dark blue and white robes—awaited them at the steps of the temple. When the carriage came to a halt, Grayson was the first to spring into action, nearly stumbling as he swung the carriage door open.

Cassandra could not help but giggle, turning to the city's royal. "Please excuse my brother's enthusiasm; he is as captivated by new travels as I am. It is our first time leaving our island, you see."

He nodded thoughtfully. "That explains the odd behaviour."

"Odd?" Cassandra raised an eyebrow in response.

Sebastian nonchalantly stepped out of the carriage. "It is clear you do not understand other nations."

Cassandra could not help but scoff. "I beg your pardon. I did my research."

A shrug accompanied Sebastian's reply. "Reading history books is not always enough; your versions might not be up to date."

He extended his hand, waiting for Cassandra to descend from the carriage. She found him surprisingly formal, yet incredibly rude at the same time. Reluctantly, she took his hand, pulling at her dress and carefully placing her foot on the ground as she stepped out. A shiver ran down her spine as her finger touched his calloused hands—hands that were likely accustomed to killing and dealing with dangerous individuals. She hated herself for being so naïve at times.

Her family was soon informed that they would be guided to their respective rooms as they were to stay the night and travel again in the morning, only this time accompanied by the Spars family.

Cassandra was assigned a servant and she followed the attendant to a lovely chamber adorned with silver sheets, intricate silver embellishments, and walls of a deep blue hue. It was a rather plain room, furnished with a bed, window, and a shared bathroom.

As the door closed behind them, Cassandra and Savannah finally allowed themselves to exhale. She could not contain her excitement, her face lighting up with a bright smile. "Savannah, can you believe it? Spade City!"

Savannah had her head poking into the restroom, unimpressed. "All this wealth and they offer nothing but a tub, sink, and a toilet. How dreadfully plain these people are."

"Savannah please, do not be so judgmental. This is a thrilling new adventure for us!" Cassandra tried to infuse her friend with the same enthusiasm she felt.

With a roll of her dark eyes, Savannah took Cassandra's arm and guided her towards the restroom. "Yes, yes, now let's freshen up before dinner."

After enduring the tense dinner talk with her rivals, Cassandra could not bear another moment in the stifling atmosphere. She excused herself to bed early, desperate to escape the prying gazes and unsettling aura that radiated off of Sebastian.

Throughout the dinner, her mind had been consumed with thoughts of what he was hiding regarding the Mercenary Games. The mere mention of it seemed to send a shiver down her spine, even though the sport's existence was unknown.

In her room Cassandra thought of Sebastian's words, how they lingered in her head and how he spoke nonchalantly about the Mercenary Games. Before she could dive into a deeper conclusion and spiral, a knock on her door pulled her from her thoughts. Startling her, she hesitantly opened the door, only to be relieved to find her brother's face peeking in. A sly smile danced on his lips as he handed her a set of servant clothing from their home, a thoughtful preparation for their undercover exploration.

"This is your final chance," Grayson whispered, his eyes filled with determination.

Cassandra nodded in agreement, silently acknowledging the gravity of their decision. With a huffed breath, she disappeared into her bathroom to change, soon emerging in the humble attire, transforming into a commoner.

As they stealthily slipped into the dimly-lit hallway, the thrill of forbidden adventure ignited a spark of excitement within them. Cassandra and her brother were determined to fulfil the most of their trip in the city. Eager to unravel the mysteries surrounding the Mercenary Games, they navigated the labyrinthine passages, careful not to attract the attention of the servants or secret guards lurking in the shadows. Their daring escape led them out of the Spade Temple and onto a concrete ground adorned with ancient bonsai trees. The two believed they were finally safe from prying eyes, but that thought was short-lived.

A sudden movement caught Cassandra's eye and she gasped, believing it was the elusive secret guard they sought to avoid. However, as the figure moved, it became apparent that he was running away from them, not towards them. He nimbly scaled the temple, leaving Cassandra with an unsettling realisation of how easily they could be caught if they were not careful.

Feet away from the shadowy figure, Grayson panted from the exertion, hands on his knees as he mumbled about wanting to stop, but Cassandra pulled at his arm, gesturing towards the shadowy figure.

"He is our way out. We need to follow him," Cassandra urged her brother, instincts pushing her to pursue the mysterious figure.

Grayson lifted his head, following Cassandra's finger that pointed towards the window the figure had left from, now standing on the rooftop of the temple. "How are you sure he is actually a *he?*"

"Look at his body. The movements are rough and direct, nothing about him screams female. Plus, the no breasts gave it away," Cassandra responded, as the first thing she noticed was his tight-fitted outfit. She quickly led the way.

They squeezed through narrow meditation areas and scaled the iron gates. Keeping a cautious distance, they followed the figure, witnessing his dexterity as he deftly manoeuvred past the guards stationed at the entry door, evading capture with skill and precision. Their hearts raced with anticipation and fear as they crouched in the concealing bushes near the iron gates, holding their breaths until they made it to the bust streets of Spade City.

They continued their hunt, following the hooded figure through the bustling crowds, discreetly pointing out his path to each other, trying to keep a vigilant eye on him. Abruptly, the hooded figure stopped, blending into the large crowd as if he were just another anonymous soul.

The two siblings formed a protective circle, backs automatically clinging to one another as they searched the crowded streets. Cassandra came to the sudden realization that without the hooded figure as a guide back to the temple they were lost in this large, unfamiliar city. She scanned the groups around them, everyone nearly looking identical. Each one held a similar bone structure, hair colour, and posture. It reminded her of King Kenji with his almond-shaped eyes and dark brown colour within.

"No…" Cassandra muttered under her breath, her voice tinged with frustration as she could not find him. "No, no, no, no, no!"

"This way." Grayson reached for his sister's hand, tightening his grip on her as he guided them out of the crowds and towards a nearby alleyway. Cassandra trusted her brother, and together they pressed through the crowd.

As they entered the narrow alley, the atmosphere grew tense and eerie. Trash bins, discarded papers, and bits of metal littered the ground. Suddenly, they heard a thud not too far away, and their surroundings were quickly bathed in a disorienting mix of white and blue lights. Cassandra's instincts warned her of the approaching danger, but before she could react, a gloved hand closed around her throat and the tip of a dagger pressed against the side of her neck. Her breath caught in her throat, causing Grayson to turn. Within sections she retracted her mechanical arm, allowing her sniper to push through. Swiftly, she directed the barrel of her weapon towards the side of the man's face, detecting a cool metal plate on his jaw.

A light hearted chuckle escaped his lips, and that was all she needed to know who the man was.

Grayson retracted his arm, allowing his mechanical bow to show. Along with that, thanks to the new piece he had gotten before the games, an arrow was formed as well. Her brother gripped the arrow firmly. "Release her, Spars," her brother grunted, his bow now aimed at their rival, arrow perfectly aligned to Sebastian's head.

"Why are you following me?" The air in the dead-end alley seemed to grow even heavier as Sebastian's response echoed between the walls, the distant noise of the street fading into oblivion, as if the city itself had abandoned them.

"We saw you leaving the temple and figured we could follow you out."

"Why?"

Neither Grayson nor Cassandra answered. They knew it had to remain a secret; this was none of his concern.

He pressed the tip of his dagger harder into Cassandra's neck. In retaliation, she pressed her weapon against his jaw harder as well. "Do that shit again. I dare you," she grunted.

"Answer me."

"You do not order me around."

Sebastian chuckled. "Cute." He moved his lips closer to her ear, breath fanning her cheek. "Tell me, Princess." He dug the dagger deeper and she felt small droplets of blood trickling down her neck. Grayson gave her a worried look, as if panicking over her wellbeing, but Cassandra did not react, nor did she care. "Why were you following me?"

"I think we both know the answer to that question" was all Cassandra said.

"You are trying to see if I could lead you to the Mercenary Games."

She shrugged. "You came to that conclusion on your own. I did not say anything of that sort, but please, do continue. Having a dagger digging into the side of my neck is very relaxing."

Sebastian did not like her sarcastic comment. "How did you know it was me?"

"We took our chances."

To her astonishment, Sebastian laughed instead of striking them down, his grip loosening, and the dagger soon gone from her neck. Cassandra cautiously stepped back toward her brother, her arm still raised and ready to defend if needed. Grayson protectively stood slightly in front of her to prevent anything else from happening.

"What is this obsession with the Mercenary Games?" he questioned, eyes sparkling in amusement. "Are you truly excited to witness a cruel game where people bleed for sport?"

"It is real," Grayson gasped.

"Hmm." Sebastian stared at his dagger, examining the small residue of blood that remained and wiping it on his shirt. He twirled the weapon, a playful smirk dancing on his lips as he took a step back. "Have fun hunting for the games on your own. You are likely to be searching all night."

With that, he started to make his way down the alley, intent on leaving the siblings behind. Cassandra and Grayson exchanged wide-eyed glances before instinctively taking off after him, determined not to be left stranded in an unfamiliar city. Sebastian turned back one last time, pulling his hood up and disappearing into the bustling crowd.

Cassandra and Grayson went back to following Sebastian. He pushed the siblings to their limits, chasing him through the winding streets and crowded boulevards. As they rounded another corner, they saw Sebastian approaching a steam-power bike, ready to speed off into the night and leave them behind. Cassandra's adrenaline-fuelled determination took over as she saw this as her only chance. She positioned herself in front of the bike, bracing herself for the potential collision.

Sebastian blinked at her in surprise, the only sign of shock visible on his covered face.

"You will take us to the Mercenary Games." Cassandra gasped for air, her heart pounding in her chest. She refused to back down.

"Why?" He raised a dark brow.

She scoffed, gripping the bike's handles tightly, determined to keep him from escaping. "Because you simply cannot leave us here alone! We do not know your nation. We do not know the streets of the city. We could get lost."

Sebastian chuckled, finding her plea amusing. He made another attempt to move the bike forward but she held firm, refusing to let go. "How dramatic are you?" he remarked.

"If you do not help us, I will inform the temple guards, the King, and Queen about your involvement in the Mercenary Games," Cassandra said, her voice firm, though she knew it was a risky move.

Sebastian's dark eyes bore into her blue ones, his expression a clear sign of irritation. "You dare threaten me in my own city and then demand for help?" he hissed.

Cassandra swallowed hard, realising that her approach was not the wisest. Grayson soon appeared, stepping beside his sister.

There was a long silence as the two stared at one another. No one moved or blinked. Heavy breaths and the sound of the streets were all that needed to be heard.

With a heavy sigh, Sebastian pointed north. "Go to the Arena and then to the nearest subway station. Wait there for me, I will help you get in. That is all I will say." He gave her one last look, eyes roaming her body as a small smirk formed on his lips before he sped off.

With the aid of some kind-hearted locals at a nearby noodle restaurant, Cassandra and her brother managed to board a traveller-sized steam-powered train. The train was equipped with twenty seats and carried them to the southern part of the Arena. The conductor explained that they were not allowed to go any further, as the Arena was restricted at night.

They bid him farewell, their footsteps echoing through the dimly-lit streets as they made their way to the nearest subway station.

With the feeble streetlights casting eerie shadows, they followed the overhead sign, its arrow and subway symbol guiding them in the right direction. As they approached the stairs descending into the subway, an unexpected voice shattered the silence, causing them to startle and swiftly pivot on their heels.

Emerging from the moonlit shadows, Sebastian's towering figure became visible, a touch of mockery lacing his tone. "I'm surprised you managed to come this far," he quipped, his hands casually tucked into his pockets.

He motioned for them to follow as he descended the steps. They fell in line, their vigilant gazes scanning their surroundings. The dimly-lit subway was awash in dingy white tiles, with feeble lights casting their glow around. Oddly, there was no sign of a subway train or any other people.

Sebastian began to explain as they reached the end of the platform, where he pushed open the yellow gates barring access to the subway tracks and nonchalantly hopped onto them. Cassandra's heart raced in her chest, her head on a constant swivel to ensure they were not walking into a trap. Grayson seized the opportunity to join Sebastian, and with a hand extended, he helped Cassandra follow suit, her feet landing softly on the concrete surface. Sebastian issued a contemptuous scoff at their cautiousness before he turned and ventured deeper into the subway tunnels.

In the suffocating darkness, their only companions were the cacophonous echoes of their footsteps on the gravel and rocks, and the occasional rustle of nearby rodents. The subway tunnels grew even darker, now adorned with black tiles that seemed to absorb the scant light. Dim blue bulbs provided their sole illumination, guiding them through the labyrinthine tunnels. Just as Cassandra was starting to fear that this journey had no end, they made a final turn and were greeted by a cacophony of cheers and shouts.

Grayson's grin widened, his grip on Cassandra tightening as he pulled her closer to Sebastian and the source of the noise. In no time, they were standing amidst a throng of people. Four tall bleachers encircled a ring set upon a raised platform. The crowd before them was filled with lowlives and potential criminals, however their excitement roared as they witnessed two men pummelling each other mercilessly.

"Alright, enjoy," Sebastian said before vanishing into the sea of people.

The fights began filling the air with the sound of clashing swords, grunts of men, and cheers of the crowd, each combatant trying to make a name for themselves. As the announcer's screeching voice echoed through the tunnels, the crowd erupted into thunderous applause when a victorious fighter left the centre. However, the real anticipation arose as the announcer called for the last two fighters— the main attraction of the night. Cassandra let her nerves settle down, her eyes everywhere as she came to the conclusion that these games were not the place to let one's guard down.

Two formidable fighters stepped into the ring. "In this corner, the thug with over a thousand kills, Hiroki Ito!" A tall, imposing figure stepped closer to the centre of the ring. Dressed in nothing but long black pants and matching boots, his dark hair buzzed close to his scalp, eyes as black as the darkest night and a tooth missing in his maniacal grin. He raised his arms, acknowledging the fans' adulation. Strapped to his back was a colossal sword, its blade capable of slicing any opponent in two with a single stroke, leaving a chilling image of its deadly power. "And in this corner, a crowd favourite, champion for the last three years, Ryo!" The crowd's anticipation reached a fever pitch as the familiar figure merged from the shadows.

Covered in black, hood up and face partially concealed, Sebastian stood in the centre of the ring, facing his opponent. Two dragon leathered daggers rested on each of his sides, shimmering in the dim light. Within seconds a clicking noise was heard and Cassandra watched in shock as Sebastian's forearms held two large iron blades, popping through his skin.

Cassandra's mind reeled from the intense spectacle unfolding before her. Grayson's shocked grip on her arm contrasted with her own stunned silence. The bell rang, signalling the beginning of the match. Hiroki took the first swing at Sebastian, who seemed to dance around his larger opponent. Despite being smaller and leaner, Sebastian's agility granted him an edge, allowing him to avoid the thug's powerful strikes. With lightning-fast reflexes, Sebastian seized every opportunity to retaliate, hurling one of his knives at Hiroki's right shoulder. The large man laughed slowly, yanking the knife from his flesh, discarding it with a smirk.

Their fight continued, each move calculated and dangerous. Sebastian's slender frame became a blur as he dodged another of Hiromi's blows, the sword barely missing the tip of his nose. In response, Sebastian retaliated with another knife throw, eliciting a roaring cheer from the crowd. Cassandra found herself swept up in the frenzy of excitement. With Grayson, she clapped enthusiastically, rising to her feet to encourage Sebastian in his fierce match. However, amongst the jubilant chaos, something caught Cassandra's eye—a deep glare, a glaze of anger. Turning her head ever so slightly, she spotted a figure standing at the bottom of the stands, near the entrance. It was none other than King Kenji himself, dressed in an attire similar to Sebastian's, with a mask veiling half his face. Cassandra suddenly felt nauseous, a pit forming in her stomach at the sight.

She felt the air grow heavy, suffocating, as if his gaze alone could pierce through her very soul. Cassandra nudged her brother, grabbing his attention. Grayson turned to her as she gestured to the bottom of the stands and Grayson turned his gaze in that direction. "What is he doing here?" her brother asked the very question she was thinking.

In that momentary encounter, the world around her seemed to fade into the background, the noise of the cheering crowd became a distant echo. Time itself appeared to pause, leaving Cassandra entangled with an unsettling trance with the King. Slowly, she tore her gaze away and was once again engulfed by the cheers of the crowd, pulling her back to the present.

As she turned her attention back to the match, a gasp of astonishment escaped her lips. Hiroki, towering over Sebastian moments ago, found himself on the ground with Sebastian's legs wrapped around his neck. Struggling to break free, Hiroki realised he was trapped, and the match was already decided. Sebastian brought his daggered arm down swiftly, and a chilling silence fell over them as the thug's throat was sliced open. Blood spilled onto Sebastian's chest, staining the dark fabric of his attire, and the crowd erupted into cheers. Sebastian, seemingly unfazed, pushed the lifeless body off him and calmly stood to his feet. The announcer declared him the winner, lifting his arm in triumph.

CHAPTER 4

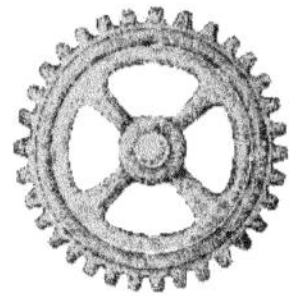

The early morning light filtered through the curtains, casting a soft glow on Cassandra's room as she lay in bed, her mind still consumed by the events of the previous night. Sebastian's victory in the intense match had left her with more questions than answers.

As the birds began to chirp outside, she could not shake the feeling of unease that clung to her thoughts. Savannah entered the room, ready to prepare for the day's travel. However, Cassandra remained still, lost in contemplation. Her mind was a maze of mysteries, especially concerning King Kenji's sudden disappearance after the match. It was as if he had evaporated into thin air.

Choosing to avoid the unnerving atmosphere at the breakfast table, Cassandra asked Savannah to bring her breakfast to her room, claiming she was feeling unwell. Although her head maid raised a curious eyebrow, she respected Cassandra's wishes and withdrew, leaving Cassandra to her own thoughts. In the solitude of her room, Cassandra could not dismiss the presence of the King.

A gentle knock on the door pulled Cassandra from her thoughts and she opened the door to find Grayson standing there in his night clothes, his dark red hair a mess, evidence of a restless night. "I could not sleep last night," he admitted, stepping into his sister's room.

Cassandra let out a sigh, making space for him on her bed. "I do not understand what Kenji was doing there. It is very hard to believe it was a mere coincidence."

Grayson's face mirrored her own confusion. "Do you believe he has something to do with Sebastian's involvement in the matches?"

She shrugged. "I cannot say for sure, but there was something peculiar about the way he looked at us, as if he knew more than he let on..."

"Do you believe Father knows?"

"No, I do not think so. It feels like this is his own secret, something he is keeping hidden from many."

Their conversation was interrupted by a knock on the door and Savannah entered the room with a tray of food. She paused, taking in the sight of the siblings sitting together. With a teasing smile, she closed the door behind her and addressed Grayson, tone laced with playful suspicion. "Let me guess, you are unwell, too?"

Grayson exaggerated a cough as he nodded. "Yes, terribly unwell."

"Well, you two need to recover quickly, for your father will be coming to check on you both in a few moments." With a knowing smile and a slight bow, Savannah departed, leaving Grayson wide-eyed and scampering after her. They knew their little charade had been exposed, and when Jaronas came to check on Cassandra, she was dismissed as healthy, alongside her brother. They were given an unexpected directive—to join Sebastian on a ground tour before their departure for the Diamond Kingdom at noon.

Once dressed, Savannah led Grayson and Cassandra to the main foyer, where Sebastian awaited them. He leaned casually against the entrance doors that led to what appeared to be a secluded garden. With a respectful bow, Savannah excused herself, leaving the trio to face each other in an uneasy silence, still affected by the events of the previous night.

Sebastian's gaze flickered between each sibling before he decided to break the silence, speaking over his shoulder as he started walking. "Follow me," he instructed and they obeyed, trailing behind him without a word.

The tour was quiet. Sebastian showed them familiar places—the grand dining hall, the vast library, the Queen's lounge, the training areas, and the tranquil vegetable gardens. Sebastian provided additional information, revealing titbits about the Spade Temple they had never known. However, he also made it clear that certain areas were off-limits and could not be explored. Consequently, the tour wrapped up in less than an hour.

As they stood at the entranceway where they had initially met, by the secluded garden, a sense of awkwardness lingered in the air. Sebastian seemed ready to part ways, his mind seemingly set on returning to the familiar confines of the training areas. "This is the end of the tour. Goodbye." He was prepared to leave.

"Last night," she began, voice trembling slightly, causing Sebastian to halt in his steps and for Grayson to protest in a hushed whisper, but Cassandra could not stop herself. She needed to know more. "We saw your father–"

"You saw nothing," Sebastian retorted, turning to face her with cold, unyielding eyes.

His demeanour was both commanding and dangerous but she did not back down. "I thought I told you to not give me orders."

"This is more than that. Nothing happened. You say nothing. You saw nothing. You remained in your rooms all night and went nowhere. Am I clear?"

"No, you cannot—"

"*Am* I clear?"

"But we saw–"

"You saw nothing," Sebastian interrupted again, taking steps closer until he loomed over Cassandra. "If you so much as speak of where you went or what you saw last night, I *promise* you a slow and torturous death."

Grayson stepped forward, placing himself between his sister and Sebastian. "Careful with your words, Spars. You are speaking to a Princess."

Sebastian's dark gaze remained fixed on Cassandra, unwavering in its intensity. "Then she should learn to keep her mouth shut," he retorted, voice laced with warning as he shifted his glare toward Grayson. "Do not think this statement does not apply to you as well."

Without uttering another word, Sebastian turned on his heel and left, his presence fading into the shadows of the Temple. Cassandra and Grayson were left standing in his wake, their minds buzzing with questions and uncertainty.

The carriage ride was suffocatingly silent. Cassandra stared out the carriage window, Grayson by her side and Sebastian facing them. His gaze seemed fixated on the Spade crest that sat above her head, as if searching for something beyond the emblem. Cassandra could feel his eyes on her, like a heavy weight upon her skin, and she fought the urge to meet his intense stare. As they neared the train station, the feeling of being watched intensified. She turned her attention to Sebastian and found his dark eyes wandering over her form, making her heart race and her cheeks flush. Their eyes met briefly and, in that moment, the confined space of the carriage seemed to shrink even further.

So much had happened, so much left unsaid. The night before weighed heavily on Cassandra's mind, but Sebastian's threats echoed in her ears, keeping her from speaking out. She averted her gaze, seeking refuge in the passing scenery outside the window, hoping her silence conveyed the message she dared not utter.

Finally, the carriage came to a slow stop and she looked out to see the impressive structure of the train station before her. Its circular base rose with elegant lines, tapering into a pointed top. Small windows dotted the upper portion, while the open base welcomed passengers and trains alike. Smaller trains let out their distinct horns, signalling their imminent departures, mirroring the ones she had seen in the city.

"Ours is the longest train," Sebastian grumbled. There it stood, isolated from the bustling crowd on the platform—the Triumph Games Train. Constructed in the early years of the Triumph Games, its primary purpose was to transport all competitors to the Forest Lands. In recent years, newer transportation methods had been made, however tradition dictated that competitors must travel by train. To align with modern technology, the Triumph Games Train underwent modifications, updating its engines to offer a quicker way to travel. Unlike the standard five-day journey to the Diamond Kingdom, this train provided the royals with the ability to reach the next nation within a mere six hours.

A grand steam-powered locomotive, its imposing frame covered in a deep shade of grey metal. The train's sides were carefully partitioned, each section adorned with a family crest, indicating their respective living quarters. At the very front were the Spars, followed by Harth, the Clubs, and lastly, the Dimond.

As Cassandra observed the arrangement, memories from her history book surfaced, replaying in her mind as if she were immersed in its pages once more. The opulence of the Diamond Kingdom's cart caught her eyes, boasting a large rounded window that adorned less than half of their luxurious quarters. From her vantage point, Cassandra could see snippets of gilded and ivory-coloured furniture, a testament to the kingdom's wealth and splendour. It was well-known that the Diamonds had financed the creation of the Triumph Games Train, insisting on having the largest and farthest quarters from the Spars.

Exiting the carriage, they entered the bustling train station, a hive of activity with people scurrying about, carrying their luggage, and determinedly making their way to their respective destinations. Amongst the vibrant atmosphere, the tension grew between the three young royals. Cassandra was well aware that the journey to the Diamond Kingdom would be relatively short, with their arrival scheduled close to dinnertime.

Accompanied by the King and Queen of Spade City, along with her father, the young royals strolled behind them, through the platform. People acknowledged them, respectfully bowed to them, yet there was no commotion or display of strong emotions from the onlookers. Everyone remained composed, as if preoccupied with matters of greater significance.

As they approached the train, the conductor warmly greeted his King and Queen, guiding them to their designed carts, which would transport the group to their secluded section. Paired up, they boarded a compact cart, taking their seats accordingly. Cassandra found herself beside Queen Suzume, exchanging a nod. Sitting silently, her hands gracefully folded on her lap, the Princess could not help but be captivated by the sight of the magnificent samurai sword resting beneath her fingers. Sebastian occupied the space in front of her, King Kenji sat beside him, whereas Grayson and King Jaronas found their places behind her.

Curiosity got the better of Cassandra, and she found herself inquiring about the sword. "How old is it?" Her fingers lightly brushed the metal bracelet gifted to her by the Queen the day before.

With a small smile, Suzume's metal fingers gently traced the fine silver of the ancient weapon. "It is nearly a thousand years old. It has been passed down through generations in my family, since the very beginning of our great name."

"It is truly a magnificent weapon," Cassandra remarked, admiration evident in her voice.

"Would you like to hold it?"

Cassandra's excitement was palpable as she eagerly nodded and extended her hands, much like a child yearning for a prized possession. The Queen carefully removed the sword from its leather sheath and placed the delicate yet razor-sharp weapon in Cassandra's hands. "Be careful, it is exceedingly sharp," Suzume cautioned, ensuring Cassandra handled the ancient heirloom with care.

Cassandra carefully held the samurai sword in her grasp, her thumb grazing the sharp blade, causing a small involuntary hiss of pain. She quickly wiped the tiny droplet of blood on her skirts, unfazed and still mesmerised by the weapon before her. A wide smile graced her lips as she took in every detail of the magnificent blade. Suzume observed with a soft smile, understanding the significance of the moment. Lost in her thoughts, Cassandra pondered the sword's history—how much blood it had seen, how many lives it had taken in wars long past. It was a powerful artefact, carrying with it a legacy of War and victory.

Upon reaching the Triumph Games Train, she reluctantly handed the sword back to Suzume, thanking her for the cherished experience that would remain etched in her memory. Cassandra bowed in gratitude before rejoining Grayson and Jaronas in their living quarters.

The interior of the train surprised her—black hardwood chairs with maroon cushions and softener adorned the space, proudly displaying the colours of her family. Cassandra appreciated the absence of dividing doors, a thoughtful touch absent in the Diamond Kingdom's design.

Settling into a cushioned maroon chair, Cassandra gazed out the train window. It was larger than the one in her carriage but wide enough that three windows sat a few spaces apart. The familiar towers of Spade City and the bustling commotion outside faded into silence as their journey commenced.

CHAPTER 5

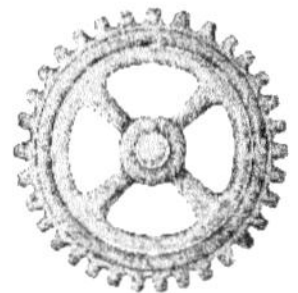

Cassandra stirred in her seat, neck crooked and feeling groggy from her short nap. Disoriented, she pulled her copy of *Beginning of the Triumph Games* off her chest. To her surprise, Savannah sat before her, holding a cup of tea and engrossed in a book of poetry. The clinking of wooden swords drew her attention to the other side of the living quarters, where Grayson practised fencing with his trainer, focused on perfecting his balance and stance. Cassandra could not recall falling asleep and found it peculiar that she had done so.

Grayson noticed his sister waking up and paused his training, walking over to her with a warm smile. "You woke up just in time. We will be reaching the Diamond Kingdom in about half an hour," he informed her. Cassandra straightened herself, rubbing the sleep from her eyes. "Father mentioned that we will get a glimpse of the Lower Tier from our train, but it will be a short moment as we leave the Rockies."

As Cassandra looked out the window, she noticed the dark grey mountains and tiny trees surrounding them, signalling their proximity to the Diamond Kingdom. Stretching, Savannah tidied up Cassandra's hair and attire before directing her attention to the vast landscape outside. As the train traversed through the Rockies, the oppressive dark grey terrain gave way to the breathtaking sight of lush greenery. Cassandra was awestruck by the sudden transformation, mesmerised by the vivid and almost surreal shade of green that greeted her. The landscape was adorned with a multitude of wildflowers, creating a seemingly endless and vibrant field of colours. But amongst this natural beauty, something caught her eye and she could not tear her gaze away from it.

"Grayson, come see this!" she exclaimed, directing her brother's attention to a sight in the distance. There it was, the Lower Tier of the Diamond Kingdom. From their vantage point, she knew that Grayson and Jaronas were able to see the vast expanse of deep green, almost muddy, grass that covered the area. However, Cassandra was the only one who could see further. Her right eye was enhanced, permitting her to see long distances. She saw more than the muddy ground and the small outlined homes. She saw the roads they walked on and various large contraptions that rested in different locations throughout the Lower Tier. Cassandra was aware that the Lower Tier was primarily associated with mining, as her books did provide a short amount of information about it, however, she never realised how horrible the living conditions were. The specifics of its operation remained a mystery to all.

Scattered around the Lower Tier were what appeared to be mining holes. Large, round, black caves with groups of men either emerging from or disappearing into the mining sections. They were covered in dirt, wearing large orange helmets with lights on top. Cassandra could not help but feel a sense of dread at the sight. The working conditions in those mines must have been awful, but what struck her even more was the apparent bleakness of the pale as a living environment. She pressed her face against the window, longing to see more, to ensure into the Lower Tier and witness first-hand how those people lived. Despite the brightness of the sun and the clear sky, everything on that side seemed gloomier, sadder. It was baffling to her how the Diamonds could allow such a grim reality to persist.

Everything came to a halt as Cassandra's eyes fixated on a colossal stone wall, seemingly dividing the kingdom into two distinct parts: one side with endless bright green grass, merging into smaller forest areas and scattered large homes, the other side concealed from her view. The houses exhibited a striking similarity in colours: beige stone walls with red roofs; while some featured black doors, others had grey ones. However, their architecture varied greatly, with some grand structures boasting towers that extended beyond the rest of the dwelling, while others being short set wide, sprawled across the vast lands they occupied.

As the train passed the Lower Tier and ventured deeper into the Upper Tier, Cassandra observed the scene and her attention was drawn to children playing joyfully in their lavish clothing. They appeared blissfully unaware of the destruction that seemed to be unfolding just beyond the imposing wall. While journeying through the Upper Tier, Cassandra's attention was drawn to a peculiar sight: towering black iron gates set right in the middle of the stone wall. It was surrounded by seven guards, as if preventing anyone from entering. Her gaze then shifted upwards, noticing an endless number of guards positioned on top of the high wall, diligently patrolling the fields below. Some faced away from her, while others kept a watchful eye on the surroundings.

She paid close attention to the eleven women who strolled the streets. They wore large gowns and adorned their heads with elaborate hats, which, to her, seemed almost comical. Accompanying the elegant women were men dressed in formal white and black attire, donning black top hats on their heads. Some of the men sported a classic moustache about their upper lips, while others had a unique style where their moustache connected to their chin, forming a continuous line of facial hair.

Cassandra found herself taken aback by this unfamiliar dressing style, which seemed strange and peculiar to her. In contrast to Spade City's loud and chaotic atmosphere, similar to her own home, the people of Spade City dressed in more practical materials like leathers and cotton. In contrast, the residents of Heart Lot opted for fabrics suitable for their island lifestyle, capable of withstanding water exposure.

Cotton and wool were commonly-used fabrics, occasionally accompanied by silk; however, upon arriving in the Diamond Kingdom, everything seemed vastly different. Cassandra found herself unable to identify the material the people wore. Whether it was silk or satin, wool or cotton, it all appeared bespoke and uniquely crafted for each individual, as if tailored to their personal preferences and needs.

"Their fabrics are created by using actual diamonds," Savannah whispered to Cassandra. She turned to her friend, wide-eyed and eager to hear more. "They have devised a method to create fabrics using actual diamonds. Silk and satin are replicated with the brilliance of diamonds, producing exquisite attire, but such luxury is reserved for the elite, while people of the Lower Tier have to make do with humble cotton and rags."

Cassandra was taken aback by this revelation and was about to inquire further when the train's deceleration interrupted them. Savannah rushed to prepare her in a more elegant gown for the upcoming occasion. They were quickly ushered into the bedroom section. Grayson and her father remained in the other room, changing as well. She found herself draped in a stunning black silk gown, its tight corset adorned with delicate straps that extended into long, flowing black silk sleeves that gracefully reached her wrists. The night-black dress was accentuated by elegant maroon designs that danced around the skirt in intricate patterns. Her footwear was simple yet tasteful, donning black flats that complemented the overall attire. Her fiery red hair was neatly pinned back, secured with a crimson elastic band.

Emerging from the bedroom section, Cassandra was greeted by Jaronas and Grayson, both impeccably dressed in matching maroon shirts, paired with black trousers and dress shoes. It was a rare sight to see them so formally attired, but Cassandra understood that it was all for the sake of making an impression on the Diamond Kingdom's royals. However, she could not bring herself to care about their opinions. Cassandra had known from the start that she would not like them.

Stepping out of the train as it came to a gentle halt, Cassandra was met with a scorching sun and an unblemished blue sky. The heat caught her off-guard but a refreshing breeze allowed her to catch her breath. As she turned her head, another door slid open and the Spars family emerged from their section. Queen Suzume elegantly tied her black hair into a tight bun and wore a deep blue gown adorned with shimmering silver sparkles. King Kenji extended his hand to his wife as she gracefully disembarked from the train. The Spade King's hair was nearly pulled back into a bun, and his attire closely resembled that of her father and brother, dressed in dark blue shirt and black trousers. Following Suzume was Sebastian, who offered a helping hand to his mother before closing the train door behind him and stepping onto the platform. Cassandra could not help but be taken aback by his appearance. His customary black leathers were replaced by a refined black suit, and his dark brown hair cascaded neatly around him.

The Dimond family did not bother with any formal greetings, leaving their guests with two golden carriages drawn by four majestic white horses. As they stepped inside, the carriages set off toward the royal palace. The journey up to the castle felt never-ending, with

Jaronas constantly lecturing his children on their behaviour, emphasising the need for flawless presentation, as the Diamond Kingdom's residents would seize any opportunity to ridicule them.

Cassandra, however, did not care.

Instead, she changed the topic of conversation. "Father, what can you tell me about the Lower Tier? I find it curious that my books do not hold much information on it." Cassandra recalled the division of the Diamond Kingdom from the *History of Our Nations*. Her mind flashed back to a page in her book. "*The Lower Tier was home to the common people, hardworking miners extracting precious gold and diamonds, which essentially fuelled the kingdom's success. On the other hand, the Upper Tier was occupied by the elites and royals who indulged in extravagant tea parties and held self-centred worldviews. The trade mainly revolved around the Hearts and occasionally the Spades, in exchange for blimps and protection. Beyond that, information was scarce.*"

Jaronas smiled at his daughter's curiosity, and delved into the reality of the Diamond Kingdom. Cassandra's book was right, allowing her prediction to be accurate as well. However, Jaronas explained how the Lower Tier's access to the Upper Tier was restricted to a few specific roles, such as housemaid and palace workers. Without a valid access card and proof of identity, they were denied entry into the Upper Tier.

"They are treated like mere commodities," Jaronas said. "The Upper Tier shows little regard for them. With an overpopulated Lower Tier, as soon as one person is gone, another stands ready to fill their place. The elites themselves control numerous mining sectors, ensuring their areas remain less crowded and allowing them to obtain the most wealth and land." Cassandra's mind raced, filling with empathy for the people she had observed from the train. Though she kept her thoughts to herself, her emotions were evident as she turned her face towards the window, staring at the stark contrast between lush green grass and the homes of the Upper Tier.

The Diamond Kingdom's diverse system, with its clear favouritism towards the Upper Tier, left her with an insatiable craving to understand more.

Upon arriving at the Diamond Castle, Cassandra was mesmerised by its beauty. Situated atop a hill, it offered a view of the sea below. Large red blimps scattered the Upper Tier. The blimps were from her own nation, an evident symbol of their trade with the Diamonds—gold and diamonds in exchange for new Heart transportation.

The palace itself was a marvel to behold, towering like three skyscrapers merged into one. Its white brick walls rose gracefully, reaching up to three majestic towers that adorned the castle's pinnacle. Cassandra's gaze trailed along the length of the palace, noticing how it seamlessly connected to a bell tower with a shimmering golden bell that chimed, announcing the arrival of guests. The building's design curved into a rectangular shape, with each level gradually reducing in size until it led to a beautifully sloping golden roof crowned by three exquisite miniature towers. Every inch of the castle seemed adorned with gold, from the roof to the bannisters, stairs and the doors. Even the crystal windows were framed in gold, exuding an aura of luxury and extravagance. The front of the palace boasted a golden statue of the Dimond family crest.

Cassandra found herself captivated by the castle's beauty, longing to explore its grounds and learn more about its history and secrets. As the carriage reached the top of the hill, she caught sight of the three Dimond Royals standing at the grand front doors, ready to welcome their guests.

Jaronas sighed. "Certain things truly remain unchanged." Cassandra observed her father who was clearly irritated by his old rival in the games. The Dimond Royals were stationed atop the staircase. As the carriages came to a complete halt, Jaronas took the initiative to step out first. He extended his hand, signalling for

Cassandra to follow suit, and then for Grayson to proceed. Cassandra lifted her gaze towards the Dimond Royals, who exuded an air of supremacy through their posture and their smug expressions indicated that they believed they were superior to the two royal families before them.

In the middle stood King Albert, a man of shorter stature compared to her own father and King Kenji, yet possessing a sturdy build. His golden blonde hair was cropped close to his head, adorned with a diamond and gold crown that sat regally atop his brow. A neatly-trimmed golden beard framed his face, and his light brown eyes bore an intense gaze that seemed to scrutinise each member of the visiting royal families.

As a result of an injury sustained during the games, particularly in a match against Jaronas, Albert had undergone a transformation. His chest had been replaced with intricate golden gears, granting him a new mechanical extension that functioned as a spinal extension along with a mechanical arm, effectively serving as a third limb. Cassandra's gaze fixated on the three-fingered claw that protruded menacingly over his shoulder, a fusion of black and gold intricacies that seemed to coil around him. On his left hand, King Albert wielded a golden hammer, a creation fashioned from pure gold. Cassandra recalled how this hammer was once a potent emblem of authority and might within his realm.

On King Albert's right side stood Princess Charlotte, a figure of smaller stature compared to her father, yet possessing a fragile yet strong presence. Her slender frame belied a hidden strength within. With cascading golden blonde locks that flowed down her sides, reaching a midpoint on her back, a round face and vivid green eyes that bore into Cassandra's form, Charlotte was a vision of elegance. Adored in a black and golden gown, the Princess of the Diamond Kingdom wore a corset that, though snug, exuded an air of royalty.

Unlike her father, Charlotte lacked a spinal extension. Instead, her right arm was enhanced with a steel retractable whip. With a mesmerising display, she playfully manipulated her golden black claw, intriguing her guests by alternating between whip and hand. Cassandra found herself staring at the retractable weapon, the ease of the whip arm, interested in the weaponized limb that could transform into a mechanical substitute.

As Cassandra scrutinised the retractable weapon, she realised its capacity to extend over substantial distances. On closer examination, she noted the tip was designed like a miniature hand, allowing her to grasp objects. The tip of her long crimson nails glinted in the sunlight as Charlotte smirked, seemingly relishing in Cassandra's gaze. On Albert's left stood Benjamin, the heir apparent. Just as Cassandra's book recounted, Charlotte and Benjamin were twins. Although Charlotte was older by three minutes, she could not ascend to the throne, permitting Benjamin to be the appointed ruler.

Benjamin, notably slender compared to his father, managed to surpass him by a few inches in height. His visage bore an oval shape, crowned by a cascade of golden hair that reached the midpoint of his neck. Resting at the bridge of his nose were round spectacles that adorned his bright green eyes, which surveyed both his opponents. In a manner mirroring his father, Benjamin also held a spinal extension, a fusion of gleaming black and gold metal that culminated in a claw-like apparatus. This appendage permitted him the ability to seize and manipulate objects, an adaptation perhaps derived from the competitive demands of the Diamond Kingdom.

Cassandra overheard Grayson's dismissive snort, directed to Benjamin. His eyes carried a distinct glare, while Sebastian maintained an impartial countenance. Standing tall with a soldier's bearing, Sebastian exuded an aura of lethal readiness, poised to strike at any given moment. Cassandra discerned that the boys were diligently studying their competitors, keenly searching for vulnerabilities that could be exploited in the upcoming tournament.

The three Dimond Royals exchanged cunning smiles, and it was Albert who initiated the descent down the grand staircase, his children trailing behind. Cassandra felt herself cringe at the three royals before her, wanting nothing more than to laugh in their face and turn away. Who were they to believe they were better than everyone else?

Worst of all, she had no idea how Kenji and her father were so calm.

The process of introductions was slightly different than the warm welcome she had received in Spade City. There were no welcoming gifts or guided tours of the residence. Instead, it was a mere nod of the head at a distance deliberately placed by the Dimond Royals. It was at this point that Albert signalled for his guests to accompany him to the garden, where an open-air dinner awaited.

Following the Dimond Royals, Cassandra made it a point to cast her gaze upward, one final time at the imposing castle before being guided to the back. The gardens, as they entered, unfolded a picturesque display of diverse-hued roses. While the majority boasted a classic palette of red and white, occasional bursts of pink and orange punctuated the landscape. Cassandra found herself stunned by the garden's panorama. Perched atop the hill, their vantage point offered a sweeping view of the kingdom sprawling below. The sun lingered in the sky, its position high enough to signal the onset of dinner—a cue underscored by the resounding toll of a bell.

Albert sat at the head of the table, disregarding his visitors' titles. Benjamin and Charlotte sat on either side, effectively discourage anyone from getting close to him.

Cassandra nearly rolled her eyes at his immaturity.

It was Grayson who noticed her annoyance and bumped his elbow against her, giving her a look. That was when she did roll her eyes.

Jaronas gestured for his daughter to take a seat beside Charlotte, a gesture of peace.

Suppressing a groan, Cassandra settled besides Charlotte, who also appeared to be annoyed.

It was clear that Charlotte hoped for Grayson to sit beside her. Cassandra was no idiot; she noticed the girl's flirtatious glances and had to fight back the waves of nausea at the thought of the self-absorbed girl beside her ending up with Grayson.

To Cassandra's right sat Suzume. With a small smile, her gaze met her son's. Grayson sat facing Cassandra, with Sebastian to the right of him. The table extended only so much that there were two seats remaining with no chair at the other end. Jaronas took his seat beside the Spade Queen while Kenji sat beside his son.

All assembled were poised, primed for the commencement of the meal. Cassandra gradually tuned out the sporadic clinks of tableware and directed her gaze towards the palace that lay ahead. The golden embellishments adorning it were indeed genuine, and the crystal windows were as real as they appeared. Yet, in that moment, Cassandra's attention was drawn to the subtle glimmers of diamond-studded accents gracing the castle's facade—undeniable testament of opulence.

The Diamond Kingdom, the first nation to be founded, stood as the foremost sovereign state, a treasury of profound history and importance. An overwhelming desire surged within Cassandra, compelling her to venture into their library, to immerse herself in the books bearing the weight of ages that extended back to the beginning of time.

Dinner eventually drew to a close, much to Cassandra's relief. Her focus had been so consumed by observing the nation's inner workings that she had neglected mingling with the fellow royals around her. Albert proposed for the young royals to stroll in the garden, prompting Charlotte to swiftly rise from her seat and offer smiles to her peers. Converging at the garden's entrance, a grand arch of gold marked their gathering point.

Charlotte immediately hooked her arm through Grayson's, ushering him through the archway. Benjamin exchanged a knowing grin with Cassandra, which she acknowledged, and placed her arm loosely in his. Sebastian, on the other hand, walked alone. His posture reflected a military bearing with hands positioned behind him.

Perched atop a lofty hill, the palace offered them an expansive view as they ventured deeper into the garden. The Upper Tier was sprawled out beneath them, whereas the Lower Tier remained at a far distance. Charlotte and Grayson engaged in lively conversation, exploring the intricacies of the Diamond Kingdom. Meanwhile, Cassandra remained bored. Benjamin did not stop speaking about himself, dismissing Cassandra entirely.

Glancing back at Sebastian, she caught him smirking at her bemused expression, resulting in a shared, secretive laugh between them.

Charlotte beamed at the group. "Behold, our favourite spot," she exclaimed, her smile radiant. "A charming little corner that offers an exceptionally breathtaking view of our kingdom."

Cassandra took one look and knew Charlotte was not lying.

Progressing past towering hedges and clusters of rose bushes, it felt as if they were entering an entirely different nation. Ahead of them, the entire expanse of the Diamond Kingdom stretched out like a tableau. The hill sloped steeply downwards, revealing a panorama that was nothing short of captivating. To the left, the ocean sparkled in shades of azure, a serene and magnificent sight. To the right, lay the land with its sprawling residences, miniature gardens, fortifications, and the laborious environment of the Lower Tier.

Cassandra was startled by Benjamin's words. She had momentarily forgotten he was still talking to her. "It is quite a challenge being a man," he mused aloud. His unexpected comment left her bewildered. "Numerous young women would consider being my wife a great honour. However, I seek someone respectable and kind. Someone like you would make an excellent match." Cassandra stared at him, her eyes wide with surprise. She could not fathom where this was suddenly coming from. "Your father will announce when you are ready for courtship and mine has offered a substantial sum to secure you for me."

Cassandra felt another wave of nausea. He must be joking.

"Is that not thrilling? We will be wed someday, and all of this will be yours."

He was not joking.

Sebastian's laughter broke the chatter, silencing the surroundings. "You hardly qualify as a man."

"Pardon me?"

"Someone as thin and undersized as you hardly embody the essence of manhood." Sebastian advanced a step. "A true man is meant to shield his woman, not flee in the opposite direction, abandoning her." He then gave a lethal smile. "I would be better suited for her than you would be."

Cassandra sensed the escalating tension between them, too stunned by Benjamin's marriage proposal and of Sebastian's retaliation. She felt Charlotte's harsh gaze, heard her steps as Grayson tried to intervene, the two Harth children playing the peacekeepers.

Benjamin boldly approached, his face inches away from Sebastian's. "Watch yourself; I know exactly what you are and I am not afraid of you."

Sebastian's lips curled into a smirk. "Your understanding is questionable."

"A genuine man embodies Princely honour, not a mere boy who fortuitously stumbled into the role and now spends his days training for some lofty importance. All to satisfy his so-called father's approval." Benjamin's smile turned sly. "Is that not the truth, bastard Prince?"

Sebastian remained composed, yet his eyes smouldered, and Cassandra noticed his hand inching toward his dragon leather dagger. She instinctively stepped between them, pushing Sebastian back, a silent command to retreat. Still, Sebastian's gaze remained locked on Benjamin, whose smug smile lingered.

"Mind your station," Benjamin seethed.

"Stay vigilant, you little schemer. I'll come for you and your tongue will be mine."

"Do not need to be so dramatic," Cassandra snapped, giving Sebastian another shove. The assassin's eyes bore into her, a fierce glare. "No more. Walk with me, cool down."

As Cassandra pushed Sebastian aside, Grayson intervened by redirecting Benjamin's attention towards Charlotte, effectively diverting their conflict. Meanwhile, Cassandra led Sebastian to a distant part of the hill, a significant distance from the other young royals and their elders.

When they were out of earshot, she reprimanded Sebastian. "Why did you provoke him?"

He simply shrugged. "It is a part of our history. It was inevitable that they would lay blame on my family for something we did not do. This incident merely provided a pretext." Sebastian's lips curled into a smirk. "Besides, I found it rather amusing. Opportunities like that are too good to pass up."

She stared at him, utterly baffled by his response. "That has to be the most nonsensical thing I have ever heard."

Again, he shrugged nonchalantly. "It is history, a role each of us plays. You and your brother, the peacemakers—a role you were destined for. The only surprising thing is how you came to my defence, when anyone else would have probably left me to deal with it alone."

Cassandra rolled her eyes. "Because I happen to possess a heart."

"Isn't that ironic?" he quipped.

"Are you satisfied now?"

"Immensely. Did you see how he pounced the moment I spoke? Truly entertaining." Sebastian's expression remained neutral, yet a spark of joy gleamed in his eyes—an emotion she rarely saw in him. She could not contain herself, giggling at his comment.

A momentary hush followed and Sebastian soon suggested that they depart. However, Cassandra was poised to pose another question, curious about Benjamin's earlier remark. Sebastian, however, did not grant her the opportunity. He strode away, trailed by Charlotte who approached them. Her smile was sugary sweet, a facade that many perceived as genuine kindnesses, but Cassandra knew better.

Charlotte's smile faded swiftly as she stood before her. "You should have ignored him," she remarked sharply. "It would have been prudent to follow your brother's example and prioritise peace between the Heart Lot Islands and the Diamond Kingdom instead of fixating on the bastard from Spade City."

Cassandra let out an incredulous snort. "I hardly need a lecture from you." Ready to go after Sebastian, she felt an abrupt tug on her wrist. Charlotte's crimson nail bit into her skin as Cassandra activated her sniper and pointed it towards the Princess. "You have five seconds to release me before I pull the trigger and watch that pretty brain of your splatter on the ground."

Charlotte was quick to release her, but her taunting smirk remained. "It would be wise to remember who your allies are."

Cassandra laughed. "That better be a warning and not a threat."

"I would do no such thing. I was simply giving advice." It was a calculated move on Charlotte's end. "Come along, let me show you and the others the grand hall and our collection of historical paintings." Without further ado, Charlotte linked arms with Cassandra and led her away to rejoin the rest of the group. Cassandra held a distinct aversion to Charlotte. She could not comprehend why Charlotte was so fixated on their shared history rather than focusing on their collective future.

CHAPTER 6

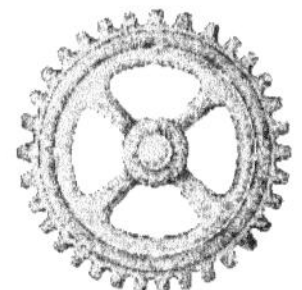

After raising their glasses to the upcoming games and indulging in desserts, the Dimond Royals guided their guests to their sleeping quarters. Cassandra's room was covered in gold wallpaper, with cream-coloured bed sheets and a large diamond chandelier. As Cassandra laid in her bed, she claimed it was the best sleep she had in years. The mattress permitted her body to sink into it.

The following day, Savannah woke Cassandra at seven, declaring it was time for them to leave. The train ride from the Diamond Kingdom to Club Caverns was a mere three hours. After eating breakfast in her room and Savannah picking out a lovely black gown for Cassandra to wear, she was guided back to the courtyard where her father and the other royals remained.

The ride to Club Caverns consisted of Grayson and Jaronas speaking of the Triumph Games and what to expect. Cassandra remained in her corner, mind absorbing the words in her book, trying to understand the nature of Club Caverns. She found the Club nation to be very interesting and unique as it once served as a nucleus for factories and pioneering scientists who relentlessly work on forging cutting-edge technology. The pervasive coal pollution had compelled them to establish an underground city. Their economic ties reached across all nations, offering innovative technology in exchange for salt and fish from the Heart Lot Islands, collaborative advancements from Spades, and a steady supply of ore from the Diamond Kingdom.

After the third hour of their ride, Cassandra began to twist in her seat, feeling very uncomfortable. It was then that she noticed the shift in the sky. The bluish-grey hue, the sun's rays piercing through the expanse of clouds. The sky began to darken, akin to a colossal cloud looming overhead. A collective gasp escaped from Grayson, prompting her to glance over to him before turning her attention back out the window. As the train tracks curved, Club Caverns came into view from a distance, its silhouette enveloped in a shroud of smog. The city appeared veiled by coal dust and smoke, with heavy layers obscuring the sunlight.

Grayson's voice broke the silence. "What is that?"

Cassandra's response was swift. "Clubs Caverns are known for their machinery and coal-based products. The city is often enshrouded in darkness due to the emissions from their industrial activities."

Her father leaned on the window ledge, adding his perspective. "And let's not forget the numerous concealed inventions they keep to themselves. They are constantly crafting new tools, withholding a significant portion of their creations from the rest of the world."

She was well aware that this clandestine approach contributed to the Clubs' dominance, as many nations heavily relied on their technological innovations.

"Can they even breathe in such an environment?" her brother's inquiry persisted.

"Some individuals have adapted to the smog, but many carry portable air tanks on their backs. These tanks contain a filtration system and a small built-in light to help them navigate within their nation," Cassandra explained. As she gazed at the extensive brown haze engulfing the surroundings and the corresponding desolate terrain, she could not help but notice the absence of lush greenery. Instead, dirt and pebbles covered the landscape, with factories sprawled across the area. Large greenish pits, presumably containing hazardous substances, were scattered throughout the region.

Jaronas chimed in, adding more context. "While some indeed utilise the tanks to breathe, it is a common practice to inhale the fumes directly from the tanks. Yet, it is widely understood that their true dwellings lie underground, where the air is cleaner and continually circulated. Although the notion of an underground city remains somewhat of a myth, despite historical records suggesting otherwise, the name Club Caverns itself hints at this concept."

In a swift sequence, the transition was immediate: from sunlight to obscurity. Breathing became notably more challenging as an alert notified passengers of decreasing oxygen levels. The message advised the passengers who did not have artificial lungs to put on gas masks that were available in the emergency kits located beside the exit doors, and to also be aware that the filtration system would commence in moments.

This filtration would permit passengers to continue to breathe in clear oxygen before placing the masks on their faces. Cassandra and Jaronas were the only two with artificial lungs, whereas Grayson was not given any, as Jaronas claimed his son would remain in the perfect human physique that was given to him. Grayson grabbed a mask and prepared himself to breathe in the oxygen; however, her father still instructed Cassandra to grab a gas mask, claiming to be safer than sorry.

Cassandra peered out in a mixture of wonder and surprise at the nation. It lay enveloped in a shroud of black mist, sporadic illumination emanating from candle-lit lampposts positioned every few paces. Darkness prevailed perpetually, sunlight obscured, rendering visibility difficult. Many individuals relied on night vision goggles, equipped with tanks fastened to their backs, and continued with their daily routines. Such circumstances were typical there. She also observed a handful of people who breathed unaided, showcasing their adaptation to the limited oxygen prevalent in the city. This adaptation hinted at their ability to process both oxygen and carbon dioxide, a remarkable adjustment; much like the artificial lungs she and her family had.

"The factories cannot be solely responsible for all of this," Grayson exclaimed, quickly donning his mask.

Savannah promptly handed Cassandra her copy of *History of Our Nations* and turned to the section about Club Caverns. The smog's origin was attributed to the ceaseless energy demand of the factories, leading to a decline in oxygen levels to the point where people had to adapt to surviving on carbon dioxide-rich air. The book delved into the establishment of underground cities for those reliant on tanks for breathing, while still maintaining a connection to the surface, enabling their lungs to acclimate to both air compositions.

"It is true, the book provides all the details," Cassandra affirmed, her voice slightly muffled through her mask.

The surface mainly accommodated factory workers, while life thrived in the underground. Initially, supplementary tanks were introduced for individuals struggling to breathe, but this evolved into a means for people to inhale the gas or fumes, akin to a form of intoxication. The tubes once used for oxygen were repurposed for these glasses, facilitating a somewhat high experience. Strikingly, the city had no natural life aside from its residents. The soil, contaminated by numerous chemicals, had become inhospitable to living organisms. Trees were replaced by lamp posts fuelled by candles, casting a dim illumination on the streets. Coal was integral to nearly every aspect of life, particularly in the transportation system.

Communal steam trains traversed both the surface and underground, symbolising the intricate interplay between these two cities.

The train station bore similarities to those in both the Diamond Kingdom and Spade City, yet its towering spire was concealed by heavy dark clouds. Upon pulling into the station, a gas mask inspection was conducted before the doors were opened. Cassandra found it odd for her to wear a mask, however, her father still wanted to keep precautions. It was then that she truly took in the scene before her. Her vision adapted to the dimness of the nation, despite the initial brightness upon their arrival, the interior was shrouded in darkness and haze. Grayson motioned for Cassandra to grasp his arm and together they descended the stairs, guided by the presence of others.

They reached the communal steam trains. These had no glass windows, only spacious rectangular compartments accommodating up to three individuals. A faint green light hung overhead and Cassandra could just make out the flickering candle inside. The journey to Club Mansion was lengthy, and upon their arrival, the reality starkly contrasted her preconceptions. In her mind, she had envisioned silver and green bricks, elegant frames, something similar to other nations. However, Club Mansion defied her imagination.

The Mansion stretched out with an imposing grandeur; its architecture was reminiscent of Cassandra's own residence. It stood adorned in sombre, robust, dark grey bricks, while sinuous veins of dark green wound their way around the exterior. These tendrils climbed the walls with an almost organic persistence, trailing over window frames and creeping up to caress the very roof of the structure. Two expansive banners, each bearing the unmistakable emblem of the Clubs family, hung like sentinels on opposite sides of the Mansion. The Club crest was meticulously etched on a deep green backdrop, a stark yet fitting contrast to the otherwise muted hues of the building.

The Club Mansion's appearance teetered on the eerie, evoking images of a place forgotten by time; a dwelling that might have been deemed dilapidated. However, this unsettling aura was intertwined with an unexpected beauty, a mesmerising fusion of the sinister and the aesthetically captivating.

Grayson leaned in, his voice carrying a hushed undertone. "It is said that beneath the Mansion lies royal machinery, where the Club royals, along with other accomplished scientists, toil away in ceaseless creation, devising new innovations and technologies. Nevertheless," he continued, his voice carrying the weight of secrecy, "these advancements are strictly reserved for the exclusive use of the royals; they remain concealed from the gaze and touch of anyone else unless granted explicit permission."

Upon their arrival at the Club Mansion, the imposing brown oak doors swung open, and the royal inhabitants emerged with genuine smiles adorning their faces. Cassandra could not help but notice that none of them were wearing oxygen masks.

King Constantine took the initiative to initiate the introductions. He was not particularly tall, roughly on par with Albert's height, with broad shoulders. Short, dark brown hair adorned his head, complemented by a neatly trimmed beard that extended to the middle of his neck. Cassandra engaged in several exchanges with the King, her observant eyes noting the unique features he carried. A mechanical implant adorned his left shoulder, furnished with intricate spikes. His left hand wielded a spiked steel ball flail, a medium-range instrument of destruction. Positioned on his right side was a large metallic fist, a well-known weapon of choice from his participation in the Triumph Games. Additionally, an oxygen tank was affixed to his left chest, serving as a vital component of his respiratory system.

His dark green eyes exude warmth as he greeted Cassandra, extending a helping hand as she disembarked from the train. "I'm delighted to make your acquaintance," he expressed, his embrace pulling her into a gentle hug, followed by a kiss on each cheek.

Cassandra reciprocated with a sincere smile, matching the respectful gesture of their encounter. "Likewise, King Constantine."

A hearty laugh escaped the lips of the Club King. "Just Constantine will do, my dear."

Next in line to extend her greetings was Queen Morana of the Clubs. She presented a short and plump figure, characterised by a distinct corpulence, in contrast to Queen Suzume's more streamlined appearance. Her dark brown hair was styled in three large circular sections with the bottom cropped to her shoulders, framed by a round face adorned with deep brown eyes. Notably, her robotic right arm featured elongated clawed fingers that expertly mimicked the movements of a human hand. Affixed to her back was an oxygen tank, complete with a straw-like apparatus that facilitated her inhalation of the air.

Standing beside her was the young Clubs Prince. Although Augustus inherited his father's stature in terms of height, his build was slenderer. His short dark brown hair and modest beard framed a countenance adorned with bulky green goggles, beneath which shone his eyes in an exuberant display of joy as he greeted Cassandra. His left arm was equipped with a razor-sharp chainsaw, embodying his persona as a mad scientist. Similar to his mother, he carried a back-mounted air tank and a straw-like device that provided him with air, which he too used to inhale the fumes in a manner akin to smoking.

However, as the greetings unfolded, Cassandra gradually gleaned the significance of his role as the new heir. A tragic incident had befallen his older brother, leading Augustus to assume the throne. The depth of his pain and past experiences were beyond Cassandra's full comprehension.

"Please, do come." Morana extended a warm smile to her guests, gesturing towards the Mansion. "Join us inside for some tea." The Dimond Royals were the first to stride through the doors, seemingly eager for a breath of fresh air. Augustus approached Sebastian, extending a friendly greeting that prompted a rare smile beneath Sebastian's gas mask. It was the first time Cassandra had witnessed such an expression from him.

Stepping inside the Mansion, the group was led to a spacious dining area for tea. Cassandra observed that they were permitted to remove their masks, greeted by a refreshing and clean atmosphere. Despite the lack of open windows, the air quality inside the Club Mansion was remarkable. Cassandra contemplated the various methods that might have contributed to maintaining such cleanliness within the Mansion.

Constantine assumed his position at the head of the table, with the other Kings encircling him. On the opposite end, Queen Morana took her place, flanked by Suzume and Charlotte. Cassandra found herself seated beside Charlotte once more, while Augustus occupied the seat to her right. The stark contrast between Morana and Suzume was evident to Cassandra. The Club Queen exuded a boisterous and humorous demeanour, engaging in playful banter with Constantine, who reciprocated with laughter or witty retorts. It was notable that they all partook in inhaling the air, a fact further exemplified when Augustus offered some to Cassandra, a gesture she politely declined.

"May I inquire if the rumours about your underground city are true?" Grayson posed the question to Augustus in a courteous manner.

Augustus responded with a smile. "Perhaps."

Cassandra regarded him with wide-eyed curiosity. "Oh, please, do consider showing us."

He playfully challenged her. "How can you be certain I am not weaving a tale? I might just be spinning a web of lies."

She countered with a smirk. "Multiple sources in my books would beg to differ."

There was a long silence as the two royals challenged each other. It was not long 'till Augustus exchanged a glance with a servant whom he then summoned with a whisper. The servant promptly hurried to Constantine, relaying the message.

With a nod from his father, Augustus leaned back in his chair smirking at Cassandra. "Now, we await."

As the tea concluded, Constantine rose from his seat, flanked by Kenji on one side and Jaronas on the other. Notably, Albert positioned himself at a distance, clearly preferring to stay within walls containing breathable air. "Please, join me for a tour of our nation," Constantine invited.

Albert declined, stating, "Thank you, but I would much rather remain in areas with air."

Constantine let out a hearty chuckle. "Rest assured, witnessing our nation would likely change your perspective." With an immediate and unrestrained burst of excitement, the Harth siblings rose from their seats, their faces animated with joy, well aware of the significance of this opportunity.

Augustus swiftly fulfilled their request and this realisation heightened their exhilaration. Positioned beside Cassandra, Augustus leaned in and softly murmured, "Express your desire, and I will attend to your every need."

An unexpected warmth coloured Cassandra's cheeks at his words; they seemed to carry an almost imprudent pledge. However, Sebastian's reaction was far from agreeable as he cast a displeased glare at the pair before him.

Following a brief discussion and an assurance of a swift return, they embarked towards what Cassandra hoped would be the entrance to the underground city. Guided through the Mansion's corridors, they arrived at another chamber. Positioned on the rear wall loomed a pair of sizable steel doors, flanked by vigilant guards. The same butler from earlier signalled with a ring of a bell, prompting the doors to groan open. Revealed before them was a steel shaft. "Hurry, gather in," Constantine instructed, his smile stretching from ear to ear, with Morana taking his arm. The assembled group managed to squeeze into the confined space of the shaft, and soon enough, they felt the platform descend.

A somewhat forceful impact upon reaching the ground caused them to stumble. Cassandra found herself holding onto Augustus, who reciprocated by offering his support, resulting in a shared chuckle. "This occurrence is rather common," Augustus reassured her with a grin.

The thought of marrying Augustus crossed her mind. If Benjamin was right and if her father was preparing to announce her to society—Cassandra shook that thought from her mind. Life was more than boys and marriage. It was about making history, learning, and creating a life that she would someday look back on and be proud of. But the thought of potentially marrying Augustus did remain in the back of her mind.

As the sliding doors opened, they were greeted by a vibrant and bustling city, reminiscent of Spade City in its lively atmosphere. The unexpected cacophony of sounds from this expansive area surprised Cassandra. The underground city sprawled out extensively, occupying nearly the same expanse as its counterpart above ground.

Enclosed by the four large main tunnels that surrounded the city, Casandra's mind linked back to her history book, fully understanding the dynamic of Club Caverns. The tunnels were created during times of war. Each large tunnel contained other miniature tunnels, each with a path of its own that extended across Club Caverns. No one truly knew how far they ventured. Some believed there were paths leading to the Forest Lands, while others claimed they travelled south to Spade City.

The city was illuminated by large white sheets, the material being extremely thin, permitting light to carry through. They hung at every corner. When viewing the city before them, it was clear that it expanded through the entire Club nation. The scene unfolded before them with a multitude of shops and stalls, offering everything from food to cutting-edge technological enhancements. A bustling market stretched out, leading to residential areas towards the back. Modest houses and small towers adorned this part of the underground domain. In the distance, a clamour of voices directed their attention to the familiar sight of the transportation train that had brought them to Club Mansion.

Before anyone could react, Augustus took Cassandra's hand and playfully nudged Grayson. "Time to explore the wonders," he exclaimed. Without further ado, they joined Augustus, venturing into the depths of the underground city. Sebastian, Charlotte, and Benjamin also joined the group, though Cassandra found their company less relevant, since the two Dimond Royals seemed to grumble incessantly. Yet, the Harth siblings revealed the experience. Augustus led them through a plethora of innovative equipment and novel products that were entirely new to them. What was more, Cassandra noted with appreciation that darkness did not encroach upon any corner of the underground expanse.

"How does the place have so much illumination?" Cassandra could not help but inquire.

Augustus, with an air of pride, replied, wrapping his arm around her shoulders. It was then that Cassandra noticed that he, too, like the other royals, had retracted his weaponry arm for a mechanical one. "We have developed a unique form of lighting, utilising compact steam-powered orbs. Coal is fed into a furnace, and the resulting heat of the coal is challenged into containers that are distributed throughout the city, generating light."

Grayson, munching on some sweets, chimed in. "It explains the stark contrast in brightness between here and the surface world."

As time seemed to slip away, the trio of explorers delved into various corners of the subterranean realm. But soon, a horn's resonant sound signalled that it was time to return to the surface. Joining the adults near the entrance, Cassandra and her brother clutched bags of candy and new robotic enhancements. Grayson had acquired a set of refined steel arrows, while Cassandra secured a batch of golden bullets designed for enhanced penetration. As they tumbled up the shaft, Cassandra noticed Sebastian standing quietly in a corner. Throughout their underground escapade, he had maintained an uncharacteristic silence, at times eluding their sight in the labyrinth city. However, it came as no surprise when Cassandra discerned a new addition to his ensemble. Another dagger graced his waist—a longer, elegantly curved piece with a sleek black hilt. Their eyes met; Cassandra found herself entranced by the deep brown gaze before her, marvelling at the unexpected allure within someone she had perceived as unrelentingly harsh.

Upon their return to the Mansion, Queen Morana announced that dinner would be served shortly. As they reconvened in the dining room, the trio of young royals nibbled on their sweets, only to receive a reprimand from Moran for spoiling their appetites. The scolding, in all its childlike simplicity, momentarily tugged at Cassandra's heartstrings, reminding her of her own mother's reproaches during similar instances with her brother.

As the dinner drew to a close, a toast was raised in honour of the forthcoming Triumph Games. With the evening deepening, they were guided back to the awaiting train. As they settled in for the night's journey, Cassandra found herself yearning for the familiarity of Club Caverns, already nostalgic for the delight it had sparked in her before the vexations of the games took over. From her window, she watched as the expanse of Club Caverns receded into the distance, shrinking steadily until the only vista that remained was one dominated by sombre clouds.

CHAPTER 7

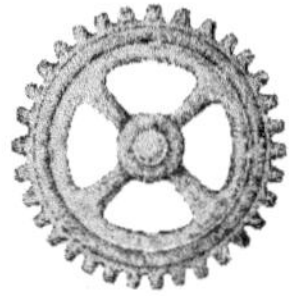

Perched in her comfortable nook, the early morning rays shone down on her. Savannah had once more woken Cassandra at an ungodly hour, claiming that they would be reaching the Forest Lands in a few short hours. Cassandra listened to her father's relentless critiques of her brother's fencing stance, now annoyed by how lost-minded her brother had to be to not understand how to stand properly. Her brother's trainer reluctantly listened to her father, making Grayson go through endless drills. Cassandra could not help but think of the games that were nearing, knowing that this win would slip through his fingers in a heartbeat.

Savannah fired questions at Cassandra about the upcoming Triumph Games. After a while, the unending canopy of shade began thinning and the verdant trees grew sparse. Jaronas directed his children's attention to the window, where the once-continuous forest gave way. In the distance, a colossal Arena came into view, reminiscent of an ancient coliseum, its imposing metal walls and bracing pipes casting an eerie impression. The Arena's periphery was studded with sprawling camps and grand pavilions, resonating with the crescendo of anticipatory roars from the assembling crowds. A fleet of hot air balloons, each adorned in their nation's hues, clustered overhead, a vivid testament to their citizens' unwavering support and spirited presence in the impending games. But as swiftly as it appeared, the sylvan curtain descended, concealing the spectacle once more.

"What is the purpose of those camps?" Grayson's inquiry pierced the air.

"They are for the spectators, the undying fans, and admirers of the games," their father responded. "Each nation possesses a connecting bridge to the island that is opened when the games begin, each bridge connecting to where the Arena stands, though we competitors are not granted access to it. The spectacle, however, must go on. It is a part of tradition, you see." His voice resonated with a sombre authority.

The landscape shifted again, revealing the sprawling expanse of the Forest Lands stretching for miles. Her father's words took on a narrative tone, almost as if reciting a dark history etched into his memory.

"The forest lands are a sprawling tribe of pacifists," Jaronas commenced, the words tinged with both admiration and caution. "There is no hierarchy here, no reigning monarchs. Just a chieftain, anointed every four years through a unique process. They can appoint the same man for every election, permitting him to always be chief until one day he passes or a new chief comes to replace him. It is a fragile balance."

"How intriguing," Cassandra could not help but murmur, her gaze fixed upon the large woodland terrain that stretched out before them.

"The very ground beneath them is fashioned from timber and logs," Jaronas continued. "They are fervent advocates of nature's bounty, relying solely on what the earth provides. The only non-natural construction within their nation is the Arena. Everything else is built with what they have closest to them."

Her curiosity swelled. "Do they possess any of the marvels of steam-powered machinery?" Cassandra inquired, a hunger for knowledge evident in her voice. "Are their workshops alive with whirring gears and intricate contraptions?"

A faint smile graced her father's lips, a glint of reminiscence in his eyes. "They do not believe in such things, proclaiming that the human body should not be enhanced. That the gods created humans in a specific way for a reason. They are not against the steam-powered technology, but they kept their distance from the rest of the world. This is also the reason why they are considered the best nation for the Triumph Games. They are the neutral ground between all nations. When stepping into their nations, it is to be a reminder of where we once were and where we are today."

Jaronas continued to paint the portrait, each stroke revealing more of the enigmatic Forest Lands. "These woodland folk are recognized for their role as impartial arbiters and judges in the games. Their neutrality assured that no nation would be unfairly favoured. While the royals influenced the selection of a few contests, the forest people held the ultimate sway in decision-making. The sovereigns' authority hardly extended beyond these boundaries."

A wistful note crept into Jaronas's voice as he concluded, his gaze lingering on the world passing by the train window. "It was only in recent years that they allowed radio broadcasts to enlighten their own nation about the games, but apart from that, their world remains deeply rooted in the embrace of nature. Their focus lies in the sanctity of humanity's natural form, untouched by the mechanical aspirations that consumed other realms."

The towering trees veiled and unveiled the sight of the village in fleeting glimpses, an ethereal dance of secrets and revelations. Cassandra's mind harked back to her readings, stories of the Town's tranquil existence, a harmonious bubble disrupted only by the intrusion of the train. Thus, it was no surprise that the train's halt was on the distant side of the Town, far from the sensitive ears of its inhabitants. Her father's explanation about the proximity of the Camps and the village, albeit a long walk, seemed a small sacrifice for what awaited.

Stepping off the train was like crossing into a parallel universe for Cassandra. The grumbles of Albert and the whining of his progeny seemed inconsequential as she revealed in the embrace of nature's bounty. The verdant trees, the untainted air, all evoked memories of her island home.

The Forest Lands' Chief stood before them, an embodiment of the land's essence. His hair, braided and black as the earth, his eyes a warm brown reflecting the sun's eternal caress on his skin. "Hello guests, my name is Onatach, Chief of the Forest Lands," he introduced himself with open arms, exuding an air of peace. "It brings me great joy to greet you all. Please, accept these tokens, crafted by our woodsmiths." He handed each of them a miniature rendition of their family crest, intricately carved from light oak. Cassandra was entranced by the exquisite detailing of the Harth emblem. She offered her gratitude as the Chief bestowed this unique gift upon every contender. "Now," he continued with a placid smile, "allow me to lead you to your awaiting carriages."

They followed the Chief as he led them to five substantial wooden carriages, drawn by robust brown horses. These carriages, resembling the miniature wooden sculptures they had received, had no roofs. The rich, dark oak wood gave them a distinct allure. Cassandra paid no heed to the subdued complaints from the Dimond Royals. To her, this setting was a blend of beauty and novelty, a place she refused to leave.

Their journey took them down a rugged trail, embraced by the verdant canopy of trees. Eventually, they arrived at the Camp.

Although situated away from the general populace, it was a private enclave designated for competitors. The Dimonds' inaudible grievances did not capture her attention. Every tent, of equal proportions, proudly bore the family crest atop. The light-hued wood, mirroring the token they had received, formed a sheltering embrace over each tent. Cassandra took her leisure, surveying the expanse of the Arena, absorbing this fresh chapter of her adventure. Arranged were four capacious tents, one for each royal family, demarcated by a central pit, illustrating the distinction. The Spars' encampment occupied the immediate space before her, a mere breath away.

On the distant left, the Dimonds' tent was positioned, although it was subtly set back a few paces, a clear assertion of their desire for solitude. At the opposite end, the Clubs claimed their spot. Grayson's call for his sister snapped Cassandra from her thoughts, and she followed Savannah into their tent. Upon entry, she marvelled at its generous expanse, easily accommodating ten occupants. The interior unfolded before her eyes, revealing a modest sitting area with finely crafted wooden chairs and a large cushioned couch. A step further and the layout shifted to a compact dining corner, furnished with a basket of fruits and vegetables, tokens of the Forest Lands' hospitality.

As Cassandra continued her inspection, she noticed the well-defined living zones. It struck her how she had her own distinct area, and this realisation expanded as she observed that her father, brother, head maid, and trainer each had their designated sections for slumber.

Grayson's concern voiced itself, his query directed at his father. "Where will I practise before the competition if the other guys are out there observing me?"

Jaronas cast a glance over his shoulder, his gaze shifting from his allocated sleeping area as he sorted through his belongings. "The Arena features a training chamber," he offered. "It is a space equipped with every requisite tool for a competitor. Our challenge, however, is securing a dedicated slot before the others."

His attention then shifted towards Cassandra, a paternal smile gracing his features. "For you and the other young women, there is a Sky Box where you can observe the training sessions, if you are interested. Of course, many sponsors will be there, assessing whom to place their bets on." Cassandra took note of the Sky Box, remembering the build and shape of it. She knew the Sky Box was able to become a detachable blimp, however, she doubted it would ever be used. She remembered her father speaking of it with his men, explaining the production costs and how it would benefit the islands. The blimp was created as a precaution unless something wrong were to happen to the royals and they needed a quick escape.

Turning back to Grayson, Jaronas added with a fatherly tone, "This place is the beginning to your great legacy, son. Make us proud." His focus pivoted back to Cassandra. His expression turned serious, his words carrying a weight of expectation. "Remember, Cassandra, the Sky Box is also a measure of your ability to show yourself as a proper young lady in our society." With that final piece of advice, Jaronas turned away, engrossed in the unpacking process that engulfed them all. Amongst the stir of activity, Cassandra was left with a bundle of nerves, a storm of anticipation swirling within her for the days that lay ahead.

CHAPTER 8

Cassandra's stomach hurt. As if it were in knots, nervous and anxious over what was to come that day. She knew her brother would not do too well in fencing; she knew that the tournament was about to begin, yet she found herself wishing these nerves were over herself and not her brother. She wished she felt anxious about the tournament's event and how she would perform, hoping she herself would do well rather than hoping for her brother to not make a fool out of the family.

Savannah stood behind her, preparing Cassandra for the better part of the morning, before the opening ceremony that would take that afternoon. Restlessly, Cassandra began to pace within the confinements of the tent, dragging an exasperated Savannah with her.

"Princess, please!" Savannah begged, struggling to keep up with the flurried movements. "You need to stop fidgeting. I need to finish your hair before the ceremony."

"I have no desire to be part of this ceremony. All I wish is to either be the one being presented or simply be at home."

With a visible display of frustration, Savannah rolled her eyes, her patience wearing thin. "Quit acting like a child. You are to be here for your brother, you are to represent that family, and you were the one that has been the most eager to explore the world. Now look where you are, look at what you saw. It is a great accomplishment."

"A greater accomplishment would be to become the first female competitor in the tournament," Cassandra snapped. "Smiling and waving to the thousands in the audience, hearing them chant my name. Stepping into the Arena for the first time and feeling the energy from the crowd—"

Savannah laughed. "You are funny."

Cassandra felt sick again. It was as if she did not hear her words.

"Come, now, stay put while I finish up. The sooner we are done, the sooner you can march off to the ceremony."

She did nothing. She stood quietly, letting Savannah finish her hair. Cassandra tried to breathe through her nose, out her mouth. Tried to control her emotions, forcing herself to not see red and feel that pain in her chest grow. Instead, once Savannah finished, she sat on her cot and opened the pages to her book, throwing herself back into her readings.

"How are you feeling?" Savannah asked as she began to clean up the tent.

"Fine" was all Cassandra said as she flipped a page. Her head maid gave her a look. Prepared to speak, she was quickly cut off by Grayson stumbled into the tent, sweat glistening on his forehead from his morning training.

His gaze fixed on his sister, face bright with a smile. "Ready?"

Nodding, she shut her book and tried to compose herself. "Of course." She gave Savannah a look, which she obliged to. Bowing, her maid exited the tent, causing Grayson to arch a brow in curiosity.

Taking a seat on the couch, he patted the spot beside him, inviting Cassandra to join him. "Come, tell me what's bothering you."

"I have already confided in Savannah," she said, opening her book once more wanting nothing more than to avoid any further conversation.

Her brother laughed, echoing through the tent. "You are not being truthful." He patted the cushion beside him once more, dark eyes warm and inviting. "Come, sit and share your worries with your little brother."

"I am quite comfortable here, thank you."

"Cass," he whined.

Cassandra looked up from her brook, giving her brother a gentle smile. "I am okay, honestly. Just a touch of nerves, but it is not something that cannot be managed."

She lied. It was all a lie. She had to. There was no other choice.

"Are you absolutely certain?"

"Yes."

Grayson's gaze lingered on his sister, a hint of uncertainty in his eyes as he debated whether to delve deeper. Eventually, he relented. With a swift motion, he rose from his seat, crossing the distance to Cassandra. He sat beside her, causing Cassandra to look up from her book, and enveloped her in a hug, his embrace both comforting and protective. "If and when you are ready to talk, I will be here."

Cassandra's arms found their way around her brother, a fleeting moment of vulnerability passing between them. "Thank you, Grayson."

As Grayson departed and Savannah returned to the tent, she completed dressing Cassandra for the impending ceremony, the two settled in the tent with cups of tea, awaiting the final touches from the men. Savannah had carefully woven Cassandra's hair into two intricate braids, framing her head. A jewelled crown, a fusion of sparkling black and orange, adorned her dresses. The dress Cassandra wore was a refined black, interlaced with silver and red accents that shimmered enchantingly. It bore a simplicity, its design graceful and uncomplicated. It draped elegantly from her waist and chest, the silk cascading down to just above her feet, a sleek line of fabric gracing the ground.

Her father, dressed in an all-black attire. A lengthy red cape hung regally from his shoulders. Grayson's attire mirrored their father's in essence, but his top boasted a rich orange hue, while his pants and boots remained obsidian. His crown, though not as opulent as his father's, held its own charm—a modest silver diadem studded with gleaming crimson gems.

After their dressing ritual, the family assembled, poised to head to the opening ceremony. They congregated outside their tents, awaiting the carriages that would transport them. Just then, the Clubs family appeared, greeted by genuine smiles.

Morana, taking the lead, approached Cassandra with warmth emanating from her. She planted sweet kisses on Cassandra's cheeks, drawing her into a tender embrace. "Good morning, my dear. You are radiantly beautiful," she praised. Morana donned an elegant attire combining black and green hues. The bodice bore a rebellious spirit, its black leather adorned with edgy spikes. A corset cinched her waist snugly, above which cascaded a verdant skirt.

Cassandra returned the compliment with genuine admiration. "You look equally stunning, Queen Morana."

The Clubs Queen's laughter rang out, a pleasant sound that reverberated in the air. "Dear, just Morana will suffice here. No need for formalities; we are all friends," she reassured her with a sweet smile.

She observed Cassandra's subtle anxiety as the carriages pulled up, noticing the young Princess's nervous fidgeting. Concern etched Morana's features. "Are you all right?"

Cassandra nodded, exhaling a shaky breath. She readied herself to join her father and brother, but Morana intervened, halting her.

"Dear," Morana called out to Constantine. "Cassandra and I will take a separate carriage." With that, Morana gently guided Cassandra into a wooden carriage and directed the driver to proceed. The boys, engrossed in their conversation, did not question the arrangement. Left alone in the carriage, Morana leaned in. "Now that we have a moment, tell me, what is troubling you?"

Glancing around at the line of carriages trailing behind them, Cassandra thought about her options. Fully opening up and informing Morana—a woman she met only once in her life, and confiding in her about her opinions regarding who should truly be participating in this tournament, or go a different route.

"Have you ever felt so nervous that it turns into nausea? I understand—the Arena holds thousands of people and everyone will be staring at me, but I cannot help but feel nervous." Cassandra felt the lie on her tongue, knew not speaking of the true thing bothering her was for the best. No one should know except for those closest to her. No one unknown should be trusted. "The thought of so many eyes watching me, ready to criticise my every move, terrifies me. I fear ending up in the newspapers, subjected to mockery. All I want is to be back home in the familiarity of my confined nation."

Morana regarded her with kindness, taking Cassandra's hands in hers and believing the lie that was told to her. "Cassandra," she started, her tone gentle yet firm. "Judgement is inevitable, no matter who you are. People often thrive on others' struggles. But you cannot let that hinder you. It is a tough reality, I admit, but you have a duty, not just to your nation but to your family. Your father and brother are probably equally anxious. Now, I am not invalidating your feelings, but perhaps confiding in him might ease both your burdens. Discover shared apprehensions that could help you both find some solace."

"Oh" was all Cassandra found herself saying.

"Or," Morana added with a mischievous grin, "you could divert your attention to the horses before you until it is over." Laughter bubbled between them, a fleeting moment of simple joy.

Cassandra's gaze shifted to the imposing Arena ahead, its metallic exterior radiating a greyish-silver hue. Banners representing each nation adorned the stadium, while a row of four flanked the front. People cheered and waved at the royals as their carriages rolled by. "Where are we headed?" Cassandra inquired, noting they were not taking the path that led to the front entrance with the other attendees.

"Back entrance, my dear. We'll prepare there," Morana explained. True to her words, the carriage veered around the Arena, coming to a stop where two imposing guards stood sentinel.

Their presence was formidable, armed with hefty wooden staff by their sides. As the carriages entered through the back entrance, the steel-covered walls enveloped them. The interior echoed with bustling activity as people swarmed around, assisting the royals to disembark while others directed them towards their designated carriages. In a precise sequence mirroring the hierarchical structure of the nations, the procession commenced. The Harth carriage led, a robust construction of red wood drawn by two sleek black horses. Following was the Spars carriage, an embodiment of dark blue wood hauled by two majestic white horses. Then came the Dimonds', their ostentatious golden carriage pulled by four resplendent horses at the front.

Morana's amused scoff reached Cassandra's ears. "Always craving attention. It is the only way we can survive this mad world."

With those parting words, Morana advanced to the last carriage, painted in rich green wood and drawn by two formidable black horses. As they settled into their carriage, Cassandra stood between her father and brother. The flurry of activity continued outside. Two men gripped the massive wooden doors and a voice reverberated through the air, announcing the imminent commencement of the ceremony.

A queasy sensation churned in Cassandra's stomach, the impulse to retch threatening to overwhelm her. This time the true nerves of the ceremony hit her. She realized her words to Morana were half true instead of a full lie. She was scared of what the public deemed of her, worried of their judgmental eyes.

The radio host's voice boomed over the steam-powered amplifier magnified by the Arena's walls. Clenching her emotions, she focused on her breathing, inhaling through her nose. She turned to Grayson, her grip tight around his hand.

"I'm nervous," she confessed, her voice a vulnerable whisper. Amidst the ongoing introduction by the radio host, Grayson regarded her with a mixture of curiosity and concern.

"Nervous? You?"

She nodded, her gaze steady on him. "I am afraid of their judgement, of becoming the next target for their ridicule in the newspapers." The cacophony of the event continued, the radio host's words intertwining with the racing of her heartbeat.

Grayson gently squeezed his sister's hand, his expression a mix of understanding and encouragement. "I share your nervousness about that, too. But perhaps, to ease your worry, would you like to hold my hand throughout the entire ceremony?" His offer was gentle and considerate.

Cassandra nodded in agreement and Grayson's hand remained securely clasped in hers. Side by side, they braced themselves as a signal prompted the grand doors to swing open, exposing their carriage to the intense illumination of the Arena. The clamour of the crowd erupted, each nation's supporters roaring with passion. Among the multitude, shouts of her brother's name rang out, mingling with cheers for all the contestants.

"Wave," Jaronas' voice reached them over the din. Following his lead, they raised their free hands and waved to the sea of faces.

Amidst the fervour, Cassandra's attention barely caught the radio host's words as he introduced each royal in turn.

"Behold, ladies and gentlemen! The Harth family takes the stage! Leading the way is Grayson, our spirited contender in the Games! And right behind him strides King Jaronas, a former triumphant of these very Games. Grayson, the burden of legacy is upon you! Best of luck!" The radio host's words seemed to strike a chord with Grayson, his stance subtly tensing at the weight of expectations.

"And here she is, folks! Our beautiful Princess Cassandra! What a sight to behold, is she not?" The crowd erupted once more, stirred by the radio host's peculiar choice of description.

As the announcer's voice faded into the background, Cassandra found herself bewildered by the simplicity of it all. Was that the extent of her introduction? Reduced to being just *beautiful* and quickly overshadowed?

She squeezed her brother's hand, this time not out of nervousness but anger.

Once the ceremonial introductions concluded, the majestic horses embarked on a nearly-complete circle, pausing midway to come to a halt in front of the imposing wooden chair occupied by the chief of the Forest Lands. Above him loomed the Sky Box, the realm of sponsors and soon-to-be-seated royals, including Cassandra herself.

With her gaze fixed on the Chief, who stood with an air of pride and his arms uplifted toward the throng, Cassandra was immersed in the grandeur of the moment. "Greetings, my children!" his vibrant voice echoed through the expanse. "Distinguished guests, welcome to the realm of the Forest Lands."

A quick glance to her left stirred the urge to look at Sebastian. He stood poised beside his parents, hands clasped behind his back and his expression resolute. His customary attire of black leather accentuated his composed stance, his dark hair pulled back with characteristic precision.

"In the upcoming fortnight," Onatach continued, a broad smile on his lips, "we shall bear witness to a fierce contest among nations, the battle of the Triumph Games, to determine who shall claim the coveted Triumph Cup!" At his side, two men carefully lifted the golden gauntlet—an impressive artefact nearly half the size of a man—causing the gleam of pure gold to dazzle in the sunlight.

"To secure this coveted cup, our valiant competitors must engage in a series of challenges, their scores meticulously recorded on our imposing scoreboard." Onatach gestured towards an oversized black chalkboard; each contender's name was etched in chalk. Cassandra let her focus wane slightly during this segment, as she knew these details were irrelevant to her. The gentle squeeze of Grayson's hand, however, snapped her back to attention, urging her to listen more closely.

"As the rules dictate, each ranking corresponds to a set of points. First place garners ten points, second is rewarded five, third claims two, while last place accrues none." The crowd erupted with cheers, and Cassandra's interest sharpened as the chief began to outline the upcoming events. "This year's sequence of Games will unfold as follows: archery, spear-throwing, fencing, the triathlon, and culminating with the combat sector."

Cassandra mentally arranged the upcoming challenges. Archery was set for the following day, followed by spear-throwing in two days. Fencing was scheduled for three days later, and the triathlon was to take place two days after that. What intrigued her most was the combat sector, marked for four days hence, leading to the climactic closing ceremony on the subsequent day.

As Onatach beckoned the competitors forward, a man appeared beside him, cradling four wooden branches in his arms. "Each of you must break a branch from the sacred oak tree and ignite the fractured end of your choice." The assistant descended from the podium and distributed a branch to each young man. Facing Onatach, they poised with anticipation. His arms remained raised, a symbol of command. "Now, break the branches!"

In synchronised movements, the boys snapped their branches and the same attendant reappeared, this time bearing a torch. He first handed it to Grayson, who ignited the fractured end of his branch. As the flames licked the wood, each contender followed suit, their flames combining to form a unified blaze. This symbolic act marked the commencement of the Games.

"May fortune favour you all! And may the worthiest Prince emerge victorious!" Onatach's words resonated through the air, a wishful declaration echoing the aspirations of not only the competitors but the entire realm.

Cassandra watched her brother smile, happy for him and for his moment. She heard her father cheer for his son, the heir, the successor, and the future victor.

Somehow, amongst it all, she found herself wondering what it would be like if it were her taking her brother's place. Soon her thoughts forged together and one phrase repeated itself in her mind.

That could have been me.

CHAPTER 9

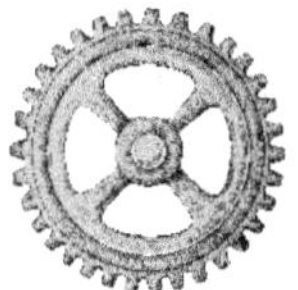

Perched in the Sky Box next to her father, Cassandra observed the chamber's interior, now filled with sponsors from various nations. The faces were unfamiliar to her, except for the presence of her father's wealthy associate, the second richest man on her island, along with Onatach and his esteemed council. The inaugural match was the archery contest, and Cassandra occupied her seat in an exquisite gown, a regal shade of black cascading down to the floor. Atop her head rested a silver crown, a demure bun securing her hair.

The announcer's voice boomed overhead, expressing gratitude to the sponsors whose contributions had made the tournament possible. Laughter followed as he acknowledged their financial support. "Special recognition goes to the Mountmonts," the announcer declared, "for their generous donation and contributing sponsors of this generation's Triumph Games."

Cassandra turned to her father, a question forming on her lips. "Father, who exactly are the Mountmonts?"

"The Mountmonts are a mystery," her father responded, leaning in as if sharing a secret. "No one truly knows their history. Some believe their presence spans generations, while others insist they are new money coming into the world. However, it was said that a father and his two sons live in a grand Mansion nestled in the outskirts of the Mountain Regions. They only truly became known to the public when they gave a small donation to the Forest Lands. Rumour has it, they help maintain its lands and rules, but no one quite knows for sure, as the Chief refuses to speak of it."

"And no one has ever seen them?"

"Only the Chief."

"How interesting."

As if on cue, a horn's resonant call echoed through the Arena, marking the commencement of the archery challenge. Cassandra knew her brother held a significant advantage here, his prowess in archery well-known. The archery segment was divided into three distinct rounds: the regular, far, and obstacle rounds.

The atmosphere was charged with anticipation as each contestant stepped out from their designated corners. Among them, Cassandra spotted her brother, Grayson, confidently placing himself in the Arena's centre. The four competitors formed a straight line—Grayson led, followed by Sebastian, Benjamin, and Augustus. A target emerged from the ground, hovering several hundred feet away.

Their challenge: to skillfully aim and strike the bullseye.

Grayson was summoned first, and in an instant, his arrow found the target's heart, securing him fifty points. Sebastian stepped up next, his shot mirroring Grayson's success, another fifty points. Benjamin, however, struggled, eventually hitting the third ring on the target's periphery, earning a mere ten points. Augustus followed suit, but his aim faltered, causing his arrow to hit the second rim of the central circle, granting him thirty points.

As the second round began, the target assumed a new challenge. Suspended on a hook and rod, it ascended into the air and moved farther from the competitors. The platform the boys stood on raised, aligning them with the target's height. Bows drawn, they focused on their shots. Grayson and Sebastian both struck the bullseye, collecting fifty points each. Augustus managed to hit the third circle again for ten points. Unfortunately, Benjamin's aim faltered entirely, his arrow missing the mark and finding the ground instead.

Then came the final round—an unpredictable test of agility and precision. The target danced between slow and rapid movements, shifting directions unpredictably. Targets emerged from various spots around them, demanding quick reactions and swift shots. Grayson's concentration was palpable, leading him to hit the centre once more, adding fifty points to his score. Sebastian's shot, while accurate, grazed the outer ring, securing him thirty points. Augustus and Benjamin encountered less luck, their arrows failing to hit the target. Augustus's arrow plummeted, while Benjamin dangerously neared the crowd.

With a triumphant flourish, Grayson emerged victorious in the archery segment. The audience erupted in cheers and Jaronas leapt to his feet, his pride evident. Cassandra, too, was on her feet, clapping for her brother, knowing that he had done well.

Under the night sky, the Harth family sat in a circle around the crackling campfire, enveloped in an aura of camaraderie. Laughter and conversation flowed freely, punctuated by talk of the day's archery challenge. Grayson, beside Cassandra, animatedly gestured with his hands, reliving the moments he had experienced.

"Father, you were absolutely right," Grayson enthused, his eyes alight with excitement. "It was an incredible rush to hear my name echoing in the Arena, to step onto that grand stage." He turned to

Cassandra, a spark in his gaze. "You cannot imagine, Cass. It was a whirlwind of thrill and excitement all at once."

Cassandra could only imagine if that was her, standing there, heart pounding in her chest as she took in the view before her. Proud to step into that Arena, raise her arm up high and hear the crowds scream her name. It was all an imagination, all a thought—never to happen. She put her hand in a fist, daggering her nails into her skin, trying to control her anger and frustration. She should be happy for her brother, proud of him for doing so well in the first challenge, but instead she found herself jealous of his success.

"One instant, I was behind those massive iron doors, and the next they were sliding open, the announcer's voice ringing out. And there I was, amidst it all. The rush hit me as I strode onto the mats, and when I saw those targets, my arrows seemed to find their mark in the centre every time. It was as though I had shut out the world around me, focusing solely on that moment." Grayson continued to recount the sensations that had surged through him; when he settled down beside his sister, Jaronas raised his glass.

"To the start of many victories," her father proclaimed.

Their glasses clinked together, the resonance of the toast mingling with the gentle crackle of the fire. As they drained their cups, the Harths revelled in the promise of success that lay ahead.

"Would you care for a little more?" a voice beckoned from outside their tent. As they turned, the Clubs family emerged into view. Constantine carried a bottle of rich red wine, while Morana held three gleaming glasses. "Wine, anyone?" he offered, playfully wiggling the bottle.

"Old friend, always a pleasure!" Jaronas responded with a genuine smile, rising to meet Constantine in a hearty handshake.

Augustus directed his attention to Grayson, his admiration evident. "Congratulations on the challenge. Your flawless marksmanship was truly a sight to behold. Remarkable." He then turned to Cassandra and gave her a quick peck on the cheek, as if greeting her. She tried to contain her blush.

Seated beside Cassandra, Morana pulled her into a warm hug. "And how are you, my dear? We missed a chance to chat yesterday. Are you feeling better? Did you take my advice and fixate on the horses' behinds?" She added a playful wink, prompting a genuine laugh from Cassandra.

"I did speak to my brother," she replied with a grin. "As for the horses' behinds, well, the aroma was enough motivation to look elsewhere."

Laughter and camaraderie filled the air, transforming the once-quiet vicinity into a space of lively interaction. Sharing laughter with their rivals, these supposed adversaries carried an unexpected warmth that felt oddly comforting. However, Cassandra harboured curiosity regarding the excessive amiability displayed between them. Despite her desire to converse with her father, he was engrossed in jovial conversation with fellow royals. Observing his interaction, which resembled familiarity with long-standing companions, held a certain fascination.

"It is odd, is it not?" Augustus remarked, tracing Cassandra's line of sight to their fathers who were seated in close proximity, their expressions marked by smiles and laughter.

"Indeed."

"They maintained a friendship throughout the duration of the games," Augustus commented, a brief smile gracing his lips. "In spite of the War Predicament, your father consistently held onto the belief of attaining peace. My own father recounted how King Jaronas stood out as the sole individual willing to engage with each competitor, refusing to let the War taint their interactions, recognizing them as the youth who stumbled into a violent affair."

"Furthermore, this situation serves as a wellspring for forging unions and alliances," Grayson remarked while passing them fresh wine. Casting a questioning glance towards Cassandra, he detected her incredulous expression, seemingly surprised by his extensive knowledge. "What? Before my arrival here, father advised me to foster amicable relations with all our competitors, for they could become essential contacts concerning the welfare of the nation."

With a gulp of wine, Augustus affirmed, "Indeed, my father echoed the very sentiment."

"Father told me to behave, and it seems he only dragged me here to see who I could one day marry."

Augustus smirked. "Does that mean I have a chance?"

Grayson gave his new friend a look but Cassandra giggled. "Better you than Benjamin."

"Oh, good lord. Not this again," her brother mumbled as he drank more wine.

It was Augustus who sat there listening as Cassandra retold the story of the events from the Diamond Kingdom, their friend now laughing.

Grayson gestured towards the Dimonds' enclosure. "They provide us with gold, diamonds, and precious gems if the need arises." He then directed attention to the Spars' section. "They arm us with weaponry, a variety of iron resources tailored for distinct arms. Our contribution lies in salt, and more recently, our airships. We must play nice despite certain people's…personalities."

"And let's not forget," Augustus chimed in with a smirk, taking a sip of his wine. "We offer technologies that stretch beyond the confines of imagination and have the genetics to create beautiful offspring." He winked at Cassandra.

"How intriguing, maybe we should put it to the test."

"Truly?" Augustus asked, seemingly too excited about it.

Grayson turned to his sister. "Must you make me nauseous? Speaking of offspring and the need for it?"

"Yes, that is how our society functions," Augustus mused. "A matrimonial alliance has proven to be an efficient method to keep peace within the nations. At last, my dear Cassandra, it is not you who I am looking to create this matrimonial alliance with. You are a good second option."

"How dare you! My soon-to-be-husband is leaving me before we reach the altar." Cassandra laughed. "But do tell, who is this special lady?"

Augustus smirked, reclining on the log where they were all perched. "Charlotte."

"The snooty Princess of the Diamond Kingdom!" Cassandra nearly exclaimed, causing Grayson to burst into laughter. Augustus shot Grayson a glare, giving him a light shove that almost sent him off the log. This moment carried an oddity, an encounter between comrades rather than adversaries. A sense of warmth lingered, as if a genuine friendship was tentatively taking shape—an unusual sensation, seemingly out of place yet undeniably fitting.

"Arranged marriages form the foundation of my nations' continuity!" Augustus repeated, his tone carrying a note of gravity. "My mother, a leading scientist among the royals, owes her presence to an alliance facilitated by my grandfather. Without his discussion of a marriage possibility, I would not be here."

"A blessing we could have been spared from," Grayson muttered, sipping his wine with a wry grin. All this playful banter reminded her of home, her summer memories with Yara and Jan, Adriana and her brothers. The chasing, giggling, drunkenly kissing.

"Were all the royal unions arranged in a similar manner?" Cassandra inquired, her gaze directed at Augustus, awaiting his response. "I am familiar with the Spars' marriage," she continued. "Queen Suzume, of royal lineage, wed King Kenji due to an obligation of protection, to stop an assassin plotting against her."

Augustus chuckled. "Oh, no, that tale has been considerably misinterpreted."

"What do you mean? My books—"

"And those books are egregiously mistaken." He leaned in, his smile sly as he rested his head on her lap. "Allow me to share what my parents imparted to me prior to our arrival." His expression carried a hint of mischief. "Queen Suzume's union with King Kenji was not for safeguarding but because he was the very assassin tasked with her elimination. He had been dispatched by an unidentified party, lured by the promise of unimaginable riches. Unbeknownst to him, Queen Suzume was pursuing him in return, aiming to ensure her own safety. It is rather romantic, if you ask me."

"You're spinning lies!" Grayson interjected.

"I assure you; I am not. Queen Suzume herself disclosed to my mother the blossoming affection she eventually developed for the now King."

"Does she not fear he might still harbour intentions to harm her?" Cassandra queried.

Augustus chuckled. "Why else do you think they opted for an adopted son rather than conceiving one?"

"He is adopted?" Cassandra's eyes widened.

"I thought he was a bastard," her brother chimed in.

"That is the rumour, at least. The other is that Sebastian is the love child of Queen Suzume and a man from Club Caverns."

"What!" Cassandra nearly screeched. The boys shushed her. "Impossible, a lady shouldn't—we aren't allowed to—oh, lord." With that she took a swing of her wine, filling her glass twice.

Grayson took the bottle from his sister as she went for a third glass. "I am still confused. Let's say Sebastian is adopted, how does it tie into King Kenji's situation?"

"It is all a rumour. The only truth I know of is Suzume confiding in my mother about her admiration and attractiveness to Kenji. Now, anything else around it is still rumoured. No one seems to know that truth. But understand, with the King's marriage exclusively to the

Queen, any child—be it by blood or adoption—retains a claim to the throne, ranking second only to a direct royal heir."

Grayson blinked and turned to his sister. "Why am I still confused?"

"Regardless if Sebastian is her true biological son or not, he is still considered a royal, making him second-in-line to the throne. Meaning that Kenji cannot rule without the Queen or an heir." She turned to Augustus, who had his eyes closed. "Is that correct?"

"Sounds about right."

"How confusing," Cassandra mumbled, taking a sip of the wine and feeling its effects in her head.

Grayson drained his cup letting out a sigh. "I am still confused and now I am out of wine. Care for a refill?" he inquired, gesturing to the two cups.

Rising to his feet, Augustus raised his cup. "I would certainly appreciate it more!"

Cassandra shook her head and observed as the two young men stumbled toward the King and Queen, seizing the wine bottle and replenishing their cups. However, her gaze soon shifted back to the Spars tent.

What secrets are they keeping? What does this mean of Sebastian? It would explain why Benjamin knew the truth about him. Too drunk and still very confused, she joined the boys, letting the night of fun continue.

CHAPTER 10

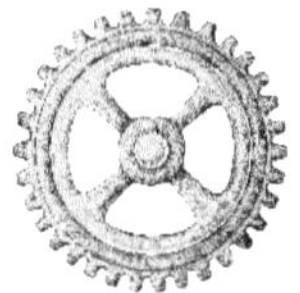

Two days had passed since the archery challenge—a span marked by observing her brother's rigorous preparation for the upcoming trial and enduring her father's incessant chastising of Grayson. Spear-throwing was a renowned test of strategy, amalgamating strength and power. Cassandra had spent the past couple of days stationed in the Arena's training area, watching from the sidelines as her brother honed his throwing technique. His proficiency was apparent, yet concerns loomed regarding Sebastian outshining Grayson in this challenge.

Sebastian had only made a single appearance in the training area and that was just prior to Grayson's practice session. Cassandra could still recall his demeanour—clad in the same dark blue jersey worn two days earlier for the archery challenge, paired with his customary black trousers. Yet, it was not his attire that captivated her attention; it was his towering stature, the beads of sweat tracing down his cheeks, and the unmistakable determination etched in his deep brown eyes—the essence of a resolute individual.

Swiftly, Cassandra dismissed the train of thought, burying her face into her pillow. Savannah promptly entered the tent, rousing her for the morning's preparations and coaxing her out of bed. For the day, Savannah opted for a cream-coloured cotton dress for Cassandra. The attire was airy, with delicate sleeves cascading to her wrists. A lightweight creation, it descended to her ankles, featuring gentle ruffles that layered around it and stopping just above her bosom. With Cassandra's hair neatly braided, Savannah readied her for the day. Despite the warmth of the morning, Cassandra welcomed it, reminiscent of the balmy summer days back in the Heart Lot Islands.

"Swiftly now," Savannah urged, redirecting Cassandra from her reverie. "Your father and brother are already at the Arena."

"Why so early?"

Savannah shrugged, proffering a white fan to her. "Your father stated they required extra practice prior to his challenge this afternoon. Hurry, you must join them."

Exhaling a sigh, she pulled open the tent's drape, greeted by the sun's inviting warmth. The low murmur of morning activities enveloped her as she surveyed the campgrounds. Sebastian was perched on a log beside the fire, savouring a bowl of oatmeal. Augustus occupied a spot on the ground nearby, engrossed in some inventive endeavour, while Benjamin lounged regally in an opulent chair outside his tent. Each of them sported the same jerseys from the archery challenge, leading Cassandra to deduce that this had become their customary game attire.

Savannah approached Sebastian, delivering a curt bow before whispering a few words to him. His dark eyes flicked to Cassandra, narrowing slightly before returning to the head maid with an unspoken question. With a shake of his head and a pointed gesture towards several vacant, pristine bowls and spoons in a bucket, Sebastian gave Savannah directions. Another bow from Savannah, a filled bowl of oatmeal in hand, and she returned to Cassandra.

"What was that all about?" Cassandra inquired, accepting the bowl Savannah handed her, her gaze trained on Sebastian. Savannah guided Cassandra towards the wooden carriages. "The Spade Prince informed me that the oatmeal was intended for the competitors, but since everyone else has already eaten, there is enough left for you."

Cassandra rolled her eyes. "Lucky me," she muttered, stepping into the carriage. She could still feel Sebastian's eyes upon her, scrutinising her every movement until she settled comfortably in the carriage. Unable to resist, she looked up, locking eyes with him, and delivering a steely glare. She had no patience for his little game. She wished to avoid the emotions he seemed to evoke with his gaze, the sly smirks he could muster, and most of all, his biting and sarcastic comments.

"To the Arena, please," Savannah instructed the driver, and with that, the carriage started moving, pulling them away from the Camp and the piercing scrutiny of the Spade City Prince.

The carriage conveyed them to the Arena, traversing a broad earthen bridge as pedestrians strolled across it, en route to the secluded island. A scattering of individuals populated the grounds, parting to make way for the carriage's passage. Friendly faces directed smiles toward Cassandra, allowing her the opportunity to reciprocate with waves.

Upon arriving at the Arena, Chief Onatach stood near the rear doors, ready to welcome her. "Your father informed me of your intention to join him and Grayson for training."

Cassandra's smile carried a gracious charm as she accepted the Chief's outstretched hand. "Indeed, though my role will be that of an observer on the sidelines, rather than an active participant."

"Ah, splendid! I do have some matters to discuss with your father. Would you mind my company as we watch?"

"Of course not."

They walked in tandem through the substantial iron doors, Onatach guiding Cassandra to the training area.

Within, Grayson emitted a loud groan moments before a spear whizzed through the air. Her father's commanding voice urged Grayson to execute another throw relentlessly until the execution reached a state of perfection. Cassandra found herself simply blinking at the unfolding tableau, exerting effort to suppress any laughter that might arise as her brother responded with evident frustration to their father's instructions. Chief Onatach shifted his attention to Cassandra, leading her to a pair of seats positioned toward the rear of the training area. In this section, they observed in silence the dynamic between them. Moments rolled by, and eventually, Grayson concluded his practice regimen. Jaronas directed Grayson to change attire in readiness for the impending challenge and Onatach, offering a sweet smile, excused himself to confer with Jaronas.

This left Cassandra alone with Savannah by her side. "What a remarkably reserved and tranquil individual," her maid observed.

Cassandra chuckled. "What do you mean?"

"Well, most leaders would seize this opportunity to engage with you, to establish some form of foundational camaraderie out of respect for your father and your nation. Yet, the Chief merely sat beside you, quietly minding his own affairs. It is almost impolite," Savannah commented, her gaze narrowing as she regarded the man conversing with Jaronas.

However, Cassandra huffed and turned to address her head maid. "Perhaps things are different here. Remember, the Forest Lands do not necessarily adhere to the conventions of the other nations; they possess their own distinct ways. It is possible he operates under the same philosophy," she mused, her head tilting as curiosity coursed through her. "Or perhaps he finds more interest in engaging with the new leaders than a mere Princess who is due to be wed within a year."

Savannah remained silent, releasing a breath as they both embraced the quietude, until the blaring sound of a horn reverberated through the speakers. This marked the herald of the upcoming challenge.

Spear-throwing shared similarities with archery, yet diverged in the fundamental mechanics. Instead of the steady poise required for an arrow's trajectory with a bow, Spear-throwing embraced the engagement of the entire body. This allowed for flexibility—bending, swaying—but most of all power. Thus, enabling participants to gauge distances and strive for optimal outcomes. Cassandra held a certain certainty that her brother would excel in this challenge. Yet, a disconcerting thought lingered: the potential for Sebastian to outperform him. As they entered the Sky Box amidst fellow royals, the roaring crowd greeted them, their cheers a welcoming wave for another gripping match. She found it intriguing how people cheered for their own royals seated and spectating, much like themselves.

Adhering to the Sky Box's decorum, dressing to impress was crucial. Cassandra's attire closely mirrored her choices back home, underscoring the significance of always presenting oneself in the best light. At least, that's what her self-help guide on *Becoming a Lady* espoused. Essentially, it was an opportunity to flaunt their most sumptuous garments and showcase them in the Sky Box. Demonstrating this sentiment, Cassandra observed Charlotte stepping toward the Sky Box's edge, a radiant smile gracing her face as she waved to the crowd. She embodied the very image of a Princess, bedecked in a floor-length gown shimmering in delicate rose gold hues, her golden hair crowned with a resplendent tiara.

Cassandra could not help but nearly laugh at the disparities between their respective nations—how understated her appearance was compared to the overt attention the Dimonds seemingly sought to command. However, her momentary amusement waned when Charlotte approached her, sporting a sly smile and insisting they sit together. With a brief glance toward Jaronas, who offered a nod signalling her to engage with the other royals, Cassandra yielded. She followed Charlotte to the front rows of the Sky Box.

During those fleeting ten minutes of occupying their seats, Charlotte skilfully wove a tapestry of snide remarks, directed first at Queen Morana's attire and then expounding upon how she would not adopt such a plainly attired or extravagantly wild fashion when she ascended the throne. In a further sally, Charlotte disparaged Cassandra, criticising her for what she deemed an excessively modest dress sense.

Cassandra found herself at a crossroads—debating whether to depart or to firmly stand her ground against this insufferable royal.

"It is wiser to carry oneself with dignity than to stand before the audience devoid of any," Charlotte asserted, sparing no restraint. "And you, dear, lack any semblance of dignity."

Cassandra bristled at the words, her thick dark brown eyebrows knitting together as she issued a scoff in response to Charlotte's comment. "I must ask for your forgiveness?"

"The statement holds its veracity."

"Then exercise caution with your words to avoid inciting offence that might reignite a civil conflict," Cassandra retorted, her blue eyes narrowing in focus.

The mutual disdain between the two was palpable and Charlotte's audacious belief in her superiority over everyone else in the room could not have been more evident. "You might perceive us as distinct, you and I," she continued. Cassandra found herself momentarily puzzled as to how this related to the offensive encounter that had just transpired. "But in reality, we share a similarity."

Cassandra paused, grappling with the connection Charlotte attempted to draw—uncertain of its relevance to the disrespect just demonstrated. "Your assertion is mistaken."

"We both hold the status of firstborns, destined for the throne and irrevocably entwined with the Triumph Games. Yet, as women, we both assume the secondary position within our families, intended merely to be married off. Our birthright to the throne was relinquished the moment we were born," Charlotte asserted, her eyes narrowing in emphasis. "We are relegated to being obstacles that prevent the birth of male heirs, destined to quickly bear the offspring that future Kings require."

Cassandra experienced a wave of discomfort, a sickening feeling rising within her. "Your choice of words is exceedingly unsettling. Must you articulate it in such a manner?"

"Should the truth not be presented in its most straightforward form?" Charlotte replied unapologetically.

Amidst the resounding cheers of the crowd, Cassandra settled into her seat with haste, her focus now captured by the radio host whose resonant voice echoed above. She loved her brother yet she knew Charlotte was right, she had been telling herself how unfair it was however it was almost odd hearing it from someone else.

"You are right," Cassandra found herself saying, catching Charlotte off-guard. "I have been thinking of such things for as long as I can remember, however there is nothing we can do. We are forced to play the game of a helpless Princess."

"I do not wish to play that game any longer," Charlotte blurted out.

The two shared a long look, eyes boring into one another as an understanding reached them both. "I wish the same," Cassandra agreed.

"It is exhausting, is it not?"

"What is?"

Charlotte sighed, reclining into the plus velvet chair. "The reality we must contend with." Her gaze turned towards Cassandra, whose wide eyes blinked in astonishment and contemplation. Charlotte's laughter rang out at the sight. "If we do not wish to acquiesce to societal norms, then we must play by them differently. Show that we aspire to stand out, to seize the attention of others—make them talk about you more than your brother. Stop standing on the side, hiding in the shadows, letting those men speak down to you, and stop reading those pages in your novels. They will not always help you. Step onto the stage, be bold, and shine. Illuminate that bloody stage like you are the star and they have come to watch you."

"Interesting advice from the same Princess who mocked my modest attire not even ten minutes ago," Cassandra retorted sharply. "This all seems to have emerged from thin air."

"Not thin air, but from the concealed truth both of us have long harboured," Charlotte responded with a smile, allowing her cunning beauty to surface.

Without further dialogue, the blaring horn marked the onset of the challenge. Overhead, the announcer enumerated the competitors and Cassandra remained seated, watching as the iron doors slid open one by one. Charlotte smiled at her, proud of her new backbone and newfound realization. Stand out, and by standing out, she must sit down, not being a part of everyone else.

The four Princes emerged, each grasping a sizable spear in readiness for the contest.

CHAPTER 11

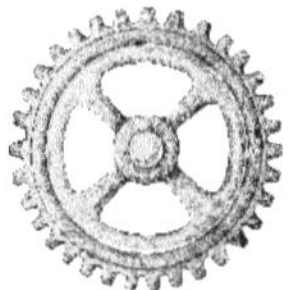

The audience erupted in cheers as Grayson's spear soared through the air. The dark wooden shaft, adorned with the emblem of the heart, landed at the furthest mark: three hundred and fifty yards. The field's layout had been reconfigured for this challenge. The four competitors positioned themselves on the far-left side, with a red boundary line indicating where they must not cross, and an expanse of grass extending to their right.

The Arena floor was partitioned into four sections, each designated by a distinct colour to indicate the distance achieved by each Prince's throw. The segments began with white, representing one hundred yards and covering the most extensive area, stretching from a few feet ahead of the competitors to a quarter of the distance. Bright yellow signified two hundred yards, encompassing nearly half of the grass field and presenting the most probable target. A bright orange section, a foot in length, represented three hundred yards, while the most challenging target was the four-hundred-yard bright red zone, a mere foot long but vivid enough to catch the competitors' attention—the precise spot where they aimed to land their spears.

Luck favoured Grayson as his spear struck the middle of the orange sector, a deliberate choice considering its difficulty. Now, he could only hope that the other contenders would not replicate his feat. Cassandra took in the cheers of his successful hit, with her father leaping from his seat behind her, exuberantly praising his son, pointing at Grayson and exclaiming his amazement. While she remained in her seat, a rigid expression affixed to her face, the weight of Charlotte's words bore down upon her, accentuated by her feline smile.

A realization dawned on her. Action was needed but the path ahead of her would always remain unclear, meaning it was to be a long life of living in her brother's shadow. Cassandra found herself clapping for her brother's accomplishment, while she internally thought of launching her brother's spear toward the very Sky Box she occupied.

It was tradition, she had reminded herself of that over and over again. The notion that was deeply rooted within their history, an acceptance that she was forced to embrace since childhood. It made her sick. How is such a thing possible? To deem every female royal is to not participate in the Triumph Games due to the myth of it being too intense.

How hard could these games possibly be?

Casting a spear a great distance, targeting with a bow, engaging in a fencing match—these were all feats she had trained for extensively alongside her brother since childhood. Her education spanned the realms of womanly grace in society and the strength required for self-defence, equipping her with multifaceted skills. However, societal expectations remained heavily skewed toward the abilities of men, deeming them as better.

In those moments, Cassandra wished for nothing more than to participate in these games, and wished for an opportunity to arise for her to be able to prove everyone wrong. Yet, if she were to wish too hard for such a thing then her brother would be the one getting hurt, something incredibly bad needing to happen to him in order for her to take his place, and she wanted nothing but for him to remain safe and healthy. Cassandra quickly took back her wish, hoping the universe did not hear her.

The time had come for Sebastian to take the stage. He exuded a composed demeanour, his gaze methodically surveying the expanse before him as he clutched the wooden spear in his hand. Cassandra could not help but observe the common thread among the players— the emblem of their respective family crests adorning the sharpened tips of their spears. Her focus remained riveted on Sebastian, her unspoken hope directed toward the outcome above, wishing that he would miss the four-hundred-yard mark. Sebastian drew a calming breath and poised the spear on his shoulder, his arm extending to the side before raising, his body primed for the throw.

As the whistle blew, he embarked on three powerful strides, channelling his might into the launch, his form nearly grazing the ground. The trajectory of Sebastian's spear traced a graceful arc through the air, evoking an anticipatory hush from the audience. Motion ceased, breaths held, until the spear finally found its destination. Cassandra's attention shifted briefly to the sight of Kenji embracing Suzume with elation—a rare display of affection between the two. However, Cassandra's expression faltered.

Sebastian had accomplished the impossible; his spear had landed precisely on the four-hundred-yard mark, propelling him into first place. An outpouring of cheers engulfed the Arena and it was then that she noticed Sebastian's self-assured smirk directed to Grayson and seemingly up to her in the Sky Box. She could have sworn his gaze was fixed on her, his expression conveying his prowess in outshining Grayson, showcasing his superior strength among the competitors. A flush of warmth spread across Cassandra's cheeks, his smirk further intensifying as he offered a congratulatory clap for himself.

The Spear-throwing challenge was one that has not been won by Spade City in years, yet Sebastian stood there with a smile on his face, fist in the air as he made history, his name soon to be in the books.

Benjamin followed with his turn, his spear falling short, landing within the initial range of the two hundred-yard markers, within the broader zone.

Charlotte responded to her brother's performance with a soft chuckle. "Embarrassment," she murmured. "I could have performed better."

Augustus stepped up, his throw mirroring her brother's, both landing within the same vicinity. Augustus secured the third spot. After performing the same throws two more times, it was evident that Sebastian was the clear winner, as his spear constantly aimed for the four-hundred-line marking. With these outcomes, Spade City emerged as the unequivocal winner. Her brother came in second place, Augustusin third, and for Benjamin remained last. Sebastian stood poised, hands clasped behind his back, offering a bow of gratitude to the audience before departing the stage.

On that night, the Spars tent was devoid of celebration—no laughter, no revelry, only an eerie quietude that enveloped their tents. The Dimonds joined them in their sombre demeanour, leaving the Clubs to gather around the campfire with the Harths. Cassandra observed the stark contrast between her father and Constantine— two Kings who embodied light-heartedness, seldom broaching the topic of the Triumph Games, instead engaging in discussions on political matters aimed at benefiting their respective nations upon their return. Seated beside Queen Morana, Cassandra was inundated with a ceaseless stream of chatter about the ever-evolving fashion trends within the Diamond Kingdom. Meanwhile, the two Princes animatedly discussed the earlier match and the impending Fencing event. The rapid friendship between the two families intrigued her, forming a distinct contrast to the distant relations among the other royals.

The upcoming match was a mere two days away, necessitating rigorous preparation and practise for Grayson. Cassandra recognized the challenge that lay ahead for her brother—striking the right balance, mastering the proper techniques. She hoped that their impromptu lessons during their boat journey had borne fruit.

As the night waned, the three bottles of wine provided to them were emptied. Cassandra's vision grew slightly blurred as she and Grayson shared laughter at their father's expense. Jaronas had drank too much, leaving the Harth siblings shouldering the responsibility of carrying their inebriated father back to their tents, bidding the Clubs goodnight before departing.

After gently laying their father in his designated sleeping area, Cassandra could not resist embracing her brother tightly. "I am immensely proud of you," she declared. "You performed excellently in the archery challenge, and today's event, even if you didn't emerge as the victor, proved your skill. I'm confident you can win this tournament." Drawing back, she offered a warm smile. "You truly deserve this, Grayson, every bit of it."

Grayson's laughter bubbled forth. "I think it is time for you to rest as well, Cass. But thank you."

Cassandra mumbled her self-doubt, "I could have certainly done better." Her younger brother guided her back to her designated sleeping area.

"Without a doubt," Grayson chuckled, gently ushering her. With goodnight wishes exchanged, he retreated to his own section.

Cassandra's slumber was interrupted by rustling sounds that initially she attributed to Grayson's restless sleep in an unfamiliar environment. She muttered loudly, assuming he was talking in his sleep, "Grayson, please, be quiet. I'm trying to sleep. Save your self-talk for another night."

However, the rustling persisted, and Cassandra heard voices. Thinking that her imagination was playing tricks on her, she was about to drift back to sleep when she heard her brother grunting as if he were in pain.

She began to cough, as if some sort of horrible smell entered her tent. Frowning in confusion, Cassandra groggily rolled over, intending to figure out where that smell came from and why her brother did not stop his restless turning. Her eyes were met with a large amount of grey smoke, almost a toxic gas. The contraption rested in the middle of the room as she tried to form words, but she froze as her eyes fell upon two large figures dragging Grayson across the tent floor. She opened her mouth to scream, but no sound escaped. She was immobilised, unable to comprehend the situation—why could she not speak, who were these intruders, why was she feeling dizzy, and what was happening?

Summoning her courage, she sprang into action, rushing to Grayson's aid. She grabbed his leg and tugged, attempting to free him from their grasp. One of the shadowy figures growled, "Get away" as he grabbed the back of Cassandra's head and forcefully flung her across the room. She landed with a jolt on her bed. Cassandra turned to her maid, shaking her to wake; however, the smell got worse and her maid did not move.

Cassandra did not understand what was happening; usually Savannah awakened at the first instant of being disrupted. But in those moments, it was odd, she did not move. She remained asleep and did not move. The gas smelled horrible and she quickly understood what that meant. This gas was not permitting Savannah to wake, as if it was some sort of sleeping gas. That only made Cassandra panic more as she was stuck in a mute state and had no idea who else to ask for help. How could she be rendered speechless in the face of such danger, especially after having been able to speak just moments ago?

She urged herself to scream, to let out the fear and protect her brother, who was being dragged away. Standing up, Cassandra quickly felt her head spin as she reached for the chair before her. Her lungs tried to take the air and filtrate it, the gears within her tried to move properly to give Cassandra enough energy, however, time was running out and her goal to wake her father was still in motion. She had to wake him, the suffocating gas seemed to not completely destroy Cassandra, but he was stronger than her. She shook him with urgency, attempting to rouse him from sleep.

"Grayson!" she managed to utter amidst her efforts to wake him.

Her father coughed. "Cassandra? What in the world..." he mumbled, eyes shutting again. However, the situation was growing dire and there was no time to explain. Grayson was being hauled out of the tent by the intruders, and time was running out.

Cassandra shook her father with increasing urgency. "Father! Grayson!" Panic gripped her as she faced the dilemma of whether to stay and awaken her father or chase after her abducted brother. Jaronas managed to get up, swinging his legs over the cot as he reached out his arm to Cassandra, as if asking him to guide her to the situation. However, the smell of the gas and the headache it caused her were too much to handle. Cassandra tugged at her father, the two shuffling out of the tent as he grunted, mumbling something about the gas, but as they reached the outside, Cassandra gasped at the sight. The entire camp was filled with that same toxic gas. No one seemed to wake up besides the two of them.

Cassandra scanned the dark area, searching for Grayson through the haze, but there was no sign of him, as if he had vanished without a trace. That was when she heard the rustle of branches and leaves and Grayson came running out of the dark forest area. His hair a mess, tangled and muddy, his clothes smeared with dirt and pieces of grass. His eyes grew wide at the scene before him: the gas that filled the camp, Jaronas and Cassandra coughing until it became hard to breathe.

"Grayson!" Jaronas screamed, but it was too late. A staff hit the back of Grayson's head, causing him to fall to his knees. Her brother grunted in pain, hands behind his head as he tried to attack the person that hit him.

Cassandra was in shock at the scene before her, her father not wasting a second to hazily rush towards his son, prepared to attack his kidnapper. Still in a daze, Cassandra did not hear the second person behind her. Her eyes trained on the staff that slammed across Jaronas' face, knocking him to the ground. Grayson did not move from his position, eyes trained on his father as he tried to reach for him, however the figure behind him grabbed the back of Grayson's neck, pulling him back and placing a cloth to his mouth and nose.

Cassandra was prepared to rush towards her brother, to get him away from his kidnapper, but two strong arms wrapped around her waist from behind and a matching cream cloth pressed to her face. It was a sickeningly sweet smell, one that invaded her senses. Her eyes widened as she struggled against the grip, managing to break free and summon the courage to scream through the muffled fabric.

A light flickered to life from the nearby Spars tent, followed by coughs and groans of the others. This only encouraged her to try again, this time with more intensity. Cassandra's mind clouded, her vision dimming as she pushed against the figure's tight grip. She screamed once more, eyes meeting Grayson's as she did so. Her brother met her gaze, eyes lazily dropping as he knew there was nothing to do to protect his sister, as his frantic moves died down.

Summoning a last burst of energy, Cassandra clawed at her captor's arms, and managed to release one final, feeble scream before succumbing to darkness. In the distance, the tolling of an emergency bell began to ring, its urgent peals echoing through the camp.

Cassandra's eyes snapped open, her head throbbing as she coughed and realised she was lying on the ground. Her father, Kenji, and Sebastian surrounded her, illuminated only by the nearby flickering light. The darkness still blanketed the surroundings.

"Oh, my dear," her father's voice trembled as he helped Cassandra to sit. "Are you alright?"

"No," she managed, the memories flooding back in. "Grayson... he is..." Her voice faltered, the truth sinking in. She had not rescued her brother; it was not just a dream, but a harrowing reality.

Shuffling and groans and coughs from the other royals made way to her buzzing ears. Loud hooves slapped against the forest ground as seven guards on horseback arrived, led by Chief Onatach. A siren blared, jolting the Forest Lands awake. An announcement instructed residents to stay indoors, and guests were to remain in their tents until further notice.

"What happened here?" Onatach demanded as he dismounted.

Cassandra hurriedly explained, "Grayson, he was taken. I tried to stop them; I really did." Turning to her father, her eyes brimming with tears, she added, "I am so sorry."

Jaronas stood, his gaze locked onto the Chief. "We must retrieve my son."

Onatach gathered the Kings around him, ready to dispense further instructions. Jaronas directed Cassandra to sit on a nearby log and wait for him.

Sebastian remained by her side, extending a hand. "Come on, let me help you up."

"Thank you," she whispered as Sebastian assisted her and guided her to the fire pit.

"I heard your scream," Sebastian revealed as they settled down. "Initially, I thought it was some wild animal, but when the noise ceased and I glanced out of my tent, I saw you on the ground with your father calling your name. My father and I hurried to see what had happened."

Cassandra nodded, too consumed by the events that had just transpired.

The two sat in silence, eavesdropping on the hushed conversation between the four Kings and the Chief. Amidst the exchange, she caught Onatach's mention of a dawn meeting, with Jaronas expected to be ready for whatever lay ahead. Cassandra's gaze shifted to Sebastian, who had also picked up on the conversation. Yet, what intrigued her more was the sight of Augustus peering from his tent, much like Benjamin and Charlotte.

CHAPTER 12

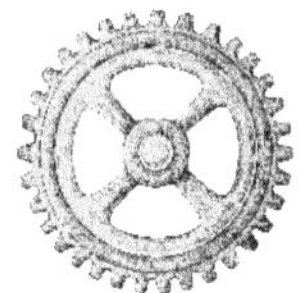

As dawn broke, Savannah remained sound asleep, along with Grayson's trainer who was producing snores from the corner. Meanwhile, Cassandra lay in her cot, observing her father's departure from the tent. He was dressed and ready for his meeting with the other Kings and the Chief. The image of her father's distress-filled outburst haunted her mind; she hadn't witnessed her father in such a state since her mother's passing. The memory was disconcerting, as if history was replaying itself.

Her father had likely thought he was quiet when exiting the tent, but Cassandra lay there, waiting for him to leave. Outside, the other Kings conversed in muted tones and soon her father joined them.

Once the echo of their footsteps faded, Cassandra swiftly rose from her bed, opting for her brother's trousers and top. A dress would only hinder her movements; this was no time for such formality. She refused to remain in the tent while her brother's fate hung in the balance. Her mind churned with plans to locate him, envisioning herself tracking his captors and retracing the events of the previous night. Trusting no one else for this task, Cassandra firmly believed she could and would rescue her brother. She understood that time was crucial, that she needed it to piece together the puzzle and devise a strategy.

Stepping cautiously, she peered outside the tent, scanning both directions to ensure no one was stirring or lingering around the fire. With everything seemingly quiet, she emerged fully into the open.

"Where do you think you are going?" A deep voice emerged from behind her. Startled, Cassandra spun around, nearly stumbling in surprise as she found Sebastian casually leaning against a nearby tree. His dagger rested at his waist, and he was clad in his customary black leathers.

"Why were you lurking there?" she inquired with a mix of curiosity and suspicion.

Sebastian simply shrugged, moving out of the shaded area, allowing the morning sun to illuminate his dark form. "I had an early training session with my father before he departed for the meeting with the chief. Seems we're not the only ones awake at this hour." He gestured toward the Clubs tent, where Augustus was emerging with a slow and dishevelled demeanour. His dark hair was a tangle, with a pair of green goggles perched atop it, serving as an attempt to maintain a semblance of neatness. Augustus wore a belt around his waist, a collection of assorted trinkets clinking softly as he adjusted them to quell the noise.

"What brings you out here?" Cassandra whispered to Augustus, causing him to startle slightly at the sudden voice.

"Me?" he retorted, holding onto his array of trinkets to prevent any further jingling. "What is your purpose for being here?"

Cassandra rolled her eyes. "My brother just got kidnapped. I thought my purpose was pretty obvious."

"Ah, right," Augustus chuckled softly to himself, as if only now realising what his previous question implied. "My bad."

"Do you have to make so much noise?" Sebastian interjected, casting a critical gaze at the jangling belt around Augustus' waist.

Augustus clutched his belt defensively. "Yes, I have crafted a new invention and I wanted to test it out. This one required ample open space." He grinned with a touch of mischief, glancing down at the tinkling trinkets. "Would you like to see how it works?"

"No," Sebastian replied curtly.

Cassandra offered a sweet smile. "I appreciate the offer, but I have other plans for this early hour."

"In other words, no," Sebastian chimed in again, offering Augustus a brief, tight-lipped smile.

Augustus raised an inquisitive eyebrow. "So, where are you headed? Can I tag along?"

Before Cassandra could respond, hushed murmurs emerged from the nearby Dimond tent. Emerging from within were Charlotte and Benjamin, both adorned in their characteristic lavish attire. Cassandra tilted her head, taking in the intricate design of Charlotte's dress, the shimmering blue fabric catching the sunlight and nearly blinding them all.

"How splendid," she muttered, somewhat sarcastically. "More company."

Benjamin came to a halt, eyeing the other three young royals before him. "What brings you all out here?"

Cassandra let out a groan, not in the mood to go through the formalities again. "I am heading to the Arena. Prince Sebastian just wrapped up an early training session and Prince Augustus was on the verge of turning the Forest Lands into chaos with his new experiment. Now, if you will excuse me!"

"Mind if we join you?" Benjamin called out, quickening his pace to catch up with Cassandra, who was already moving away.

"No."

"Well, why not? We were planning to eavesdrop on the meeting anyway," Charlotte retorted, causing Cassandra to pause.

"Excuse me?" Cassandra's eyes widened in shock. "How does this concern you? It is about my brother who was abducted."

Benjamin gave a nonchalant shrug. "True, but there is a chance for us to be introduced with a new competitor, one as a replacement until Grayson is found."

"Are you truly speaking of such a thing right now?" Cassandra scoffed. "My brother has been taken–kidnapped, and you are here speaking about a new competitor! How much of an entitled brat must you be to be thinking of such a thing at a time like this!"

Sebastian took a step forward, completely disregarding her outburst. "A new competitor?"

Cassandra groaned, feet marching faster on the dirt ground. The young royal's voice was a faint reminder of the situation she was in–of the situation her family was in. Grayson was gone, taken before her very own eyes, and these suffocating royals only cared for a competition.

"Indeed!" Benjamin almost exclaimed from a distance. "According to the rules, if something were to happen to the first competitor during the tournament, the nation can designate its second son as a replacement. And if there is no second son, the nation has the option to appoint a temporary replacement until the first competitor is fit to compete again. If not, the nation is forced to withdraw from the Triumph Games."

Augustus stood with his mouth agape. "You must be kidding."

Charlotte frowned. "Would the three of you please stop talking! The poor girl lost her brother. Are you forgetting she was *there* last night when he was taken? Sebastian found her on the ground unconscious, no less." She scolded them, eyes narrowing at their childish behaviour. "If I hear so much as another word about the competition from any of your mouths, I will have your tongues." A small smirk took up the corner of Charlotte's lip, sharp eyes fixing on Cassandra. "Besides, the Heart Lot Princess would be the best option to take her brother's place in this tournament."

"Mind your tongue!" Cassandra exclaimed, head darting over to the group behind her. "No one is replacing my brother and that is final! I will do everything in my power to find him and bring him back!"

"Then you will be disqualified." Benjamin smirked.

Cassandra glared at him. "You so much as mention another word about this tournament and I will feed you to the kraken that lives in the depths of the sea near the Heart Lot Islands."

"So!" Charlotte declared, quickly changing conversation. "Shall we go find out what the meeting has in store?"

Augustus raised his hand. "I am so in!"

Sebastian simply shrugged, suggesting he was joining the expedition as well. With a resigned groan, Cassandra set off, trailed by the Diamond siblings. Augustus seemed all too pleased to be in Charlotte's company, while Sebastian pondered over who the new competitor might be.

Cassandra signalled for the group to keep quiet as they stealthily moved through the corridors of the Arena. Their fathers' distant conversations acted as their guide to the Chief's office. Careful not to be spotted, they took cover behind a distant wall. She knew they needed to eavesdrop on the conversation without raising suspicion from people.

Augustus extracted a trinket from his belt, wearing an innocent smile as he approached the door, slid a metal rod underneath, and quickly rejoined the group. "Behold the magic," he announced, sliding the rod into an old miniature radio and giving the box a few shakes until a loud noise burst forth.

Sebastian shot him an annoyed glare. "Must you make such a racket?"

"Quiet down," Augustus countered, adjusting the volume and tuning into the conversation unfolding inside the meeting room.

The meeting had just commenced, with Onatach elaborating on the same points Benjamin had shared earlier. Cassandra could sense the smugness in Benjamin's expression. "Given your lack of another male heir, introducing another competitor seems the most viable solution," Onatach's voice resonated soothingly. "Jaronas, I am giving you one extra day to find your son; you have until the fencing matches, but understand that a replacement is to be kept in mind in case you do not find Grayson within those respective days."

Kenji chuckled. "There is barely enough time to find a suitable replacement."

"The most fitting candidate would be your daughter," Constantine chimed in.

This elicited hearty laughter from Albert. "You are beginning to sound like my own daughter!"

"A woman cannot partake in these games," Kenji snapped, his tone laced with hostility. "Placing a woman in such a physically-demanding environment is unnatural."

Jaronas mused, his tone firm. "That is an interesting viewpoint."

Kenji's retort was cutting. "Women have no place in this competition. My wife stands as an example—why, I had to compete for her. She was far too delicate."

"Are you implying that my daughter is too delicate to join the tournament?"

"What I am stating is that it is ethically questionable to subject her to such an unfamiliar setting."

"You sound threatened, Kenji," Constantine chuckled. "Are you concerned that a young woman might outshine your son?"

"Watch your words!" King Kenji's voice boomed through the small radio.

"Cassandra will take Grayson's place in the Triumph Games," Jaronas declared, voice low and tired, "only if my son is not found before the next challenge."

A heavy silence fell upon the room and Cassandra felt her heart plummet. It was impossible. She was not prepared; in the past she had taken training, yes, but purely for self-defence. Never for a tournament. Some sickening part of her remembered her wish from the night before, hoping to participate, and hated herself for even thinking it. Her wish came true and she was to be a part of the tournament that she was unprepared for.

The Princes all turned their gaze toward her, wide-eyed, struggling to comprehend what had just transpired, their shock rendering them momentarily speechless.

Charlotte wore a wide smile, evident in her prideful hug as she embraced Cassandra. "You could become the first woman to compete!"

Cassandra was caught between shock and excitement, her emotions a whirlwind. She felt both unprepared and elated. Amongst the ensuing argument among the Kings, attempting to brainstorm alternative solutions, Cassandra found herself on her feet. Now that the opportunity was hers, she was to claim it. Sebastian attempted to restrain her, his touch brushing against her wrist, but she evaded his grasp. Determinedly, she moved toward Chief Onatach's office.

"Cassandra!" Sebastian's hushed voice echoed down the hallway. He started to rise, an intention to follow her evident in his stance, and Augustus promptly acted on the same notion. He clasped Cassandra around her waist and lifted her off her feet.

"Let me go!" she hissed, striking at Augustus's arms and attempting to free herself from his hold.

Sebastian intervened, gripping her wrists to prevent her from causing further harm to Augustus. "You might regret your actions."

"No, let me go!" She arched her head backward, unintentionally colliding with Augustus's nose. He grunted, releasing Cassandra, his hand cupping his bleeding nose. She quickly wriggled free, manoeuvring past Sebastian, and shoved open the office doors. The rest of the young royals hurriedly followed, stumbling into the office.

The Kings sat in a stunned silence at Cassandra's impulsive entrance, yet she remained resolute, standing tall. "I demand that a search party be launched immediately to find my brother. It is not right that you four are sitting here, bombarding my father, as we are trying to grieve from the situation."

Kenji scoffed. "Watch your tongue, girl."

"You mind yours!" she seethed, turning her attention to Chief Onatach. "I demand that you gather your finest men and be at my father's disposal."

Onatach looked at Cassandra with a sort of satisfaction. "Yes," he said, turning to Jaronas. "My seven best warriors are yours."

"However, there is still the matter of a replacement!" Albert exclaimed. "I will not have my son in a tournament against a girl. It is absurd!"

Cassandra fought back tears, pushed the lump back down her throat. There was no way King Albert was going to take this opportunity away from her. Balling her fists, feeling her nails dig into her palms, she controlled her breathing, calmed her emotions, and listened to Albert and Kenji bicker with Onatach. Her father sat staring at the wall, Constantine gazing over at his friend whose mind was elsewhere. All these men cared about were the games, not that her brother was missing, and too worried that a girl might be in the tournament instead.

"I will step into the Triumph Games if my brother is not found within a three-day request of searching for him," Cassandra declared, causing Jaronas to snap his attention towards his daughter, eyes wide in shock as he saw the single tear that fell down her cheek. "All you men care for are these Games, meanwhile there are two people who took my brother! If it is so important to you, then yes, I will compete!"

Kenji scoffed and rose from his seat. "You do not know what you are talking about. This tournament is not meant for women."

Cassandra returned his gaze with unwavering resolve. "Yes and it was not meant for you either when you competed in these games." An insult to a King was a form of high treason, it was a form of war. However, Kenji just glared at her, biting his tongue before he turned away.

Albert chuckled. "There is a better chance for me to win now."

Onatach remained silent, his dark eyes sweeping across the room before he exhaled deeply. Her father nodded in approval, already to his feet as he made his way to his daughter. "We are leaving now," he mumbled to Cassandra, who nodded and followed her father out the door.

"Welcome, new competitor." A warm smile adorned Onatach' face as he observed Cassandra, impressed by her audacity and determination.

In that very moment, Cassandra understood she was making history. She realised that her name would be etched into the annals of history books, recounting the first instance in years when a woman had entered the competition. However, none of that was for certain until she found her brother. And they had three days to do so.

CHAPTER 13

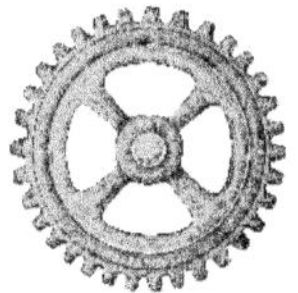

It had been three days since the matter was decided, hours of wallowing and searching for Grayson. Jaronas had taken Chief Onatach's warriors and searched for three days straight. During her father's leave of absence, Cassandra did nothing more but remain in Grayson's cot, crying over her lost brother and continuously blaming herself for his kidnapping. She did not know how to control her emotions. She blamed herself for his kidnapping, blamed herself for the wish she made, and thought it was the gods above playing a dirty trick on her, forcing her to accept the consequences.

She woke up in frantic states, believing that those men had come back for her. However, it was on the last day of his search when her father had returned. His eyes were hollow as he shook his head. He had followed the path his son was taking, tracking the dragged dirt and occasional footsteps, however it all came to a dead end. It was within those last hours of the day that the Kings had another meeting with the Chief, declaring that Cassandra would take her brother's place in the tournament as Onatach's men and her father continued to search for Grayson.

When being given this sort of information, Cassandra nearly passed out. Not believing her father's words, not believing it were true. She struggled to breath, tightness gripping her chest as she could not accept the reality of what happened, of what she had wished for. The opportunity she always wanted was here and yet, it was at her brother's disappearance that helped her.

Three days had gone by too quickly and now she was to participate in the Triumph Games. This tournament belonged to Grayson; despite her wish and her hoping and dreaming, it belonged to him—and by some twist of faith became hers.

She felt sick again.

In a matter of hours, Cassandra would find herself in the Arena, where countless eyes would be fixated on her. She was to become the first woman to step onto the stage of the Triumph Games, and it did not feel real nor right. This marked a historical moment, but her brother was missing. It was an event that was destined to be recounted not only throughout this era but for generations to come.

Guilt washed over Cassandra as her father encouraged her to take fencing lessons with her brother's instructor. Her challenge was the next day, and as hard as her father tried, Cassandra was not able to leave Grayson's cot.

Both Jaronas and Savannah tried to pull Cassandra from the cot, but it was no use. She was confident in herself; she knew how to fence—hell, she taught her brother on the train ride over. However, her father made it perfectly clear that training with her brother versus the other Princes was not the same thing, that her confidence would only take her so far before reality struck her.

She continued to ignore him, closing her eyes and praying to the gods for Grayson's safety and finding him quickly. The mere thought of everyone's eyes on her was what compelled Cassandra to truly stay in bed. Fear mixed in with her guilt, soon overtaking her. The thought of everyone laughing, saying they were right to not have women compete, only made her nervous. She was the future.

As the hours ticked by, her father grew more worried. Cassandra had not eaten dinner and immersed herself in her favourite book, *Beginning of the Triumph Games.*

The next morning, in a gentle manner, he entered the Harth tent, sat by his daughter, and wore a reassuring smile. "Cassandra, dear, I understand that being a competitor was not in your plans during this trip. But please, understand that if you do decide to participate, it would be for your brother. It would be for our family. If you truly decide to join this tournament, you can save your brother's score before he permanently gets disqualified."

"I said I would participate; I won't go back on my word. Just leave me be." Cassandra turned to her side, back facing her father.

Her father shook his head and quietly exited the tent once more. He met Savannah at the entrance. "Make sure she eats something today. If she changes her mind, you and her will be sent back to the Islands where it is safe." Savannah nodded and bowed to her King as he left, feeling truly defeated.

Cassandra curled in a ball, hearing her father's whispers, stomach turning as she tried to sleep off the bundle of emotions washing through her. The fencing challenge was scheduled for the late afternoon; her early morning wake-up gave enough time to train if needed and she wondered if she was truly meant for this tournament. Maybe it was all a mistake, maybe it was a learning lesson and for her to help find her brother.

Or maybe it was her chance to prove everyone wrong.

That thought alone had Cassandra sighing as she turned to Savannah, who walked into the tent. "Please inform the trainer and my father that I will be waiting for my training session. They have twenty minutes to prepare." The maid's dark green eyes widened as she ran out of the tent, charging towards the King to inform him of his daughter's wishes.

It took a few moments for her to transition from her nightgown to Grayson's training attire. As Cassandra held the jersey in her hands, she could not help but feel a sense of longing and connection to it. The deep red colour, the prominent golden heart on the back, and her brother's name elegantly scripted above their family crest evoked a mix of emotions within her. She then glanced at the identical jersey laid out on her bed, the new outfit designated for the Triumph Games. However, Cassandra was hesitant to put it on—it felt odd to don something that was meant to be Grayson's. Nevertheless, the exhilaration of participating in the event lingered, creating a complex amalgamation of feelings. It seemed both improper and fitting at the same time, as if she were claiming a part of it as her own.

Before long, Cassandra rendezvoused with the trainer for a brief practice session. They focused on refining her stance, enhancing her launching technique, and maintaining a state of constant readiness against potential attacks. The instructions centred around standing tall and composed, projecting an air of unwavering confidence.

Suppressing a chuckle, Cassandra knew she was well-versed in fencing techniques, having taken lessons herself. She restrained herself from reminiscing about the time aboard the ship to Spade City, where she had assisted her brother in refining his fencing skills. Cassandra's mind started to drift, her thoughts consumed by her missing brother and began to spiral. This led to her focus wavering, causing her trainer to notice. He observed her shifting attention and how she became increasingly unsteady in her stance. Recognizing her distraction, he instructed her to find a spot in the shade and gather herself.

Following the trainer's guidance, Cassandra left the training area within the Arena and wandered aimlessly through the corridors. Eventually, she stumbled upon a rear exit that led to the bay. Despite the potential consequences, she disregarded them and stepped outside, settling herself by the water's edge. Sitting there, Cassandra's thoughts were consumed by her brother's disappearance and the events of the previous night. The memory of how he had been abducted replayed in her mind, and a strong urge to return to the Camp and investigate the tracks seized her.

Despite knowing her father would likely follow the trail left by Grayson, Cassandra felt a compulsion to reach the camp first. Acting before she could second-guess herself, she was already in motion. Her legs carried her swiftly toward the camp grounds, her eyes scanning the surroundings until she arrived at the site of the extinguished campfire. As she gazed at the gap between the Harth and Clubs tents, a sense of clarity washed over her. Despite the short distance separating them, it felt vast in that moment. Cassandra took a step forward, descending onto the path where the ground was freshly disturbed, the earth still retaining the imprints of footsteps and dragged marks.

Following the trail, her eyes locked onto a cream-coloured cloth that stirred a memory from the previous night. She traced the path of the dragged dirt, observed the arrangement of footprints alongside and behind it, until suddenly the dragging ceased, and the tracks seemed to vanish into thin air, much like what her father described to her. The realisation struck her that the footprints led in a northern direction, possibly toward Clubs Caverns. An uneasy shiver ran down her spine.

Clutching the cream cloth in her hand, Cassandra understood that only one person could assist her in unravelling this mystery.

Although she knew she should inform her father immediately, she hesitated, considering his involvement in a crucial meeting. Cassandra reasoned that she should gather more evidence before involving him further. Deciding to share her theory once she had solid proof, she turned on her heels and retraced her steps back to the Arena.

As the morning progressed, the trainer eventually announced that he would prepare lunch, creating an opportunity for Cassandra to make her way toward the Club tent. Sebastian sat on a log near the campfire, casually munching on an apple as he observed Cassandra walking past him. She paused before Augustus, who was engrossed in his latest invention while sitting cross-legged beside his tent in the shaded area. Holding up the cream-coloured cloth, Cassandra addressed Augustus with determination.

"I need your assistance."

Augustus did not look up from his work, his attention focused on his invention. "No."

"Why not?"

"Because in the span of three days, you have become my competition."

"Lies. You became my friend. What happened since is out of our control."

"You could have said no or could have *not* run into the meeting."

Cassandra shot him an annoyed glare. "Oh, so now I am your rival. But when you were interacting with my brother, it was a different story."

Augustus remained absorbed in his work. "Because I actually enjoyed conversing with your brother."

"More like you felt threatened by him," she retorted. Augustus chose not to respond, prompting Cassandra to roll her eyes. Taking a seat in front of him, she knew she needed his help, given his intelligence when it came to analysis and dissection. Displaying the cloth once more, she presented it to Augustus.

"This cloth was used on me the night my brother was abducted," she explained. "I thought you could run some tests and help me determine who took him."

With a scoff, Augustus shook his head. "And why should I assist you?"

"I will do anything you ask," she blurted out, causing Augustus to smirk. "Nothing inappropriate," she added quickly, resulting in a disappointed pout from the Prince. This led Cassandra to scowl at him. Suddenly, a voice called out from the Harth tent, her trainer summoning Cassandra for lunch. Panicked, she cast a pleading look at Augustus.

Sighing, Augustus extended his hand, allowing Cassandra to place the cloth in his palm. "I will help you on one condition: you have to be my lab rat, testing out any inventions I come up with."

Accepting the condition, Cassandra kissed Augustus on the cheek. Thanking him before departing. He sat there stunned, a small smile forming on his lips as he watched her walk away. Sebastian continued to watch her, his gaze following Cassandra with a sense of concern, even as she moved forward and returned to the trainer's area.

By mid-afternoon it was time for the next challenge. Cassandra completed changing into her attire and just as she was ready, her father entered the tent. He informed her that he would be accompanying her down to the platform, the same spot where Grayson had once stood before each challenge began. Agreeing to his guidance, Cassandra and her father set out toward the waiting carriages that would transport them to the Arena.

During this moment, Augustus caught up with Cassandra, matching his pace to hers and allowing her to slow her steps. In a hushed tone, he began to share his findings. "I have discovered traces of blood," he whispered, displaying the cloth in his hand and pointing to a small drop on it. "It belonged to one of the kidnappers. Moreover, I identified the use of a chemical—a type of anaesthetic gas. It employs multiple compounds to prevent dizziness, but when combined in excessive amounts, it can induce complete unconsciousness. The effects can last for up to three hours."

Cassandra's mind raced, connecting the information to her brother's experience. She placed her hand on his. "Thank you, Augustus," she whispered.

Taking the cloth from him, she held it in her own hand. Augustus responded with a brief smile before walking away. This allowed Cassandra to quickly rejoin her father's side and enter the carriage preparing to carry them to the Arena for the challenge ahead.

It was not long before she stood in front of the imposing iron doors, positioned on the same platform where her brother had once stood. She was dressed in a pristine white fencing outfit, awaiting her entry into the Arena as the crowd's deafening cheers filled the air, echoing the name of her absent brother. Her father stood beside her, giving words of reassurance. His hands rested on her shoulders, and his smile radiated encouragement.

"You will excel, my dear," he assured her, his voice calm but firm. "Remember, the noise might overwhelm you initially. But over time, you'll learn to block it out and focus solely on your opponents."

Cassandra nodded briefly, absorbing her father's advice. He leaned down and pressed a gentle kiss on her forehead, murmuring words of strength and confidence before stepping away to join the other royals in the Sky Box.

As he left the platform, Cassandra's nerves surged to the forefront. The reality of standing before those massive iron doors began to sink in and a sense of panic started to creep over her. There was no way she thought it could be this easy. She was in over her head. She should back out—even if there were women and little girls cheering for her.

She hated her mind. Hated how right it was at times. She could not leave, she had to do this for them.

Above, the announcer's voice boomed through the Arena's speakers, breaking the tense silence.

"Thank you, honoured sponsors, for gracing us with your presence this afternoon," the announcer's voice echoed. "And a special thank you to the Mountmonts, who are making their inaugural appearance in the Triumph Games. I assure you, this match will be one for the records, as Cassandra Harth takes her brother Grayson Harth's place after his recent disappearance." A wave of nausea rolled over Cassandra, her stomach churning.

The crowd erupted into cheers, their voices creating a cacophony that reverberated throughout the Arena. The announcer continued, introducing each of the competing Princes from the various nations. The sound of their gates opening, accompanied by the screeching noise, grated on her ears.

Cassandra remained the last to be introduced, a deliberate suspense building around her. Her nerves tightened and her heart raced as her turn approached. "Last but certainly not least, the moment you've all been waiting for! Cassandra Harth! Princess of the Heart Lot Islands! The first female competitor in the history of the Triumph Games!" The announcer's exuberant declaration was met with a renewed surge of applause, cheers, claps, and screams from the crowd.

With a subtle shift, the platform beneath Cassandra seemed to nudge her forward, urging her toward the grand stage positioned at the centre of the Arena. The cheers of the crowd surrounded her, enveloping her in a swirling mix of anticipation and exhilaration.

The fencing segment of the competition proved to be relatively straightforward—a one-on-one challenge. The initial matches would determine the two winners, who would then contend for first place, while the remaining two would vie for third. From her vantage point, Cassandra spotted the three Princes on the fencing stage. The floor was covered by a large blue mat and the contenders were clad in the customary fencing attire.

The first match was between Augustus and Benjamin. Cassandra observed the proceedings, assessing their strengths and styles. It became apparent that Benjamin's physique and agility were well-suited for fencing, evident in his balanced movements and the assistance provided by the robotic extension on his back. In contrast, Augustus seemed better suited for activities such as spear-throwing or future combat phases, his build favouring strength over agility. Yet, the match passed in a blur for Cassandra. She struggled to suppress her anxiety, focusing on her breathing as Benjamin swiftly manoeuvred on the mat, consistently landing blows on Augustus. This dominance culminated in Benjamin's victory.

Cassandra's stomach churned as her own match against Sebastian approached. As she and Sebastian stepped onto the mat, she knew it would not be easy. She was going to lose, but she couldn't let her mind get the best of her.

At the referee's signal, they began circling each other, a tense dance of anticipation. Cassandra grew impatient and decided to take the initiative. Advancing and extending her arm, she encountered Sebastian's defences, his eyes locked onto her every movement. Amidst their actions, not a word was exchanged. Sebastian's dark eyes bore into hers with a subtle smirk and swiftly, he managed to strike her, landing a hit right in the centre of her chest.

For the second round, Cassandra assumed her stance. Sebastian lunged at her, hoping to catch her off-guard. However, she had anticipated this manoeuvre, recognizing his inclination toward overconfidence. She deftly manoeuvred around his attempts, even evading his extended leg meant to trip her. With a quick tap on his shoulder, she declared him out, resulting in a tie and a third round to decide the victor.

As the third round commenced, both participants lunged toward each other, driven by the desire to win and the surge of adrenaline coursing through their veins.

"You won't win. You can't. This tournament is not meant for you." Sebastian attempted to undermine her confidence.

Cassandra ignored his words, focusing her energy on their duel. She pushed back against his blade, causing him to momentarily stumble. Sebastian maintained his composure, taking a deep breath. In that moment, something within him shifted, a transition from casual engagement to a more earnest contest. The Mercenary Games flashed in Cassandra's mind, stirring a hint of unease. Sebastian's movements became more graceful, his actions swift and poised. She struggled to keep pace, feeling slightly overwhelmed. Their clash led to Sebastian exerting his body weight against hers and both competitors found themselves on the mat. Despite the referee's whistle, they disregarded its call, continuing to press their blades against each other with unyielding determination, determined to emerge as the victor.

Cassandra harboured no sentiments of remorse or romantic flutter; her sole focus was on winning. Nevertheless, she had not anticipated Sebastian's swift manoeuvres, his blade grazing her shoulder with a gentle touch, granting him victory in the match.

With a smug grin, Sebastian rose from his position and extended a hand in a gesture of sportsmanship. "Good match," he offered.

Cassandra swatted his hand away with her sword and rose to her feet. "Prick."

Sebastian's win secured his place in the final round alongside Benjamin. With a fifteen-minute break before the ultimate clash, Cassandra took the opportunity to catch her breath. Surveying the Arena, she realised the previously overwhelming noise had faded away, her anxiety subdued after facing Sebastian. In that moment of respite, her gaze was drawn to the vast expanse of the Arena from her vantage point. However, her attention was swiftly diverted as she spotted a figure—more precisely, a tall individual shrouded in a hood—standing atop the Arena. She squinted, attempting to discern the identity of the person. She questioned her own perception, doubting the possibility of someone occupying such a high position.

The piercing sound of the whistle marked the end of the fifteen-minute break, signalling that it was time for Augustus and Cassandra to compete for third place. Cassandra was confident that this round would not be too challenging, as Augustus lunged forward first. This gave her the advantage of anticipating his footwork, predicting his movements, and landing a hit on his back during the first round.

As the second round commenced, Cassandra's nervousness began to wane. She had gained insight into her competitor's tactics and knew that she needed to play the unexpected role. Sidestepping with agility, she swiftly traversed the mat. With a fortunate twist of fate, she found herself positioned behind Augustus, primed for a strike. However, her victory was short-lived as he managed to touch her first, his blade sliding between his arm and grazing her stomach.

The third round posed a greater challenge, as Cassandra's energy diminished. Yet, she preserved with determination, driven by the desire to emerge as the winner. In the final round, Augustus made his move, lunging forward, swords poised in preparation. The clash of metal reverberated as they engaged in combat. Cassandra calculated her strategy, waiting for the right moment when Augustus placed excessive pressure on his leading right leg. He leaned heavily, but she swiftly sidestepped, causing him to stumble. She was determined to secure third place, aiming to touch his back, but when he twirled around, their swords clashed. He swatted her sword away and reached for her stomach, trying to score a point. She, however, continuously stepped back, evading each of his attempts as Augustus struggled to land a hit on Cassandra. As she saw him falter again, panic in his eyes, Cassandra believed victory was within her grasp.

But as she stepped backward once more, her footing gave way. She slipped on the map beneath her and ended up on her back. Seizing the opportunity, Augustus stood over her and tapped the tip of his blade to the centre of her stomach, signifying the Clubs' victory in third place. She groaned in annoyance, berating herself for letting her arrogance get the best of her. Cassandra grumbled as she rose to her feet, with Augustus wearing a triumphant smile and extending his hand.

"Better luck next time," he said with genuine kindness.

Cassandra tightly gripped his hand, her eyes narrowing as she applied more pressure. She remained silent, allowing her eyes to convey her message, watching Augustus swallow hard and quickly withdraw his hand. She was undoubtedly furious, disliking the taste of defeat once more. With that, the two opponents stepped off the mat.

It was then that Cassandra knew what she had to do. She had to train harder and better. She was a woman, yes, so she had to train like a man. They already knew each other's strengths and weaknesses; she was the odd one out, which gave her an advantage. In just a few seconds her mind was made up on what to do and how to go about it.

In moments, the next match began. Her focus quickly shifted to the upcoming duel between Benjamin and Sebastian. The tension between the two Princes was palpable. The whistle pierced the air, marking the beginning of their match and propelling both contestants into action. They circled each other warily, biding their time for the right moment to launch their attacks. Unable to restrain himself any longer, Benjamin made the first move, thrusting his sword towards the agile assassin. Sebastian smoothly sidestepped Benjamin's charge, causing the Dimond Prince to whirl around in an attempt to strike him. Instead, Sebastian blocked the attack and their swords clashed, with Benjamin exerting his strength to push against the assassin.

As the match unfolded, Cassandra's mind raced, aware that there were still two more rounds to come. Cassandra's focus remained locked on the intense duel between Benjamin and Sebastian. From the Sky Box, Albert shouted feedback to his son, offering guidance on his movements. This momentary distraction worked in Sebastian's favour as he exploited the opportunity to launch an attack. However, Benjamin's rapid reflexes enabled him to avoid Sebastian's strike, causing Benjamin to lose his balance and tumble to the ground. Seizing the advantage, Sebastian delivered several quick strikes. Sebastian's tactics succeeded in distracting Benjamin just enough to secure a tap on his opponent's shoulder, marking his victory in the first round.

In response to the sight, Albert erupted in frustration, passionately encouraging Benjamin to perform better. Charlotte, unfazed by her father's outburst, simply rolled her eyes and blocked one ear with her hand.

Fuelled by a surge of anger and determination, Benjamin patiently waited for the bell to ring. Sebastian remained cool, a small smirk on his face. Cassandra noted the arrogance and wished him luck, as she hoped he would not have the same fate as she did. As the bell signalled, the start of the next round began. Benjamin, once more lunged at Sebastian, who skilfully avoided the incoming hit; however, instead of tumbling to the ground, Benjamin retaliated by delivering a kick to Sebastian's knee, forcing him to step back and regain his footing.

The referee intervened, declaring a temporary halt to the match due to this illegal manoeuvre. Both competitors were cautioned to maintain a fair and clean fight. Sebastian responded by swinging his sword and cracking his neck, readying himself for the continuation of the match.

A shift seemed to occur within Benjamin, transforming him into an entirely different person. Once more, they engaged in their relentless dance of blocks and lunges, with Benjamin attempting to strike Sebastian. Nevertheless, Sebastian had foreseen Benjamin's manoeuvre and skilfully countered by aiming to strike his opponent down. Unfazed, Benjamin remained resolute, fully aware of this anticipated move. Within moments, he quickly avoided Sebastian's targeted attack towards his shoulder and delivered a precise hit to the assassin's thigh, signalling the Dimonds' triumph in the second round.

Cassandra heard the crowd cheer, the ground nearly shaking.

During the third round, the two contestants engaged in a fierce and animalistic clash. Benjamin utilized his extensions as a supplementary aid, effectively enhancing his mobility. Armed with this advantage, he made every effort to disconcert Sebastian and score a hit. However, both Princes were determined to win the fencing challenge, making it difficult for either of them to be easily distracted. Both competitors lunged and circled, their determination evident. Benjamin exhibited patience, biding his time for Sebastian to make a move. After circling twice, his impatience surfaced, and he impulsively lunged at Sebastian. The intensity of their competition was clear, showcasing their remarkable skill and strength as two of the strongest contenders.

Cassandra could not help but scoff at herself, fully acknowledging how blinded she was by herself. These boys had trained their entire lives for this moment, to prove they are the best. Fighting for the glory of their nation. It made sense that she lost. She only properly began training a few hours ago. Some part of her felt like backtracking, helping to find her brother quicker so he could take her place, but that was not why she should be looking for him. She should be searching for him because she wanted him to be safe, not to save her. She could save herself; she could train harder and become faster and better.

Both competitors managed to eliminate each other simultaneously, Sebastian hitting Benjamin's leg and the Dimond Prince striking his opponent's abdomen. The unexpected spectacle left Cassandra blinking in sheer astonishment, while the Arena erupted in cheers. The referee reviewed the captured images, ultimately declaring Benjamin as the victor of the Fencing challenge.

Amidst the crowd's mixed reactions of cheers and boos, Sebastian made his way towards Cassandra, his hand extended in a gesture of camaraderie. "I underestimated you," he confessed, prompting the Princess to firmly shake his hand. "I understand your determination to locate your brother."

Cassandra's curiosity led her to question, "So, you overheard my conversation with Augustus?"

Sebastian's response was nonchalant. "I was merely observing."

Slightly irritated, Cassandra pressed, "What is the purpose of this conversation?"

With a smug smile, he stated, "I would like to offer my assistance, but it comes with a price." Cassandra raised an eyebrow, her patience evident. "Throw the Games. Get the title of first female competitor and let us win. But know that if you get in my way, there *will* be consequences."

In response, Cassandra could not help but express her exasperation, retorting, "Just when I thought you were trying to be nice." She pulled her hand away from his grip. "Prick."

Sebastian's chuckle filled the air as he nodded. "Well, I can be fair, but my terms remain. I am genuinely willing to aid you." A subtle tilt of his head was accompanied by another chuckle. "It has become quite evident that you could use some assistance."

Although Cassandra was wary of Sebastian's potential hidden motives, she acknowledged his expertise as an assassin, particularly in tracking abilities.

Letting out a sigh, she challenged him. "I won't throw the Games, but when we are to go up against each other, I'll make sure to put all my efforts into beating you."

He chuckled. "I like that. A new challenge. Deal." He extended his hand, and without a second thought, she squeezed it, promising herself to beat him and the rest of the Princes here. Prepared to prove them all wrong.

CHAPTER 14

After the Dimonds secured their victory in the game, a surge of frustration over her conversation with Sebastian drove Cassandra to swiftly exit the Arena. A newfound determination to locate her brother now consumed her thoughts. Assisted by Augustus, she understood that retracing the path where the cloth was discovered would likely lead her in the right direction.

Her mission became clear: find her brother, bring him home, and keep a good distance with her fellow competitors. It was the only way for them to all win and get what they wanted. However, part of her knew it was best to try and find Grayson before the combat sector took place.

With a sense of urgency, Cassandra hurried out of the Heart Lot gates, only to be intercepted by Savannah and her trainer. They quickly spoke of her father looking for her, and as Savannah began to lead Cassandra away, her attention was quickly captured by the figure turning the corner–Sebastian. Accompanied by his trainer, it was clear that he was focused, refusing to permit any distractions to come his way, however his stern gaze managed to fall upon her.

Despite their recent alliance, the reality of the two remained. They were competitors first, allies second. Cassandra felt a short pain in her chest at the thought; the reality of their situation hung in the air as she watched him walk past her. Their eyes did not break away. Cassandra's stance communicated that she was no easy target, that she was to not back down, however her brother's face flashed through her mind. She must not disappoint her brother, she had to find him, no matter the alliance with Sebastian.

Shaking her head, Cassandra refocused her thoughts and followed Savannah to the Sky Box, where her father stood, a smile adorning his face.

"You were exceptional, my dear!" he exclaimed, enveloping his daughter in a warm hug. With a motion, he introduced two gentlemen standing nearby. Stepping aside, he gestured toward the identical twins. "Allow me to introduce you to the Mountmonts." The pair of men were tall, though one was slender compared to the other.

The leaner of the twins possessed a mane of thick, dark red hair that closely mirrored her own. His eyes, a deep shade of brown, shone with enthusiasm, and his unusually pale countenance seemed almost ghostly. Cassandra noted the near-alabaster hue of his skin. "A pleasure," he greeted with a broad smile, extending his hand. Cassandra accepted the handshake and then turned her attention to the other twin, who bore the same pale complexion. This sibling, however, differed from his brother. His build was slightly broader, his shoulders more imposing, and his hair was a shade of near-midnight black. The dark brown eyes that met hers bore a striking resemblance to her brother's.

They greeted Cassandra with smiles that seemed overly broad, creating an uncomfortable sensation within her. Jaronas introduced them, mentioning that they were at the tournament in place of their parents who could not attend. The slimmer of the brothers seemed to fixate on Cassandra, his gaze following her every movement. His silence prevailed for most of the time, giving off an impression of intense observation. On the other hand, the bulkier brother engaged in conversation with Jaronas, discussing the games and various topics of casual small talk. Despite his efforts, Cassandra couldn't divert her attention from the slender brother, finding it difficult to tear her eyes away due to a growing sense of unease.

"How does it feel to be the first female competitor?" inquired the larger brother, his grin equally unsettling.

"Nerve-wracking to say the least. Though I am relieved it is over for now," Cassandra replied.

The bulkier brother nodded thoughtfully. "I shan't detain you any longer. Rest must be essential." He offered a slight bow. "It was a pleasure to meet you." With mutual smiles, Jaronas and Cassandra took their leave, the twins waving as they departed. Cassandra couldn't help but notice that the brothers continued to gaze at her, their stares unyielding. Just before she left their presence, she glanced back, finding their unbroken stares. A shiver ran down her spine as their giggles rang out like eerie hyenas.

As the evening concluded, her father spoke with Cassandra within the tent regarding the upcoming triathlon. He explained his plan to depart early in the morning instead of during the night to search for her missing brother. Her father believed that daylight would aid their efforts. Jaronas drifted off to sleep mid-sentence, prompting Cassandra to realise it was her cue to leave. She swiftly changed into Grayson's trousers and top, donned her boots, and grabbed a lit candle. Her intention was clear—to venture into the forest and retrace the path, hoping to uncover further clues.

Cassandra moved with stealth, taking care to avoid making any noise. Just when she believed she was in the clear, the clearing of a throat startled her, and she spun around, sniper raised, to find

Sebastian standing there. Leaning against a tree, he was clad in his customary black leathers, a sizable samurai sword resting on his back, and a dagger in his hand, twirling it idly as if it were a mere toy.

In a hushed tone filled with surprise, Cassandra asked, "What are you doing here?"

Sebastian's response came with a chuckle. "I had a hunch that you would be up to some nighttime adventure. You seemed rather on edge earlier, ready to bolt. And that glare you shot my way was quite the spectacle." Stepping forward, he returned his dagger to its sheath at his waist. "To top it off, you were conspicuously absent during dinner."

Cassandra offered Sebastian a sly smile. "You seem to be keeping a close eye on me."

He scoffed, narrowing his dark eyes. "Nonsense. I merely possess a keen awareness of my surroundings, which includes noticing even the minutest details—like your absence from dinner and your restless pacing around your tent—"

"Your presence here is unnecessary," she cut him off, gesturing toward his tent. "You can leave now."

"Absolutely not."

"No, leave."

"You're a woman, and regardless of the circumstances, women need protection."

"That's nauseating."

"Moreover, the likelihood of you injuring yourself without my presence is far higher than if I were here."

Cassandra stared at him, dumbfounded by the words that had escaped his lips. Eventually, she found herself chuckling. "You will invent any reason to be close to me."

"Absolutely not!"

"Very well, you can stay then."

Sebastian seemed flustered and Cassandra took the lead along the dark path, with only the faint light of the candle and moon to guide them. Along the way, she described where she had found the cloth and indicated the starting point of the tracks. Sebastian held back from asking questions for the time being, but she knew his curiosity would get the better of him sooner or later.

So, she began to recount the events of the night when Grayson was abducted. "I hold myself accountable for not being able to do more to assist him," she confessed.

Sebastian's gaze lingered on her for a brief moment after she spoke those words. In his eyes, there was a sense of understanding and sadness, as if he could empathise with her sentiment. In that fleeting moment, she became entranced, her attention fixated on the moonlight casting a glow on his dark hair and attire. Cassandra realised that beneath Sebastian's enigmatic exterior, there was an underlying truth.

Their moment was abruptly interrupted by the sound of a breaking branch nearby. Both of them tensed, ready to react and their eyes turned to Augustus, who stood there with a smile, casually waving at them.

"I have been searching for you," he stated, his focus on Cassandra as he handed her a new invention. "This is a candleless illuminator. It is gas-powered, with a small bulb emitting bright light through a white screen." His smile faded as he regarded the two of them. "Where are you headed?"

"Leave us," Sebastian retorted, his arms crossed.

Cassandra turned to Sebastian. "We need his expertise."

"Fine." Stepping forward, Sebastian addressed Augustus. "But do not pry."

Cassandra knew that Augustus cared more about the invention than any potential trouble he could get into. Together, the three of them followed the trail south, with Cassandra utilising the new invention as a guide. As they reached the trail's end, she pointed out that the footprints seemed to vanish completely. Sebastian instructed them to split up and search for hidden traps. It was at this point that Augustus unintentionally triggered something—a metallic plate that seemed to function like a hatch. He pressed his foot on it, and Sebastian joined him, clearing away leaves and dirt to reveal the hatch underneath.

"What's this?" Augustus questioned.

"An underground shelter," Sebastian confirmed. "These are scattered throughout the Forest Lands, remnants from the War— places of refuge."

Sebastian struggled to open the hatch, growing frustrated with its resistance. Augustus chuckled and pushed Sebastian aside. "Allow me," he announced, activating his chainsaw extension. The loud noise reverberated through the dark forest as he began to see through the hatch. After a brief but intense effort, the hatch was finally pried open.

As she readied herself to descend first, Augustus swiftly jumped down, producing another candleless illuminator and gesturing for them to follow. Sebastian offered his hand to Cassandra, aiding her as she descended the ladder. As she looked around the steel chamber, her fingers brushed against the metal surface. It was during this exploration that she came across a switch, and she instinctively flicked it on. Instantly, the room was bathed in light, causing Augustus to open his eyes in surprise.

"This is nearly identical to Clubs technology," he murmured, his gaze fixed on the illumination. "It functions almost the same way as it does back in the Caverns. It is very old Club technology, but still… similar."

The trio stood there, astonished by the discovery, a shared eagerness to continue further into the tunnel. Cassandra was resolute; nothing would deter her now. She was determined to follow the endless passageways—this was a promising lead, and she was resolved to pursue it. Yet in those moments, Cassandra's concern was non-existent as she strode purposefully down the tunnel. Tracing the unending glow of light, she had covered half the distance when the sound of footsteps reached their ears from above.

"What's that?" Sebastian questioned, his mechanical arm now replaced by a dagger popping out of his forearm, quickly poised to his side, and his eyes fixed on the now sealed hatch.

Then, as if choreographed, the echo of hooves resounded over their heads. "The Chief's search party?" Augustus speculated.

"No, that's not until morning," Cassandra replied, her gaze still tracing the tunnel's contours. Suddenly, a realisation struck her—the potential reason for the commotion. "It could be guards trying to locate us. Perhaps our fathers have realised we are not in our beds." The muffled shouts from above seemed to confirm her theory, men urging one another to proceed northward in their search. She shrugged. "Oh, well. They will just have to wait." Without another word she continued her descent along the illuminated passage.

Augustus gave her an odd look while Sebastian continued to watch her, finding her behaviour peculiar. She led the small group down the endless tunnel; it was then that she caught sight of the immense emerald light that beckoned to her. Her feet pressed against the metallic floor as her hands slightly shook, but she quickly formed them into fists, squeezing them tight and taking slow breath. *Control,* she told herself.

It was the realization that whoever had taken Grayson could be awaiting them at the tunnel's end—for some reason she was prepared to face them.

"Perhaps we should consider turning back," Augustus suggested.

"If you wish to go back, go ahead. But I'm staying," Cassandra responded, rounding a corner, the vivid green light intensifying slightly.

Augustus tried to reach out to Cassandra. "We really should go."

"No. My brother is somewhere down here and that light is likely guiding the way," she declared, determined. The echo of hooves and men's shouts persisted, growing louder. Then, a metallic clanking sound reverberated, like the striking of metal against metal. Cassandra snapped her head down the tunnel, eyes widening. "Grayson?" she whispered, ignoring the commotion above. The clanks persisted, growing heavier with each step they took. Gradually, the rhythm of the clanks started to falter, with longer intervals between each occurrence.

"Cassandra," Augustus urged.

Sebastian hushed him. His enhancement gleamed in the dim light and Cassandra found interesting how large the blade on Sebastian's forearm was, nearly fascinated by it, and slightly forgetting where she was. She became curious to touch it, but too cautious and worried of getting cut. He kept close to her, offering his protection whether their alliance was solid or not. Meanwhile, Augustus trailed behind, his mechanical arm snapping and allowing his chainsaw to string through, each of the royals with their robotic pieces ready.

As they followed Cassandra through labyrinthine tunnels, she suddenly came to a halt, causing Sebastian to nearly collide with her. They had reached a dead end. "Is this a maze?" Cassandra muttered, her frustration evident as she stared at the stubbornly glowing green light. "Are you kidding me? It is a maze!" Her frustration boiled over and she fired her gunned arm at the light, shattering the glass and sending shards clattering onto the ground, the noise resonating through the tunnels.

"Cassandra! You are making too much noise!" Sebastian admonished, gripping her gunned arm to prevent further damage. "We need to be quiet."

As if his words triggered a realisation, the clanking sound persisted, reverberating through the tunnels. Cassandra pivoted, her determination unyielding. She had to find Grayson; it was a relentless need burning within her, a determination to bring her brother home safe and sound. And so, she pursued the elusive sound, navigating through an array of dead ends, destroying every green light she encountered.

After her fifth target, Sebastian suggested they retreat back up through the hatch. "We are lost down here and our impulsive approach is not working. Going back and planning meticulously will give us a better chance."

"No! I have to find him," Cassandra insisted, her eyes ablaze with intensity.

"Yes, but you will not locate him in a single night," Sebastian reasoned, stepping forward. "This requires time and strategy." He looked down at her, a towering presence against the backdrop of the persistent clanks. "Whoever is creating that noise is luring you in; you need to be smarter than them." He placed his hands on her shoulders. "Let's return and formulate a proper plan."

Cassandra pulled away. "I am not a child!" she began to protest, but her words were truncated by a low murmur, like the hushed conversations of people. Without a second thought, she sprinted in the direction of the voices, the boys' calls fading into the distance against the cacophony of clanks and murmurs. She kept racing through the tunnels, the passages leading her eastwards. Eventually, another green light came into view and Cassandra followed it.

The noises of gears and a gust of wind caught her off-guard, causing her to slow her pace. The clanking ceased, replaced by the crescendo of voices. The green light became brighter as Cassandra ventured deeper within the tunnel. Turning left, Cassandra felt her breath catch in her throat as disbelief washed over her. The dark green tunnel led to a wide landscape of the Club Caverns. She was not in the heart of the caverns like when visiting with the other royals, however this time, she was in the outskirts of the city. The tunnel was on a small mount overlooking the outskirts that lay before her. In the distance, Cassandra saw the underground city. Its buzzing voice echoing through the tunnels and the green radiating off the lights from within.

The Club Caverns were truly in front of her and Cassandra had a hard time believing it was true—or even real. Her body froze and a chill ran down her spine as she stared. Augustus—could he really be the one who orchestrated this with his nation to abduct Grayson for the sake of winning the Games? The thought left her bewildered, her senses suspended in disbelief. Uncertainty gnawed at her, preventing her from fully confirming his involvement. Perhaps it was his parents, or maybe he had a role in it. The entire situation seemed impossible, her mind struggling to come to terms with the shocking revelation.

As her mind grappled with the overwhelming complexity of the situation, she failed to hear Sebastian approaching from behind. "You demand not to be treated like a child, yet you dash around like one," he commented, grasping her arm. However, he halted his attempt to pull her away upon seeing the scene laid out before them. The sprawling underground expanse of Club Caverns met his gaze.

"You are seeing this too? I'm not going mad, am I?" she asked him, hoping for reassurance.

She heard him swallow, his grip loosening. "It cannot… You don't suppose?"

"I don't know."

"It could be a possibility."

"I don't know. We need proof."

Sebastian then gently led her away, his hand wrapping around hers as he guided her backward, her gaze still fixated on the city below.

"Where is he?" she murmured, her steps continuing as she pressed herself against Sebastian's warm chest.

"I instructed him to return to the hatch, assuring that we would meet him there," Sebastian explained to Cassandra. She nodded in response. "We will return," he reassured her, guiding her away from the echoing city. "We will come back without Augustus and conduct a thorough investigation." She wanted to believe his words, but a part of her could not fully trust him.

As they reached the end of the short tunnel, Cassandra's steps came to a halt. Sebastian let out a sigh, and without hesitation, he lifted Cassandra up, a move she did not resist. Her mind raced, mapping the twists and turns in her memory, mentally charting the path back to this very spot.

Observing Sebastian manoeuvre through the tunnels with ease, Cassandra could not help but question his sudden act of kindness and how he knew his way so well. Curiosity ran through her, watching as he turned and mapped out and knew where he was going all too easily. It was not long before they were brought back to Augustus, who anxiously awaited by the ladder. Throughout their journey, Cassandra found herself conflicted—despite her urge to question him, she could not deny a sense of calm settling over her as she nestled in Sebastian's arms. She regulated her breathing and heartbeat, her gaze fixed upon him. His cool eyes looked ahead and the metal piece framing his jaw was taut.

Augustus inquired about Cassandra's choice to run down the tunnel, but she offered him nothing more than a disdainful glance before extracting herself from Sebastian's embrace. It was Sebastian who ascended the ladder first, clambering up through the hatch and then extending his hand for Cassandra to follow suit. She did not hesitate, joining him up the ladder, and the trio eventually made their way back to camp, enveloped in silence. Augustus assumed that Cassandra's lack of words stemmed from heartbreak, yet her true emotion was far from sadness—it was seething anger directed at him.

Sebastian maintained a composed demeanour as he walked between the two, seemingly convinced it was the optimal approach. Cassandra found herself torn between conflicting feelings. She was grappling with whom to place her trust in; Augustus was rapidly slipping down the trustworthiness scale, while Sebastian's position remained ambiguous, his intentions and loyalties leaving her utterly perplexed.

Upon their arrival at camp, the early morning hours were nearly upon them. Cassandra entered her tent quietly, taking a seat on her cot and fixing her gaze on Grayson's vacant bed. Her father stirred from his sleep and was taken aback to find his daughter sitting so intently, her attention locked onto the empty space.

Her father informed Cassandra that he was to leave soon, leading a group of men down the path. He further explained that another group had ventured out during the night to survey the area for the morning's early ride. Cassandra acknowledged this with a simple nod, her focus unwavering. Sitting beside his daughter, Jaronas suggested that she should try to get some rest. Responding with a tired nod, Cassandra settled onto her cot and drifted into slumber.

Hours later, Cassandra awoke to find herself alone in the tent, the aroma of lunch cooking filling the air. Soon, her trainer and Savannah entered, her maid holding a dish with an enthusiastic smile. The trainer conveyed that Cassandra needed to prepare for the triathlon scheduled for the day, though there was a mere two-day break before the subsequent challenge—a woefully insufficient timeframe for her to adequately prepare.

And Cassandra knew she had to train, to become better and to prove them all wrong. She had to redeem herself for the events of the fencing challenge. It was a promise she was going to see through.

The trainer proceeded to outline the intense nature of the upcoming challenge to her. Each competitor would be required to hoist their flag to the summit of a mountain, utilising any machinery they carried and employing it against their fellow participants. The task would entail traversing hills, navigating through a river by swimming, and ascending a rugged mountain slope to plant their flag. On the surface, it did not appear overly daunting to Cassandra. Her endurance had always been a strong suit, and her swimming skills had been honed since her childhood. She reasoned that scaling a rocky mountain must be akin to climbing a boat's mast, with the main difference being the presence of competitors, particularly the boys who would vie against her. Cassandra understood she'd likely be the prime target and thus devoted her entire afternoon to rigorous training.

Their training session unfolded within the woods, with the trainer employing unconventional methods to push Cassandra beyond her limits. Scaling trees and maintaining her balance became paramount, as ascending a mountain amidst strong winds posed a different challenge compared to tree climbing. By simulating a condensed mountain environment within the trees, her trainer aimed to enhance her agility and pace. He hurled objects at her, demanding swift evasive action, and emphasised maintaining concentration despite the chaos. Most importantly, he stressed avoiding looking down—an essential principle for both climbing boats and scaling mountains.

As they paused for a late lunch, Cassandra seized the opportunity to inform her trainer of her intention to work on her swimming technique near the Arena. The relatively shallow waters there would facilitate practising her movements against the current, refining her glide and stroke efficiency.

With a renewed determination, Cassandra knew she had to win the triathlon, motivated by her desire to secure victory for both her father and her missing brother. Nonetheless, her thoughts frequently gravitated towards the path leading to the underground bunker she had discovered. Back at the tent, her resolve solidified, and she began to pack a bag, intent on returning to the tunnels. The urge to be alone and delve further into her discoveries proved irresistible.

Taking a moment to survey her surroundings, Cassandra spotted her trainer engrossed in a conversation with Charlotte's maid, who sat beside the spoiled Princess, who was occupied with her knitting. Cassandra could not help but roll her eyes, sensing that her trainer was more interested in flirting with the maid than keeping tabs on her. Exploiting the distraction, Cassandra steered herself towards the river, acknowledging her trainer's wave in passing but knowing he would likely remain occupied.

Making a deliberate choice, Cassandra opted to take a different route. Instead of heading towards the river as expected, she veered left and navigated her way down to the entrance of the tunnels. Her determination propelled her onward, unfazed by the possibility of venturing alone into the depths of the underground passages.

CHAPTER 15

Cassandra's task was clear: revisit the underground city and meticulously investigate the area for anything she might have missed previously. There had to be some hidden clues waiting to be discovered. She was determined to trace Sebastian's steps, eager to calculate the distance from the campgrounds to the underground city.

As she ventured a few yards away from the camp, Cassandra detected a sense of someone trailing behind her. Not one to be easily rattled, she carried on, eventually positioning herself behind a tree to survey her pursuer. She activated her gunned arm, prepared to use it as a scare tactic. She contemplated whether the follower could be Sebastian or Augustus. As the sounds of rustling leaves and breaking branches grew nearer, Cassandra emerged from the shadows, her weapon aimed squarely at Charlotte, who let out a startled scream before unsheathing her metal whip.

Perplexed and wary, Cassandra questioned Charlotte's presence. "Why are you here? Why did you follow me?"

"Bored of knitting," she retorted with a huff. "Endless yarn can get quite tiresome."

"You should have minded your own business. Go back and leave me be," Cassandra admonished, her arm lowering as she retreated behind the tree to retrieve her bag.

"Where were you planning to go?" Charlotte inquired, her gaze fixed on Cassandra, who displayed a bag meant for swimming.

"I needed to clear my head. Swimming helps."

A smirk formed on Charlotte's lips as she retracted her whip. "It is quite intriguing how you're heading north, yet you mention the lake, which is to the south." She took a step forward, observing Cassandra's bag. "And your bag seems more suitable for hiking than swimming. If you do not tell me your true destination, I will inform your trainer."

Cassandra let out a heavy laugh and brushed past Charlotte. "Go right ahead. He is far too preoccupied flirting with your maid to notice my absence."

"Then I will inform my father about this and he will surely talk to your father."

"Feel free to do so! My father will return tomorrow from his expedition," Cassandra retorted, her tone defiant. As Charlotte turned and walked back towards the camp, she took advantage of the situation and began heading back towards the hatch.

Navigating through branches and dirt, Cassandra managed to lift the lid of the hatch and pry it open. After casting a final glance around, she leaped in and swiftly closed the top. Once inside, she activated the lights and proceeded down the passage. The route seemed somewhat familiar, but as she continued along the seemingly similar path, Cassandra slowly realised that she was becoming disoriented and not making any progress. With an exasperated sigh, she decided it was wise to retrace her steps to the entrance and pinpoint where she had gone astray.

However, in the midst of turning a corner, she collided with someone. Another scream escaped Charlotte as Cassandra groaned in frustration.

"Do you have no sense of when you're not wanted?" Cassandra exclaimed, her irritation evident as she addressed the unwanted guest.

Charlotte smirked. "This would make for quite the tale to tell my father."

"Keep your mouth shut!" Cassandra shot back, taking a step closer. "If you even breathe a word about this, I will have my dog on you." While Cassandra did not actually have a dog, she considered Sebastian to be a formidable enough ally to handle any situation, should he be compensated accordingly.

The revelation took Charlotte by surprise and she readily promised to keep the secret. However, this only meant that yet another person was now privy to the knowledge of the underground bunker and the purpose behind Cassandra's journey into the depths. The two of them continued through the tunnels in silence, navigating the twists and turns. While Cassandra recognized that they were getting lost, she was determined not to admit it. Amidst the maze of tunnels, the green lights caught her attention. Seeing an opportunity, she decided to follow the lights once more. Yet, like before, they were met with a dead end—a wall that formed part of the labyrinth she had momentarily forgotten about.

An hour passed, and the two Princesses found themselves back in the same tunnels they had started in. "Why not try the left tunnel instead of the right?" Charlotte suggested.

Cassandra was ready to counter her suggestion with an argument, but something held her back. Curiosity about what her companion might know overcame her, leading her to consider the possibility that not only Augustus, but perhaps another nation as well, was involved in Grayson's disappearance.

Agreeing with a nod, Cassandra led them down the left tunnel. After a short while, they encountered another dead end. "Let's turn back," she proposed, about to pivot.

Charlotte grasped her arm and redirected her attention. "No, look," she urged, pointing to a ladder tucked in the corner, its top leading to a hatch. Cassandra had grown so accustomed to the unvarying greyness that she had mistaken the grey ladder for a section of the wall.

Cassandra retrieved the candleless light from her bag, and with a grin, ascended the ladder. She exerted effort to push open the hatch and glanced back at Charlotte. "Don't just stand there, lend a hand," she urged.

"Right!" Charlotte responded.

Together, they worked to free the stuck hatch, and after some exertion, they managed to swing it open. A weighty sensation pressed down on them as they realised that a carpet was laid on top of the hatch.

"What a charming abode," Charlotte remarked.

Cassandra could not help but scoff. "You are utterly crazy."

"I am not!" Charlotte whispered back. "The interior design of this place is exquisite. The drapery is made from materials that haven't been used since the War. I must take a closer look." With that, the two Princesses manoeuvred themselves out of the hatch, carefully rolling back the carpet. They tidied up their surroundings, attempting to leave things as orderly as possible. Amidst their actions, an urgent question occupied Cassandra's thoughts: Where had they ended up?

Examining the foyer, Cassandra took in the oak-panelled walls and the hardwood floors. Her gaze travelled over a bookshelf and a table that stood before an imposing staircase. An ornate diamond chandelier hung overhead. Beside three expansive windows that offered a view of the Mountain Regions, she noticed an intriguing sight.

"What sort of home is located this far?" Cassandra inquired, her attention fixated on a robotic device resting on a small wooden table near the window. "Would it be the Mountmonts' Mansion?"

Charlotte shook her head, eyes adorning the tapestries and designs. "Nonetheless, this residence does not match the expectations for someone of such elevated status. It appears to be much too rustic and worn-down." Charlotte replied. "However, it is puzzling. The interior designs, carpets, and tapestries here reflect styles from the old Clubs Castles, dating back to the era before they became a fully technologically-advanced nation. It bears striking similarities to the luxurious ways of my own nation."

Cassandra regarded Charlotte with a questioning look. "How do you possess so much knowledge about this?"

"I had to study the living styles of various nations. My education focuses on interior design and lifestyles—a subject my father deems exceptionally practical." She let out a scornful murmur. "Prick."

Cassandra smirked at the remark. Her mind began to race as she thought of the endless possibilities of what this home could be used for. Whether it was abandoned or not she did not know. As the conversation quieted, she found herself gazing out of the window at the Mountain Regions, and Cassandra's attention shifted to the robotic extension before her.

With its frayed wires and a rustic reddish hue, it bore a resemblance to Grayson's extension. However, what unsettled her most was that upon picking up the device, it transformed into a bow. A sickening sensation enveloped her as she moved to place it back down, only to notice a pool of blood on the small wooden table. A rapid thudding echoed in her chest as she stared down at her hands, now stained with blood.

"Charlotte," Cassandra's voice trembled as she called out to her companion. She could not tear her gaze away from the blood that dripped onto the floor, staining her boots and fingers—a dark, unsettling red.

When Charlotte approached, her gasp mirrored the shock that Cassandra felt. "Put it down," Charlotte urged, leading Cassandra to the pool of blood on the table. Despite her efforts to remain composed, panic began to seep into Charlotte's demeanour. Cassandra, on the other hand, was spiralling into a state of distress. Her mind raced, questions about her brother's fate flooding her thoughts. She struggled to recall every detail of his extension piece, to imagine it attached to his arm. Her anxiety escalated, her breath grew ragged, and her heart raced uncontrollably. Fainting seemed imminent, the world around her beginning to blur.

Charlotte took Cassandra's blood-streaked hands into her own, disregarding the mess. Unexpectedly, she provided comfort, guiding Cassandra through controlled breaths. "Follow me, that's it. Breathe, through your nose and out of your mouth."

After what felt like an eternity, Cassandra managed to regain control of her breath and stabilise her engine heart, yet her gaze remained fixated on the blood that now tainted both of their hands. Charlotte gently directed Cassandra back down the hatch, moving deliberately to avoid triggering further distress. As they descended, their ears caught the sound of rapid footsteps from above, accompanied by eerie giggles. Fright exchanged between the two Princesses, spurring them to hasten their descent into the tunnels.

Cassandra clutched a handful of Charlotte's black dress fabric, propelling them forward. While the fabric absorbed more blood, the stain seemed insignificant in the face of their imminent escape. They navigated twists and turns, the ominous laughter and footsteps trailing closely behind them. Spotting the hatch that led back up to the camp, they pushed forward. Cassandra boosted Charlotte upward and tossed her bag to her, allowing the Princess of the Diamond Kingdom to catch it. With a rush of determination, they scrambled up the ladder, landing with laboured breaths. They sealed the hatch behind them with leaves and dirt, ensuring that whatever malevolent presence had pursued them remained trapped below.

Facing each other, they found themselves laughing—a mixture of relief and tension. Charlotte wiped her hands clean on her gown. "Guess we'll have to burn it."

Cassandra used the moment to catch her breath, a small smile curving her lips as she acknowledged Charlotte's words. Yet beneath the surface, her mind churned with unsettling thoughts. The tunnels had led them to disparate places: Club Caverns, the Mountain Regions. Cassandra could not help but wonder how far those tunnels extended—could they reach the Diamond Kingdom or Spade City? Could they possibly stretch across the ocean to the Heart Lot Islands? The giggling persisted in her mind, an eerie reminder of the enigmatic tunnels that held secrets waiting to be unveiled.

"A map would have been incredibly handy," Charlotte breathed out, rising from her spot on the ground. Cassandra mirrored her actions, fully agreeing with her companion's sentiment.

After returning to camp, Cassandra sought solace in her tent. Shedding her soiled clothes, she exchanged them for a simple blue cotton dress. Settling onto her cot, she gathered ink and paper, focusing on crafting a map of the mysterious tunnels. By the time dinner approached, she had finished her task, her eyes scrutinising every detail of the intricate sketch. As Savannah brought her meal, Cassandra quickly concealed the paper, guarding her newfound information.

The night hours elapsed, the campsite buzzing with conversations from outside her tent. Yet Cassandra remained within, her mind preoccupied with thoughts of her impending venture back into the tunnels.

With the tent flaps drawn open, she felt an unnerving sensation of being observed. Lifting her gaze from her map, she peered into the darkness of the forest, her heart racing. A rustling of leaves and the entrance of Savannah into the tent nearly startled her, the fleeting image of a man watching her fading as quickly as it had appeared—merely a trick of her imagination.

When the moment was opportune and the Camp had settled into slumber, Cassandra cautiously poked her head out of her tent, scanning the surroundings before embarking on her secret return to the tunnels. "Where are you off to this time?" a voice emerged unexpectedly from behind her, causing Cassandra to start.

Sitting nonchalantly beside her tent, an apple in hand and his dagger slicing through its flesh, was Sebastian. His untamed hair partially veiled his face, his appearance eliciting a sudden freeze in Cassandra's movements.

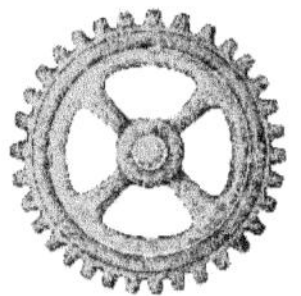

"Why do you insist on following me?" Cassandra nearly screamed, frustration evident on her face.

He merely shrugged, calmly slicing another piece from his apple. "You amuse me," Sebastian replied, offering her the piece. "Want some?"

"So I am just a source of entertainment for you?" she scoffed, taking the slice and stuffing it into her mouth before turning to walk away.

Sebastian rose to his feet, trailing behind her while continuing to cut more slices of apple. "Not solely that," he commented, his tone casual. "I also came to inform you that I overheard Charlotte talking to her brother about today's events."

Cassandra halted in her tracks, slowly pivoting to face him. "What?"

"They were planning to venture into the tunnels tonight," Sebastian revealed, munching on another piece of fruit. "Thought you might want to know. Consider it a heads-up." His words hung in the air, sinking in. Cassandra struggled to grasp the implications. Why would Charlotte involve Benjamin? Was there more to their involvement in her brother's disappearance?

"Why tell me at all?"

His response came with another casual shrug. Downing the last piece of his apple, he bit around the core. "Well, we did agree to explore the tunnels together, and I have a gut feeling that tonight might turn out to be quite eventful."

"You are delusional," she scoffed, ready to walk away. Yet Sebastian's grip on her wrist stopped her abruptly.

"I am not," he asserted, stepping closer. "More often than not, when I get these feelings, I am proven right."

Her breath hitched as Sebastian's fingers delicately encircled her wrist. The moonlight painted his features once again, casting a familiar glow akin to the previous nights. Cassandra could feel her crush deepening, the proximity between them more palpable than ever. Against her strongest resolve, she could not avert her gaze from him and found herself studying his visage intently. Her attention traced the curve of his lips, noting the slight cut on his upper lip—a remnant of a mishap, no doubt. Cassandra examined the contour of his nose, the faint scar just above his right ear, the way his dusky hair framed his face, and the intensity in his eyes as they locked onto hers. It was a mutual observation, a silent connection forming between them. In that fleeting moment, the world seemed too quiet, as if a serene harp melody played in the background, lulling her senses.

However, reality swiftly pulled her back; she withdrew her wrist from his grasp and uttered, "Yes, almost always" before turning away. With her departure, she left Sebastian in a reverie similar to the one she had experienced just moments before.

The journey to the bunker unfolded in silence, Sebastian maintaining a vigilant presence behind Cassandra, his forearms clicked and sharp iron daggers pushed through his flesh. He was prepared for any potential threat and Cassandra knew to follow his lead.

When distant voices reached their ears, Sebastian moved swiftly to her side, a subtle shift in his posture indicating his readiness. Their synchronised steps advanced towards the scene that unfolded before them: Charlotte and Benjamin engaged in a heated exchange with Augustus, the open hatch beckoning. Cassandra could not help but groan at the sight, a reaction that Sebastian found amusing. As they drew closer to the trio, Cassandra's initial resolve wavered. Regret trickled in.

"There are no creatures in the tunnels!" Augustus retorted, clearly exasperated with Charlotte, whose dishevelled demeanour betrayed her lingering fear from their earlier escapade.

"You were not there! You cannot understand the terror we felt!" Charlotte's voice held an edge of frustration and anxiety.

"It is not about feelings but reasoning and logistics! Where is the evidence of any such creatures? There are none!" Augustus countered.

Benjamin chimed in swiftly, advocating for his sister's perspective. "Hidden records might exist, detailing things concealed from the other nations—creations that we are unaware of."

Augustus was taken aback by this accusation, his tone shifting. "Are you insinuating that Club Caverns is behind these so-called creatures?" He chuckled and stepped closer to Benjamin, head inclined slightly. "If I wanted to create a creature, I would have already."

Charlotte positioned herself between the two, her gaze unwavering as she looked up at Augustus. "Mind your tone." The tension was palpable as the two locked eyes, a standoff that emitted a menacing energy. Cassandra pondered whether she should retreat before they noticed her arrival, but Benjamin's voice preempted that possibility, causing both rivals to direct their gaze at her.

Sebastian could not help but mutter a soft observation, his hidden grin betrayed by the corners of his lips. "Well, well."

"Can you people not give me a moment of peace?" Cassandra's voice held a hint of exasperation as Augustus, Charlotte, and Benjamin approached her, their words clashing in a chaotic jumble. Sebastian maintained his position at her side, his mischievous grin a constant fixture as he watched the spectacle unfold. The trio began to argue fervently, each vying to be the chosen one to accompany her into the bunker. However, their reasons were far from convincing, and Cassandra found herself growing impatient.

As the bickering continued, Cassandra's tolerance reached its limit. With a swift clap of her hands, she signalled for the cacophony to cease. "Enough of this. How about a compromise? None of you will join me and I will venture into the tunnels alone."

Sebastian's sly remark cut through the tension. "I will be joining you." His smirk conveyed his intent to provoke a reaction.

Cassandra sent him a glare, annoyed by his behaviour.

Charlotte's scoff echoed in the air. "Why would she need the company of someone of lower standing when she has me, a true Princess?"

Sebastian's retort was swift. "Because nobody wants to endure your ceaseless complaints all day long."

Augustus chimed in, arm raised. "Take me instead. I have new inventions that could prove valuable." The exchange hung in the air, the implications of each statement lingering. It was a verbal tussle that showcased not only their differing personalities but also their underlying motivations and desires. Amidst the commotion, Sebastian's smirk remained firmly in place, his eyes dancing with amusement as he continued to watch the unfolding drama.

The ceaseless bickering came to an abrupt halt as a nearby branch snapped, sending a shiver of tension through the group. Charlotte and Benjamin shrieked in fear, causing the two to clutch onto each other in an attempt to find some sense of security. Augustus, on the other hand, tightened his grip on his bag and activated the ominous hum of his chainsaw. Beside him, Sebastian mirrored the defensive motion, expertly drawing two daggers from his arms. Meanwhile, Cassandra remained poised and unflinching, her eyes scanning the surroundings with calculated scrutiny.

The sound of approaching footsteps echoed, accompanied by the eerie churn of gears shifting into position. It was the unmistakable cadence of someone preparing for a confrontation. Cassandra's gunned arm sprung to life, the sniper scope lining up with her intent gaze, scanning the vicinity for any sign of the impending threat. A sudden movement from Charlotte and Benjamin, punctuated by their screams, sent them teetering on the brink of panic. Reacting quickly, Charlotte's impulsive shoved Benjamin, sending him down the open hatch with a startled groan.

"Everybody, down the hatch!" Sebastian's voice broke through the chaos; his authoritative command spurring the others into swift action. Charlotte did not hesitate, following her brother into the depths without sparing a thought for what they might find below. Augustus followed suit, urgency evident in his movements.

Cassandra shot a pointed glare at Sebastian, her back pressed to his as they moved cautiously in a circle. "This mess is your doing," she accused him in a hushed voice, the weight of their situation amplifying her frustration. "If you had just left, they might have followed. Now we are stuck with two insufferable children and a mad scientist."

Sebastian's laughter was quiet but edged with amusement. "I anticipated something like this would happen. You need protection."

Cassandra scoffed at his response. "Why should you care? We are rivals. Spare me the notion of you caring about my wellbeing just because I'm a Princess. I can handle myself just fine."

Sebastian's response was cool and confident. "I have my reasons. You do not understand the extent of the threat. I have been trained to handle situations like this and to react swiftly."

Footsteps reverberated behind them, causing them to spin around in a tense circle, their gazes darting around as they searched for the source of the disturbance. But the true danger seemed to be taunting them, always lurking just out of sight. The continuous churning of gears, a sinister prelude to an attack, forced Sebastian into action. Reacting with instinctive speed, he shoved Cassandra to the ground just as three bullets whizzed through the air, narrowly missing their intended targets.

Cassandra's breath hitched as Sebastian's body pressed against hers, his weight anchoring her to the ground. This proximity was entirely new to her, and in this charged moment, she was aware of every contour and line of his face. She could feel the strategic placements of his daggers, the subtle bulges of metal that adorned him, and the unyielding strength of the leather armour that clad him. The intimacy of their closeness was such that she could almost conjure the blended scent of wood, the fragrance of freshly-crushed herbs and the subtle traces of exotic spices that clung to him.

His gaze scanned the terrain ahead, his earlier sense of ease vanishing as he abruptly stood and hauled her up with him. "Go down the hatch," he commanded, and just as those words left his lips, a barrage of bullets and arrows descended upon them. "Now!" Sebastian's voice surged with urgency as he yanked her toward the hatch.

With heads lowered, they sprinted toward it, Sebastian deftly retrieving shurikens from his leather attire and expertly hurling them at the attackers. Each shuriken sliced through the air, and as new incoming arrows flew toward them, each were struck down with deadly precision by Sebastian.

Cassandra came to a stop beside him, her arm raised, aligning her sights with the source of the gunfire. "What are you doing? Get down the ladder!" Sebastian's exclamation echoed, urgency etched in his tone.

She fired rapidly, focusing through a narrow gap and targeting wherever threats loomed. "I am not leaving you behind."

"Yes, you are! Get down!" he barked, yanking her down once more as a massive wooden staff with spiked ends hurtled their way, embedding itself into the trees behind them.

"Okay." Without hesitation she leaped down the hatch and found herself in Augustus' grasp.

Sebastian followed swiftly, his shurikens a whirlwind of defence as he descended the ladder. Grasping the hatch's edge, he wrestled it shut and hung there, his mind racing to secure it against intrusion. In moments, Augustus had set Cassandra down on the ground and pulled a torch from his bag. Ascending the ladder, he joined Sebastian in welding the metal shut, sealing off any potential entry from above.

"Now how do we get out of here?" Charlotte's panicked voice pierced the air.

Augustus chuckled as he descended the ladder, followed closely by Sebastian. "I will cut it open. Do not worry."

Charlotte's scoff rippled in response to his statement.

CHAPTER 17

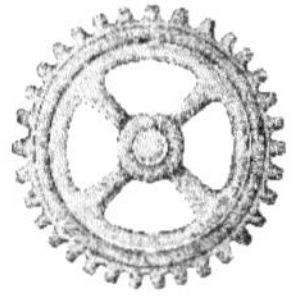

After a long argument, a plan was made.

It was Cassandra who proposed the idea of splitting up the group to explore the tunnels individually before rendezvousing at the hatch. She reassured Charlotte that it would not take more than a few brief hours. Concealing her map from Charlotte's vision, Cassandra pleaded that she did not know anything about it, opting to keep her intention veiled. She wanted to test her companions' trust, as it was the first time all five of them travelled through the tunnels together.

"The goal is to reach the Mansion located in the Mountain Regions," Cassandra began, outlining the mission. "Charlotte and I familiarise ourselves with the route earlier today, but given the extensive network of tunnels, there are likely multiple paths leading to it. Once we arrive, our goal is to search the Mansion for any clues related to Grayson."

She continued by pairing people: Charlotte and Benjamin, Sebastian and Augustus, while she remained alone. Despite their objections, Cassandra insisted on the separation, and before they could voice further objections, she abruptly veered down a tunnel, taking a sharp left, then right, and repeating the pattern with another right and left.

As time passed, Cassandra found herself disoriented, bewildered by how she had managed to become lost. There was no way to locate anyone else within the next few hours. Considering her options, Cassandra decided it was best to keep walking. She held onto the belief that she would eventually stumble upon some clue that would guide her back to the group. Lost in her thought, she failed to hear the approaching footsteps. She abruptly halted, her back instinctively pressed against the cold, unyielding iron wall behind her. Ears attuned to every sound, she strained to discern any movement.

Once again, the footsteps echoed, but they were not composed; they were rapid and drawing closer. Fuelled by panic, Cassandra wasted no time in activating her sniper and fleeing down the labyrinthine tunnels. She pivoted and twisted at every opportunity, her pace quickening as she sought to distance herself from the relentless footfalls shadowing her. Mid-flight, she cast a swift glance over her shoulder to gauge whether anyone was in pursuit. In doing so, she inadvertently chose another tunnel and nearly collided with a sizable wooden door.

The sight was startling, as amidst a subterranean landscape dominated by iron and metal, this was an incongruous wooden structure. Notably, a vivid green glow emanated from beneath the door. Her hand hesitated above the knob, wavering between caution and curiosity. Could it be a trap, perhaps leading the unknown pursuer to her very location? But the allure of uncovering the mysteries behind this enigma proved irresistible.

With resolve solidified, Cassandra pushed open the door and an overpowering stench of blood immediately assailed her senses. The scene that greeted her was that of a grim laboratory, replete with towering tools and instruments strewn about. In the centre of the room sat a blood-soaked metal chair, its surface an epitome of unspeakable horror. Instruments and tools bore traces of crimson, leaving for Cassandra to assume they were meant for a sinister purpose—to cut and dissect. Nausea swelled within her, a physical reaction to the grotesque tableau before her. Every instinct urged her to flee, to escape the suffocating weight of the room, but the thought of Grayson's potential suffering in such a place compelled her to remain.

Summoning her willpower, Cassandra pushed the door shut behind her, shutting out the world beyond momentarily. She stood poised on the precipice of panic, determined to resist its grip. Though her impulse was to flee, she stood her ground. She desperately searched the room for an exit. In the midst of it. Cassandra's gaze fell upon a disturbing collection of glass jars, each containing grotesque specimens–clear indication of a scientist at work. One jar held preserved eyeballs, another housed a mishmash of severed lips, while more lingered the shelved. Each jar contained a body part, something so striking that Cassandra suppressed the urge to vomit.

Shaking off the nausea and disgust, she could not understand how people enjoyed living in such a way. The idea seemed so abnormal to her–creating, crafting items that were meant to replace body parts felt almost unnatural to her–yet Cassandra could not help but laugh as she took in her appearance.

It was then that her eyes then alighted on an unsettling sight—a brain resting on a counter, its neural connection tethered to a machine by a network of wires. Disquiet surged within her, intensifying as she continued to scan the room in search of an escape route. Luck favoured her when her gaze settled upon a sealed metal door tucked away in a corner of the confined laboratory. Obstructed by towering shelves brimming with rows upon rows of jarred body parts, the door seemed almost concealed. Determined, she manoeuvred through the cramped space, her determination unwavering.

Pushing at the door, she was met with resistance. Attempt after attempt yielded no success, and her growing frustration propelled her to fire at the hinges, seeking to force the door open. Eventually, her efforts paid off, and as the door swung open, a gasp escaped her lips. Before her stretched a sprawling room, bathed in a muted beige hue, dotted with countless cells. The layout bore resemblance to a colossal holding area—a grim relic from the era of the war, a chamber designed to confine and incarcerate. Within this vast expanse, Cassandra was drawn to a peculiar sound, the scratching emanating from a cell positioned at the far end of the corridor. Instinctively, she activated her weapon, steadying her aim while her heart raced with both trepidation and anticipation.

The suspenseful silence was broken by a hacking cough followed by a muttered curse. In that moment, Cassandra's heart seemed to seize as she recognized the source of that deep, resonant voice.

"Grayson?" Her voice quivered with hope, her words scarcely more than a breathless whisper.

The tapping ceased, and in its stead, a shuffling sound reverberated, something being dragged across the cold floor. The air seemed to constrict around her as a familiar voice responded, "Cass?"

The single syllable was laden with surprise and disbelief, laced with an underlying wave of emotion that threatened to engulf them both.

Without a moment's hesitation, Cassandra rushed to Grayson's cell, her body nearly collapsing to the ground in front of the iron bars that confined him. A gasp escaped her lips as she surveyed the grim cell before her. Its walls and floor bore gruesome streaks of blood, an unsettling scene that made her stomach churn in queasiness. Her faze focused on the drops of blood trickling from Grayson's battered form, an image that sent shivers down her spine. With his back pressed against the wall, Grayson was shackled, chains wound tightly around his wrist, ankles, and torso, each link marred by the same crimson hue. His cuffs seemed to dig into his flesh, causing rivulets of blood to seep between the metal and his skin.

His typically dark red hair was now untied and fell down to his shoulders, his posture reflecting a sense of both physical and mental torment. Machines of various kinds were scattered around him, wires protruding his head and chest like harbingers of his captivity. Cassandra's heart clenched at the sight of his shattered and mangled state; his suffering was all too real and she blamed herself for his state; if she had worked harder and faster, she would have found Grayson sooner.

Drawing herself closer, she noticed the grotesque details—the dislocated shoulder, his left arm that once held his bow replaced by a newer one. The bow stood activated, adorned in gleaming new metals and fabrics. The design exhibited a more pronounced curve than his previous one, facilitating the launch of multiple arrows simultaneously. Cassandra could not help but observe the metallic embellishments on his chest, gears and a furnace now embodied him—and the faceplates that concealed portions of his nose and neck. The once-pristine figure she had known was now transformed, replaced by steam-powered enhancements.

A surge of panic washed over Cassandra, eyes frantically searching for their mother's leather that once bounded around her brother's bow handle, resembling the leathers on her own sniper. Grayson appeared to grasp Cassandra's intention, his response coming as a hushed murmur. "It's in my pocket," he mumbled, voice strained. "Mother's... It's with me."

Cassandra rose to her feet, determination propelling her forward, mind refusing to work properly as her fingers fought with the lock mechanism. She activated her sniper, prepared to puncture it. She had to get her brother, she had to bring him back to her father—he had to be safe.

The shot reverberated through the confined space, leaving her ears ringing in its aftermath. Simultaneously, the intrusion triggered an alarm, a piercing sound that set Grayson off into a panicked scream. His distress echoing off the walls. Hastily, Cassandra managed to open the cell door, though the noise it generated only added to her mounting sense of urgency.

"Grayson, let's go!" Cassandra's voice rang out, a mix of fear and urgency. She tugged and strained against the chains that held Grayson captive, her shots aimed at the anchor points on the walls, the metal clanks mingling with the sound of her racing heart. Each shot seemed to resonate with a palpable desperation as she fought to free him, the links stubbornly refusing to yield. "We need to get out of here!"

Grayson's initial panic seemed to subside, his features shifting from turmoil to a hardened resolve as he absorbed the situation. His gaze settled on the empty cell, a strange calm settling upon him. In stark contrast, the approaching footsteps, growing ever closer and more rapid, spurred Cassandra into heightened anxiety. Caught in the crossroads of instinctual fight-or-flight impulses, her mind raced to make a decision that could determine their fate.

Her heart wrestled with the dilemma before her, torn between leaving her brother or standing by him in his dire state. Yet her internal conflict was abruptly disrupted as the door to the cell room was forcefully flung open, revealing Sebastian and Augustus charging in with their weapons in place, ready for action.

At the sight of their arrival, a mixture of relief and urgency surged within Cassandra, the words escaping her lips in a near-plea. "Over here!" she called out, her arms frantically waving to draw their attention.

Sebastian was the first to close the gap, his gaze rife with a storm of emotions as he took in the scene before him. Frustration mingled with concern as he berated her. "You could not keep quiet, could you?"

Cassandra had little room for explanations, her primary focus being on the dire predicament at hand. "Save the lecture for later! Right now, I need your help!"

Augustus joined them shortly after, his eyes falling upon Grayson who remained unnervingly still, seemingly lost in his mind. Her friend assessed him, voice low and filled with worry. "We should leave. He does not seem well."

Cassandra, feeling a mix of desperation and determination, rose from her position by her brother's side, her plea directed at the newcomers. "Please, assist me in helping him."

Both Sebastian and Augustus complied, stepping cautiously into the cell and tending to Grayson. Her brother regarded the two Princes with a mixture of curiosity and confusion, his attempts to unshackle himself met with limited success. Yet, his efforts were secondary as Augustus brandished his chainsaw, slicing through the restraints with swift efficiency. Meanwhile, Sebastian carefully navigated the network of wires attached to Grayson's body, each cut drawing forth a stifled groan of discomfort from him.

As the final strands of restraint were removed, Grayson continued to mutter under his breath. Cassandra attempted to overlook his behaviour, focusing instead on coordinating their actions. She directed Sebastian and Augustus to assist her brother to his feet, positioning themselves to lift him. Once Grayson was to his feet, Cassandra began to explain their plan of escape. However, in a moment, Grayson's demeanour changed, as if something had been switched on, awakening something within him.

In a rapid and uncanny display, Grayson broke free from the boys' hold, causing him to stumble. He quickly positioned himself against the wall, narrowing his eyes at the group. His bow emitted an abnormal click, signifying readiness for a fight.

Grayson moved with a sense of disorientation, fingers gripping the wall as he struggled to lift his bow. His movements were strained, as if he was using all his strength to lift his mechanical arm. In response, Augustus acted on instinct, drawing Cassandra close and assuming the role of a protective shield against the imminent threat. Grayson's once-warm brown eyes were now obscured by a clouded darkness, signalling an unsettling transformation. In a matter of seconds, he lunged towards Cassandra, his right hand clenched into a fist and raised high above his head. However, Sebastian swiftly intervened, blocking the punch and initiating a wrestling match between the two.

Grayson, unable to maintain his balance under the force of the Spade Prince's strength, quickly faltered. Blood dripped from his wrist, and his muscles began to tense, the two adversaries nearly colliding heads as Grayson harnessed his newfound strength. Cassandra, processing the abrupt sequence of events, struggled to comprehend Grayson's unexpected aggression towards her.

With a resounding grunt, Grayson's eyes flickered towards his sister, radiating pure rage and hatred. Sebastian successfully pushed Grayson back, his body colliding with the wall. Grayson, now hunched over, took deep breaths, his long hair draping over his face. It seemed as though he had depleted his energy in the brief skirmish. However, as his eyes met Cassandra's once again, she sensed that this was merely the inception of something more profound and unsettling. His heavy breathing prompted Augustus and Sebastian to position themselves as her guards, readying their weapons in case he attacked again, forming a defensive triangle.

Grayson stood tall, abruptly gripping the long silver chain that once encircled his torso. As he pulled at it, the group witnessed the chain breaking free from its fixture on the wall. In a swift motion, he launched the extended chain towards Sebastian. The chain's tip hit the side of the assassin, causing Sebastian to groan and collapse to his knees. The impact appeared to disrupt Grayson's focus and he huffed under the strain of the additional weight, grunting and stumbling in the aftermath.

After a brief pause, Grayson wielded his chain once again, with Augustus as his new target. However, Augustus moved quickly, using his chainsaw to block the attack. The tiny blades of the saw sliced through the chain, taking a large chunk of the chains, leaving nothing more than half. Grayson groaned once more at the impact, fingers gripping the chain tightly. Cassandra noticed that her brother seemed to have momentarily overlooked his bow, relying solely on his strength to confront the Princes.

Sebastian, back on his feet, activated his iron blades. His forearms clicked as the chain hurtled towards him. He skilfully dodged its trajectory. Closing the distance to Grayson, Sebastian understood that the only way to conclude this confrontation was by cutting the chain to its very end. However, aware of the chain's movements, Sebastian knew it would be a challenging task. In seconds, the chain recoiled towards him. Reacting quickly, he slid to the ground, arching his back as he sliced through the middle of the chain. Most of it was severed, leaving Grayson with only a small section.

Grayson bellowed as his body toppled to the side, his head lightly colliding with the cold ground. The trio stepped back, observing and analysing his next move.

They witnessed Grayson spitting out blood and adjusting his wrist, allowing the remaining chain to coil tightly around his fist. Cassandra understood that the chain could inflict damage, but the extent was uncertain. Her brother rose slowly, his knuckles almost turning white beneath the silver chain wrapped around his right fist. The sequence of events unfolded too quickly for Cassandra to fully grasp.

Sebastian, however, anticipated what was about to transpire. Engaging in a graceful dance with Grayson, his movements formed a symphony of calculated strikes, causing her brother to falter. Although Grayson's chained fist managed to land a few solid punches on Sebastian, he displayed no signs of pain. The clash of metal against metal resonated within the confined space.

Augustus was not far behind, his chainsaw roaring to life with a menacing growl. It was evident that Grayson could not effectively combat both Princes. His eyes darted frantically from one opponent to the next, his movements growing feeble and his body clearly drained from the multiple attacks. Sparks flew as Augustus swung his chainsaw in a wide arc, meeting Grayson's bowed arm—a demonstration of raw power and unwavering determination.

Cassandra, her heart in a tumult of fear for her brother and determination to protect her comrades, joined the fray. Her sniper remained steady as she aimed with precision, the reticule fixed on her brother's slow movements. His attacks were relentless as he pushed against the two Princes. Augustus lost his grip on Grayson's bowed arm, permitting him to reach for another chain. Gripping it tightly, he was prepared to whip it at Augustus, but Cassandra allowed her bullet to fly, watching as it hit Grayson's chain-wrapped hand. Dark, hollow brown eyes whirled towards Cassandra, as if Grayson momentarily lost concentration on the task at hand. Before he could do anything more, before the cell room became a battleground, Cassandra seized her chance. She aimed her sniper once more, this time at the room's ceiling. With a precise shot, she dislodged a heavy metal pipe, sending it crashing down to block one of the exits.

As the pipe crashed down, Sebastian and Augustus seized the opportunity, their movements swift and strategic. Sebastian lunged forward with a deceptive feint, his dagger aimed for Grayson's mechanical arm. Augustus followed through, chainsaw roaring. The combined force of their attacks caused Grayson to groan, his hold weakening and eyes nearly rolling to the back of his head.

Yet her brother's actions took an unexpected turn. With determination, he managed to extract an arrow from his own chest. Cassandra stood in shock, gaping at her brother and the new enhancements he possessed. Grayson was never one to have enhancements; his body was the definition of perfection, yet there he stood before her with arrows forming in his chest due to the furnace that was now installed. Cassandra grew slightly nauseous at the thought of her brother being taken in the first place, making it all so clear now–Grayson was the only competitor with one enhancement on his body, making him the perfect toy for improvements.

She heard Augustus swear, while Sebastian remained quiet, carefully assessing the situation. Cassandra remained in her thoughts, not uttering a word as her body froze. Grayson, the brother she once knew all too well, was not the man standing before her. The embodiment of perfection was now a creation of new steam parts and engines. Grayson was enhanced to his fullest, demonstrating what humans could do if they were willing to give up their entire body to science and be completely transformed. Cassandra found herself grappling with the sheer impossibility of his newfound abilities, watching as he pulled four arrows from his chest, all generated and crafted perfectly—and suddenly aimed at her.

As her brother prepared the four arrows on his bow, Sebastian sprang into action, launching an attack to incapacitate Grayson. However, her brother swiftly evaded, kicking the assassin aside and expertly repositioning the arrows on his bow before releasing them. Cassandra's perception seemed to slow down as the arrows sped towards her. In the matter of a second, she managed to drop to the ground. But beside her, a cry of agony echoed as Augustus clutched his right hand, where an arrow had pierced through. He fell to his knees, cradling the injured hand, and Cassandra joined him, inspecting the wound. Sebastian wasted no time as he lunged at Grayson once more. She carefully instructed Augustus to cut off both ends of the arrow, leaving only the thin wooden shaft. Then, she guided him to count to three before they removed the arrow from his hand. Augustus winced in pain as Cassandra tore pieces from her shirt and gently wrapped them around his injured hand.

Seizing the moment, Grayson took advantage of the chaos and pulled himself to his feet. Kicking Sebastian back to the ground, her brother pulled another arrow from his chest and placed it on his bow. His eyes narrowed on Sebastian as he pulled back his arm, prepared to shoot. The room held its breath in anticipation, the air thick with tension as the confrontation reached a critical juncture.

Cassandra swiftly assumed a combat stance and fired her weapon at Grayson. The sharp crack of the gunshot reverberated throughout the room, the bullet finding its mark in Grayson's back. For an instant, her heart raced with hope that her intervention would stop him. Cassandra watched as her brother faltered, hoping it would do some damage, but instead, she watched in shock as her brother remained motionless. Her eyes widened as the bullet dropped to the ground, leaving her mind reeling with realisation and disbelief. The new metal plates that laid on his chest and back, covering his upper organs. The gears and engine that occupied his body.

In a shocking turn, Grayson's eyes bore into Cassandra with a twisted intensity. Without hesitation, he angled his arrow and let it fly.

The arrow's trajectory was swift and merciless, its aim unerringly accurate. It found its mark in Cassandra's shoulder, sinking deep into her flesh. Pain lanced through her, but she refused to succumb to agony. Determination ignited her actions as she fought to maintain her stance. As Grayson stumbled, breaths heavy and gears screeching, Augustus took the opportunity to unleash a gas bomb that filled the chamber with a thick, green, choking haze. The room was engulfed in swirling fumes, casting an eerie, surreal atmosphere.

Seizing the chance to escape, Sebastian swept Cassandra into his arms, his quick movements guided by equal parts urgency and concern. His heartbeat pounded in tandem with hers as he navigated through the fog, finding their path towards freedom. Their departure was a hasty retreat, the clang of the metal door signalling their exit from the chaotic battleground.

As they emerged from the haze into the dimly-lit corridor, Cassandra leaned against Sebastian, her wounded shoulder throbbing with each heartbeat. The echoes of the fierce battle lingered in the air, a testament to the intensity of the clash they had faced. In this moment of respite, Cassandra clung to Sebastian's support, the strength of their connection forming a lifeline amidst the turmoil.

CHAPTER 18

Cassandra replayed the events of the previous night in her mind, repeatedly attempting to grasp how rapidly her brother had transformed. The notion of Grayson being the embodiment of change seemed utterly absurd. Her thoughts swirled, unsure of what to believe. She ventured into various mental territories, attempting to discern the true from the false. Her mind clearly played tricks on her, creating imaginative explanations as to why her brother's captors would take him—the concept sounded dreadful. Transforming Grayson into a superior being seemed like something from the pages of one of her novels.

However, Cassandra knew that was exactly what they did. They made his physical being better than the average human with enhancements, something no one has ever seen before. The very notion of it made her sick, shaken to her core. The image of his arrows, once aimed at her, played on a loop in her mind as she laid on her cot, her injured shoulder wrapped in clean white bandages. It was moments like this when she was grateful for her father's absence.

Her thoughts raced incessantly, dissecting each moment of that fateful encounter. She combed through her memories, watching his faltered steps and actions, trying to identify the pivotal moment when he had tried to strike her.

Before her thoughts could delve any deeper, Savannah slipped through the tent's opening, her expression marked by a deep frown as her green eyes locked onto Cassandra with an accusing glare. "The Spade Prince dumped you in your cot when he woke me up. Care to give me a reason why you were with him?" Ignoring Savannah, Cassandra shifted away, her back turned towards the maid. "Get up. You have visitors." Without another word, she left.

Cassandra remained where she was, her gaze fixed on the expanse of the white sheet that enclosed her tent. "Some way to say hi to old friends." A voice disrupted her reverie, accompanied by a soft laughter. Her heart raced as she twisted around to see Yara, Adriana, and Nora standing before her. An overwhelming surge of emotion surged through her, and she hurriedly rose from the bed, embracing her friends in a tearful hug.

"What brings you guys here?" Cassandra's voice quivered with a mix of surprise and gratitude.

"Our fathers were summoned to aid King Jaronas in his search for your brother. We requested to accompany them to ensure your wellbeing," Yara explained, a faint smile playing on her lips. "Father said King Jaronas and the Chief's men found another path, one that could potentially lead them to Grayson."

Cassandra felt her stomach turn; she had to speak with her father. She promised Sebastian.

Adriana chimed in, a playful wink in her light green eyes. "And we could not resist the chance to witness a female contender in the Triumph Games."

"Not well enough, clearly. When did this happen?" Nora gestured towards Cassandra's wounded shoulder.

Cassandra felt an inner conflict, knowing she should confide in her friends about the events of the previous night, yet she sensed that they would become overly protective and possibly obstruct her plans, which she could not allow. "I had a mishap while training for the triathlon yesterday. Clumsiness at its finest."

Nora chuckled. "Some things never change. Now, enough of that. How about introducing us to this mysterious Sebastian we've been hearing so much about?"

"Absolutely not," Cassandra replied firmly.

Adriana's expression morphed into a pleading pout, her eyes wide and innocent. "Please!"

As Cassandra prepared to respond, Sebastian entered the open tent, accompanied by Augustus at his side–hand bandaged tightly. "Cassandra, are you—" His words tapered off as two highly excited young women beamed at his arrival.

Yara could not help but step closer to the Spade Prince, a sly smile dancing on her lips. "And who might you gentlemen be?"

"Augustus Clubs, ma'am." He introduced himself with a respectful bow.

"And Sebastian Spars, Miss," their friend added, bowing in a similar manner. "And who might you be?"

"Friends of the Princess, naturally," Yara answered, mischief glinting in her dark eyes.

Augustus took a step forward, his gaze fixed on Nora. "And what might your names be? I must say, I hope to attach a name to such a lovely face." A faint blush warmed Nora's cheek, while Adriana responded with a delighted giggle.

Nora extended her hand, her raven-black hair elegantly pulled back in a bun, her smile directed at Augustus. "Nora, at your service. These are my companions, Yara and Adriana."

"Pleased to make your acquaintance," Augustus replied, his attention captivated by her. However, this unexpected interest from

Augustus prompted Cassandra to give him a perplexed frown. Was he not showing interest in Charlotte just a few days prior?

Sebastian cleared his throat, snapping Augustus out of his reverie. Sebastian's hand on Augustus's shoulder guided him back to the present moment. "Ladies, if you would not mind, we would appreciate a moment to speak with the Princess."

Adriana assented with a nod. "Certainly. Let me fetch Savannah." Before Sebastian could interject, Adriana left the tent and returned shortly with Savannah by her side. The girls bid Cassandra farewell, informing her that they would be waiting on their boat by the bay, urging her to join them soon. With a brief nod, they departed, leaving the four of them behind.

Savannah huffed audibly, her arms crossed in a stern posture. "Would anyone care to explain why my Princess returned at such an ungodly hour, and more importantly, why she is wounded?" A heavy silence lingered. No one spoke first and no one dared to make a move, but Savannah was not about to let it go. She rolled her eyes, her hands finding their way to her hips. "Very well, if no one is forthcoming, I shall not hesitate to discuss this matter with the Kings."

Sebastian positioned himself in front of the determined head maid, effectively blocking her exit. His intense gaze bore into her, his commanding presence towering over her smaller frame. "Please, have a seat. We are here to explain."

Despite his attempt, Savannah stood her ground, resolute and defiant. She held her head high, meeting Sebastian's stern stare with her own piercing glare.

Cassandra was well aware that Savannah was loyal to her family, but she was loyal to her King first. "I encountered Grayson last night," she began, causing a look of shock to cross the head maid's face. "We stumbled upon a hidden bunker in the woods."

Savannah's astonishment was evident, but her concern was mounting. "Why did you not bring him back with you?"

Cassandra's voice carried a sombre tone. "He was not himself. He attacked me—he attacked us," she revealed, causing Savannah to take a step back, her mind racing with the implications of this revelation.

"Do the Kings know?"

The group fell quiet once more, causing Cassandra to shift slightly under Sebastian's hard stare. "I will speak to my father...eventually."

"You have not told King Jaronas yet?" Savannah gasped.

Cassandra rolled her eyes. "As I said, I will speak to him eventually."

"Why have you not spoken to him yet?" Augustus questioned.

"Why are we speaking about me not informing my father when we should be focusing on my brother?"

"Because whatever reasoning you have is not a good enough reason as to why you shouldn't be telling Jaronas," Sebastian grunted, causing Cassandra to scoff at him.

Savannah smiled lightly. "How about, you write your father a letter informing him–"

Cassandra huffed and turned to the group, anger boiling. "I will speak to my father before the triathlon, now can we please focus on my brother!"

Sebastian tilted his head, curiosity filling him as he watched Cassandra's outburst, but it was Savannah who held her hands and spoke to her lightly, explaining that there was nothing to do until the Kings were involved. Furthermore, Cassandra urged Savannah to not say a word about it and swore that the next time they were to venture into the tunnels that she could cover for them. Reluctantly, Savannah found herself agreeing, and in a matter of moments, they began discussing strategies to rescue Grayson, a short plan until the Kings were involved. Cassandra did not like the idea at all, as she did not want to trouble her father with such things. However, she knew that Jaronas wanted to find Grayson–a father would stop at nothing to find his son. And yet, Cassandra was somehow in the way of it, not understanding why.

As the conversation evolved, the topic shifted to the two Princes voicing their concerns about Cassandra's potential participation in the triathlon scheduled for the following day. She brushed aside their apprehensions, insisting that they leave her be. Savannah joined in the conversation with a laugh, assuring Cassandra that she would quickly heal her wound before the tournament.

With Savannah leaving to gather herbs, Cassandra settled into her cot, her mind consumed with plotting ways to unmask the traitor among them that night.

On that particular night, Cassandra remained within her tent, anticipating her father's arrival. He entered with a brief "goodnight," accompanied by a gentle kiss on her forehead. He murmured well wishes for her upcoming participation in the tournament and soon retired to his own cot, exhausted from the day's efforts to locate Grayson. Savannah, already asleep close to Cassandra's cot, breathed softly. Cassandra chose not to inform her, feeling it necessary to confront the situation alone. Having prepared a small note detailing her intentions in case Savannah awoke, Cassandra slipped out of her tent with the utmost stealth, her every movement calculated.

"Where are you going?" a voice called from behind. Cassandra groaned in response, knowing exactly who it was.

Turning around, she saw Sebastian sitting before the now burning fire. The light bounced off his reflection as Cassandra huffed in annoyance. "What are you doing here?"

"The wine helps me sleep," Sebastian said, his eyes wandering over her. "And I see you are going back to the tunnels." Holding up a mug, Sebastian extended it to her. "Want some?" Cassandra rolled her eyes as she made her way towards the Spade Prince. Sitting beside him, she grabbed the mug and downed the wine that filled it.

Suddenly, Sebastian's tone shifted, and he asked a rather unexpected question. "How did you find the lab and the cell room?"

Cassandra cleaned her face of the wine, holding the mug tightly in her hand as she felt a sense of unease queasiness in her stomach. "Why do you want to know?" she retorted, her guard up.

He shrugged casually, eyes gazing up at the starry night. "You know, it is hard to see the stars at night from Spade City. It is nearly impossible. The bright city lights always manage to ruin the experience, but here, I am able to look up and see infinite constellations and watch as they light up the night sky." She blinked at him, shocked by what he had just said. "And to answer your question..." His head fell to the side lazily, eyes meeting hers. "Curiosity, I suppose."

Cassandra found herself leaning back, eyes gazing up at the stars. "Back on the Heart Lot Islands, we use the stars to guide our ships home." She thought of her home, pictured the bright stars and the constellations she and her mother had named. "You have never lived if you have not seen the stars shining down on the sea. The view... It is truly something to remember." As Cassandra shared tales of her home and the mesmerising starlit nights over the sea, Sebastian found himself captivated by the genuine passion in her voice.

The flickering firelight played on her features, casting a warm glow that seemed to intensify the connection between them. As the night unfolded and their conversation deepened, a subtle shift in the air hinted at the unspoken tension between the two. Sebastian, normally reserved and composed, could not help but be drawn to Cassandra's authenticity and the beauty of her words. There was an unspoken understanding, a connection that transcended the differences between their worlds. As they sat under the starry canopy, the distant echoes of the town replaced by the gentle crackling of the fire, it felt like time itself had slowed.

In this moment of shared vulnerability, Cassandra turned to Sebastian, her eyes reflecting the dancing flames. Sebastian, sensing an unspoken invitation, leaned in closer. The air between them crackled with anticipation, and as their breaths mingled, the unspoken tension reached its zenith. In the soft glow of the fire, their lips finally met. The kiss was a revelation, a gentle merging of two souls beneath the vast expanse of stars. It was a tender exchange, a silent acknowledgment of a connection that could not be ignored. In that stolen moment, surrounded by the serenity of the night and the comforting warmth of the fire, they allowed themselves to be enveloped in the magic of an unexpected, and perhaps inevitable, connection.

As they broke the kiss, Cassandra's eyes held a newfound intensity. The vulnerability that had been shared in that intimate exchange lingered in the air. In the flickering firelight, she confessed, "I went alone to find Grayson because I feel that it is my responsibility to do so." Cassandra did not know what possessed her to say such a thing, especially after a memorable kiss.

Sebastian pushed back strands of her red hair, eyes gazing from her lips to her eyes. "You do know that I am here to help. You do not have to do this alone."

She knew he would run to her aid as he had done it countless times before, however it was the bitterness that surfaced first, the sour taste in her mouth of having to search for help when she knew she was capable of doing it on her own. "I will ask for your help when I see fit. Until then, thank you but no thank you." She was quick to her feet, making it past her tent and towards the forest. She followed the path towards the tunnels.

Keeping her back turned, she thought over Sebastian's words, not understanding how someone could say such a thing. She knew he was being kind and understood he was only trying to help, but Cassandra did not know why it was so hard for her to accept his help and admit that she needed it. Cassandra's attention was abruptly shattered as a hand gripped her wrist, spinning her around, her back was to a tree while Sebastian stood before her, out of breath and eyes narrowed.

"You walk extremely fast when you are mad" was the first thing he said to her, causing Cassandra to scoff. Sebastian loomed over her, his imposing stature pinning her against the tree as his intense gaze bore into her.

"Maybe because I no longer wish to speak with you?"

Sebastian smirked, head tilting down. "No, that cannot be it. Why would anyone not want to speak to me?"

Cassandra rolled her eyes. "Why did you follow me?"

"Because our conversion was not over."

"Yes, it was."

"No, it was not."

She huffed in annoyance as Sebastian smirked. "It is as if I am speaking to a child." She tried to push past the Spade Prince, but it was no use; he remained still, body stiff and practically caging her in. She knew there was no way out unless she gave him what he wanted. "Alright, go ahead."

Sebastian smiled slightly, knowing he won their little game. "Why not mention any of this to your father? Would you not want his help in finding your brother? Would you not want to show him the tunnels?" He managed to step closer, their bodies so close to each other that it made it extremely hard for her to breath. He smelled of spice and green tea, causing Cassandra to nearly sigh in satisfaction.

"I–I do not know why–it has crossed my mind."

"Your brother is missing; his son is missing—you do see the flaw in this, do you not?"

"I understand." Cassandra nodded her head, inhaling his scent and focusing on her fast-beating heart. "I should tell him, I know I should, and for some reason, part of me finds it so difficult to accept help and I understand that–I just..." She was at a loss for words, knowing he was right and knowing very well that her brain was fogging up.

Sebastian raised a dark brow. "You just what? Will you speak to him?"

Cassandra nodded her head, her control no longer being a factor in this equation. "Yes."

"Yes what?" He knew he was toying with her, but Cassandra struggled to find the words.

"Yes, I will speak with my father about the tunnels."

"And?"

"And I will ask for help when needed."

Sebastian smirked, fingertips scaling the side of Cassandra's neck. "Good girl."

Cassandra could no longer contain her urge, his scent nearly suffocating her. It was thrilling to break free from the game he constantly played, and taking the opportunity, she grabbed the sides of Sebastian's face and planted a kiss on his lips. Sebastian blinked in shock as Cassandra pulled back, her own realisation hitting her. "I don't know why I did that, I'm sorry—"

Before she could finish her sentence, Sebastian's eyes filled with intensity as he breathed heavily. His body pressed against hers as he passionately kissed her, their lips moulding together. Sebastian's hand cupped the back of her head while the other wrapped around her waist. He kept her pinned against the tree, their lips parting as his tongue brushed against hers before he reluctantly pulled away. Both of them were left panting; Sebastian stood tall as his eyes filled with desire and his lips laid in a sly smirk.

Sebastian mumbled, "We must do that again."

Cassandra nodded, letting out a heavy breath. As she brushed her hair out of her face, she gazed up at Sebastian and knew that she was about to make the right decision. "Do you want to come with me to the tunnels?" Sebastian was taken aback by her words; he simply nodded as the two walked back to camp for the Prince to collect his things.

As they walked down the path that led them towards the tunnels, Sebastian and Cassandra made sure to keep a safe distance from the tunnel's mouth. She found a fallen tree of considerable size, surrounded by concealed bushes. The duo sat quietly behind it, weapons readied, and observing the hidden bunker. The night passed slowly, an hour stretching by as they maintained vigilance and patience. Cassandra's attention was abruptly shattered as she realised they were not alone. In a swift motion, Sebastian placed his hand above her mouth, finger to his lips to indicate her to stay quiet. He activated an attachment, blades poking out of his skin as Cassandra readied her gun. That was when she heard it—the soft, muted sound of footsteps crunching on aged leaves and branches. This was the culmination of her waiting, the pivotal moment she had anticipated. Yet, to her surprise, it was not one of her competitors who emerged. Instead, a cloaked figure, draped in a deep black cloak with a hood drawn over their head, emerged from the shadows. The figure surveyed the surroundings, a hefty staff resting by their side.

Sebastian acted swiftly, hand on her mouth; he focused on the hooded figure, while Cassandra found herself lost in a daze as she gazed up at him. Their eyes met briefly, and for a moment, everything else faded away. He whispered something to her, but she was entranced by the depth of his eyes, their hue holding her captive.

Sebastian withdrew his hand from her mouth, causing her breathing to become unsteady. His fingers brushed down her neck, gently tucking strands of hair behind her ear, all while his voice carried a whispered plan to her. An idea to ensnare the cloaked intruder before they could vanish into the tunnel's depths. As he spoke, Cassandra regained her composure, her focus sharpening on his proposal.

Following the plan Sebastian had devised, he promptly tossed a rock to the opposite side. The hooded figure pivoted, drawn toward the sound, providing Sebastian with the opportunity to ascend a nearby tree with agility akin to that of a monkey. He nimbly ascended the tree's branches, reaching a height of ten feet. In this advantageous position, he sprang down on the cloaked figure. Seizing the moment, Sebastian released a small shuriken from his grasp, expertly aiming it to strike the figure's shoulder, causing a grimace of pain.

This signal prompted Cassandra to emerge from her concealed position, her gun trained on the hooded figure. A shot from her firearm struck the figure's hand, forcing them to relinquish the sizable staff they held. Despite their injury, the figure turned toward her, poised for confrontation. Yet, with swift precision, Sebastian leaped from the tree, landing on the figure's back and swiftly forcing him to the ground. A knife, poised close to the cloaked figure's throat, solidified Sebastian's control over the situation.

Cassandra advanced, her body twitching as she readied her gun, prepared to extract answers by force if necessary. But her intent was abruptly interrupted as a sudden impact knocked her to the ground. Whipping around, her eyes fell upon another figure, masked with a black fabric that concealed half of their face, and mirroring the stance of the other assailant, they clutched a staff in their grip. In a fleeting moment, understanding dawned on Cassandra. These were the very individuals who had seized her brother, and she stole herself for the impending confrontation.

Without hesitation, Cassandra raised her sniper, honing in on her target, and released a shot that struck the man's thigh. A cry of agony pierced the air, yet the altercation was far from over. Springing to her feet, she directed a powerful punch toward the figure's face, swiftly followed by a forceful kick to their stomach. As she aims her gun once more, her focus shifted as a sharp blow landed on her back; the other hooded figure–the one who had been aligned with Sebastian–now assaulted her. Turning, she observed Sebastian on the ground, his body battered and bloodied, struggling to rise.

Fear surged through her when the figure she had been grappling with lunged at her anew, fingers constricting around her throat, blocking her airway and making it agonisingly difficult to breathe. Desperation compelled her to claw at his grasp, though her efforts proved futile against his unyielding grip.

Darkness encroached on her vision, punctuated by flickering spots of light, her consciousness wavering on the precipice. In an unexpected twist, Sebastian reemerged, delivering a decisive strike to the assailant's forearm with his weapon. The wound was not profound, but it was sufficient to elicit a cry of pain and compel him to release his hold on Cassandra, granting her precious relief from the suffocating grip.

As the second hooded figure lunged towards them, Sebastian sprang into action, vaulting over Cassandra's prone form and sending his shuriken hurtling toward the man's thigh. The weapon found its mark, embedding itself into the very wound that Cassandra's previous shot had created, and Sebastian drove it deeper with a swift, calculated motion.

Cassandra felt her consciousness waning, her surroundings spinning as her body collided with the unforgiving ground. Struggling against the encroaching darkness, she vaguely registered Sebastian's presence. He knelt by her side, his strong arms supporting her faltering form. But before he could fully lift her, the unexpected strike of a staff against the back of his head sent him toppling forward.

The passage of time was hazy as Cassandra gradually regained awareness. The soft songs of birds indicated that dawn had broken, and as her senses cleared, she became aware of Sebastian's weight resting upon her. His head rested upon her chest, and despite the gravity of their situation, she could not help but groan at the awkwardness of the situation. Glancing around, she noted the absence of the hooded figures.

Gently shaking Sebastian awake, he stirred with a muttered curse. Cassandra informed him of their departure, to which he responded with a self-blameful admission. "This is all my fault. I should not have been distracted."

Cassandra was momentarily taken aback by his admission, a flicker of empathy crossing her features. However, she opted not to comment, instead suggesting they return to Camp before anyone discovered their absence.

Before Sebastian could respond, she was already moving away, resolute steps leading her back towards the campsite.

CHAPTER 19

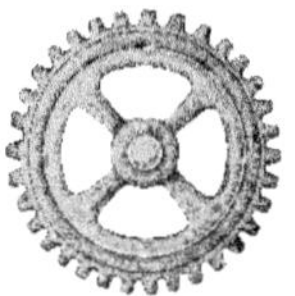

Several hours had passed since the intense confrontation, and an uneasy tension lingered between the two royals. Sebastian and Cassandra continued to steadfastly ignore each other, their frustrations with one another simmering just below the surface. Sebastian was grappling with the weight of his miscalculations and his undue focus on Cassandra during the encounter. On the other hand, she harboured resentment towards him for his harsh words and his unjust blame regarding the loss of the two hooded assailants.

Despite the strained atmosphere, Cassandra carried on with her morning routine. She engaged in a last-minute stretching session before the commencement of the early-morning challenge: the triathlon. This particular trial was set to unfold across various stages, spanning from the Arena to the outskirts of the Mountain Region.

At the onset of the challenge, participants would be furnished with coloured flags, each representing their respective nations. The task involved starting from the Arena, making their way to the river they would swim across, and subsequently navigating through the rugged terrain of the Mountain Region. Their objective was to ascend the first mountain, affixing their flag at its summit. In this demanding endeavour, competitors were granted the liberty to utilise any integrated mechanical enhancements on their bodies, provided that these augmentations were extensions or had been seamlessly incorporated into their bodies.

While on route to the carriages that would transport them to the Arena, Cassandra and her father observed Benjamin receiving additional sets of robotic arms. The sight brought to mind Cassandra's prior readings on this subject. Albert had elevated this augmentation to a symbol of achievement, a pinnacle of refinement and prowess. Achieving the status of six robotic arms underscored a level of sophistication and dominance that left many of the other competitors at a distinct disadvantage.

Jaronas playfully nudged his daughter. "Do not be concerned. This does not prevent you from replacing your existing enhancements with something new."

Upon arriving at the Arena, Cassandra realised her father's insight was spot-on. Standing by the imposing iron gates were Mees and Yara, each holding new contraptions in their hands. After embracing both companions, Mees delved into an explanation of the newly designed grappling hook, which was slated to replace her sniper. As Mees outlined the mechanics, Cassandra activated the device, allowing him to carefully extract the old one and install the new piece.

"It is a grappling hook," Mees began, making adjustments. "Much like your sniper, it transforms upon activation."

Yara winked. "Plus everything's waterproof."

Cassandra giggled as she turned towards her father. "Do you think these enhancements will be sufficient? I am worried that the Princes will have more advanced gear than I do, that they might outperform me."

Her father chuckled. "That is why we are replacing almost every bit of metal on your body. We are enhancing your steam engine." He eyed the new piece in Yara's hands. "The engine you have now is not meant for your new active lifestyle, causing it to drain and be the reason for why you have not been performing well. However, the new engine will enhance your performance."

Yara began to tweak the new engine before them, eyes checking over the part one last time. "Keep in mind that this engine is only for the tournament, so once we return home, I will be able to change your engine once more."

Cassandra nodded, realising her father had planned to counter any advantage her competitors might possess.

In a passing scene, Sebastian walked alongside King Kenji and Queen Suzume, accompanied by his trainer, who was carrying new extensions for him. Cassandra and Sebastian exchanged a brief tense gaze, the air between them heavy with unspoken words. Since that morning, they had not exchanged any conversation, and Cassandra had come to the conclusion that it was wiser to maintain a distance rather than risk further interactions. She accepted the consequences of her earlier actions and chose to bear them.

"It is best to keep your distance," her father remarked, noticing the exchanged looks between the two young royals. "He is concentrating on the match, much like you are. No time to be friendly." Once Yara and Mees completed the installation of her new extensions, they headed to the Sky Box, leaving Cassandra alone with her father. He placed his hands on his daughter's shoulders, offering words of encouragement for the upcoming challenge.

Cassandra took this time to breathe, her mind rushing as she remembered her promise to Sebastian. "Father," she began, catching his attention. As the two rounded the corner, she spotted the Mountmont brothers. They smiled at the Hearth's, encouraging her father to guide her towards them. "I must tell you something," she urged.

"It can wait 'till after the triathlon, Cassandra." He smiled. "Right now, we must speak to the sponsors."

"No, it cannot–" She was cut off by the brothers' greetings, causing Cassandra to huff in annoyance.

"Ah! The Mountmonts!" her father exclaimed, shaking hands with the brothers. "So good to see you again."

The red-haired brother smiled all too widely, reminding Cassandra of their odd behaviour. "So good to see you as well. We would not want to miss this challenge."

The black-haired brother quickly jumped in, his smile cracking widely as well. "We have a surprise." He giggled. Cassandra perked at the noise, shivers running down her spin. The eerie giggle sounded all too familiar. "With our generously large donation, the Triumph Games were able to turn the Sky Box into a blimp. Is that not wonderful? That way the royals can keep an eye on their children throughout the tournament and not have to patiently wait for them to return."

Jaronas let out a heavy laugh as he slapped the brother on his shoulder, his black hair flopping to the side as he slightly hissed. "That is a wonderful idea. Who would have thought such a thing?"

"It is the creation of new things that fascinate us," the red-haired brother said. "It is the improvement of the nations, the bettering of society that thrills us. As society is a blueprint to perfection."

"An example would be the human body," his brother chimed in. Cassandra perked up at his words. "As it was once a simple body with organs and blood flow, today, it is one with steam-powered attachments. There was improvement for it to grow. Now, with the creation of a steam-powered person already in existence, why not tweak it and turn it into something more? Why not permit absolute perfection?"

Cassandra's stomach stirred at their words, not liking how they were similar to her thoughts about her brother and his recent upcoming change. They spoke all too excitedly about the change of humans, as if they knew much on this subject. Their intricate descriptions painted vivid pictures in her mind. She listened and drew parallels between Grayson's transformation and the Mountmonts' vision of perfecting the human body through mechanisation.

A stillness overcame her, her heart coming to a halt. Cassandra's eyes locked with theirs, a revelation passed between them, and their grins widened, confirming her suspicion.

Cassandra took a step back, feeling sick. She watched as the brothers bid her father goodbye, limping slightly as they moved. Her heart began to beat fast, feeling her blood coursing through her veins. Could it be? It was not possible; it could not be. The idea was absurd and unimaginable. The Mountmont brothers could not be her brother's kidnappers. They did not know him, they did not meet him, and yet Cassandra could not find a better reason as to why it would not be them. Or maybe she was completely wrong and she was creating more false accusations, adding another name to her list.

"I–I need a moment," Cassandra mumbled to her father. As she moved away from the iron gates, she kept her head down, vision blurred, and unintentionally collided with Charlotte. Struggling to catch her breath, Cassandra could not contain her panic.

"Are you alright?" Charlotte asked, but Cassandra turned her gaze to the brothers once more, studying their movements. Their slight limps, their scrunched faces as they stepped wrong. Worse of all, when they stepped into the elevator, they each had a knowing smirk as they faced her. Charlotte followed her gaze, brows furrowed. "Thomas and Charlie Mountmont?" Cassandra shivered at their name, watching as the door closed and feeling herself go pale. Rushing for the washroom, Charlotte followed suit.

It did not take long for Cassandra to vomit, the thought of it all overpowering her and making her sick. Charlotte was quick to pull back Cassandra's hair, holding it tight enough for the loose strands to not fall into her face as her head was hovering over the toilet.

"What happened?" a voice said from behind, startling the two. Sebastian was there, eyes wide as he analysed the situation.

Cassandra managed to stand, going to the sink to wash her mouth. "I am not sure," Charlotte said. "She had seen Thomas and Charlie then rushed to the washroom."

"Who are Thomas and Charlie?"

"The Mountmont brothers."

"Which is which?"

Charlotte stared at him in confusion. "Charlie is the black-haired, Thomas is the other– how do you not know this?"

"Because I labelled them as creepy and creepier." Sebastian pushed past Charlotte, leaving her completely speechless. His concerns lied with Cassandra, who had spat the water out of her mouth and let out heavy breathes. "Take a breath," he instructed, but Cassandra paid him no mind as her mind ran over what she had witnessed. "You need to tell us what happened, Cass." Sebastian pushed a strand of red hair out of her face, tucking it behind her ear.

Words seemed to elude Cassandra, her mind still racing all too fast for her mouth to articulate the turmoil within her.

"The Mountmont brothers?" Sebastian prompted, making her flinch. "What did you see?"

"They were speaking about blueprints and society and the perfect human," Cassandra ranted, but it was when her gaze locked onto Sebastian's that realisation seeped through him. "They…They were limping,"

Charlotte appeared perplexed. "What does that signify?"

"They were the ones who took Grayson," Cassandra exclaimed, the revelation settling in with a heavy weight. "They had to be. There is no other explanation for this."

Sebastian nodded. "Alright, but we still need proof. Some type of evidence that makes your statement true."

"What do you mean? I can tell my father now and have them taken by the authorities."

"Yes, however the Mountmonts are a wealthy family. This type of accusation will need proof," Sebastian said, arms crossed over his chest. "Do not worry, there is a way to find it. We just need to figure out how."

Cassandra nodded her head, fingers curling around the metal sink. Sebastian saw how overwhelmed she was, and knew she was to crumble at any moment. Tears pooled in her eyes, and before she was able to let out a cry, Charlotte was by her side. Arms wrapped around her, embracing her tightly. "We will do everything in our power to find your brother, Cassandra. We are here for you."

Cassandra returned the gesture, arms tightly wrapped around her waist and head buried into her shoulder. Sebastian stood not too far behind, watching the two. He was not one for affection, especially with other people present, however he watched with worried eyes as Cassandra squeezed Charlotte before letting go.

A resounding trumpet-like sound signalled the commencement of the challenge, a reminder that it was time to pull herself together. Cassandra knew she could not afford to falter now. This challenge was her opportunity to honour Grayson. Despite wanting to rush off and rescue him immediately, Cassandra reminded herself of her duty towards her people and her father.

She knew in order to save her brother a plan must be made.

CHAPTER 20

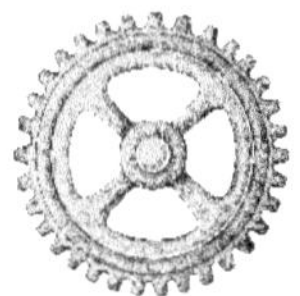

Upon their return to the Arena, the competitors stood in a line at its centre. Onatach's men proceeded to hand each royal a flag, donned in their house colour. The middle of the flag held their respective family crests. Cassandra held up her red flag with the black Heart crest in the middle, wondering how long it took for someone to sew. Not missing a single detail.

She watched as the Chiefs men lined the floor with white markings, demonstrating for each competitor to position themselves at the end. Sebastian stood a few paces to her left, followed by Benjamin and Augustus to his. Everyone was equipped with new extensions attached to their bodies. The triathlon had a time limit of eight hours and thirty minutes for completion, and the first individual to place their flag at the top of a mountain within that time frame would secure first place.

Cassandra took care to secure her flag in the pocket of her training pants, sealing it safely with a zipper added by Savannah. Her father, along with their friends who occupied the Sky Box, cheered and clapped, Yara, Adriana, and Nora being the loudest of them. Yet Cassandra found it difficult to focus on these expressions of support, her attention firmly fixed on the Mountmont brothers seating the Sky Box, their broad smiles directed at her. The Sky Box would follow their every move, floating overhead and permitting a front-row view to their challenge.

Amongst the crowd's roar, Cassandra's heartbeat pounded in her ears, her breath becoming her sole awareness. Then, a gunshot signalled the commencement of the challenge and the Princess marvelled as the Sky Box began to float. The motor whirled at an incredible speed, lifting the royals and prepared to follow the competitors.

With determined strides, the competitors surged forwards, exiting the Arena with determined strides. Massive iron gates swung open, relieving the bay adjacent to the Arena. Sebastian became her guide, with Cassandra trailing behind him, using him as a reference point for her surroundings. The first segment of the Triathlon involved swimming across the bay that connected the Arena to the rest of the Forest Lands. Swimming was Cassandra's specialty and she accelerated.

She picked up speed, watching as Benjamin converted his back extensions into one large water propeller. Augustus followed suit, enclosing his head in a clear circular glass resembling a bubble, he pressed buttons on his air tank causing lights to appear and providing light to the murky bay—permitting perfect vision for himself and the competitors. Additionally, two large propellers at the bottom of his tank allowed him to navigate through the water.

As Cassandra raced past them, she witnessed Sebastian assuming a diving position. His calves transformed into an underwater engine, and his feet turned into metallic fins. Trying to ignore the modifications made to the Princes, she focused on herself. Approaching the edge of the bay, she allowed the transformation to take place. Leaping ahead of Sebastian and the others, she soared through the air. In mid-flight, Cassandra fused her legs into a single, mermaid-like tail, inspired by the mythical creatures of the Heart Lot Islands' waters. As she plunged into the water, her legs seamlessly transformed, with clicking mechanisms and whirring gears orchestrating the change. This groundbreaking technology was an unprecedented innovation tailored exclusively for the Heart Lot people.

The river's embrace brought her home, a sanctuary where she felt most secure. Cassandra sensed the water's motion and heard three splashes behind her, but she had already surged far ahead. Immersed in the water, she found solace as if her troubles had dissolved. It felt like ages since she used to swim the island's currents to evade her governess's educational sessions. Nevertheless, she felt the tide approaching, the water merging with the dry land, and soon she emerged from the river, drenched from head to toe, hoisting herself up.

Applause and gleeful shouts reached her ears from above. Her gaze shifted upward, revealing the Sky Box suspended in the air. Her father and friends clapped and smiled in approval. It was then that she noticed the Mountmonts wearing sly smirks. Cassandra regretted not informing her father about the Mountmonts before the challenge. She shouldn't have let herself break down after learning the truth about them. However, she acknowledged that it was her regret to handle, and she understood that the sooner she completed the challenge, the sooner she could address the issue with her father. Muttering curses under her breath, Cassandra allowed her gills to return to their place, and her legs carried her forward as she followed the designated path. The route included passing by the Train Station, navigating through the town, and then heading northeast toward the Mountain Region. Along the way, they were required to follow the trail marked by white flags for safety and to stay on course.

As she went up the trail, Cassandra heard the gasps of breaths, the pulling of water and the muttering curses of the boys. She knew it would not be long 'till they were near her but Cassandra kept pushing. She proceeded along the route, past the Train Station, feeling her lungs burn as she transitioned into a light jog. Augustus followed closely, his footsteps echoing on the dirt path just a few paces behind. Benjamin maintained a moderate distance, audibly panting and groaning as he jogged.

However, Sebastian's presence was stealthy and graceful, making it hard for her to pinpoint his location until he smoothly overtook her and jogged straight toward the town. Her mind was preoccupied with recent events, preventing her from calling out to him or asking questions.

As she pushed forward down a hill that provided an overlook of the town, she realised it was her first time actually being within it. She had seen it from a distance but had never been drawn by the lively atmosphere filled with chanting and laughter. Cassandra had been too fixated on Grayson, too absorbed in the possibility of her brother's demise, to fully appreciate anything else.

As they weaved through the town, crowds cheered from behind barriers, each carrying flags representing different nations. Cassandra attempted to take in the surroundings, to absorb the town's charm— the wooden homes and shops lining the streets, the sound of children's laughter and adults' smiles, and nearly everyone dressed in shades of beige, white, and brown. Yet her focus remained on what steps to take next, how to rescue her brother and bring him back home.

After passing through the town, Sebastian maintained his lead with long, graceful strides. Cassandra made an effort to keep up, but Augustus and Benjamin had fallen too far behind, leaving her an opening. As she picked up her pace and caught up to Sebastian, she called out his name.

"What?" he responded, not missing a beat in his steps.

Cassandra pondered, "What do we do now that we know who the Mountmonts truly are? What is our plan?"

Sebastian scoffed. "For now, I will focus on winning this race, while you try not to get in my way."

Cassandra furrowed her brows, puzzled. "Why the sudden change in attitude? Just a few hours ago, you were by my side helping me."

"I was being polite."

"Does being polite include pressing someone against a tree for a kiss?"

Sebastian scoffed. "You are proving to be a distraction from my goal. Why jeopardise my chances because of a girl?"

"It is not my fault you're constantly distracted by me," she retorted with a smirk on her face. However, Sebastian rolled his eyes and carried forward, leaving the conversation to die.

As the minutes went by, the two engaged in a spirited race against each other, challenging the other down the path marked by white flags. However, during these sudden sprints towards the edge of the Forest Lands, Cassandra could not shake the feeling of being watched from beyond the forest grounds. She looked up, almost assuring herself that the Sky Box was there. To her relief it was and her father sat with a wide smile on his face, almost instantly calming her down. It was then that she heard ruffles of movement. She turned her head and glimpsed a figure moving as swiftly as she was, his body becoming a blur as he darted behind the trees and then disappeared altogether.

"Did you see that?" Cassandra inquired to Sebastian, who scanned their surroundings. When he shook his head, she felt it crucial to draw nearer to him, seeking a measure of protection in case something was to occur. Initially, Cassandra considered it might have been a product of her imagination, but she sensed it was more than that. As they progressed, they swiftly arrived at the base of the mountain.

Sebastian was quick to use his daggered arms, their razor-sharp edges gripping onto the uneven surface of the mountainside, propelling him upward with remarkable agility. Cassandra, amused, could not help but stifle a laugh as she swiftly activated her grappling hook. Its metallic hum resonates against the rugged terrain. Approaching footsteps heralded Augustus's arrival, his breathless greeting falling on Cassandra's ears just as Sebastian commenced his ascent. Augustus pressed a sequence of buttons on his forearm, triggering a propeller once more from his air tank. As if summoned by his actions, handholds promptly materialised prepared to guide him up the mountainside.

Taking this as her cue, Cassandra expertly launched her grappling hook, its metallic arc slicing through the air as she began her climb. Benjamin, not to be outdone, swiftly followed suit, activating his robotic arms. Their metallic fingers gripped onto the mountain's edge, seamlessly hauling him upward. Together, the four embarked on their upward journey, each determined to step closer to the top and win the triathlon.

However, just as their ascent gained momentum, an arrow streaked down towards Cassandra, sending her into a panicked scream as she skilfully dodged its deadly path. All four competitors instinctively redirected their gaze upward to the mountain's peak, where the ominous silhouette of a figure emerged, clad entirely in black leather, with a mask covering half of their face. The mysterious figure wielded a taunt bow, one that caught Cassandra's eyes. She had a suspicion about the figure's identity, but she remained quiet and in denial. She tried to tell herself otherwise, that it was not him, but as he pulled three more arrows from his chest, Cassandra swore.

She had to move forward. Proceeding up the mountain, she dodged each arrow, twirling and jumping, ultimately downing that she could do nothing else but reach the top. The Princes were ahead of her now, but all of that changed when an arrow sliced through the rope of her grappling hook. Her eyes widened as she watched the rope break in half, feeling her body be dragged down by gravity.

Letting out a loud scream, she braced herself for the impact of the hard ground, but she was swept to safety just in time. Two massive iron claws, operated by Benjamin, cradled her body and whisked her away from the danger.

His eyes wide with panic, Benjamin glanced from Cassandra to the enigmatic figure perched atop the mountain. "Who is he?"

Augustus wasted no time in chiming in. "Could it be Grayson?"

Sebastian said nothing as his eyes remained on Cassandra, who muttered, "I think I'm going to be nauseous."

"But how can we be certain it's him? What if it is one of the Mountmont brothers?" Sebastian joined in, posture relaxed against the mountain's edge.

Augustus's curiosity manifested in furrowed brows. "What connection would they have to Grayson?"

Sebastian subtly nodded in Cassandra's direction. "She figured it out. I was merely trying to get her to stop crying."

Cassandra scoffed, folding her arms defensively. "I was not crying."

Benjamin looked around, bewildered by the ongoing discussion, but the conversation abruptly ceased as another volley of arrows descended upon them. Sebastian reacted by hurling two daggers, aiming to time them to intercept the man.

Augustus was determined to fly up and identify the figure. With most of the royals lacking weapons to retaliate, their situation quickly devolved into a defensive struggle to evade the deadly arrows. They skilfully navigated through the barrage, advancing toward the top.

CHAPTER 21

Cassandra sprang from Benjamin's claw-like grip and lunged at the leather-clad figure. He aimed his bow but she quickly dodged the shot. She activated her new weapon, using the rope of her grappling hook to her advantage. The rope became a whip, striking the man and deflecting his incoming arrows. Benjamin swiftly joined her, utilising his claw-like hands to wrest the bow from the man's grasp. Cassandra and Benjamin worked together as Sebastian used his enhancements in a hand-to-hand combat with the man.

The chaotic scene escalated further as, from the corner of her eye, Cassandra observed Augustus positioning himself just beside her, body slightly tilting forwards, his face filled with sorrow, as he uttered, "I'm sorry, but I need to win this challenge for my brother."

With that, he sprinted towards the small podium at the opposite end of the mountaintop and planted his green flag in the stand. A small trumpet sounded, signalling the claim of the first-place marker. The three other competitors started in shock, providing the man an opportunity to launch arrows at them. Cassandra gasped loudly as she ducked, feeling a sting on her ear. Touching the tip, she glanced down at her finger to find blood; the man had grazed her. Looking up, she observed Benjamin and Sebastian running towards the podium.

Not wanting them to win, Cassandra swiftly rose in motion and ran after them. Arrows flew in her direction as she ducked. When she ran beside Sebastian, she sensed a winning chance. However, the man quickly jumped in front of the three and unleashed more arrows in her direction. Sebastian grabbed Cassandra and threw them both to the ground, using his body as a shield. Arrows whizzed over their heads as Benjamin utilised his claw-like extension to place his flag on the stand, securing second place.

Amongst the chaos, Augustus positioned himself behind the figure clad in leather, chainsaw at the ready. Its blades buzzed fiercely, creating a deafening cacophony that nearly overwhelmed Cassandra's senses. She could not fathom why he had chosen to intervene at this moment. He had already won the challenge; why persist in the fight?

Sebastian firmly gripped Cassandra's arm, rolling her beneath him to prevent another arrow from hitting her. "You need to be more careful," he advised.

A brief blush crossed her face, relishing the closeness for a moment before Benjamin grabbed the man's leg, pulling him away from the two.

"We worry about the competition later," Sebastian instructed her. "Right now, we focus on the attacker."

As the two stood, the group of young royals initiated their attacks on the man. Benjamin and Augustus worked in tandem, distracting him while Sebastian took a moment to silently analyse the unfolding situation. Understanding that the two Princes would serve as ample distraction, Sebastian saw an opportunity to approach unnoticed.

Seizing this chance, Cassandra glanced up at the Sky Box, witnessing panic ripple through the Kings and Queens as they stood from their seats. Her father pounded his hands against the protective glass, and King Constantine resorted to kicking at the pilot's door. The other two Kings stood behind the Mountmonts, their attachments activated, while Charlotte held her whip at the ready, pointing towards the Mountmont brothers. This clear gesture communicated who they were and what they were planning. Amidst the chaos, the Mountmonts remained seated, their hidden smiles betraying their glee as they peered down at Cassandra.

A grunt was heard by the man as Sebastian took his final soft steps, launching himself onto the figure's back. However, the man proved quick as his reflexes alerted Sebastian's presence. Grabbing Sebastian by the throat, he threw him onto Augustus and the two tumbled back, bodies edging the top of the mountain. Yet the outcome was inconsequential, for in Sebastian's hands, the figure's mask revealed a sight that sent shockwaves through their bodies.

A sinking sensation enveloped Cassandra as she shoved Benjamin aside, her focus unwavering on the unmasked man.

Grayson stood with a scowl etched on his face. Their eyes locked on Cassandra, who was observing in an eerie slow-motion as he advanced. However, Benjamin swiftly stepped forward, almost forming a protective barrier in front of Cassandra.

Without hesitation, her brother pressed forward, extracting arrows from his chest, yet it was Sebastian who interposed himself in Grayson's path. Shurikens glided between the Spade Prince's fingers as he directed them toward Grayson. Her brother adeptly sidestepped each blade aimed at him. However, the relentless onslaught of shurikens obscured Grayson's view of the assassin. He failed to notice Sebastian's swift escape as he slid towards Grayson, hurling two shurikens directly at his head. In a deft move, her brother caught them and promptly threw them down toward Sebastian. The shurikens grazed past Sebastian's head as he seized Grayson's ankle, tackling him to the ground. With a new blade at Grayson's throat, Sebastian struggled to keep him subdued.

In that brief moment of advantage, Cassandra seized the opportunity to interrogate Grayson. "Why did the Mountmonts do this to you?"

Her brother promptly shoved Sebastian away, positioning the assassin beneath him with his hand and dagger pressed against Sebastian's throat. "I am destined to be the perfect human. The flawless amalgamation of steam power and humanity. I am to embody mechanical perfection!"

Cassandra staggered on her footing as she reflected on her conversation with the Mountmonts. Her head spun and this singular phrase proved to be all the confirmation she required. When she looked back up at the Sky Box, she observed an unexpected altercation unfolding. The Queens stood poised and prepared, while the Kings pushed through the barrier on the blimp. It was then that Cassandra gasped, witnessing the Mountmonts as the adversaries against whom the Queens and her friends were in battle. Charlotte used her metal whip to her full advantage, launching it toward each brother, making sure to snip both of them. Their grinning faces stretched widely and unnaturally. The individuals in the Sky Box were well aware that the Mountmonts were responsible, as evidenced by the fact that they would not be engaged in combat with them otherwise.

Abruptly, an alarm blared, signalling the last five minutes of the challenge. Cassandra felt the flag in her pocket, eyes turning from Sebastian to the podium. He had instructed her that the challenge would only be an issue later on, knowing that the attacker was much too important. Panic seized through her and she screamed as her ponytail was gripped tightly. Grayson twirled the hair in his hand before launching Cassandra across the ground, her back hitting the small stand. Seizing the opportunity, Sebastian reached for two more shurikens and embedded them deeply into Grayson's chest. The grating sound of metal against metal indicated the formidable protection at the front of her brother.

Cassandra groaned loudly, back and head in pain as she rolled onto her side. She watched in a haze as the boys fought against Grayson, one attack after the next, and not stopping until she was up and prepared to fight again. Unfazed by the pain, Grayson extracted the two throwing stars from his chest, prompting Cassandra to notice the small dent in his chest. Unhesitatingly, he sneered down at Sebastian, who attempted to slip out of her brother's hold. Grayson swiftly thrust one shuriken deep into Sebastian's shoulder, while the other lodged into his left bicep, rendering his attachment on that arm inoperable. The blades cut deeply, eliciting a grunt of pain from Sebastian. It was at that moment that Cassandra decided what to do next. She knew that Grayson would only stop his fighting for a split second due to loud noises.

With that, Cassandra placed her red flag just beside Benjamin's golden flag, signalling another jarring alarm to be triggered, demonstrating that it was the end of the triathlon.

Cassandra acted swiftly after that, employing the rope as a whip to lash Grayson's back and ensnare him. Her brother turned slowly, his eyes ablaze with intensity, his bowed arm poised for an imminent attack. Benjamin pulled Cassandra's waist with his claws to the other end of the mountain top. Her brother's piercing gaze followed them. Benjamin moved swiftly, his robotic arms executing rapid motions in an attempt to seize Grayson. Yet her brother proved nimble, managing to grasp one of Benjamin's arms. Despite Benjamin's efforts to free his arm, her brother effortlessly crushed it with his hand. Benjamin grunted in response to the unexpected strength displayed by Grayson. Sensing an opportune moment, Cassandra wielded her rope, tightly wrapping it around her brother.

"You're going nowhere," she grunted as her brother struggled to rip at the tightly-wound ropes. Glancing upward, she smiled as her father and the other Kings landed atop the mountain, weapons at the ready.

Grayson remained silent, his dishevelled hair framing his face as he strained against the tight bonds. However, as if responding to an inaudible cue, Grayson began to scream, exerting immense force to tear the ropes apart. Cassandra struggled, finding his relentless efforts too much to handle, causing the ropes to snap and sending her—along with the tattered remains of the bindings—to the ground.

Her brother swiftly pulled arrows from his chest, aiming them squarely at Cassandra. However, her father intervened, launching a fish knife at his son and shielding his daughter. The knife struck Grayson's thigh, prompting him to groan and stumble slightly. Cassandra's wide-eyed gaze fixed upon her father, struggling to believe that he had finally laid eyes on Grayson since he was taken. A rush of guilt and pity washed over her, realising she should have told her father sooner, regretting her previous fear. Her father froze, a sense of realization taking over as he saw that his son was the unfamiliar figure.

"That is enough!" her father roared. Grayson pulled at the knife, his eyes entranced by the sharp ends. "Lower the bow, son." He positioned himself protectively in front of Cassandra. Augustus swiftly pulled her back, her concern for him and Benjamin evident as she focused solely on what was about to transpire with her brother.

The other two Kings swiftly converged around Grayson, forming a protective circle. King Constantine took his place beside her father, his spiked steel ball flail poised, as if ready to strike at a moment's notice. His right metallic hand was clenched into a fist, prepared for combat. King Albert positioned himself behind Grayson, his gleaming golden hammer catching the sunlight. He too stood prepared for a confrontation. However, King Kenji's whereabouts remained a mystery to Cassandra, as he was conspicuously absent.

As Grayson tried to move forward, a dagger landed just in front of him, as another pierced his thigh. Her brother grunted as he pulled the blade from his skin and threw it to the side. Kenji quickly appeared on the mountaintop, accompanied by Sebastian. A lengthy, flexible metal whip wrapped around Grayson's metallic chest, its sharp edges grazed his shoulders, temporarily impeding his mobility.

In a matter of moments, Grayson wrestled free from the constricting whip and launched arrows at Jaronas. Arrows whizzed in all directions, Grayson making note to keep the Kings at a distance. Cassandra understood that her brother's strength was long-range shooting and that did not change, as whenever a King stepped too close, he released an arrow. Her father wasted no time in responding; he raised his spear and squared off against his own son. He grappled with the moral dilemma of the situation, fully aware that he could not bring harm to his own flesh and blood. However, an unsettling realisation struck him—the scars inflicted in this battle could heal, wounds could be repaired, and for some inexplicable reason, Jaronas understood that the figure before him was no longer the child he had raised.

"Step aside," Constantine advised the young royals. "You do not want to be caught in the crossfire."

Cassandra heeded the warning and retreated a few paces with the others, ready to activate their enhancements if necessary. Grayson assumed his position on the mountain's edge, his intentions becoming apparent. The elevated vantage point offered him an advantage, as it allowed him to oversee the approaching Kings. This emphasised his strategy of maintaining distance and underscored his recognition of being outmatched in a direct confrontation. Constantine swung his spiked steel ball flail with such force that it hurtled toward Grayson's bow. Her brother deftly sidestepped the projectile and observed as the ball flail recoiled. Cassandra marvelled at the remarkable distance the weapon covered, making it nearly impossible to evade. Meanwhile, Grayson continued his relentless barrage of arrows, specifically targeting Albert and Jaronas, recognizing their expertise in close combat. Kenji wasted no time, hurling daggers at Grayson while expertly avoiding the incoming arrows. The air was filled with the whooshing of arrows and the exasperated sighs of the Kings.

Albert, growing increasingly frustrated at being unable to close the distance to Grayson, swatted away the arrows targeting him as he activated his enhancement. In contrast, Jaronas, still somewhat in shock at the unfolding chaos, held back his unique weapon, using it only as a last resort.

Augustus, sensing the urgency, said, "We cannot just stand here. We need to assist."

Sebastian, however, responded with a roll of his eyes. "We were instructed to stay put. It's usually safer to be the backup rather than the primary target."

Cassandra observed as Albert's extensions nimbly weaved through the flurry of arrows, closing the distance to Grayson. His claw-like attachments extended in an attempt to seize Grayson's mechanical bow. Constantine joined the advance, stepping forward and launching his flail ball, focusing on the mechanical bow as his target. However, it was evident that Constantine intent was not to harm her brother but to dismantle the bow, effectively disarming Grayson.

However, what the two Kings failed to realise was that Grayson had anticipated their sudden shift in determination. In a swift move, he latched onto Albert's claw, his fingers coiling around the claw's throat. Simultaneously, he did the same with the ball flail. The Kings struggled to retract their enhancements, attempting to pull Grayson with them. Her brother battled to maintain a grip on both enhancements, his heels digging into the ground as the Kings slowly dragged him towards the mountain's edge.

When he was halfway down, Grayson released his grasp on the flail ball, causing Constantine to tumble backward, his own weight insufficient to prevent the fall. He landed near the edge of the mountain, clutching the ground with his left hand to steady himself. Albert continued to pull harder, compelling Grayson to follow him. Her brother's hold remained firm on the enhancement, propelling Albert towards Constantine. Grayson then exhaled heavily, doubling over and placing his hands on his knees.

Albert's robotic enhancement clung to the mountainside as both he and Constantine tumbled over the edge. Benjamin stared in shock at the harrowing sight, unsure of what to do. Meanwhile, Augustus wasted no time; he dashed towards Grayson, while Benjamin rushed towards the two fallen Kings. Cassandra accompanied Benjamin, helping Constantine to his feet as Albert managed to rise on his own. The other Kings shouted at Augustus to stop and Grayson continued to rain arrows down on the older royals.

However, he allowed Augustus to approach within a few feet before launching an arrow that pierced Augustus' collarbone, causing him to stagger backward. Despite the onslaught of arrows, Augustus pressed on, his chainsaw roaring to life as he launched an all-out offensive against Grayson, who moved with eerie agility. Unlike his earlier sloppy shots, Grayson now seemed prepared, as if he had anticipated what was to come.

Amidst their intense battle, Grayson managed to land a powerful punch on Augustus's face, causing him to emit a deep, painful groan as he stumbled. In a matter of seconds, Grayson swiftly swept his leg beneath Augustus, sending him tumbling over the edge toward the rest of the group. Cassandra rushed to his side, assessing his injuries. His eye and nose were now bloodied, and the arrow had penetrated his flesh even further.

Without hesitation, Sebastian and Benjamin sprang into action, disregarding the Kings' demands to stop. However, Grayson made sure to keep the older men at bay by continuously launching arrows in their direction. Meanwhile, the assassin hurled dagger after dagger at Grayson, attempting to wound him. Benjamin used his extendable arm to thrust into Grayson's side, aiming to pluck the bow from his mechanical arm.

Cassandra gently pulled Augustus closer, her delicate fingers gripping the arrow deeply lodged in his collarbone. A pained groan escaped him as she contemplated ways to staunch the bleeding. She swiftly extricated Augustus from the intense skirmish, tearing a piece of her jersey to apply as a makeshift bandage for his injured eye. Her father remained by her side, eager to provide assistance, but Cassandra gently pushed him away.

"Father, please," she implored, her tone filled with determination. "Go and stop Grayson. I will manage here." Part of her hoped that the Sky Box would contain some sort of medical kit, as she knew her jersey would not be enough.

As she glanced upward, the ground violently shook, causing the Kings and Princes to sway unsteadily. Her gaze darted over her shoulder, where a massive explosion had erupted, sending dark smoke billowing into the sky, illuminated by fiery reds and oranges. Cassandra quickly surveyed the scene, her heart sinking as she spotted the Mountmont brothers revelling in their victory, while the Queens and Charlotte appeared defeated. Without wasting a moment, she turned to King Albert and Constantine, who were making their way toward her.

"You need to head to the Sky Box! There was some kind of explosion and the Mountmonts may be involved!" She urgently gestured towards the jubilant smiles of the brothers.

King Albert swiftly extended his claw toward the small platform that typically facilitated the Kings' descent from the blimp. King

Constantine, without hesitation, grasped his companion's arm, and in unison they propelled toward the Sky Box, determined to chase down the Mountmont brothers. Meanwhile, Jaronas positioned himself in front of his daughter, his eyes reflecting his admiration for the person she had become. Kenji, who had arrived at his side, pondered whether he should join the pursuit.

"Do as you see fit. I will stay here to confront my son," her father stated, turning his gaze toward Grayson, who was currently embroiled in a heated confrontation with Sebastian and Benjamin.

Kenji nodded in agreement and remained by Jaronas's side, readying his weapons. "Then I shall stand with you to face him as well."

Sebastian, still standing his ground against Grayson, bore the marks of a brutal struggle, his body displaying visible bruises and bloodied wounds. Benjamin persisted in his efforts to get closer to Grayson, snapping his claw whenever he could to intercept the arrows that incessantly flew from Grayson's bow. Sebastian managed to maintain a much closer proximity to her brother than Benjamin, raising questions about his tactics. He allowed the young royals to remain in such close quarters, but kept a constant distance from the older Kings.

Cassandra could not help but wonder about the relative strength of the Kings compared to Grayson and just how powerful her brother truly was in contrast to the young royals. Lost in her thoughts, she observed Grayson releasing arrow after arrow, primarily targeting Benjamin and the two Kings. His focus seemed intent on keeping Sebastian close, perhaps aiming to drain the assassin's strength.

In a disheartening turn of events, Sebastian's once lightning-quick movements dramatically slowed, eliciting a horrified scream from Cassandra. The shocking transformation continued as Grayson managed to catch the dagger that had been hurled towards his head and swiftly retaliated with an arrow that Sebastian barely managed to dodge. However, the unexpected dagger strike landed, its blade plunging deep into the assassin's chest. Sebastian paused, an expression of shock etched across his face as he locked eyes with Cassandra.

Grayson took measured steps towards him while Kenji screamed and hurled dagger after dagger, and Benjamin made a desperate dash to reach Sebastian. But their efforts were in vain as her brother seized Sebastian by the collar and hurled him over the mountainside.

"Sebastian!" Cassandra's anguished cry pierced the air and it felt as though time had momentarily frozen while her heart skipped a beat. Tears welled up in her eyes as she scrambled to her feet and sprinted toward the edge.

Kenji followed closely behind; their gazes locked on Sebastian's falling form. But at that critical moment, five claws extended gently, forming a protective cradle to catch the falling assassin. Benjamin successfully rescued Sebastian, utilising his single extension to support the assassin's body. The roar of engines resonated through the Mountain Region as the Sky Box gradually descended, finally landing at the mountain's base. Gently, Benjamin placed Sebastian before Cassandra and Kenji.

She expressed her gratitude with a nod and Benjamin reciprocated, recognizing the significance of the act. It was a gesture of saving a friend, transcending the boundaries of competition.

King Albert soon joined Kenji's side, inquiring about the cause of the explosion. "There was a bomb detonated in the Arena. More than half of the spectators have been injured and the Mountmonts managed to escape us. They are incredibly cunning."

"It's unfathomable that two individuals could outwit the Kings," Cassandra grumbled, her eyes narrowing as she turned to face him. "How is that even possible?"

Albert shifted his gaze from Augustus to Sebastian, his concern evident. "Cassandra, this is not the time for discussion. Right now, our priority is to gather the injured and return to the Arena. Your safety is a priority."

Kenji glanced over the edge to check on the Queens, specifically his wife. "What about the Queens?"

"They're planning to go back to the Arena to assist at the Recovery Tent," Albert informed him, and Kenji nodded in agreement. As Albert held Augustus and Benjamin cradled Sebastian, they began their descent down the mountain. Benjamin returned, this time with Charlotte following behind.

Benjamin turned to Charlotte. "Would you like to join us, or do you prefer to stay here?"

Cassandra's gaze turned to her father, who battled with evident frustration. Amidst the emotional whirlwind he was caught in, he had no choice but to stand his ground, defending himself and ensuring the safety of the other Kings and Princes. He confronted Grayson in a bitter father-son duel, their weapons clashing as the weight of their duty hung heavily in the air. Jaronas's anguish was unmistakable, but he was fully aware of the obligation that needed to be fulfilled.

Cassandra shook her head and faced Benjamin. "No, you head back to the Arena. This is something I need to do with my father."

Benjamin nodded and departed, leaving Cassandra behind. "Someone has to ensure your safe return," Charlotte commented with a smirk.

Charlotte's intentions weren't the sole acts of the heart, as Kenji also chose to stay with Jaronas. He joined the fray against Grayson, who quickly shifted his fighting style to a more defensive stance. Arrows flew from his bow as he tried to fend off the two challengers.

Within seconds, the Princesses entered the fray.

As a continuous barrage of arrows fell upon them, Cassandra took the initiative, growing weary of the distance Grayson had maintained. With determination in her eyes, she charged towards her brother, who held his ground at the mountain's edge. As he released four arrows in her direction, Cassandra adeptly dodged each one. With swift grace, she slid between his legs, executing an old move she had often used during their defensive training back on the Heart Lot Island. This manoeuvre, which she had perfected over time, had always proven challenging for her brother to counter. Cassandra's intuition proved accurate, as she now replicated the same tactic with the same results. She landed behind her brother and quickly leaped onto his back.

Her arms coiled around his neck in a desperate attempt to halt his destructive rampage. Kenji managed to sweep Grayson's feet from under him, causing him to tumble to the ground. In the process, Cassandra fell with him but remained steadfast, clinging to her brother in an effort to reach the vestiges of his humanity.

Just as Grayson lifted his body and slammed it down to the ground, Charlotte came to the rescue. She grabbed his ankles with her iron claw, dragging him away from Cassandra and hurling him against the small podium stand for the flags. The wood crumpled under his impact, and Cassandra breathed out a thankful acknowledgment to Charlotte.

"Grayson!" her father shouted. "You need to stop this foolishness and come back to camp!"

Grayson slowly lifted himself up, his body tense as he spat out blood, and a twisted smile formed on his face. Teeth stained red made Cassandra feel queasy. Kenji, displaying agility on par with Sebastian's, swiftly manoeuvred around Grayson. Jaronas launched another knife at his son, who deftly dodged it and sprinted, focusing on his father.

Without hesitation, her father joined forces with Kenji, pushing against Grayson's arrows. Charlotte and Cassandra lent their assistance, throwing in their whips, and together, they began to gain ground against Grayson's quick movements and throws. They managed to push him to the edge of the mountain when suddenly a whistle blew, resembling the sound of a human calling for their dog.

In mere moments, Grayson ceased his combat, his gaze locked onto the sound originating from his right. He started to retreat. Cassandra stood in astonishment as engines materialised on the backs of his calves, seemingly poised to propel him from the mountaintop.

"Grayson!" Cassandra's scream echoed after her brother. "Don't you dare!"

She pulled at his shoulders, desperately attempting to halt his progress, but he pushed her away, resolute in his advance. Charlotte attempted to intervene by wrapping her whip around his torso, but the effort only resulted in both of them sliding along the ground. Heels dug into the earth as Charlotte tried to anchor herself, yet the force prevailed. Meanwhile, Kenji hurled an iron whip, swiftly seized by Grayson, who promptly threw it back at the Spade City King. Undeterred, Kenji threw another, successfully ensnaring Grayson's ankles and causing him to fall once more.

Charlotte relinquished her grip on Grayson, joining Kenji in their efforts to pull him away. However, Grayson retaliated by viciously grabbing Charlotte, hurling her to the side. Her head made a harsh impact with the ground, her arm becoming scratched and blood beginning to trickle slightly from her nose. Kenji, too, faced Grayson's wrath, as he was seized by the collar, hands wrapping tightly around his throat.

Her father, witnessing the perilous situation, launched a final knife at his son's arm, the sharp end sinking deep into the skin. Grayson released Kenji to the ground, redirecting his focus to his sister and father. Another whistle sounded, causing Grayson to turn his head slightly toward the noise.

Seizing the opportunity, Cassandra jumped onto her brother's back, wrapping her arms around his neck once more. She attempted to use her rope to her advantage, pressing it deeply against his throat to cut off circulation. However, in a powerful motion, Grayson grabbed the back of her head and flung her to the ground. Her head collided with the unforgiving rocky surface, pain surging through Cassandra as she felt blood pooling on the side of her head. Her vision blurred as she observed her brother and father continue their struggle, witnessing Grayson land a hard punch to the side of their father's face.

Gradually, she observed him departing from the mountain's summit, disappearing into the shadows with only the engine's billowing smoke as a trace.

CHAPTER 22

Several hours had passed since Cassandra regained consciousness. Whispers resonated in subdued murmurs throughout the room, and as she gradually reopened her eyes, Cassandra noticed the stir of conversation. She found herself in a small medical bed, her head swathed in gauze, a hint of dried blood still lingering in her hair.

"I won for my brother—I had to. You understand that, right?" Augustus said, worry and panic lingered in his words.

"I understand, my dear. Do not worry." Charlotte responded, back turned to Cassandra as she perched on the edge of Augustus' bed.

"Do you think Cassandra and Sebastian will forgive me?"

Charlotte chuckled lightly. "It is as if you forgot about the Triumph Games entirely."

"You know it has never been an ideal of mine. Just one of my brother's and father- but mainly for my brother–this win was for them."

It was quiet for a few more moments before Charlotte inquired, "Are you feeling alright?" Cassandra was taken aback, a sense of shock coursing through her, as she could not fathom how the Diamond Kingdom Princess found herself beside her kingdom's enemy, their hands intertwined. "Are you experiencing any pain?" Her slender, fair fingers gently grazed the wounded area around Augustus' eye.

Augustus wore a faint smile, brushing a strand of his golden hair away from Charlotte's face. "I am perfectly fine, darling," he assured her.

Cassandra was bewildered by what she had missed, unable to comprehend how these two had seemingly developed a bond and begun using pet names. She blinked repeatedly, convincing herself that it was a figment of her imagination as she witnessed Charlotte lean down and plant a kiss on the top of Augustus' head. "Let me know if you require anything. I'll return once Cassandra wakes up."

Too concerned about disrupting their intimate moment, Cassandra observed as Augustus pressed a kiss on the top of Charlotte's hand, muttering something softly as he watched her depart. It was at that moment that Cassandra noticed that Charlotte wiped away a few stray tears before glancing back at Augustus and then leaving.

After a few moments, Cassandra believed it was time for her to sit up.

Gazing at her surrounding shock settled in—she was in the Recovery Tent. It contained a total of twelve beds, now holding only her, Sebastian, and Augustus.

Augustus had been the first to rouse from the effects of the amnesia-inducing dose the doctors had administered to aid in his eye's healing.

Cassandra followed, waking up a few hours after Augustus's operation. However, Sebastian remained unresponsive, his inert form occupying his bed, eyes closed, and breathing shallow. Machines and medical equipment enveloped Sebastian. She had overheard hushed conversations between the doctors. The blade that had pierced him had damaged the gears on his chest, crucial to his breathing.

Additionally, it had punctured a vein near Sebastian's heart, leaving a fragment of the dagger's steel embedded within him. The mere thought of never seeing him again made Cassandra queasy. His smell, his smirks, and smiles, his eyes always following her. Despite his annoying and cocky demeanour, she couldn't help but worry about his well being and wanting nothing more than for him to be safe and healthy.

Her thoughts came to an abrupt halt as the radio emitted a faint scratching sound, interrupting the soft music that had been playing. Augustus and Cassandra exchanged a quizzical look, their attention drawn to the radio. "You both performed exceptionally well today," Charlie's voice emanated from the radio. "We had every confidence in your ability to achieve great things in the triathlon."

In the near-empty Recovery Tent, save for the three injured competitors, a chill ran down Cassandra's spine. She wondered how they had managed to use the radio to communicate with her and how they knew she was in the tent. Since their disappearance, the camp had been on complete lockdown, maintaining high alert.

Thomas chuckled with a voice reminiscent of a hyena. "However, our master is not happy. He is quite furious at how quickly you are recovering. Things are about to become more challenging in the next round. New rules have been implemented."

Cassandra widened her eyes. *Master?* Someone is telling them to behave in such a way.

"I'm not one to shy away from a challenge." Augustus sat up, his bruised and bloodied eye narrowing.

"In that case, I suggest you grasp the patterns swiftly before it becomes too late," Thomas responded. "Our leader has a surprise for you two." Cassandra's eyes widened in shock; they were able to hear her. Augustus, too, looked between her and the radio, trying to make sense of what had happened.

"Which is it? Master or leader?" she found herself saying.

Their giggle made her skin crawl. "Does it really matter?" Charlie said.

"How about you just get lost and crawl back into the hole you came from?" Augustus retorted, testing to see if there was some sort of wire connected. His eyes searched the room, his mind racing.

Charlie chuckled. "Look who got his confidence back."

"Why did your *leader* take my brother?" Cassandra asked, her mind running. "Out of everyone here, why him?"

"Oh, don't act like you don't know, Princess," Thomas replied. "You've already pieced it all together."

"So, I was right. You took him to turn him into a superior human?"

Charlie clicked his tongue. "Not exactly, my dear. We had orders and we followed them through. Your brother is an example, a lab rat, if you will. A way to show the world that someone with few extensions could be transformed into something great. The perfect mechanical being."

"Lab rat! You are subjecting him to tests and experiments for fun? How could you do that to a person?" Cassandra felt defeated, her head spinning, wanting to cry and begging for everything not to be true. She refused to believe what was happening.

Unfortunately, it was true and Thomas was the first to reply, causing Cassandra to freeze. "Oh, we can't just give that type of information away so easily. Everything must come with a price."

"What kind of price?" she inquired cautiously, Augustus soon pointing towards a wire that was attached to the back of their beds, indicating how the Mountmonts were listening.

"Our leader would like to know why your brother's brain is so impervious that no programmed information could fully penetrate it!" Charlie stated rapidly.

"Your brother is not fully developed," Thomas cut in, his dark brown eyes narrowing on her. "There are a few things that need to be taken care of."

She scoffed. "How is this my issue?"

"Is he not your brother? The person you have been trying to get back from us?" Thomas replied. "It is quite easy, you help us, and—"

She had heard enough. Cassandra wanted nothing more of this conversation. "You will not try to threaten me! Tell your master or leader or whatever you call him that I will not help you use my brother as leverage to some sick and twisted experiment. I know it will be used against me as motivation for you to achieve what you want. However, I will get my brother back, and when I do, you will both pay for it." Cassandra let out a determined breath. "And that is a promise."

Charlie chuckled after a few moments of silence, seemingly finding her statement hilarious. "Your brother is set to become the poster child for a groundbreaking experiment, a new era of technology, showcasing how enhanced humans can be further upgraded."

"Their vitals, their programming, their extensions, and existence could all be doubled in capacity," Thomas added. "This, your brother, is being used to help us. It's all in the name of science. People will flock to us once they witness Grayson and we will be the new pioneers, no longer in the shadow of our father and his outdated extensions and experiments. It will be us, and our cutting-edge products."

Cassandra blinked in confusion, struggling to grasp the full meaning of their words. In contrast, Augustus gasped, as if the gravity of the situation had finally dawned on him. "It cannot be..." he mumbled.

Charlie chuckled. "Ah, so you do remember who our father was."

"Your father was responsible for escalating the war," Augustus muttered bitterly. "He created enhancements for the human body solely for profit, using my lands, my home, as the base for his underground enterprise! And now, you stand here ready to rub it in my face?"

"I really could not care less," Charlie expressed. "Well, we will leave you to recover and inform our leader of your poorly-chosen words."

With that, the radio scratched once more, and soft music began to play. Cassandra quickly felt a knot in her stomach, replaying the conversation in her head as she questioned what the Mountmonts had in store.

After the Mountmonts' radio conversation, her father entered the Recovery Tent, along with Constantine and Morana. Jaronas appeared stern, his eyes narrowing at his daughter as he inquired about her wellbeing, confirming with the nurse, who had also entered the tent, whether Cassandra was ready to leave. She anticipated what was coming next, her gaze shifting hopefully to Augustus, who was surrounded by his own parents, and then to Sebastian, who remained still in his bed, fast asleep.

"Charlotte explained what happened," her father stated as he returned to her bedside, his figure imposing. "She informed us that you and the other youngsters have been wandering around in the underground tunnels. You knew where your brother was, you knew who did this to him, and you chose not to tell me, not to inform the other adults," her father voiced his displeasure with sudden sternness.

Cassandra sat in silence; her head hung low, fully aware that her actions had been wrong. She knew she needed to provide her father with a proper explanation, and so she prepared herself to do just that.

"Why would you keep such a thing from me?" he inquired, his tone laced with frustration.

Cassandra attempted to respond, her mouth opening, but she found herself unable to articulate a valid reason. Her mind drew a blank because there truly was no valid justification for her actions.

She opted to stick with the truth, as she should have done from the outset. "I intended to tell you, I truly did," she began. "Sebastian and the others advised me that it was the right thing to do."

Her father's voice rose slightly as he retorted, "Yes, and somehow you didn't!" His raised voice drew the attention of the Clubs and nurses in the vicinity, but Jaronas was too irate to care about the onlookers. "Explain everything to me—how you first saw him, where it was, provide me with every single detail, without omitting a thing."

Cassandra complied, taking the next hour or so to recount the events that had unfolded since her brother's disappearance. She began by detailing the discovery of the cloth and then proceeded to the initial confrontation with Augustus, followed by her encounter with Sebastian. She provided insights into the hidden passages, the bunker, and the laboratory. Her narrative continued, covering the most recent developments where they had deduced that the Mountmonts were responsible for Grayson's abduction. Cassandra explained the Mountmonts' plans for her brother and their realisation that if they returned to the Mountmont Mansion in the Mountain Region, they could effectively rescue Grayson without the fear of being caught or rushing to save him before being discovered. As she spoke, her father's fury intensified, his eyes narrowing in anger as they bore into his daughter.

When Cassandra finished her story, and her breath steadied, Jaronas turned his gaze to the Club King, who simply nodded in agreement. King Constantine left the Recovery Tent and returned with Albert and his children, as well as Kenji and Suzume. Benjamin and Charlotte were guided to the beds next to Cassandra, while the older royals maintained an ominous silence. Jaronas, ensuring his words were unambiguous, spoke on behalf of all the elder royals.

"From this point forward," her father declared, his voice resolute, "you are on lockdown. None of you," he stated, turning toward the children throughout the room, "are permitted to leave this tent until further notice. We will have guards stationed around this tent, and the only individuals allowed to exit will be the nurses and us. Even when you are well and able to leave, you will remain here. Food will be brought to you, and a guard will accompany you to the washroom. If, at any point, we discover that any of you have left..." His gaze honed in on his daughter, well aware she might be the first to attempt an escape. "You will be disqualified from this tournament and immediately sent back to your respective nations. Your parents will then decide what steps to take."

Augustus's eyes widened and Benjamin let out a scoff. "This is unjust!" Benjamin protested, rising to his feet. "I have not done anything wrong! I only found out about it after they did. How am I being penalised for information I had no knowledge of?"

Jaronas shifted his attention to the young Prince. "I do not care. Your father agreed to your stay here. If you want to argue, take it up with him."

Benjamin looked at his father, who advised him to sit and stop complaining like a child.

"We are extremely disappointed in all of you," her father continued, addressing his daughter directly. "We had higher expectations. We expected you to act responsibly. Despite the challenging circumstances, you all behaved like children rather than leaders. You are supposed to seek guidance, regardless of your age. Instead, each of you deceived us, delaying the rescue of my own son, and there will be consequences." He then turned away without another word, leaving Cassandra feeling heartbroken in more than one way. "No one leaves. That's an order."

With that, the elder royals departed, and Jaronas did not glance at his daughter. The shift of multiple guards outside the tent confirmed their confinement, regardless of their desires.

As night descended, Jaronas and the other royals remained absent from the tent. Dinner was served, and an eerie silence enveloped the room. The operation on Sebastian unfolded without a hitch, the medical team labouring tirelessly, committed to ensuring Sebastian's recuperation.

The atmosphere remained tense, each minute passing like an agonising eternity. However, with the arrival of the first rays of dawn piercing through the tent's fabric, a wave of relief washed over Cassandra.

When she opened her eyes, Cassandra was greeted with a heart-warming sight. Sebastian was there, alive and awake, engaging in hushed conversations with Benjamin, Charlotte, and Augustus. The immediate wave of joy that surged through Cassandra was indescribable. Without hesitation, she lunged out of her bed and rushed to Sebastian's side, her face adorned with a radiant smile, her eyes gleaming with happiness and tears. The moment Cassandra reached him, she could not help herself but pull Sebastian into a tight embrace. Her arms wrapped around him, clinging to him as if she feared he might disappear if she let go. The feeling of his warmth, the steady rise and fall of his chest and the softness of his breath against her skin were all reassurances that he was truly there, alive and well.

She could not find the words to express her relief and happiness. Instead, she held onto him, her heart fluttering with a mixture of emotions. It felt like a weight had been lifted from her shoulders, and a soothing sense of serenity settled in its place. Seeing Sebastian awake, speaking, and breathing on his own felt like a small miracle. The pain she had been harbouring within her chest, a dull but constant ache, seemed to dissipate, leaving behind an overwhelming sense of gratitude and contentment. Cassandra squeezed Sebastian in her arms once more, silently thanking whatever forces might be at play for his recovery and their reunion.

Although they still faced countless challenges ahead, in that moment, surrounded by the warmth of Sebastian's presence and the unwavering support of her friends, Cassandra could not help but believe that they would overcome whatever trials awaited them.

Sebastian found himself taken aback by Cassandra's initial reaction, the suddenness and intensity of her embrace catching him off guard. He wasted no time, though, and reciprocated her hug with a tight embrace of his own. However, his physical condition could not be ignored and a series of painful coughs racked his body, forcing him to pull away from Cassandra's comforting hold.

"My chest," he managed to utter between coughs, concerned furrowing Cassandra's brow as she hastily scanned his chest for any visible signs of injury. Sebastian, sensing her worry, placed a reassuring hand on the side of her neck and gave a slight nod, placing her hand on his heart allowing her to feel his steadiness. "I am alright," he assured her, the relief evident in Cassandra's eyes as she nodded in acknowledgment.

Sebastian slowly shifted to perch on the edge of his bed and Cassandra settled beside him, prepared to recount the events of the previous day. "You missed quite the show," Augustus grinned.

Sebastian gazed at Cassandra, wordlessly prompting her to begin or clarify what he was referencing. Cassandra sighed before she commenced her narrative, starting with the radio conversation and proceeding to the lockdown ordered by her father. She made sure to include the agreement of each royal.

When she concluded, Sebastian shook his head. "You should have told him before he found out."

She gave him a pointed look. "Yes, and I've learned from my mistake. Now, let's focus on the situation. What do we do?"

"We do nothing for now. Right now, we stay here and follow orders."

Cassandra was taken aback by his response, her expression reflecting her shock. "You can't seriously believe that. We cannot sit here and wait for further instructions."

Sebastian's voice remained resolute. "Yes, we can and we will. Last time I checked, we are injured. We cannot fight at the moment. We need to let our wounds heal and formulate a plan."

"No, we need to get Grayson."

"Enough with that!" Sebastian's frustration showed as he snapped, causing Charlotte to jump slightly. "Every time we have gone into those tunnels, something bad has happened. *Every* single time. We are supposed to rest between the tournament days, and we should be focusing on the tournament, not on saving your brother. This whole situation could have been easily avoided if you would have just talked to our parents! But you did not, and now look where we are. In a Recovery Tent, under constant surveillance."

A nurse approached Sebastian, notifying him that his parents were here to see him. The group dispersed and returned to their designated beds.

He gave her a look, causing her blood to slightly boil. "Let it go, Cassandra. I mean it. Let your body rest for now."

How could something so sweet become bitter so quickly?

The group of five lay in silence inside the Recovery Tent. The air was thick with tension, making it difficult for anyone to find words to speak. King Kenji and Queen Suzume had just left to fetch the other Kings, mentioning that they needed to have a conversation with the young royals. Lunch was about to be served shortly, and afterward, the elder royals would return to speak with them.

As nurses entered the tent, setting up tables on the beds for their meal, Cassandra found it hard to comprehend Sebastian's reaction. She could not simply stay still; it wasn't in her nature. The responsibility for her brother, whether he was in trouble or not, had always fallen to her. She believed it was her duty to take care of him. Yet, here she was, ordered to sit and stay put as if she were a pet. Her gaze shifted to Sebastian, who stirred his soup and sipped it quietly. Even in this seemingly relaxed state, he remained calm, which only served to frustrate her more. How could he be so composed with the Mountmonts and their leader?

Benjamin was the first to break the tension, still clearly frustrated by the recent events. "This is your fault." He addressed Cassandra with his attention, glancing at her over his left shoulder, while Charlotte sat in the middle of them, Augustus on her far right, and Sebastian facing her.

Cassandra shifted beneath the sheets, raising an eyebrow. "My fault? How could this possibly be my fault?"

He scoffed. "Were you not in this tent when your father put us on lockdown due to your childish behaviour?" He shook his head. "I could be training right now, preparing for the final challenge."

"You can still train. Go stand in the corner and throw punches at the air. It will be the most productive thing you have done throughout this entire tournament."

Augustus almost choked on his bread, trying to conceal his smile.

Sebastian took a sip of his soup and added, "He is right."

Cassandra turned her attention to him, her voice heavy with resentment. "Excuse me?"

"Did I stutter?" Sebastian took another sip and looked up at her with hooded eyes. "I said he was right."

In a matter of moments, a heated argument erupted between the two, neither willing to yield in their views on the situation. Cassandra wasted no time in asserting that she was the one with a missing sibling and Sebastian was not far from advising her to find her place and keep quiet. Charlotte, feeling the need to join the dispute, offered her own perspective on how Sebastian should be more considerate, but

Augustus interjected, suggesting that she was overreacting to a minor comment.

Benjamin quickly chimed in, reminding everyone that the argument was happening because of Cassandra. This ignited a chain reaction, with each participant blaming the others, voices growing louder in the midst of the argument, all striving to make their point and overpower anyone who had wronged them.

Time dragged on and they persisted in their arguments, with no one pausing to catch their breath. At one point, Augustus flung a bread roll at Charlotte, leading to a gasp of surprise from Charlotte who promptly retaliated by throwing it back at him, declaring him the true child in this scenario.

Amid the ongoing clash of words and emotions, Cassandra couldn't help but recognize that these individuals, who were now her friends, were driven by genuine concern and affection for one another. Augustus was protective of Charlotte, Benjamin was infuriated by Cassandra's naïveté, Charlotte wanted to stand up for Cassandra and support her, Sebastian aimed to open Cassandra's eyes and highlight her errors, and Cassandra herself was willing to sacrifice everything for their safety. It was an unusual, surreal sensation, a somewhat foolish way to view the situation, as the argument continued and Sebastian sat undisturbed, sipping his soup with a knowing smirk, his gaze locked onto Cassandra.

"Would you look at this lot," Constantine commented as he strode into the clamorous Recovery Tent. The other royals filed in behind him, forming a line by the entrance, their gazes unwavering as they observed their children.

Jaronas, the last to enter the tent, kept his focus entirely on Cassandra, monitoring her actions. "I see you are in the midst of an argument."

"Yes, because—"

"We do not care, Benjamin," Albert interrupted his son. "We are here to discuss your punishment."

"Are we allowed to leave?" Charlotte asked, a glimmer of hope in her eyes.

"No," her father responded flatly, quashing her budding smile.

"Tonight, I am assembling a team of men to conduct a reconnaissance mission around the Mountmont Mansion," Jaronas started. "Meanwhile, the other royals will be in a meeting with Chief Onatach to deliberate our next steps."

"We are informing you of this because we expect no mischief during our absence. You will remain restricted to this tent, but after some deliberation and a vote, you will be allowed some fresh air while you dine tonight," Constantine concluded.

Jaronas approached Cassandra, handing her a letter. "Yara, Adriana, and Nora have sent word," he began, giving her the message. "Only family members are allowed inside the Recovery Tent."

Cassandra nodded.

"Keep in mind, this outdoor dinner is a test," Jaronas addressed the group. "It does not grant you permission to venture off in search of Grayson. Any hopes of assisting are futile. This is simply to see whether we can trust you to be left alone. However, that trust is hanging by a thread at the moment." Her father ensured that his words were directed towards his daughter as he fixed his gaze upon her. "Fix it."

Without another word, he departed. Cassandra clutched the letter tightly in her hand, anger raging within her, and somehow, she held back angry tears. She did not understand this new feeling; it only enraged her more. She was unable to comprehend how something as simple as telling her father the truth could lead to such severe consequences. He had looked at her coldly—her own father. Cassandra knew she deserved it, viewing it as her punishment until they could retrieve Grayson.

Slowly but surely, Cassandra felt her hope dwindling.

CHAPTER 23

Cassandra had requested paper and a few pencils from the nurse. She was determined to create different versions of the map she had previously made. She understood that her efforts would not aid the Kings directly, but perhaps these small acts of kindness could contribute to the search for Grayson in some way. Her father had left for his scouting mission and the Kings and Queens had departed earlier to meet with the Chief.

The sun was slowly setting, casting a golden orange glow over the camp. Cassandra basked in the warmth on her back, sending shivers down her spine as she continued to sketch.

The group sat outside, awaiting the commencement of dinner. Augustus had begun working on a new project that had suddenly inspired him. The only thing he muttered about was a talking radio, causing Charlotte to grow concerned for him.

She sat beside Cassandra, assisting her with the various map drawings–Cassandra had gone back to her tent, accompanied by two guards, to retrieve the map. Sebastian was busy throwing daggers at a nearby tree, hitting the bullseye on target with each blade.

Cassandra wondered how he had managed to access his weapons. Benjamin lay in the grass beside the logs, his hands clasped beneath his head, gazing up at the darkening sky. He watched as the stars emerged, and the world prepared for slumber.

Charlotte interjected with a random observation as she continued sketching the tunnels. Cassandra looked up at her, leaning over a log while Charlotte sat neatly beside her. "I find it strange how the Mountmont Mansion held so much detail of the Club Caverns."

Augustus, still seated in the dirt by the dying fire that provided them light in the dimming sky, quickly chimed in. "Why do you care?"

Charlotte elaborated, "I wonder what their origin story is."

"They are the ones who took my brother; there's your story," Cassandra grumbled as she drew out the tunnels.

"No, Cass," Charlotte interjected, catching her friend off-guard. "I mean, where do they come from? What nation did they originally come from?"

"Who cares," Augustus muttered as continued to play with his new creation, swearing as a piece of his invention did not fit together. "They are deranged scientists who listen to an even crazier leader who wants to blend steam-powered gears with the human body for fun."

Cassandra sat still, her mind racing upon hearing his words. She had heard that sentence before, or something very similar to it. Her eyes took on a distant look as she fixed her gaze on Augustus, who continued his conversation with Charlotte. She watched as his body tensed, his eyes filled with fear as he spoke quickly, as if he were hiding something from them.

It took a few moments for Augustus to realise her abrupt silence, and when their eyes met, Cassandra thought back to her home, to the conversation she had shared with her father.

"What is it?" he inquired, his eye still bandaged.

"My father shared with me a tale concerning Club Caverns," Cassandra began, her gaze locked onto Augustus. "He recounted the story of a *deranged scientist,* one who sought to *blend steam-powered gears with the human body.*" She observed as Augustus's expression shifted, his eyes comprehending the gravity of her words.

Charlotte, perceptive as ever, detected the sudden change in Augustus's demeanour. "What role did your nation play in this?"

Augustus shot Cassandra a withering glare, attempting to discourage her from continuing her narrative.

Nonetheless, Cassandra pressed on. "During the War, the scientist not only sold his inventions to Spades City–the Clubs allies, but also to his nation's enemies. Heart Lot Islands and Diamond Kingdom," she elucidated. "The scientist profited from the nations' destruction. As the War escalated, it unleashed a new era for humanity, showcasing how with these newfound enhancements, we could fend for ourselves and no longer require allies for assistance."

Augustus warned her, telling her to stop, but that was all she needed. His reaction alone proved that he was hiding something. She knew the truth and she was not afraid to say it, but it was his story to tell, a tale of his nation's mistakes and misery. Nevertheless, he knew the truth, and it had not sunk in until now. She had not realised that her father's history lesson two weeks ago would come in handy at this very moment.

Cassandra leaned forward as Augustus continued to glare. "What do you know about the Mountmonts, Augustus?"

Benjamin sat up at her words, Sebastian froze after throwing another dagger at his target, his body tensing up. Charlotte sat beside her with wide, horrified eyes. The information was a mystery to them, one that was not necessarily horrific but was a crucial piece of knowledge that needed to be shared. The camp grew quiet, the guards surrounding them on edge due to Cassandra's words.

"Do not say a word," he cautioned, swallowing hard, his green eyes filled with anger.

"I won't," she replied. "But you need to tell them the truth."

Charlotte looked between the two, clearly confused.

Sebastian approached the fire, sitting on a log beside Cassandra. A few paces behind him, Benjamin sat on the ground on the other side of the fire. She sat quietly, waiting for Augustus to speak. He continued to stare at her, a mixture of hatred and fury. He did not want to speak of his nation's dark past, reluctant to speak the truth; Cassandra was determined to have him speak, ignoring the questions that followed the Dimond siblings.

Finally, Augustus sighed, admitting defeat. "What do you know?"

"My grandfather was the first to break away during the War, leaving the Diamonds at a disadvantage," she explained, turning to Charlotte and Benjamin and offering an apologetic smile. "However, during this period, there was a scientist who created amazing things, innovations that we wear today. And once it was proven that this scientist was profiting off the War and causing even more destruction to be made, the Clubs were forced to put a bounty on his head. The first person to find him would receive a large sum from the Club King himself. This forced the scientist to go into hiding, only to be discovered weeks later. The day he was found, it was said that the Kings from each nation were to gather for his execution at night. However, the scientist vanished without a trace. Since then, the Clubs have been unable to locate him."

Augustus rolled his eyes. "You could have just said you know the story."

Cassandra narrowed her eyes. "Not all of it; there is still more to be said. I am providing a general understanding. Everything else is up to you to explain. After all, it's not my story to tell, Augustus."

"Then why bring it up in the first place?"

Cassandra replied, "There is something you are not telling us about the Mountmonts. And right now, my brother is in their custody. So I would like to know how to stop them."

He remained silent once more, taken aback by Cassandra's words.

"This is ridiculous," Benjamin chimed in, his eyes widened in disbelief. "This cannot be true. History and treaties exist for a reason."

Cassandra let out a wry laugh but kept her mouth shut as she looked at Augustus. She knew the true meaning behind the treaties, and clearly, so did Augustus. Sebastian remained wordless, his eyes keenly observing the unfolding situation.

"There is more?" Charlotte questioned.

Cassandra kept her gaze on Augustus and refused to participate any longer.

"Does this concern the treaties?" she continued, her eyes moving from Augustus to Cassandra.

The two royals were locked in a silent battle, waiting to see who would break first and speak. Cassandra stood by her words as she smirked at Augustus. She knew it was his turn, his story to tell. She wouldn't utter a word unless he asked her to speak on his behalf. When he nodded his head, it was the signal she needed to continue, no matter how stomach-turning it felt.

"There were treaties—" Cassandra began.

Augustus interrupted, realising the need for discretion. "Cassandra, I beg of you, this was sworn to secrecy. They were ordered never to discuss it again. This information must not be revealed," he implored, glancing around at the guards. "At least not in the open with so many eyes on us."

She considered his words and offered an alternative. "Alright, then what do you say we do? Write it down?"

Augustus smiled at the idea.

"Are you insane! I cannot—" she began, her voice filled with urgency and fear.

"Guards!" Charlotte quickly stood up. "If you can do us the favour of taking twenty paces back. We wish to speak in private." One of the guards mentioned that the cook would be arriving soon with their meals, and with that, the guards all stepped away. "There, easy," Charlotte said as she sat back down.

Once they had some privacy, the young royals huddled together. Cassandra began to open her mouth, prepared to speak on Augustus' behalf, but he raised his hand and smiled. "It's alright; I will explain it."

"Thank goodness," she said with a smile.

"The scientist was a childhood friend of my father's," he began, voice low. "His close friend who was driven solely by greed. He devastated our nation. If not for him, my nation would not be shrouded in a cloud of smog, causing constant illnesses among us." They all sat in shock by Augustus's sudden choice of words in the beginning of the story. Charlotte gently placed her hand on his, squeezing it tightly. "There were two treaties, one presented to the public, intended to convey that the War had concluded and the reasons behind it. But there was a second treaty, concealed from the public, meant exclusively for the royals. They were bound by an oath of secrecy regarding what truly occurred that night."

"My grandfather revealed the truth to my father, who then passed it on to me," Cassandra admitted.

"And your grandfather broke that vow," Augustus shot at Cassandra. "He was aware of the repercussions, and you are here freely discussing them?"

"What repercussions?"

"That we are all dead if the truth were to ever come out!" Augustus shouted slightly. Cassandra remains confused, tilting her head in curiosity as he scoffs. "Do not act innocent with me Cassandra. You know exactly what I am talking about." She shook her head, still not understanding. "The Mountmonts' father was *the* Jacobs! The mad scientist, the rogue who only cared for wealth. He had changed his name, created a family—my father discovered their hiding place months ago, but—"

Charlotte widened her eyes in shock at his words, leaning back slightly. "W-What?"

"You knew?" Cassandra gaped. "All this time you knew?" Sebastian sat quietly beside her, gripping her hand tightly.

Augustus realised the impact of his words, his eyes darting toward Charlotte. "Charlotte, darling, please. My father—it was his friend. He—"

Charlotte responded with anguish, her green eyes fixated on him as she shot to her feet. Her voice hushed. "How could you not tell me? How could you not share this information with us? How could you keep silent and watch?"

"It was a secret, darling–"

"Yes, a secret that could have aided Cassandra. You knew all this time and said nothing! And all you did was stand there quietly, in shock, as we unravelled it all and you just simply knew. You knew where they were located, you knew what they were capable of—you most likely knew where their Mansion was located and did not tell us."

"No, I did not know of their whereabouts. All of that was a mystery to me. I did not know what they looked like, nor what their intentions truly were. But, please, you need to understand–"

"No, I refuse to listen to another word you are saying. You betrayed us! You betrayed me!"

Augustus raised his hands in defence. "Please, darling, it is not–" Before he could finish his sentence, Charlotte slapped him hard across the face. Despite his efforts to maintain composure, it was evident he felt the impact.

"You lied to me! You've kept a secret from me, and you have been doing it since the moment I truly understood you," she ranted, not allowing Augustus a moment to speak. "How could you do such a thing? I am not another maid you can use and discard. I am here to listen and understand you, and we have been doing that for almost two weeks, yet here you are, continuing to keep secrets from me."

With every word, every hushed shout and angered pant, Augustus still reached for her. Getting to his feet as well as he tried to step towards her. "No! What are you doing?" His arms eventually embraced her, squeezing her to him tightly. "Do not touch me! You have no right to!" But he did not let go.

He clung to her tightly, as if offering a silent apology, before he mumbled the words that silenced her. "The Mountmonts are responsible for my brother's death."

Cassandra's eyes widened upon hearing Charlotte gasp. "How can this be true?" she questioned, her arms enveloping Augustus. "Your brother's death was due to a lab experiment gone wrong. Unless…"

Cassandra's mind raced, her voice piercing through the stillness. "Unless there was more to it."

Augustus withdrew, focusing on Charlotte, prepared to disclose the concealed truths. "Several months ago, my father received word from one of his private investigators that they had located the Joker family. They had been in hiding since the end of the war, and my father had refrained from contacting them ever since. Clues had suggested that my father's old friend had a wife but no children, while others discovered there was no wife and children. It was my brother's idea to establish contact with them, as he had always been intrigued by the concept of steam-powered human creation." Augustus shook his head, a sense of defeat in his expression. "I warned him against sending any letters, emphasising that it was our father's decision, not ours. But my brother, well, he was always quite headstrong."

He chuckled softly, as if reminiscing about his brother, his finger tracing over the dark green goggles hanging from his neck. "On that fateful night, shortly after my brother had sent his letter, we were in his laboratory. While conducting experiments with various chemicals and test tubes, there was a knock at the door. A man stood there, holding a letter and a vial of purple liquid, accompanied by a note. The note expressed the Jacobs' desire to meet for dinner to catch up and to offer the purple liquid for use in their experiments involving steam-powered human creations. My brother was elated and insisted on trying it immediately, despite my reservations about these mysterious individuals. Yet again, he did not heed my warnings. Instead, he experimented on himself. As the purple liquid mixed with the other chemicals, the lab erupted in an explosion."

He shook his head, his gaze fixed on Charlotte, who reached up to cup his cheek, her eyes filled with empathy. "If only I had tried harder, if I had pulled that vial away instead of just standing there and watching, my brother would still be alive. He would be participating in this tournament, not me."

She cupped his face in her hands, smiling lightly. "It is not your fault," Charlotte murmured to Augustus. "You cannot carry the blame for this."

He offered a resigned shrug. "You can say that, but words can never fully capture the weight of the actions I could have taken differently." Pain was evident on Charlotte's face, but she pulled Augustus back into a hug, the two falling silent.

As dinner was served, the group remained silent once more, processing the wealth of information they had received. Cassandra experienced a complex blend of emotions, with anger and frustration being prominent among them. She recognized that it wasn't entirely Augustus's fault for not sharing the information, but at the same time, it was. She should have made the connection sooner, recalling the story her father had told her the moment her brother was kidnapped. Such knowledge could have saved time and, in her case, prevented unnecessary drama.

As dinner concluded, the young royals seized the opportunity to enjoy the open air, extending their dinner conversation for an extended period, deliberately informing the guards that they were not finished with their meals.

Cassandra remained seated on the log, meticulously completing her map by the flickering firelight. The sun had dipped below the horizon, and the moon now cast its glow upon them. They were aware that the Kings and Queens would return from their meeting with the Chief at any moment. Cassandra's thoughts drifted to her father, and she fervently hoped for his safe journey to the Mountmont Mansion.

As she finished the final map, she surveyed her surroundings, pondering what to do next. Charlotte and Augustus continued their conversation beside her, Benjamin reclined on the ground, stargazing, and Sebastian returned to his daggers and the tree. It seemed like the perfect moment to engage with the assassin, seeking some comforting words and gaining a fresh perspective on their current predicament.

Cassandra rose from her perch on the log, striding over to Sebastian. The assassin maintained his focus, hurling dagger after dagger into the night. "Yes?" he queried as Cassandra halted beside him.

"Can we have a conversation?" she asked.

Sebastian spun his dagger skilfully, casting a glance at Cassandra's attire—brown pants paired with knee-length black boots, a snug black corset enveloping her torso, and her brother's white shirt tucked beneath it. "About what?" he retorted, resuming his dagger-throwing routine.

"I wanted to discuss a plan," she said.

Sebastian's leather-clad form shifted as he launched another dagger. "Why?"

Cassandra huffed and distanced herself, frustrated by Sebastian's unresponsiveness to her attempts at small talk. She had hoped to discuss their shared kiss and what lay ahead after the tournament. With little else to occupy their time in the camp while awaiting the return of the adults, her mind finally delved into the contemplation of their relationship.

Seating herself by a nearby tree, she leaned against its trunk, casting her gaze into the dark forest. The moon cast a gentle glow on the lush greenery, reminiscent of her home. Although missing the ocean, the Forest Lands' deep green woods would have to suffice for now. A rustle behind her signalled Sebastian's approach, and he took a seat beside her. In the quietude, they shared a rare moment of peace, absorbing the tranquil scene before them.

"I have a question for you," Cassandra found herself saying, her mind debating whether to broach the subject of their relationship or shift to an entirely different topic—one that had been bothering her for nearly two weeks.

Sebastian nodded, appearing ready for her inquiry.

"Since everyone is sharing secrets, care to explain why you participated in the Mercenary Games? It is very unlike you to be a part of something like that."

"And that is opposed to you knowing me so very well?"

Cassandra shrugged. "It is an observation I made. Yes, you are an assassin; however, you would not go out of your way to willingly kill someone. So, why participate?"

"It is none of your business," Sebastian concluded.

"Oh, come on," she nudged him slightly. "You can tell me. I won't say a word."

He shook his head. "It is not that easy. I cannot simply tell you and hope that you do not go off and tell someone. This involves others who should not be named and I would prefer not to say anything about it."

She stared at him. "Alright, then let's talk about this."

"This?"

"Us."

Sebastian scoffed. "I would rather discuss the reason behind me being a part of the Mercenary Games."

"Alright," Cassandra said as she leaned on her palms, head inclined to the dark sky above. "I believe it is your father who is behind it all. I saw him that night, and your reaction alone, well, it made it seem that you were scared of him."

"I am not scared of that man," he said quickly. "It is easier to scare you into saying nothing rather than it being a spectacle for everyone to know about." Sebastian shifted in his seat, moving closer to Cassandra. Her heart fluttered slightly. "The Mercenary Games are a secret to everyone. It is to remain a secret to anyone outside of my nation, so, you being the only outside visitor, I had to make sure you told no one about what you saw or where you went. And, if you were to say anything, you would have to face Kenji yourself."

"Kenji?" She questioned. "Not Father?"

Sebastian rolled his eyes, the dark brown shining in the dim moonlight. "As if it is not that obvious. We look nothing alike."

"I'm sorry," Cassandra found herself saying.

He smiled, no shine behind it. Just a brief smile as she looked from her to the empty dark forest. "Suzume is my real mother." Cassandra said nothing, following his gaze to the empty forest as she let him speak. She knew it would be the only time he would open up to her and she vouched to stay quiet. "I am the love child of my mother and a man she met at the Triumph Games. From what my mother said, she described my father as tough, sarcastic and kind-hearted. She said I look like him. I never knew him, never had the chance to meet him." He smirked and shook his head. "She told me they got closer in the months following the Games, having bonded over the war and the peace that followed. She told me he had a love for the sciences, admired the new technology that came about after the war. My mother knew he was the Club Caverns, which explained his admiration for technology but never went into detail. It was only when he came to her one night, appeared in her bedroom and told her he was fleeing his nation, wanting to run away with her, too. When she couldn't leave her city... that Night they consummated... Me."

Cassandra giggled at his choice of words. 'Consummated' instead of 'making love'.

"After that night, she found out she was pregnant. She became a target by an assassin and confided in Kenji, who became her good friend after the Games. She told him of her pregnancy and of the target on her back. In return, Kenji offered to kill the assassin if my mother would take his hand in marriage. She agreed and Kenji raised me as his own... Or at least tried to."

Cassandra placed her hand on top of his, squeezing it tightly. There was so much she wanted to say yet words were not able to be formed.

He pursed his lips, nodding his head as he thought to himself. "Kenji never saw me as his own; he considered me a burden. A bastard son that no one wanted and that he was stuck with–" He stopped himself as he swallowed. Cassandra felt her heart drop, feeling it shatter for him. "My mother was always by my side, caring for me, but I saw the distaste in Kenji's face. Wanting a child of his own, but my mother... She could not provide any for him. She had so many miscarriages... He was stuck with me."

"What Kenji said, about no one wanting you, he was wrong," Cassandra stated firmly.

Sebastian sighed, running his fingers through his hair. "No, he was right," he replied sombrely. "I am destined to be utterly alone as a bastard child."

Cassandra shook her head with determination. "Well, I am here for you, then. No matter the kill, no matter the loneliness, I am here to keep you company. That way, the darkness does not seem so dark."

A genuine smile crossed Sebastian's face, a beautiful toothy grin that made Cassandra's heart swell with joy. She felt an overwhelming sense of excitement knowing that she had brought that smile to his face. Without hesitation, she pulled Sebastian into a tight hug, laughing as he reciprocated, holding her even closer.

She understood the deep meaning behind the insults Sebastian had to endure as a child. They were reminders of how beneath he was from Kenji; however, she vowed to remind him otherwise. Every day till the end of time, she would remind him of how wanted he was, of how perfect he was, and of how cared for and loved he was. Cassandra would find ways of sending him letters, writing and writing until her very last one. He would not be alone in this.

Sebastian opened up further, admitting, "What interested me the most was when I was injured and thrown off the mountaintop. I saw the way Kenji panicked, how quickly he moved, and even heard him giving orders to ensure my safety. But part of me believes it was all an act, as if to ensure that his precision creation would not be lost."

Cassandra listened intently, her heart racing and her emotions in turmoil.

He continued, "But I heard you, too. I heard you scream my name; I heard the pain in your voice as if you had lost something dear to you. I even saw you run toward the edge and look at me the entire time until you went back to fight for your family."

She smiled again, feeling a mixture of excitement and anxiety. "I cannot lose you that easily." His fingers found hers, laced together; he gave her palm a tight squeeze.

Sebastian whispered softly, "The feeling is mutual," and placed a gentle kiss on her lips. It was the first true act of emotion she had ever seen from him. One that was not in secret but in the open.

"What are you doing out of the tent?" The two turned to find the Kings and Queens standing in the Camp, arms crossed and frustrated. "I thought we said you would be out for dinner," Morana said.

"And would you look at that," Albert chimed in, pulling out his pocket watch. "It is no longer six o'clock but nine!"

"Technically," Augustus said with a smile as he rose from his seat beside Charlotte, waving his plate in the air with partly-eaten vegetables still remaining. "We are still eating."

Constantine narrowed his eyes. "Don't be clever with us, boy, you know the conditions; return to the tent. All of you."

Cassandra and Sebastian walked towards them, the only thing on her mind being Jaronas and his scout of the Mountmont Mansion. "Any word from my father?"

Morana shook her head. "No, dear, I'm sorry."

"Then is it alright that I stay up waiting for his return?"

"Yes, of course. But you can do it in the tent," Constantine retorted. The young royals wanted to stay out a little longer, while the elder royals were too strict on their emplaced rules.

Quick footsteps and the sound of snapping branches to her right, emerging from the direction beyond the Clubs' tent, prompted an immediate alert within the group. Sebastian swiftly moved by Cassandra's side, his dual daggers poised at his hips, positioning himself as a protective shield. Augustus was to Charlotte's side, Benjamin not too far off as the Kings and Queens stood at the ready. All enhancements were activated as the guards eyed the dark forest. Everyone watched to see who it was. Cassandra's heart raced within her chest as she questioned whether the approaching figure could be her father.

Then, she spotted the tall silhouette and closely-cropped hair. Her breath caught as she realised just how much Bran looked like his father. "Dirk?" she mumbled.

CHAPTER 24

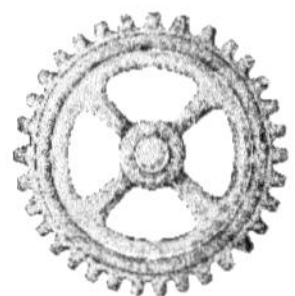

Dirk emerged from the thick forest foliage, his Heart Lot marine uniform dishevelled and stained with dirt. His sleeves bore the marks of recent cuts, dried blood tracing a path down the side of his neck, drenching his ear.

Cassandra could not help but gasp in surprise as she rushed to meet her father's friend, preventing him from stumbling to the ground. She turned back to Sebastian with an urgent plea. "Don't just stand there! Help me!" With Dirk in tow, they made their way toward a log, and Cassandra's mind raced with concern.

The royals gathered around the first as Sebastian assisted and guided Dirk to the log. "Are you alright?" Suzume asked.

"What happened to the scouts?" Constantine demanded.

"We were ambushed," Dirk replied, his voice heavy with strain as he took his place on the log.

Cassandra found it increasingly difficult to catch her breath. "Where is my father?"

"I need to speak with Onatach. Your father requested it," Dirk said, meeting Cassandra's anxious gaze. "He also instructed me to inform you of the attack."

She clutched Dirk's shoulder in desperation. "Dirk, where is my father?"

"We were near the Mansion," Dirk explained to the royals, his words coming slowly as he recalled the harrowing events. "We could see it through the trees as we approached. Upon getting closer, we stopped behind some bushes to plan our next move. But there was an unfortunate misstep by one of Chief's men, which likely triggered a silent alarm. Suddenly, four large, almost enhanced hounds came running at them. They were vicious creatures; whenever we tried to kill them, three new ones would appear. Several men are dead or injured. That was when he appeared–Grayson had calmed the dogs to his side. We barely held our ground."

Turning to Cassandra, Dirk continued with sorrowful eyes, "Your father instructed me to return to camp. He, Mees, and Loris decided to stay and fight. I refused to leave, but my King gave me orders."

"This is ridiculous!" Albert exclaimed. "You are telling me you lost to a bunch of dogs?"

"You weren't there," Dirk breathed. "Those creatures were not your ordinary lap dog that you are used to, no, these things were created somehow. They held enhancements like us, they knew when to strike and kill–and Grayson commanded them to his side at his own free will." Cassandra's entire body felt numb; it was impossible to accept. She could not fathom losing both her brother and father. "By the time I reached the end of our well-charted path," Dirk said, voice laden with anguish, "a strange, unsettling smell filled the air. It made my head spin, and when I turned back, they were gone. All of them, taken–some alive, some not."

"What do we do now?" Augustus questioned no one in particular.

"King Jaronas instructed me to seek an audience with Chief Onatach. I intend to fulfil his wishes."

With a nod to one of the guards, a bell rang, summoning the Chief. Soon after his arrival, Chief Onatach presented a plan for rescuing Jaronas, Grayson, and the other warriors held captive by the Mountmonts. Cassandra struggled to keep her composure as she listened to the discussion. Her heart ached from the loss of her brother, and the thought of losing her father as well was nearly unbearable. She could not comprehend how this could be happening and refused to accept it.

As the group continued to devise a strategy to save the captured men, the Kings insisted that the young royals stay at Camp with the Queens. Augustus was quick to make a remark, saying it was unfair; however, Cassandra stepped in, saying it was alright, and quickly handed them each a map of the underground tunnels.

"Where are the tunnels?" Kenji asked, eyeing the drawn-out sheet before him.

"East."

"No," Charlotte chimed in, finger on her chin. "I believe it was south."

Benjamin shrugged. "I thought it was north?"

Augustus shook his head. "No, no, it's in the town."

"No, you are all mistaken," Sebastian said. "It is northwest."

Cassandra smiled at their tactic, knowing this was all a strategy to throw the Kings off, overall frustrating them. King Albert was the first to begin to argue, but he was quickly cut off by Dirk, who insisted on the young royals' presence, claiming if they knew where the tunnels were and they refused to give it up, they should be permitted to join. Each King said their own version of no.

"I would not mind showing them where the tunnels are," Cassandra smiled sweetly. "However, we want to join."

"Yes," Dirk said flatly.

"No!" the Kings said in unison, glaring at their children.

Dirk shook his head. "Fine, they don't join, but so help me, if I lose both male heirs to the Heart Lot throne, it will be on each of your heads. And you will be the ones to live with the consequences." Without another word, he turned towards Cassandra and nodded. "Grab your weapons, be prepared, we leave at midnight."

The final plan was established: the Queens, including Yara, Adriana, and Nora, would remain at camp with Chief Onatach and a selected group of warriors to provide protection for the Forest Land and the camp. Dirk would lead the older royals above ground to the Mountmont Mansion, while the young royals would go through the tunnels. That way, they could conquer more ground. The only job the young royals had was to get Grayson and somehow manage to reprogram him; the Mountmonts were in the hands of the Kings.

With everyone agreeing to this plan, they began to get ready for the upcoming departure.

Dirk was quick to pull Cassandra aside, eyes looking around as he spoke to her. "You will also be searching for Jaronas. You are to rescue him from wherever he is. He and his troops will stay with you." Cassandra nodded. "I do not trust these other Kings; however, I trust that they want the same goal. Once you fix Grayson, get out of there." Dirk kept a stern face as he gazed down at her. "You are not to be injured; you are to be in one piece. Simply put, you go in and go out."

"Yes, I understand that. But why the need to speak about this in private?"

"As I said, I do not trust these people."

Cassandra gazed over at them, smiling slightly. "I trust them."

"All of them?"

Her eyes went solely to Sebastian, watching as he spoke with his hands behind his back and with his parents. He was the one she could only ever trust fully, the only outsider in her life that was not a part of her family or island. "No." Dirk followed her gaze and rolled his eyes. "The Dimonds are useless, Spars seems as though he has a hidden agenda, and… Well, Clubs seem like the only useful recruits."

"Please?" Cassandra smiled sweetly.

Dirk glared at her. "Fine, but you are my only concern. If I lose you due to their stupidity, it means war."

"Thank you!" She then hugged him.

Before leaving the tunnels, maps were properly secured and Cassandra explained the ways of the tunnel. Augustus distributed miniature radios, the invention he had created that night, aimlessly working on them. Cassandra realised this inspiration could have come from the Mountmonts and communicated towards them in the Recovery Tent.

Augustus explained how he had designed them to allow each group to communicate over a considerable distance, along with such a small earpiece to each person to allow them to speak or listen when needed. Augustus emphasised the importance of everyone remaining on Channel Two of the miniature radio, so as to ensure effective communication.

With the radios in hand, they made their way to the tunnels. Dirk reminded the young royals of their plan to rescue Grayson and to only focus on him; he also did not fail to give Cassandra a pointed look, as if to tell her that Jaronas was her duty that he passed down to her.

Upon reaching the tunnels, they bid the Kings, Dirk, and the assembled army of the Chief warrior goodbye before descending through the hatch into the tunnels. Dirk was the last to close the hatch, nodding at the group before marching towards the Mountmont Mansion with the rest. Cassandra pulled out her map, explaining that they were to enter the lab together and then use the door that connected towards the back to the cells. She emphasised on first securing her father, wanting to save him before getting Grayson. From there, they would leave Augustus and Benjamin behind as the remaining three searched the Mansion for Grayson.

Sebastian felt indifferent about the plan, emphasising that he did not want to break up the group once more. However, it was Augustus who reminded him that it would be much easier to do so, as it would allow him time to work on Grayson's reprogramming. Augustus made an effort to explain how this additional time would allow the group to bring Grayson, and all that would need to be done would be to fix him. Sebastian remained reluctant to the thought, truly not wanting to separate, as past experiences showed how their theory was usually wrong.

Charlotte was the one who made the suggestion, explaining how they would be in contact with the boys. So once Augustus was done with his reprogramming, he could join the group with an effective amount of time left. That way, together, they would be able to get Grayson and bring him back. Cassandra found all of this talk ridiculous, absurd even, not understanding how something as little as separating was such a bad thing in Sebastian's eyes.

Folding the map, she glared at him. "Sebastian, I understand your concern, but it would help us not take up too much time. Dirk said we need to be in and out. We should not waste time here. However, I agree with Charlotte. The boys stay in the lab and then once Augustus is done–whatever it is he does–he and Benjamin can join us. We are in contact all the time, thanks to these new devices that Augustus created. So let us not worry about this any longer and begin this rescue mission?"

Sebastian nodded his head, understanding that it would be easier, but he let it be, as he knew there was no way for Cassandra to turn back on her words. He vowed to himself to make sure the group would get together once more, reluctant on wanting no one to get injured or lost along the way. He was happy that he was to be with the girls, as it always seemed to be those two who caused the most danger, and he viewed it as a way to ensure their safety, rather than keeping an eye on them.

As Cassandra led the group down the endless twists and turns, their map guided them to the lab. They pushed through the doors, and although Cassandra was expecting blood to once more litter the room, the lab was spotless, as if cleaned and polished. She looked over at Sebastian, who seemed to understand her thoughts; it was odd how neat this lab was. Augustus did not waste a second and began his work, grabbing the brain that was once on the tray and securing it in a jar. He began tapping on devices around him and mixing liquids together. Charlotte looked at the map Cassandra created and spotted the door to the cell room. She manoeuvred through the tight space, but Benjamin was quick to move things around to permit more room in the area.

The door became vigilant, wide, and large, leading to the cell room where her father was. However, the sick gut feeling of this lab did not sit well with Cassandra. When Charlotte pushed open the door, Cassandra was half-expecting something horrible to pop out, but nothing did. The echoes of harsh coughing filled the air as Sebastian stepped through the door first.

Inside, they found that each cell was occupied by three men, maybe more. Leaving only one cell to be empty–Grayson's. Cassandra realised he was not there. The sickening feeling in her stomach turned. He was somewhere in the Mansion, somewhere within these walls or outside with the other men. Cassandra walked slowly, passing the cells of men, injured and dead alike put together. That was when she spotted Loris and Mees, leaning against the wall, their eyes closed. Jaronas had his back turned to them, face pressed against the bars of his cell. In Grayson's cell, his eyes roamed over them, looking at the stained blood wall and ground, his eyes trained over the new bloodied chains and the scattered pieces of the old ones that littered in a corner. Cassandra picked up the pace, not wanting her father to remain there any longer than he already was.

"Father!" Cassandra cried out, racing toward him.

Jaronas snapped his head up, looking toward the cell door as he sprang to his feet, extending his arms through the bars of his cell as Cassandra gripped his hands. "You received my message." He smiled.

Cassandra nodded, looking toward Sebastian and Charlotte, instructing them to open the cell doors. Sebastian moved to the neighbouring cell, activating his enhancement and cutting through the locks. Charlotte used her whip to rip the locks off the doors.

"Step back," Cassandra said to her father as she fired a few shots at the lock, allowing it to open. Once each man was free, Charlotte and Sebastian searched for their weapons, and once found tucked away in the far corner, they handed each Forest Land warrior their weapon. Cassandra quickly handed Jaronas a miniature radio, map, and earpiece. She explained the device's function and gave instructions on how to rendezvous with Dirk and the others.

"I am not leaving you," Jaronas said firmly. "We find Grayson together." Mees and Loris were short behind as Charlotte handed them each a map, earpiece, and miniature radio. Before Cassandra could disagree, the ground shook beneath them, causing chunks of cement to fall from the ceiling. King Albert urgently radioed for help, requesting Sebastian's assistance in the ongoing fight, along with any men that were willing to aid.

"You can have the warriors," Jaronas said into the earpiece. "But I am staying with my daughter."

Sebastian nodded at his words, looking toward Cassandra. He gave her a kiss on the forehead before saying, "Do not do anything drastic 'till I get back."

She nodded. "Go through the hatch," she said, pointing toward the hatch on the map; she instructed Sebastian that it would be an easier way to reach the Kings.

"It will take too long, there must be another way in."

One of the men quickly shouted for the royals as he pressed against a brick, and an entrance to a small passageway appeared. Sebastian moved quickly, Cassandra shortly behind. The small passage held stairs leading up. Looking back at her, Sebastian moved delicately until he reached the top, where a wooden door rested.

Pushing it open, Sebastian looked both ways before looking back at her. "Cassandra." The Princess was short behind, going up the steps and looking around. They were in the foyer where she and Charlotte once were.

"It is alright. You guys can go through here. The door is just through there."

Going back down, Sebastian explained to the warriors what they would do and where they were to go. He created a plan within seconds of analysing the area.

Jaronas tapped Cassandra gently on the arm, pulling her away from Sebastian as he spoke to the men. "Loris and I will do a sweep of the foyer with the men; if there is an upstairs, I will do the same thing. Until I radio you, you will remain down here with Mees."

Cassandra was prepared to argue; she opened her mouth prepared to tell her father otherwise when Sebastian called for the warriors to move. Jaronas looked over at Loris, who nodded, and together they moved with the men. Cassandra and Charlotte stared at each other, confused by what had just happened.

"Cass!" Benjamin quickly stepped into view of the door; she furrowed her brows, questioning why everyone had been calling her that; it was a nickname secured for her brother. However, she did somewhat enjoy how easily it rolled off her friends' tongues.

"Cassandra, Augustus is nearly finished with whatever it is he is doing. We will join you soon."

She nodded. "Thank you, Ben."

"We are using nicknames now?" Charlotte smiled.

Cassandra shook her head. "No, gods no, I did not like that at all." Charlotte laughed, and in moments, Jaronas and Loris were calling for them to join.

Reaching the top of the stairs, Cassandra informed the men as to what was going to happen, what their mission was. Together they searched the Mansion for Grayson, yet they did not find him. They searched every room on the first floor and every room on the second before reaching the foyer once more in a huff. An hour had passed, Augustus and Benjamin nowhere in sight. Charlotte had informed the group that it would be a little while longer until they were to join.

"Maybe we should search the first level once more?" Charlotte questioned the group. "Maybe we missed something." Nodding, they retraced their steps, and Cassandra contemplated returning to the cell room to explore it further for clues about Grayson's whereabouts. Jaronas instructed the girls to search downstairs as the boys were in the lab, and if anything were to happen, to call for them, and that they were to continue searching the first floor. Nodding, the girls descended to the cell room.

Cassandra noted that the lab door was shut, probably due to all the noise they were making, and Augustus needed his peace. When the girls reached Grayson's cell, it remained eerily vacant, just as they had last left it. Sharing an exasperated sigh, they turned to head back upstairs. However, when Charlotte reached for the doorknob, it refused to budge, sending a wave of panic through them as they realised they were locked inside with no apparent means of escape.

Malevolent giggles erupted from the other side of the room, chilling the girls to their core. Slowly, they turned to confront the sinister grins of the Jacobs, who loomed ominously on the opposite end. Cassandra questioned where they had come from, her eyes searching the room and thinking that there were other passages such as this one.

"Cassandra!" Augustus's voice crackled in their earpiece. "I've done it! I've done all the experiments needed on the brain that was on the tray. After testing it, everything came back alright. I've successfully reprogrammed it. We need Grayson to do the proper testing and to make the data effective!"

Cassandra and Charlotte remained immobile, too terrified to respond to Augustus's calls. The Jacobs, with their eerie silence, drew closer, prompting the girls to activate their enhancements.

"Cassandra? Are you there?" Augustus wondered.

"Cass?" Sebastian began, out of breath from the fight that occurred outside the Mansion. "Are you alright? Where are you?"

The girls did not respond, their instincts taking over as they carefully watched the Jacobs. Charlotte instinctively reached up to activate her earpiece, allowing the group to listen in on the unfolding scenario. Cassandra followed suit, and soon the sinister voices and laughter of the Jacobs filled their ears, providing the group with sufficient information.

Charlie giggled. "You have brought us guests," he began, smile growing by the second.

Augustus mumbled. "Charlotte? Cassandra?"

"Char?" Benjamin's voice chimed in.

Cassandra could not contain her fury as she confronted the Jacobs. "Why would you do this? Why tear apart families, destroy nations, all for the sake of perfection?"

Thomas stepped forward, his smile widening. "Oh, it is not us who make the rules; our leader has a great mind, wanting great things. He wanted to perfect the human body! We wanted to prove to our father that we can be just as great as he was. Our names will be etched in history as visionaries who ushered in a new era of steam-powered technology—a future for the world!"

"Girls, keep him engaged in conversation," her father's voice urged urgently through their earpieces. "I am on my way to you."

"Your leader is an idiot," Cassandra stated.

"That's not what I meant, Cassandra!"

The girls quickly acted on instinct when the Jacobs stepped too close. Cassandra raised her sniper and took the first shot. The bullet skimmed the side of Charlie's head as Charlotte activated her iron whip. She snapped the whip around Thomas's ankle and yanked him to the ground.

The brothers burst into laughter, one extending a hand to help the other regain his footing. "It's adorable that you think your battle is with us," Thomas remarked, rising to his feet.

Another deafening blast resonated from above, causing the ground to convulse, with distant shouts muffled by the Mansion's walls. Charlie glanced up at the ceiling with a sinister smile, while Thomas sported a smug smirk. "That, my dear Princesses, sounds like our cue."

In the blink of an eye, Charlie disappeared, leaving Cassandra and Charlotte alone with Thomas. It happened so abruptly; one moment Charlie was sprinting, and the next, Thomas hurled a small, round, black device in their direction.

Cassandra's eyes widened as she grabbed Charlotte's arm, quickly pulling her towards the door. Kicking at the door, they burst through it just in the nick of time. The subsequent explosion violently rocked the Mansion. Both Princesses lost control of their bodies and were flung across the floor. Cassandra's head struck against glass, followed by the thud of a painting. Charlotte landed on her back near the stairs, her neck snapping backward, both of them groaning in agony.

The enormous chandelier above them swung violently before plummeting to the ground, shattering into a rain of diamond and glass shards. Instinctively, they shielded their faces and heads, shards of glass scattering around them. Cassandra felt the pieces of diamond pierce her hands and hands, her groans of pain muffled by her hands.

The voices in her earpiece informed Cassandra that Sebastian was on his way, with Augustus and Benjamin also shouting for updates. Benjamin mentioned that he was en route to their location, while Augustus safeguarded the precious brain.

As she fought through dizziness, Cassandra's mind seethed with vengeance against the Jacobs, her resolve hardening to obliterate them once and for all.

The minutes dragged on agonisingly slow as they waited for help to arrive. Cassandra could feel the stinging pain from her wounds, her fingers gingerly trying to extract the diamond shards embedded in her skin. In the dim light, she could hear Charlotte groaning once more, the sound of her discomfort cutting through the tense atmosphere.

"Are you alright?" Charlotte called to Cassandra, concern lacing her words.

Cassandra grunted in response as the sound of doors swinging open and the rush of hurried footsteps filled the room. Jaronas swiftly made his way to Cassandra's side, while Benjamin approached his sister. Her father picked at the pieces of glass that stuck to Cassandra's skin, all of which covered her back and legs. With each shard taken away, Cassandra felt the weight of her injuries slowly lessen. Once they removed every fragment, her father gently helped her stand and she turned her gaze toward Charlotte, who was still covered in glass shards on her arms and the right side of her body. The Dimond siblings worked together to remove the remaining fragments.

Helping them, Cassandra could not help but ask, "Where are the Jacobs?"

Her father, still holding her up, responded with a furrowed brow. "I am not sure, but I do believe the men outside are fighting the Jacobs' new inventions."

"Where is Sebastian? And Grayson?" she asked.

"I did not see either of them."

"He's supposed to be here," Cassandra muttered. "Something must have happened."

"Then they are all in the Mansion," Charlotte grumbled.

Cassandra nodded as the Dimond siblings joined them. She inquired, "Did Augustus figured it out?"

Benjamin nodded in response. "I am not sure what he did. I simply stood guard and occasionally watched as he played with endless wires and used multiple vials before jumping in excitement," he explained, which earned a chuckle from Charlotte. "I am going to return to him," Benjamin continued. "I want to make sure the Jacobs did not get to him—"

Suddenly, banging on the front doors of the Mansion interrupted his words, and the group turned their attention to the commotion. In a rush, Dirk pressed himself against the lower window, hands rapidly slapping the glass. joined by the other men who had been fighting outside. Sebastian hurried to the door, attempting to pull at the knob, but it stubbornly refused to budge. In moments, he pulled for his daggers and began to pick at the knob, trying to get it open.

Cassandra, despite her injuries, quickly hobbled towards the window to assess the situation outside. Jaronas followed her, pulling for his radio, Dirk following his actions. "What happened?" The men, including the Kings, were in a terrible state, their bodies smeared with blood and their finely-tailored clothes now ruined.

"It was Grayson!" Dirk breathed heavily, his words reverberating through the earpiece. "The Mountmonts set countless traps, and Grayson welcomed the others at the Mansion gates. Making it this far was nearly impossible, and now he is gone, and we cannot find him." The men persisted in striking the windows and door with desperation, eager to retreat into the Mansion.

"Did you see Sebastian?" Cassandra asked.

"I thought he came in to help you?" Dirk questioned.

"What? Where is my son?" Kenji stared at Dirk and grabbed the radio. "Sebastian, where are you?"

There was a screech on the radio. No answer. Cassandra felt her stomach turn, only thinking of the worse, not understanding how he could have gone missing in a matter of minutes. Her mind turned on how Grayson could have grabbed him, taken him, and killed him, but she refused to think of the worst. Her body shook at the thought alone.

"Out of the way," King Albert commanded, shoving Dirk aside as he raised his hammer, prepared to break the glass. However, the glass remained unyielding, not breaking at the impact. Albert stood stunned, questioning what had happened.

King Kenji approached the window next, lightly tapping it with his fingertips. Pressing his earpiece, he glanced towards the group inside the Mansion. "It is impenetrable, as if specifically designed to be this way."

King Constantine stepped towards the door, knocking on it, and observed the wood. "In the Club Caverns, we have created doors and homes like this for the purpose of protection in case of any scientific explosion," he explained. "It appears that the entire Mansion is constructed in a similar manner, designed to withstand dangerous forces."

"What does that mean?" Cassandra inquired.

"It means there is no physical way for us to enter," Constantine concluded.

"He must be wrong. There has to be a way to get in." Benjamin tugged at the doorknob once more. "You can obviously unlock the door. It cannot be that hard!"

Charlotte frowned. "Clearly, you have trouble listening. King Constantine just explained that there is no way–"

"It does not matter what that man said–"

"Yes, it does matter!" she interrupted, her tone firm. "Last I checked, he is the only one among us who knows about these homes. But, if we ever need help in a golden castle, we will send word for you. As for right now, the doorknob is jammed and nothing is working."

Cassandra absorbed Kenji's words, listening to his instructions. He explained how a group would be sent down to the tunnels while the rest searched the area for a way in. Jaronas nodded and spoke to Dirk and the other Kings.

Cassandra turned to the others. "Benjamin, you need to go to Augustus. He hasn't said anything in a while. I am worried something bad might have happened."

He nodded and swiftly disappeared down the hall. Jaronas separated the groups; King Kenji, Dirk, and three of Chief Onatach's men would venture to the tunnels to seek an alternative way in. This left King Constantine and Albert behind, accompanied by more than a dozen other men.

Once her father finished, Cassandra spoke into the radio once more. "Sebastian, please tell me you are alright. Where are you?" There was no answer. She tried again. "Sebastian?"

"I am on my way to the lab," Benjamin instructed on the radio.

"Do you see Sebastian?"

"No."

"Benjamin? Son? Where are you?" Albert called from his radio. Cassandra looked over her shoulder and found Albert standing beside Constantine, earpieces on and listening to the conversation. A distressed cough from Charlotte briefly interrupted their conversation. The group listened intently as Benjamin described his approach to the lab door.

A gasp emanated from his end.

"What? What is it? Is it Sebastian? Is he alright?" Cassandra nearly screamed.

"It—it's Grayson," Benjamin breathed, continuing to recount the unsettling scene before him.

"Impossible, he was just outside," her father said, confirming Dirk's previous mention of his son.

Her father cleared his throat and Charlotte had another coughing fit, but Cassandra remained completely absorbed in Benjamin's narrative. He trembled while describing the numerous arrows scattered throughout the room and how Grayson had Augustus in a chokehold. "Let him go!" Benjamin shouted before dropping the radio.

Her father coughed and a strange interference caused the radio to malfunction, leaving the group to hear Grayson's chilling chuckle and the activation process of his bow.

"Grab the brain!" Augustus's voice carried urgency and desperation, accompanied by the sounds of snapping claws and flying arrows, followed by a thud to the ground. "He wants to destroy the programming. Grab it and run!"

"Benjamin!" Albert called out over the radio, the subsequent noises indicating that a fierce battle was taking place. Then the sound of two snapping claws suggested that Benjamin had secured something.

"I have the brain!" Benjamin gasped into the radio as his footsteps echoed through the tunnel floors.

Charlotte reached for her own radio, letting out a cough that drew a perplexed glance from Cassandra. "Augustus, what is happening down there?"

"He's behind me!" His voice was filled with panic.

"Keep running and I'll find you," Augustus groaned, and both their radios fell silent.

"Benjamin, tell me where you are. I will find you." Her father gave the two Princesses a nod and ran after Benjamin.

Cassandra pounded her radio with her palm while Charlotte readied her whip. Loris and Mees were short behind in following their Princess. They cleared their throats and coughed, scanning every corner of the grand foyer. Cassandra observed as Albert and Constantine conversed, and proceeded to speak to Dirk over the radio.

Lowering the volume, they spoke about finding Benjamin and her father trying to help the young royal find him.

While in the tunnels, Augustus' voice was the only thing she heard, causing her heart to stop. "Back up! I need back up! —You? What are you—"

The radio scratched once more.

"Go find Augustus!" Cassandra ordered Mees and Loris.

Mees began. "But your father ordered—"

"I don't care! I am your Princess. I order you to find my friend and make sure he is alright." Without another word, the two bowed and ran toward the tunnels.

Her attention was abruptly seized by frantic coughing.

A green smoke began to envelop the room and an eerie laughter echoed from the top of the grand staircase.

Cassandra looked up, her heart breaking into a million pieces. Charlotte gasped, deep red nails covering her mouth. The sight before her made her want to throw up. It brought tears to her eyes, almost refusing to believe it to be true.

It was impossible, he could not do that, he was not capable of it. Please let this be a dream, wake me up. I want to wake up. Please. Wake me up.

Sebastian laid at the top of the stairs, body bruised and beaten, blood dripping from his nose and mouth.

Above him, Thomas and Charlie smiled wickedly, so much so that it made her sick.

"I believe this belongs to you," Thomas said as Charlie reached for Sebastian.

Before Cassandra could react, before Charlotte could scream, Sebastian's body was flung down the stairs.

CHAPTER 25

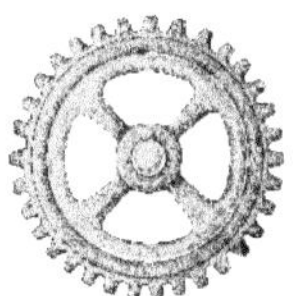

Cassandra watched Sebastian's tumble; his body did not fight to stop and get up. He let himself fall down the stairs, and only did stop once he reached the bottom. It felt as though it were all in slow motion; when he did reach the bottom, she reacted too late. Her strides felt slow, her movements almost imaginable.

Charlotte was by her side.

The two crouched down before Sebastian, Cassandra reaching for his head first making sure that he was alright. Charlotte inspected his bruises. "Come on, Sebastian, say something," Casandra muttered to herself. She could not tell if there were any serious injuries. She looked up to the brothers. "You are monsters! He's innocent! How could you—Why would you..."

"Innocent?" Thomas giggled, smile growing. "He is hardly innocent."

"No, you are wrong! He is, and you nearly killed him!"

"Oh, you are all but wrong," he sang. "He is the mastermind behind it *all*."

Charlotte frowned. "Impossible. You are simply saying this to buy yourselves some time."

"Oh, are we now?"

A giggle erupted. Not from Thomas, nor from Charlie. But from the body below her.

Sebastian gazed up at her, his smile almost evil as she scooched back. Charlotte stood up as if wanting to get away from him as quickly as possible. His aura changed; it was no longer one of sarcasm and cold features, but one of a maniac and ideologies so disturbing that could tear this world apart if they were to ever become true.

The voices on the radio became distant as Sebastian gave another giggle. His body moved in a way that seemed wrong and sat before her, leaving her to not understand who this man truly was. His evil smile only grew. Cassandra wanted to break everything in that Mansion. Her emotions taking over her body, her breathing became faster by the second, eyes watering and hands shaking.

"Sebastian?" was all she managed to say.

She watched as the man she thought she cared for, the man she saw as something special and with whom she would hopefully create a good relationship with after the Games, sat before her only smiling. "In the flesh." was all he said, his teeth as sharp as the knives on him.

"How could you?"

Sebastian did not say anything as he rose to his feet, hand extended to her as if waiting for her to take it.

"I don't need your help."

He kept his hand out, his eyes never leaving her—something he had always done, observing her and watching her every move to see what she would do next. It was clearer now that his sudden pop-ups were planned, that he would find her in those random places due to not only distracting her but to protect himself. He played dumb, let her be the fool in this game of cat and mouse.

However, her eyes remained on his outstretched hand, the hand that she for a second thought might be worth her while. Holding onto it and thinking, even for a second, that she could change him— then reality hit and she knew she could not change someone that did not intend to change.

She stood on her own, lifting herself up as Charlotte stood behind her, wanting to remain close. "You owe me an explanation."

"Blood over anyone else" was all he said, causing her mind to turn at his words.

It took her a few moments to comprehend his words, to fully run through each one. Until those minutes turned to seconds and Cassandra's eyes widened in fear. "No…"

His father. His true father, the man that disappeared and the one Sebastian claimed to never know, was a Jacobs, the father of the Mountmonts, leaving Thomas and Charlie as his half-brothers.

Charlotte gave Cassandra a look, hoping for her to explain, but Cassandra could not say anything, her body frozen and trying to not break down.

He tilted his head to the side, nearly laughing at her. Sebastian stepped close, something that once made Cassandra's heart flutter but now made her stomach queasy and her head spin. In a matter of moments, his hands went to the side of her neck, tilting her head up. His body pressed against hers. She knew Charlotte was prepared to attack, but for some reason, Cassandra knew no harm would come to her. Not yet at least.

He leaned down and kissed her. Their lips moulded together, a once-beautiful moment turned sour. "This was a lot of fun, but now the games are about to truly begin," he said, pulling away.

That was when Cassandra's mind clicked; it was a distraction. It was a way to make them lose focus on the now-green smoke that rose to their knees. Thomas and Charlie stood at the top of the stairs with a smile on their face, walking down to meet their brother.

Thomas' face grew wider at the green smoke rising, the delight shining in his eyes. He brandished his staff, one black and the other red. "You really thought you would win?" he grinned, taunting them. "You honestly believed this was your game to win?"

"News flash!" Charlie cheered, throwing his hands in the air, his dark eyes filled with excitement. "This is *our* game! We are the only ones who come out on top!"

They stood beside their brother as Sebastian unleashed his weapons.

The girl's coughs grew more frequent and Charlotte observed her companion amidst the rising smoke. She gritted her teeth. "What have you done?"

"You've noticed the smoke!" Thomas grinned, dark red hair tumbling over his forehead. "Not so clever, are we?"

Cassandra mumbled, "What is that supposed to mean?" However, the Jacobs seemed to pay no attention to them, their joy overshadowing what was about to unfold.

"*We* choose who's a part of this game," Charlie chimed in from his perch on the grand staircase, hand running through his black hair. "And we choose who isn't."

The smoke rose higher and higher, gradually enveloping them. Charlotte sank to her knees, clutching her throat as she struggled for breath. Cassandra was by her side in seconds, trying to make sure she was alright. That was when footsteps were heard; Loris and Mees were coughing loudly as she heard her father's grunts. They came back. This meant they did not find Augustus or Benjamin.

Sebastian wasted no time; he turned to his brothers, grabbed the back of both their heads, and pressed their foreheads together. "Forgive me for what I am going to do. But I will make Father proud of us." His half-brothers nodded.

In seconds Charlie used his staff and pressed the sharp steel edge into Sebastian's stomach. Cassandra watched in horror as Charlie continued to press the steel into his own brother. Sebastian let out a loud scream, one that was most likely to play the act of the victim, and she knew it would work as her father and his friends ran into the foyer, weapons at the ready and shouting as they watched the scene before them.

Cassandra gripped Charlotte's shoulders. "We need to find the boys and get the hell out of here." Her friend nodded in agreement.

The green smoke became much denser, making it hard to breathe. She coughed loudly, as did Sebastian when he hit the floor. Mees and Loris held each other up, coughing terribly. Jaronas remained the sole figure standing, his gaze fixed on the Jacobs as he aimed his spear at them. His determination to fight, inflict harm, and even kill was evident. In typical circumstances, Cassandra would have chosen to retreat, leaving her father or brother to confront any impending danger. However, this time was different. She was ready to stand by his side in the fight, eager to bring the Jacobs to their knees and force them to beg for mercy. She wanted to bring an end to it all.

Cassandra heard pounding at the windows by the door; she turned to King Albert and King Constantine, who attempted to communicate with the group. Dirk also tried to convey messages through the radio, but Cassandra remained unresponsive to their words, seemingly distant, fixated on the unsettling laughter of the Jacobs. They all missed the truth; they did not know who the real villain was. Sebastian knew his brothers would not make it out alive and knew he was to take the burden of becoming the greatest with him. Benjamin's voice boomed on the radio as he struggled to catch his breath and informed the group that he had lost Grayson in the tunnels, that he was alright and was prepared to head back to them.

The green smoke thickened, obscuring her vision entirely. The Jacobs turned into blurry figures, obscured by the enveloping haze. Cassandra and Jaronas seized the opportunity, relying on their enhanced lungs, allowing them to breathe normally despite the choking smoke. Cassandra distributed the portable gas masks that Augustus had prepared for them in the event of such a situation.

"Oh, Cassandra!" taunted Thomas.

"Jaronas!" Charlie sang out her father's name.

The Jacobs' footsteps echoed through the smoke-filled foyer. Cassandra secured a mask on Charlotte's face, making sure it was alright before turning to Sebastian and contemplating doing the same. She knew if she did not place one it would look suspicious and her father would question it, but for some reason she knew they had to fight one thing at a time, and Sebastian's turn would come soon. So she did the same. Her father did the same, helping Mees and Loris.

"You played us all; how could you do such a thing?" she whispered to Sebastian.

"Was I supposed to say sorry? You got in my way and I warned you there would be consequences if you were to ever get in my way."

"I will go to the Chief; I will tell your mother and tell the Kings."

Sebastian chuckled. "No one would believe you."

She hated how right he was. It would be his word against hers, and despite him being a terrifying man, this accusation could also start a war that has been avoided between each nation for all these years. She knew he would walk away freely.

To release some more anger towards him, she tightened his mask so much that it became impossible to remove.

"Come out, come out, wherever you are!" Charlie's laughter rang out as he waved his staff through the dissipating smoke. The smoke expanded until it reached the ceiling, where it halted and began to dissipate, becoming less dense. Cassandra could finally see the blurry figures of the Jacobs. Charlie let out a shout, swatting at the dissipating smoke around him as he located the group in the foyer. "There you are!" he exclaimed.

Thomas joined him, and that was when Sebastian sprang into action. His half-brother smirked, knowing it was going to be a fun sprawl. Activating his enhancements, Sebastian cut through the smoke and was the first to attack, slicing Charlie on the bicep. Charlotte swiftly followed, deploying her whip with blades that sliced the inside of Thomas's right thigh. Both Jacobs yelped in surprise as the smoke cleared, revealing Charlotte and Sebastian, now wearing gas masks.

"You seem surprised?" Cassandra smirked, her sniper rifle at the ready as Jaronas helped his friends to their feet. "Did you truly think we'd not come prepared?"

In a swift and coordinated move, Sebastian launched himself forward, his attention fixed solely on Charlie as he initiated the fight. Jaronas was quick to follow, spear raised as he slashed it down on Charlie, who dodge the hit. Loris joined the fight, aiding in any way he could. Thomas widened his eyes in shock at Sebastian's attacks, ducking to the ground and rolling towards his brother. His smirk grew.

Cassandra seized the moment and aimed her sniper rifle at Thomas. She watched as her bullet dug deep into his forearm. His eyes widened in surprise but the smile on his face remained undaunted as blood dripped down his hand. Besides her, Charlotte leaped into action. As Thomas swung his staff around, Charlotte released her whip upon him. Mees stood by Cassandra's side, nodding as he was prepared to join her in the fight.

Together, the three put forth utmost effort to inflict damage on him. Charlie, still by his brother's side, assisted whenever necessary, and together, they managed to maintain a steady defence against the group. Their staff skilfully deflected incoming weapons, and they used their surroundings to hurl various items toward their opponents. They would share low glances to each other and then to Sebastian, as if planning something.

Charlie took the initiative and threw a vase at Loris, striking him on the side of the head. The man groaned loudly and collapsed to the floor, holding his bloodied face. Thomas retaliated by hurling a priceless chair at Cassandra and Mees, causing the two to grunt in pain. However, Charlotte's luck was better than the group's, as she managed to land a few hits on Thomas.

As Cassandra finally caught her breath, she pulled at the small splinters that pierced her left arm. Mees stood to his feet, pulling her with him. "Are you alright?" he asked.

She gave him a nod.

With blood coursing through her veins and adrenaline surging, Cassandra became aware of Benjamin's absence. Charlie blocked Sebastian's blade and danced around Jaronas. Thomas did the same, blocking Charlotte's whip as Mees stepped into the fight once more.

Cassandra was prepared to shout into the earpiece to call out his name, but a chilling scream reverberated through the echoing halls, and that was when Benjamin emerged from the cell room door. He stepped out, full of sweat and his eyes locked onto hers. His expression registered the eerie green haze that filled the room. He began making his way towards her.

Cassandra shouted at Benjamin in alarm, arm raised as if to stop him from moving. "No!"

Thomas exerted force against Charlotte's whip and turned his gaze to Benjamin, who clutched the jar containing the programmed brain. Cassandra understood that Augustus had invested all his testing and hard work into that brain. Augustus only needed to replicate the exact procedure to ensure the same outcome for Grayson, to revert him back to normal. Charlie smirked as he managed to push Sebastian away, his focus solely on Benjamin.

Benjamin held the jar in one of his mechanical claws, with another clutching the radio. Jaronas seized this opportunity to swing his spear, striking Charlie on the side of the head. Thomas widened his eyes in shock, staring at the Heart King in disbelief before being tackled to the ground by Sebastian.

Sebastian and his half-brother rolled on the floor, Jaronas watching in case he needed to interfere; however, it was Thomas who made the noise. Hearing him whistling loudly as if to summon a dog, Cassandra widened her eyes.

"Run, Benjamin! Run!" she shouted at him. Without hesitation, Benjamin sprinted in the opposite direction. However, in that very moment, Grayson burst through a nearby wall, the nearest to Benjamin. His heavy breaths and focused eyes were fixed on the fleeing Benjamin, who raced down another hall. Grayson gave chase, Benjamin's cries and screams echoing through the corridor. Charlotte pulled away from the fight and shouted for her brother, prepared to go after him and help.

Cassandra marvelled at the vastness of the Mansion, but as the green smoke dissipated and the Jacobs continued their coordinated assault, there was no time to dwell. Her first instinct was to retaliate, to fight back, however the pounding on the window intensified and the voices of the men became discernible over the radio.

Augustus emerged from the cell door, his head swivelling as he searched for Benjamin and Charlotte ran to him. She pointed in the direction Benjamin had been chased and Augustus moved quickly with Charlotte close behind. Mees took matters into his own hands as he faced Thomas, Jaronas aiding his friend. Cassandra thought of a plan, a better plan to get them out of this mess.

At the very moment, Charlie pushed Sebastian off of him and took the higher ground. His staff pressed against Sebastian's throat, its metal handle cutting circulation as he whistled once more. Shouts and grunts echoed in the Mansion as Grayson emerged from the nearby hallway with Benjamin dragged behind him. Charlotte and Augustus were nowhere to be seen, and the brain was now in Grayson's grasp.

"Bring us the brain!" Charlie ordered.

Cassandra gasped loudly, making it noticeable as she extended her arm, aiming her sniper rifle at Grayson. She shot once, the bullet finding its mark in Grayson's shoulder. "Charlotte? Augustus? Where are you?" she said into the earpiece as Grayson grunted and shifted his gaze toward his older sister.

"Bring it to us, Grayson!" Thomas ordered as well.

Her brother remained still, as if contemplating whether to listen to his masters or not. His eyes darted down to the jar in his hands and back to Cassandra.

"You don't need to," Cassandra found herself saying. "You do not need to destroy it. We are here to help you, Grayson. We are here to bring the old you back."

"It's a lie!" Charlie shouted as he pressed his staff's handle deeper into Sebastian's throat. "They are trying to take away your strength, wanting you to be nothing but ordinary again."

"Do you want to be imperfect?" Thomas chimed in as he held his weapon against Jaronas. "Do you want to be weak and pathetic? Or would you rather be the embodiment of mechanical perfection?"

Augustus and Charlotte stumbled into the foyer again, breathless as they analysed the situation before them. Cassandra nodded at them, as if signalling for them to attack. Grayson took too long to answer, his brain whirling as there was clear vision within, but he shook his head and began to open the jar.

Cassandra found herself shoved at how easily Sebastian was about deliberately wanting to hurt his friend.

In that moment, Augustus entered the fight, charging at Grayson with his chainsaw roaring to life. Charlotte wasted no time as she focused on Charlie and slashed her whip against his back. This permitted Sebastian to gain momentum and push the Joker off him. Cassandra took aim once more and fired a shot at Grayson, hitting the metal plate on his chest. Augustus lunged at Grayson, who had managed to get the jar to open.

Cassandra panicked, trying to think of ways to not let Augustus' experiment go to waste. Augustus continued his attacks, making sure not to hit the jar as he went along. Before she realised it, she was charging towards her brother, making sure not to be in the way as she grabbed Benjamin by the collar and pulled him away.

Exiting the fight, Cassandra released Benjamin, who stared at her with wide eyes. "The brain! We need the brain!"

Cassandra glared at him. "Do you not think I know that!"

Taking a breath, she raised her arm once more, observing how Grayson held his ground against Augustus. This time, her bullet struck his mechanical bow. Her brother grunted as the Club Prince used that as his opportunity to grab the jar. Grayson narrowed his eyes at Cassandra as she pushed Augustus to the ground, the jar still in his arms as he settled it on the table nearby. Stepping towards Augustus, Grayson grabbed his leg and threw him across the room, landing just beside Benjamin.

Charlotte seized that opportunity to lunge for the jar, but she didn't get far, as Charlie grabbed the back of her head, pulling her back. He quickly slammed her face down on the floor before sliding her toward Cassandra. Charlotte cried out in pain as blood trickled down her nose. Sebastian was quick to Charlotte's side.

With Thomas finishing off Mees and throwing him to the ground beside Loris, he used his staff to block her father's spear and quickly kicked him in the stomach before jabbing the Heart King in the collarbone. Jaronas screamed in pain, and Cassandra watched in shock as Thomas pulled the staff from her father's body.

Cassandra rushed to her father's side, placing her hands on her father's open wound. She looked up at the Jacobs who stood side by side on the other end of the foyer. Grayson made his way towards them, the jar in hand. Cassandra swallowed her unease and prepared herself, and soon, the five young royals stood together, forming a line against the Jacobs and Grayson. Her brother handed Thomas the jar as he flexed his bowed arm, swinging it around once and testing it for functionality.

"We need the brain," Cassandra grumbled.

Augustus opened his mouth, prepared to say something about the brain; however, he was cut off by Charlie who only smirked at Cassandra. "Not going to happen." Looking towards Grayson, he pulled out the brain. Some form of blue and green liquid was dripping from his fingers as he held it up to Grayson. "Destroy it."

"No!" Cassandra shouted as Grayson took it in his hands. He looked up at his sister, then to his father.

"*Do it,*" Thomas gritted out.

Without a second thought, Grayson dropped the brain to the ground and within seconds stomped on it, crushing it beneath his foot. Cassandra screamed at the sight; Augustus remained still. The Jacobs smiled wickedly at the sight, enjoying the destruction they caused.

"Eliminate them," Charlie ordered.

It was when Thomas lifted his finger, pointing towards Cassandra, that he said, "I'd like to conduct some experiments on her next."

Cassandra felt her body go cold, her grip tightening on her father. Sebastian instinctively stepped forward, positioning himself protectively in front of her, blocking Thomas's line of sight. Not a word was said by the assassin, but his eyes warned everyone. A death wish was promised upon Thomas if he were to touch her.

Grayson reacted swiftly, launching an arrow that forced Sebastian to pull Cassandra away from her father. "Help me grab him," she breathed. Nodding his head, the two pulled her father up as Charlotte wielded her whip, attempting to strike Grayson. He managed to grip the whip's blades, reeling her in close and flinging her against the grand staircase with a painful cry.

"Charlotte!" Augustus screamed, but nothing else seemed to matter as Grayson had eyes only for Cassandra and Sebastian, disregarding the group entirely.

The Grand Mansion's tension hung thick in the air, as if the very walls were holding their breath, waiting for the impending storm. Mees shook Loris trying to wake him, as he looked up towards Charlotte, who grumbled from her position on the staircase. With Loris unconscious, Mees aided Charlotte, and the Jacobs defended themselves as Augustus and Benjamin attacked.

Grayson stepped over the crushed brain, strategically calculating possible steps and patterns his opponents could make, while never letting his guard down. He unleashed a barrage of arrows towards Cassandra and Sebastian, who had just placed Jaronas on the back wall besides the door. Each shot was executed with precision, causing Cassandra to panic, whereas Sebastian hurled throwing stars at Grayson, his calculated efforts shown, too.

Her brother dodged it with an agility that Cassandra could never possess and left Sebastian in a fit of frustration. Charlotte and Mees joined the fight against the Jacobs, Charlotte skilfully using her whip against Charlie. Its snaking length delivered lightning-fast attacks to keep Charlie at bay. The energy in the room became a clash between the young royals and the Jacobs. Each move was persistent, every attack strategic.

Charlotte's skill with her whip was nothing compared to Sebastian's precision with his weapons, as he activated his enhancement and permitted his daggers to work against Grayson, who continued to keep a distance.

"Pity what happened to your experiment." Thomas smiled. "But you do hold incredible talent. Have you ever thought of–"

"Save it," Augustus grumbled. "Your father already ruined relations with my family by killing my brother. I am here to repay the favour."

Thomas's smile grew. "Ah! So, you did receive our gift!"

Augustus saw red as he readied his chainsaw. He and Benjamin held up a good fight, however he mainly took over the brawl as he wanted nothing more than to make Thomas regret his words. He lunged forward and sliced through the air, grunting at every shot he made towards him.

Cassandra, however, found herself in a different role. She realised that her abilities might be most useful in the next moment. She intently watched Sebastian, recognizing that his prowess against Grayson would be key to their success.

As her brother prepared another arrow, she dropped low to the ground with ease, narrowly escaping Grayson's deadly arrows, which hissed through the air above her. The arrows whizzed by and her heart pounded in her chest. As she crouched on the floor, her mind raced with a strategy. She could not afford to miss, but her opportunity had come.

Amongst the chaos, Cassandra's moment arrived. Time seemed to slow as she made her move, her thoughts flashing towards her mother's memory. Her eyes drifted towards her injured father, who struggled to stand but refused to back down from the fight. Her trained instincts guided her as she sprang to her feet, her sniper rifle aimed squarely at Grayson, who was absorbed in the deadly game of cat and mouse with Sebastian. As the battle raged on, Grayson released another arrow, intended for Sebastian. However, he had not counted on Cassandra's precise shot as she struck down the arrow, its tip inches away from Sebastian's face. Another shot soon rang through the room as she struck him in the shoulder.

All movement on his enhanced arm stopped. Wounded and momentarily incapacitated, Grayson staggered backward, clutching his arm in pain.

Cassandra watched as her brother fell to his knees, breathing heavily as blood dripped through his fingers. Thomas was taken aback, shocked by the sudden turn of events. He had not been prepared, as Augustus punched the right side of his face, his fist connecting with his cheek. Thomas's sinister smile faded, and he stepped back, the side of his face marked by the strike. Charlie, however, kept on his attack towards Charlotte.

"Take care of it!" Charlie cried to his brother. However, Thomas was still in shock, trying to think of a way to fix this situation.

Sebastian seized the opportunity to strike Grayson on the side of his neck, targeting a pressure point that caused her brother to instantly lose consciousness. "Benjamin, grab him!" Cassandra ordered, her voice filled with urgency, as Augustus wasted no time dashing toward the cell room and the lab. Without a moment's hesitation, Benjamin reached out, his mechanical extensions seizing Grayson's ankle. Cassandra instructed Mees to go with them and together, they followed Augustus.

Thomas and Charlie exchanged a quick, uncertain glance as they watched Grayson's retreating form. They were prepared to chase after them, intent on reclaiming their experiment. They could not whistle for Grayson; they could not do anything besides watch him be dragged away. Charlie stood frozen in a mixture of shock and anger, while Dirk's voice came through the radio, indicating he was in the tunnels and on his way to the foyer.

"You are going to regret that." Charlie grunted as his attention turned to Cassandra.

Jaronas managed to stand, grunting as he activated his spear. "I don't think so."

Charlie only smiled as Sebastian was the first to move, launching a throwing star as he slid on the floor, leaned back as the staff swung over him. Jaronas met Charlie's staff with his spear, grunting in pain.

Charlotte and Cassandra looked around the room for Thomas, who had managed to slip away from them. "Did he go after the boys?"

"I doubt it," Cassandra said. "He is somewhere–" Before she could finish her sentence, Cassandra was forcefully knocked to the ground by Thomas's staff. The unforgiving wood struck her head with brutal force, eliciting a painful scream from her. Charlotte was quick to act, muttering under her breath as she launched her whip towards Thomas, who dodged it. Cassandra groaned as she watched Sebastian and Jaronas fight against Charlie in the foyer.

Sebastian was quick to take him to the ground, Jaronas huffing as he held his arm. Cassandra was a little impressed at how level-headed Sebastian remained. Another injury had been made. Charlotte stumbled to the ground as Thomas seized the back of Cassandra's head, yanking her up before brutally slamming her face back into the unforgiving ground. In a desperate attempt to free her, Charlotte grasped Thomas's arm and pulled with all her strength, but the Joker's grip on Cassandra's head tightened, causing the Princess to cry out in agony.

Sebastian swiftly turned upon hearing Cassandra's painful cry. Shock and alarm filled his widened eyes as he witnessed the distressing scene unfold before him. His focus, however, was abruptly shattered when Charlie punched him square in the face, resulting in a spurt of blood and a sharp surge of pain that darkened his gaze. Fuelled by fury, Jaronas aimed his spear at Charlie's back, however before the King was permitted to strike, Charlie rolled off of Sebastian, causing her father to falter in his attack. Charlie was quick on his feet and used his staff against Jaronas who grunted in annoyance.

Despite the relentless blows and the throbbing pain, Cassandra's fighting spirit remained undiminished. With her body still on the floor, and with Thomas's back facing her, Cassandra took the fight into her own hands. In a heartbeat, she managed to fire a shot, allowing the bullet to pierce a hole into his rib cage. Cassandra breathed out as blood dripped to the floor. She expected him to give up, to falter, however, Thomas, exhibiting an eerie resilience, did not yield.

Cassandra began to feel lightheaded, her vision blurring as Charlotte kept a good pace against Thomas. However, in a quick series of moves, Charlotte was back on the ground, hands holding her stomach as Thomas slammed his boot against her chest, causing her to gasp for air. Cassandra tried to move forward, shaking her head and trying not to let it get to her. However, as she aimed her sniper rifle once more at him, Thomas only smirked as he stepped on her arm.

With a staff raised menacingly, he taunted her with a chilling smile. "You are mine now."

With instinct guiding her actions, Cassandra had no time to contemplate her response. She reacted swiftly, poised to defend her life. A resounding gunshot echoed through the tunnels, accompanied by a guttural groan, and felt the warm blood splatter onto her face. It was Charlotte's scream that jolted Cassandra into opening her eyes, revealing the grim scene before her. She had achieved a deadly bullseye—her bullet lodged firmly between Thomas's brows. Blood dripped down his face as his eyes widened in shock, the staff slipped from his grasp, and he collapsed on top of her.

There was blood, too much blood, and it was of her doing.

Overwhelmed by a sudden surge of panic.

Blood, there was too much blood, blood that was not her own.

Cassandra could not comprehend what she had just done. It clung to her, stuck to her clothes and hair, the metallic scent in the air.

She had taken a life—a man, someone's son and brother. The most she had done was kill animals, but that was for food. To survive. Somehow, this was the same thing; it was to be killed or kill. She had to survive, and she did.

A heart-rending scream from Charlie and Charlotte hurried to help Cassandra push the lifeless body off her.

The two girls observed the unfolding scene with bated breath, their chests heaving with anxiety as Charlie unleashed a brutal blow with his heavy staff, sending it to Sebastian. The assassin, in his lightning-fast reflexes, had missed the Joker's reaction and landed on Jaronas. Coughing hard pain coursed through his body as Jaronas held Sebastian.

Charlie rushed to his fallen brother's side, his anguish palpable as he cradled the wounded brother. Cassandra watched as Sebastian stood in near shock, his composed body not revealing anything but his eyes saying it all. "No, no, no, no. Not my brother!" Charlie's cries reverberated through the tunnels, a desperate and heart-wrenching lament.

Suddenly, his gaze snapped back to the girls, and his voice morphed into a deep, menacing tone. "You worthless little Princess! You ruined everything!" His words dripped with venom and anger, as if a switch had been flipped within him.

In response, Cassandra stood resolute, her posture unwavering, with Charlotte steadfastly by her side. "That is the price you pay for destroying my brother–"

"And for killing my brother!" Augustus cut her off.

The remaining Jacobs child promptly rose to his feet, his staff now resting loosely by his side. His fingertips were stained with blood, and his right forearm dripped with crimson. His voice, too, began to rise in intensity with each step toward the girls. "You know," Charlie began, "my brother and I have endured an immense amount of suffering. We've weathered our father's relentless demands for perfection, our mother's cries of abuse, and our father's insatiable thirst for experimentation, always striving to make us superior, the ultimate creations."

With every advancing step, the intensity in his voice grew, causing the girls to retreat, their apprehension mounting. "And yet,"

Charlie continued, "somehow, my younger brother could not even handle two insignificant Princesses!"

Cassandra chuckled defiantly. "Perhaps you should think twice before underestimating us 'useless' Princesses."

Charlie responded with a chilling, early giggle that sent shivers down her spine. He advanced a step, prompting Charlotte to launch herself at him, attempting to slice him with her whip. However, he emulated his deceased brother's movements, snatching the iron blades and pulling Charlotte in close before delivering a powerful punch to her face.

Without wasting any time, Charlie raised his staff, targeting Cassandra. As he swung it down, she agilely sidestepped and fired a shot at him, hitting him squarely in the chest. However, instead of stopping him, it merely provoked more of that eerie, deranged laughter. He reached for the bullet that hit his chest with a ping, he knocked on the metal chest plate.

"I was created to be unstoppable!" Charlie bellowed at Cassandra, discarding his staff and seizing her sniper arm, which was still raised. He twisted her arm and pushed the sniper behind her back, preventing her from taking another shot. Yanking her close, Charlie seethed at her, spitting in Cassandra's face. "I was meant to be the one to introduce the world to the new breed of humans! It was supposed to be me!" Another unsettling chuckle escaped his horrifyingly smiling lips.

Cassandra saw her father pull Sebastian to his feet and just as he took a step in her direction, Sebastian stopped him.

"But it was all ruined. And when our father died, we were left with a legacy to uphold, and you just had to ruin it, didn't you?" Charlie squeezed her wrists tightly before forcefully hurling her to the ground, stomping on her stomach. "Didn't you!"

Refusing to yield, Cassandra fought back, summoning the strength to rise once more, spitting blood from her mouth. Her head spun dizzily, but her determination remained unshaken. "You picked the wrong 'useless' Princess to tangle with."

With her defiant words, Charlie unleashed a scream of rage and delivered a brutal punch to Cassandra's face, sending her crashing to the floor. Struggling to defend herself, she desperately attempted to push him away. Just as his hands closed around her throat, threatening to snuff out her life, a slick, sharp sound pierced the air.

Sebastian's dagger swiftly slid across Charlie's throat, causing a fresh spray of blood to splatter onto Cassandra's face. Charlie glared down at her with a sickening smile, his teeth stained crimson as he landed on top of her.

She could not believe it; he killed his own brother. How could he do such a thing?

"Why do they always end up on top of me? Get him off!" Cassandra screamed in frustration.

Reality crashed down upon her all at once. Her head grew increasingly light, dizziness overcame her, and her mind throbbed with pain. Amongst the chaos, she took a breath and heard Sebastian inform the Kings outside what had happened.

Her father came rushing to her side, pulling her into a tight hug.

CHAPTER 26

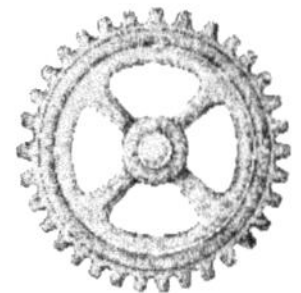

Cassandra knew, despite two threats being taken care of, that there was still one more remaining. She looked over to Sebastian,

She found herself recounting the previous events multiple times, reliving and explaining the story to the other Kings, Dirk, and their accompanying men. She was meticulous in her retelling, leaving no detail unshared—that was, everything regarding Sebastian remained a secret. He was right, no one would believe them, but it was up to Cassandra to speak with Benjamin and Augustus, to inform them of what happened. Maybe together they could find a way to lock Sebastian up for good, but as of right now there was nothing else she could have done. She felt hopeless.

Furthermore, she directed the King's outside to rendezvous with the others at the hatch, ignoring Sebastian and his evil ways. Guiding Dirk and the rest of the men back into the tunnels, Cassandra explained the dire situation and the need to return to Augustus and Benjamin.

As they navigated the labyrinthine tunnels and drew closer to the lab, a chilling sight met their eyes. Grayson was strapped to the cold metal table, still unconscious as Augustus worked and worked.

Looking over his shoulder, he smiled, but it faltered for a second as his gaze went over Cassandra's shoulder and to Sebastian. He cleared his throat and put on a tight smile. "Good, you are here."

She knew Augustus must have known something. He had to; nonetheless, Cassandra step[ed beside him, Charlotte following suit. The two tried to keep as much distance from Sebastian as possible. "I thought everything was lost?" she mumbled as she stepped into the room.

Charlotte was quick to Augustus' side, planting a soft kiss on his cheek.

"Not necessarily," Augustus smiled as he mixed more liquids together. "You see, I was prepared for something wrong to happen. I knew the Jacobs wanted to destroy the dummy-brain; it was evident that they wanted to. So I had memorized the formula before Grayson burst through the doors. I also salvaged and hid liquids and tools I would need. This was good, as Grayson did destroy everything, but it was all the wrong things. They were useless items, merely a distraction from the real thing."

He went back to work, tapping on the back of Grayson's head and working on the gears within. Benjamin was the first to hug his sister, gripping her tightly as she explained what had happened. She muttered to him, "We need to talk" before pulling away and giving Cassandra a nod.

Her eyes followed the men in the room, making sure everyone was alright. Mees stood by her father and Loris, who clung to his friend's shoulder and explained everything Augustus had done, entirely fascinated by the young Prince. Sebastian was off in the corner, arms crossed as he observed everyone. It made her skin crawl that he was able to get away, leaving her at such a disadvantage, but part of her knew she had to try. She had to tell someone, anyone of the older men in the room.

She turned to her father. "Father, there is something I need to tell you."

Her father smiled at her. "Yes?"

Cassandra gazed at him, hands shaking as her eyes went back to Sebastian, who now stood tall with a smirk on his face. She gazed back at her father. He followed her gaze to Sebastian and back to her.

"Is everything alright?"

She could not find the words to tell him. Her gaze returned to Sebastian one last time, who now held some sort of remote in his hand. His finger lightly pressed over a button. She narrowed her eyes on it, not understanding what it meant. As Sebastian pressed the button, Grayson began to furiously shake. Cassandra's eyes widened.

Augustus swore as he asked people in the room to help keep him still. Her father ran to Grayson, holding his head still, Mees and Loris grabbing his arms as Benjamin used his long extensions to keep the body still, covering all spaces.

Sebastian's gaze never left her. Their eyes on each other as they heard Grayson shaking furiously. She looked over at him quickly, watching her brother shake so hard it scared her to death. Walking up to Sebastian, Cassandra grabbed his wrist, the one holding the remote. "Fine. I won't say anything."

His smile turned evil for a split second as he leaned down to kiss the side of her cheek. "Good girl."

Those words made her skin crawl. Those once-beautiful words now irritated her to the core.

Sebastian clicked another button, which stopped the shaking.

It was not long before Augustus was done and explained that it would take time for Grayson to heal, and that he would wake up in a week's time, maybe longer or shorter depending on how his body would react to his changes.

Jaronas nodded and instructed his men to carefully remove Grayson from the table. Cassandra watched as her brother was carried out. Her father hugged her once more as the men carried Grayson's body out of the lab.

"It is over," Jaronas muttered as he kissed the side of his daughter's head. "He is safe, he is home."

Cassandra nodded lost in her own thoughts.

"What was it that you were meaning to tell me?"

She shook her head, eyes meeting Sebastian as she put on a tight lip smile. "Nothing. I forgot" Her father smiled and walked off.

Cassandra watched as the men carried Grayson out of the room. He was safe, he was alright—he would be alright and that all that truly mattered. She found herself letting out a breath she did not realize she was holding. As her father let go of her, he followed the men out of the lab, his eyes trained on Grayson's unconscious body the entire time.

Sebastian was quick to put his arm around Cassandra's shoulders, giving her a smile and a kiss on the top of her head. His own stab wound being completely disregarded, leaving for some part of her to wonder if he was even injured at all. "You follow orders extremely well."

She shoved him. "Don't touch me."

The five young royals were left alone in the room, causing Charlotte to use this opportunity to grab her brother's arm. "Ben, I need to tell you something."

But before she had the opportunity to tell him, Augustus swung a right hook to Sebastian, fist colliding with his cheek. Benjamin was prepared to go help but Charlotte held him back and explained what truly happened and who Sebastian really was. Cassandra watched her friend's hushed words and Benjamin's slow realization.

"You bastard!" Augustus nearly yelled, voice low enough that the men outside would not hear them. "You nearly killed me! All for what? A sport? A game?"

"For science," Sebastian said, surprising Augustus. "Have you never wondered what could have happened if we enhanced the steam-powered gears and extensions within us? Have you never wondered what more we could do?"

"But why my brother? Why hurt me—us, in the process?" Cassandra needed an answer.

Sebastian turned to her, smiling widely. "He was my personal guinea pig, you knew that. As to hurting you, that was not my intention. The others, however…" He turned to the three. "They need to show me how useful they are."

Cassandra could kill him; her friends could kill him.

"Are you kids alright over there?" Jaronas called from the hall.

"Yes, we're coming now."

Cassandra narrowed her eyes on Sebastian. "I don't know what your game is, but if you so much as touch my brother again, I will kill you."

He stepped close, smiling. "Promise?"

Scoffing, they walked away. Augustus and Benjamin stood behind the girls, almost making a barrier from Sebastian.

Charlotte wrapped her arms through Cassandra's. "How are you doing?"

"I'm doing alright."

She shook her head, pulling her into a tight hug. "I do not believe that for a second."

"How can someone deal with all of this? It feels impossible, like…As if my heart is breaking into millions of pieces and I cannot control it."

Charlotte smiled. "I tend to do breathing exercises, that helps me. Or reminding myself that everything happens for a reason, that it was all a life lesson that could change me for the better rather than the worse."

"How do you deal with killing someone? With death? How are you supposed to feel?"

Her friend shook her head. "Sadly, I am not someone you can go to for that. The most experienced person here is the one who tried to use your brother as a tool, but I will say that dealing with death—eventually you will find peace with it."

Cassandra looked over her shoulder at Sebastian; she wanted to ask him but she knew it was not the right choice.

It had been five days since Grayson's rescue.

Augustus and Constantine had come in with the nurses and doctors to check up on him, seeing if he was healing properly and if Augustus's reprogramming had worked; however, they would never know for sure until Grayson was to wake up. For the past five days, Cassandra and Jaronas took shifts staying by her brother's bedside.

It was her turn to sit by Grayson's bedside that day, relieving her father from his night shift and allowing Cassandra to sit in the warm early morning sun as she flipped through the pages of her book. She had finished *Beginning of the Triumph Games*, the history book being of great use to her during her times in the games, along with *History of Our Nations*, and thought it a good idea to get back to her self-help guide on *How to Become a Lady*.

Laughing, she made it a point to underline when something seemed so ridiculous to her. Her father had thought it of good use to bring this book with her, to help her become a proper lady throughout the tournament, when in reality, she should have brought her brother's books on defence and fighting tactics.

"Whoa."

Cassandra shot her head up from her book, heart beating fast as Grayson was staring down at his body. Arms extended as he looked at the new piece, touching his chest and shoulders and feeling the new things that were added to his body.

Grayson looked at her, smiling sweetly. "Hey, Cassy."

"Oh, my–" She jumped to her brother, giving him a tight hug. "You are alright, you are okay, you are you!" she cried out, tears running down her cheeks as she held Grayson tightly.

"Of course, I am. Why wouldn't I be?" He smiled cheekily.

She was prepared to ring the bell by his bedside table but something stopped her. She had to find out now, she had to know. "Do you remember who did this to you?"

Grayson remained silent. "That depends on how much information you know."

They shared a look. "Spade City was always known for being cruel and distrusting."

Her brother nodded. "That they are. Especially with the Prince being just as cold-hearted."

Those words alone set some reassurance in her. She proceeded to ring the bell. "Good, I had to know."

"Is he locked up?"

"No."

"Why?"

"There are reasons that I will fill you in with later, but as of right now, do not say a word."

Nurses and doctors began piling into the room, checking the monitors around Grayson.

"You'll never do that again!" Cassandra screamed as people now came into the room, wanting to change the atmosphere. "Do you hear me? Never again!"

Her brother nodded his head, pulling his sister into another hug. Their father was quick to the tent, eyes filled with sleep as he looked at his two children hugging and smiling. It was not long before he joined the two, wrapping his arms around his family.

Augustus and Constantine joined the nurses and doctors, trying to help in any way they could with Grayson being awake.

"What do you last remember?" Augustus asked Grayson, as he pulled up a chair and notepad, his father leaning over his shoulder to see the questions written down on the paper.

"I remember being taken," Grayson admitted, holding his sister's hand tightly, squeezing it as if remembering every moment. "From there it was flashes, really, blurs of different things. More than half the time I was in this room—"

"The lab?" Grayson nodded at Augustus, who quickly jotted down notes.

"Yes, there were jars lingering around. Anyways, I was never conscious for long to truly understand where I was. I do, however, remember a brain? Is that correct?" He looked towards his sister, who nodded. "Yes, then, a brain, and I remember seeing Cassy and Sebastian Spars and you, and Charlotte Dimond and Benjamin Dimond— you were all there, with Father. Why?"

"It was to get you back," Cassandra smiled. "It was to make sure you were able to return to us."

"What happened to them?"

"To whom?" Augustus asked, jotting down more notes, his hand moving quickly across the page.

"The men that took me."

Augustus stopped his writing, eyes already locked onto Cassandra, who squeezed her brother's hand, smiling tightly.

"I took care of them."

"What do you mean—"

"*I took care of them.*"

Augustus made a gesture to slice his finger across his throat, causing Grayson to widen his eyes at his sister. "No!"

Clearing his throat, her father looked towards the Clubs. "Let's move on, shall we?"

Augustus asked a series of more questions before having Grayson sit up and try to move his new enhancement, to if he was comfortable with the new additional pieces the Jacobs added to his body.

Augustus continued to test to see if Grayson was properly able to stand, if he was able to fix his mobility, and after a while, it turned into physical therapy, trying to see if Grayson could work his new body properly. He was no longer the Prince he was before the Games, but he changed—drastically changed.

Augustus said it would take a few days before Grayson was able to fully understand his body again; however, he recommended doing some training again, allowing his limbs to get used to it. He then proceeded to list things that were new to Grayson's body. Cassandra thought of it as the appropriate time to get her brother some food, as he must have been hungry. Jaronas looked to his daughter and nodded, Constantine saying he would walk with her as a fresh pot of soup had been made over the fire by the Queens.

Exiting the Recovery Tent with Constantine close behind, the two spoke of what to do to aid Grayson, sharing and discussing if he was truly back and how long it would take before he was fully healed. However, as they reached the fire, they were bombarded with questions by the others. Yara, Nora, and, Adriana sat by their fathers as they conversed with Onatach.

Constantine instructed Cassandra to get Grayson some soup and her friends were quick to her side. Nora pulled Cassandra into a hug first, Charlotte quickly following afterward. Adriana had poured a cup of soup for her, handing the Heart Princess the bowl as she spoke of Grayson's current state.

Queen Suzume and Queen Morana pulled Cassandra to the side, hugging her tightly. "I hope my bracelet protected you in those times," Suzume said to Cassandra, tapping the metal band on her wrist. "It was meant to protect the warrior who wore it, and since you are here standing before me, I believe it did its job."

Cassandra could not help but smile at the thought, looking down at the samurai sword that reflected the one the Queen of Spades wore around her waist. "Yes, it did protect me. It helped me very much."

"Wisdom is a precious thing," she smiled.

Cassandra bit the inside of her cheek, wanting to tell her so much, but forced to stay quiet.

Someone tapped her shoulder gently and as she turned; Sebastian stood there smiling at her. "Is it possible for us to speak?"

She nodded her head and called for Charlotte, asking if she could bring the soup to Grayson. Agreeing, Charlotte gave Sebastian a glare before making her way towards the Recovery Tent. He guided her to the edge of the camp, sitting under a tree as the midday sun shone down on them. Hours had passed since Grayson woke up, and it still did not feel real to her.

Looking around, Cassandra took in the area. Their spot overlooked the forest before her, bright and full of light. She stared at the bushes and the trees, gazing at the small path that was made, and breathed in the gust of wind that passed by her. She recognized this spot, the same place where she and Sebastian once sat. The only difference was that, when they sat here, it was at night and Dirk had come through the trees and bushes on the other side, injured and explaining to them what had happened to Jaronas and his scouts.

The difference remained that they were no longer the same people they once were at the beginning of the games. Truths were revealed and now Cassandra sat with unease.

"How are you feeling?" he asked after a pause of silence.

"Alright. Happy but alright. Why do you ask?"

Sebastian kept his eyes forward, his usual leather attire replaced with simply black pants and a dark blue top. "Curious, that is all."

"Are you alright?" she asked, not really caring for an answer but wanting to know his true intention behind this chat.

"I want you to join me."

Cassandra was taken aback by his words, eyes wide as she gazed up at him. His dark eyes met hers. She blinked a few times, processing his words.

"Wha—why would you ask me such a thing?"

"I believe there is some darkness to you. Some sick and twisted part of you that you did not know about yourself until you killed my brother. I think you do not know how to go about killing someone and you need guidance. I can be that guidance. Together we can change the world."

Cassandra scoffed. "I will never join you. To willingly kill innocents—"

"My brother was innocent."

"No, he was not, he was a mad scientist that was easily influenced…" Cassandra heard the words coming out of her mouth, heard the way it sounded. "No. You cannot manipulate me into believing otherwise."

"You just admitted to him being easily influenced. Making him an innocent."

"That is not what I meant. You manipulated him into believing otherwise. It made him just as evil."

Sebastian said nothing, just nodding his head. They sat in silence a little longer.

"How do you deal with it? The killing, I mean."

"I view them as animals. Stepping onto this earth to help someone else rather than themselves."

Cassandra felt disgusted by his response, almost shocked that he would answer so quickly and easily.

"It'll help you sleep at night knowing you killed an animal rather than a human. With animals, people do not think twice about it, but when killing a human, for some reason, people cannot live with it."

"Do you believe this could have worked out?"

"What do you mean?"

Cassandra turned to Sebastian, eyes no longer filled with tears and pain but with determination. She controlled her emotions, composed them, and allowed herself to not give in to them. "Us. Do you believe we could have worked?"

There were a few moments of silence that followed her question, Sebastian taking in her words before turning to her. "I am certain of it."

"Then why become this? Why do this?"

He did not say anything; instead he stood. Eyes meeting hers, he said, "Find me when you've made up your mind." With that he left without another word, leaving Cassandra to her thoughts.

A few days had passed since Grayson woke up. She spoke to him about Sebastian, informing him on what he missed. He recovered relatively quickly, getting acquainted with his new parts and pieces. Cassandra did her best to assist him, and the trainer played a similar role. It became evident that Grayson's strength was as robust, if not stronger, than before. Augustus mentioned that his new enhancements gave him a potential edge in the tournament, but the boys embraced the new challenge with enthusiasm.

Cassandra stood at the gates of the Hearts in the Arena, her father beside her and her brother's trainer conversing with Grayson. The time had come for him to re-enter the Triumph Games and Cassandra thought it a perfect time, too, as the tournament was a beautiful moment but being a part of the combat section was not something she was looking forward to.

"Are you sure you do not want to enter? Your brother is not completely healed and the Chief informed me that his new advancements could give him a disadvantage when getting points," her father asked Cassandra one last time.

"Having those boys willingly ruin this beautiful face? Absolutely not," Cassandra laughed.

They were silent for a few more moments before her father spoke again. "You should participate. You and Charlotte. That way it could be an even match."

Cassandra stood there in shock as Grayson overheard their father's words and cheered in agreement. Before she could understand what was happening, Savannah was preparing Cassandra in her tournament attire.

Onatach walked past them with Albert and Charlotte, who beamed at her friend. "See you out there!" It was the first time Cassandra saw Charlotte truly smile like that, a smile so wide and big that it gave her shivers.

Grayson bounced on his toes at the gate waiting for Cassandra. After being dressed in the similar dark red attire as her brother, her hair braided behind her, she stood before the gates, heart beating fast as her smile grew.

"Imagine. For the first time in history there will be a female competition in the tournament," Grayson said.

"Imagine," Cassandra countered. "Not one but two female competitors making history and changing the ways of the Triumph Games."

"I like mine more," her brother smirked.

Jaronas came to his children, gripping both their shoulders and smiling. "I am so proud of you, both of you." He turned to Cassandra. "I never got to say thank you for competing, for taking your brother's place and stepping up to the challenge. It shows me just how strong you are. Just like your mother."

She bit the inside of her cheek, nodding her head. Their father pulled them in for a group hug before departing to the Sky Box with the other royals.

"Are you nervous to face Sebastian?" her brother asked. She had not spoken or seen the Spars royal in the following days since their last conversation. She had not told anyone of what was said, ignored the questions altogether when they were being asked.

"Promise me one thing?"

He hummed in response.

"Kick his ass for me?"

Grayson smiled wide and wickedly. "You know it!" They high-fived and the Arena roared to life as the hosts voice boomed. "Are you ready?" he asked as the host began to introduce each nation.

"I've been ready all my life for this."

She heard the first gate open; Augustus' name being shouted around the Arena. Followed by Benjamin and Charlotte—announcer making sure to inform the audience that it would be the first female combat section—and Cassandra silently hoped for it to be incorporated later on in future Games. Sebastian was next to be called, then lastly it was them.

"Last, but certainly not least. You know them, you love them! Grayson and Cassandra Harth!"

The large iron gates began to open. The platform before them pushed them forward as red smoke sprouted before them. The crowd roared with excitement. The siblings held each other's hands, raising them into the air as they waved to the thousands of people who screamed their name. Cassandra could not help but gaze over to the Sky Box where all their friends now sat. Bran, Micha, Yara, Adriana, Jan, Nora, Hendrik, Mila, and Lars. Their friends cheered and stood clapping, their father beside them with their fathers, cheering for the Harth siblings to win the tournament.

A sense of pride and realization washed over Cassandra. She had come so far since the beginning of the tournament. She not only learned more about herself but about the people around her. She had come so far and just ahead of her lay the future. Her name was to be written down in the history books, and she promised herself that the future of the next generation would be changed, not the same as hers. Rules, regulations—all would change if needed.

The referee stood in the middle of the ring, golden cup in hand. Cassandra had never wanted anything more in her life than this. To be known not only as the first woman in the tournament, but the first woman to win the Triumph Games cup. She looked over to Charlotte, who only smirked, the two sharing the same thought.

It would be a fair match indeed.

Sebastian caught her eye, offering a wink that made her go cold. He was the one thing that bothered her. He did all this bad, all this wrongdoing, and yet the people who stood in the Arena were the only ones who had to know and were forced to stay silent. Cassandra vowed to make him pay for what he did to her brother. Her revenge would be sweet and cruel all at once. She was going to play him the same way he did her.

As the referee went over the rules, Cassandra bounced on her toes. The adrenalin kicked it. It was all too much, yet not enough. She was excited, thrilled even. As the sun rays shined down on them, she pictured her mother's face smiling at her, congratulating her on how far she had come, and watching her during these Games.

As the piercing sound of the whistle echoed through the Arena, the epic showdown had officially commenced to determine the winner of the Triumph Games, and Cassandra was determined to win.